SEE THROUGH
Deception

SEE THROUGH
Deception

JERMANE J. ANYOHA

SEE THROUGH DECEPTION

This is a work of fiction. All of the characters, names, incidents, organizations, and dialogue in this novel are either the products of the author's imagination or are used fictitiously.

iUniverse books may be ordered through booksellers or by contacting:

iUniverse
1663 Liberty Drive
Bloomington, IN 47403
www.iuniverse.com
1-800-Authors (1-800-288-4677)

ISBN: 978-1-5320-2764-2 (sc)
ISBN: 978-1-5320-2765-9 (e)

Library of Congress Control Number: 2017910439

Print information available on the last page.

iUniverse rev. date: 08/09/2017

CLASH IN THE JUNGLE

"*N*o ... I couldn't protect them," Jadeleve moaned, sprawled out on the ground in the cave as she tried to gather her bearings. Her purple T-shirt and purple shorts were torn. Her purple combat boots were muddied, and her golden locks were disheveled. It felt like her skull had been split in two.

The inside of the cave was blocked by a pile of boulders as if there had been an explosion. Outside the cave, the air was dense with moisture. Tropical trees seemed to stretch endlessly in all directions. Strange animal noises floated throughout the thick ecosystem from tree to tree, carried by the wind.

Where am I?

The group was nowhere to be found.

All right then.

This wasn't her first rodeo. She had already traveled halfway across the world. With that in mind, she left her fear of being without her companions behind and stepped out of the cave.

As soon as Jadeleve started to fly, she was overcome by dizziness and fell to the ground. It felt like her lungs had popped, and she began to wheeze uncontrollably.

Luckily, thanks to plentiful sunlight, Jadeleve could soak up the solar energy like a sponge. Soon, her strength returned.

Pure, electrical green energy began to envelop her body. The supply was vast, and Jadeleve could use it at her disposal however she pleased. She started to feel weightless, as if she were fast enough to outrun lightning. Her vision became so sharp that she could see the slightest rustle of a leaf a mile away. This was the power that her ancestors passed on to her. This was the most powerful energy in the universe: *zeal*.

Jadeleve was able to fly on her second try, but even while drawing energy from zeal and solar energy simultaneously, she was spending it faster than she could replenish it. As the sunlight diminished, so did her strength. She could not remember the last time she had eaten, so she decided to take a break and look for food.

Jadeleve had experience finding fruit from her voyages through the forest back home, but this was a *jungle*. She quickly realized it was close to impossible to see anything through the thick fog with the dim light that the setting sun provided.

Fog is just a cloud that's really close to the ground, so all I have to do is blow it away.

With a sudden burst of spunk, Jadeleve tapped into her energy reserves. She concentrated on changing the shape of her lime-green aura from its usual flickering candle shape into a sphere. The lime-green energy sphere expanded, enveloped around her body. Using the sphere's larger surface area, Jadeleve flew as fast as she could to create a draft that would cut through the surrounding fog.

Jadeleve finally spotted two lojels. Lojels were round turquoise fruits that grew on Jupiter before humans arrived and introduced foreign fruits like apples. She also found bananas, a big grapefruit, and one coconut from a high treetop. She sat against a grand tree with a trunk about fifteen meters wide and ate slowly. Finally, she washed it all down with the milk from the coconut. After sitting there with a full belly for about ten minutes, Jadeleve felt rejuvenated. With renewed drive, she stood up once more and disposed of her leftovers beside the tree trunk.

A deafening screech erupted throughout the misty jungle.

Oh boy, Jadeleve thought. The scent of the fruit must have attracted an unwelcome predator.

Abruptly, Jadeleve felt a stabbing pain in her head. Getting weaker by the minute, Jadeleve reactivated the zeal.

"Energy Force Field!" An electrical current was enough to startle her enemy. She quickly swung her head around to identify the creature; it was a gigantic brown leech with wings. A green snake protruded from its mouth like a tongue. This was a Being: a descendant of Earth animals that mutated after they were brought to Jupiter. The Being must have been absorbing her energy with its snake tongue. Reluctant to kill, Jadeleve taunted the creature, forcing it to fly away.

The sooner she escaped the jungle, the better. What was the most efficient way to travel and elude enemies simultaneously? *Using the After-Image Technique is the best way to avoid opponents. And for traveling …*

After a flash of lightning, a fire illuminated the jungle. Before the conflagration could get any worse, the clouds began to cry and douse the embers.

That's it! I could make a sonic boom by drawing energy from the thunder's sound waves and the lightning's electricity. And since water conducts electricity, the rain is the perfect fuel. I could use that energy so much longer than if I used my own. If I'm going to get out of here, I'll need to use my surroundings.

Jadeleve raced to the skies, trying to promote electrical activity in the atmosphere by sending zeal energy into the clouds. Due to the zeal's nature, if Jadeleve was ever attacked with zeal, she could automatically absorb it. Her hope was that her zeal energy would fuse with the lightning's energy so that when she was struck by lightning, she could absorb the combined energy of the lightning and the zeal, and she would gain more power back.

Confident that this would work, the young warrior put her grand plan into play. She shot a beam of zeal energy into the gray smog above her head, creating electric charges within the clouds.

When the lightning struck, Jadeleve significantly decreased the speed of descent using the Slow Motion Technique. Finally, Jadeleve withstood the astounding force of the lightning with her bare hands and attempted to harness the dense energy in her palms.

"Nngh!" Jadeleve screeched at the effort. Gritting her teeth, she positioned her arms in front of her, facing her back in the direction she wanted to go, and released the pulsing, pent-up energy inside her palms. A great sonic boom erupted from her hands and propelled her forward at a blinding speed. To quicken her pace even more, Jadeleve used her bodily aura, which would make anyone looking up from below think she was a shooting star.

For hours, Jadeleve flew at this relentless speed without stopping. The silver haze served as a constant reminder of her silver-haired sisters. Even so, Jadeleve's endurance prevailed, and she was able to glide straight through the darkness, clinging to the hope of being reunited with her family again.

As the first rays of morning light streaked across the sky, Jadeleve guessed it was a quarter to six in the morning. The sky was mostly clear, which would have been good under different circumstances; now, however, she could no longer draw from the electric energy.

Jadeleve wrestled with her hunger and her desire to stop flying so she could take a break, but she knew she was daydreaming if she thought she could get away with that. She kept thinking, *There has got to be a better way.* The Zeal Possessor continued to question all the possible ways she could double her traveling speed. At least it kept her mind awake as she sailed through an endless blue blanket in one direction.

Jadeleve finally gave into her thirst, which was amplified by the eighty-five-degree temperature. She drifted down toward the column of trees below, collected the water vapor from the surrounding fog, and turned it into a nice, refreshing drink, using excess water to pour on her head in an attempt to keep cool. Drawing from aqua energy was not her strong suit, but she was able to manage the task. Finally, she resumed her flight.

Once she was comfortable, she let her mind relax. She persisted throughout the day, but sleep deprivation began to dull her senses

4

around sunset. Her eyes drooped and drifted downward until she landed serenely on a treetop. *Five minutes of shut-eye never hurt anyone*, Jadeleve lazily thought before blacking out.

A harsh buzzing sound woke Jadeleve with a jolt. Before her vision even cleared, she took her fighting stance, a maneuver that had been drilled into her through years of training. A refreshing but humid breeze from the north tousled her golden hair. It was only then that she realized that the sky was dark and she had been sleeping for hours. Jadeleve also noted that if not for the buzzing, she probably would have slept on that treetop for days.

Despite the dusk, the green-brown moonlight from Europa illuminated the landscape, allowing Jadeleve to see clearly. A swarm of black-and-white-striped insects flew overhead. These were Reebees, one of the few Beings with an official (provided by the royal family) name. Jadeleve had never seen one, but she knew about them from Zenon, who had showed her a picture of one while they were traveling together through the Land of See-Throughs. Zenon wanted to know about all kinds of Beings and their abilities. From these conversations, Jadeleve knew the Reebees' strengths but none of their weaknesses.

Reebees were extremely fast, could grow up to two inches with five-inch stingers, and were nearly impossible to evade. They stored energy in their stingers and stung their opponent's vital spots while vigorously vibrating in place. Vibrating allowed them to spread their poisonous energy throughout the foe's body even faster. Their poison was not deadly but could cause hallucinations.

Realizing that the smart decision was to escape, Jadeleve bolted at full speed. As she predicted, the Reebee swarm caught up to her in a split second. However, Jadeleve was prepared to defend with all her might.

"Energy Force Field!" she bellowed. The rapidly rotating sphere of green energy could burn enemies and gave her a 360-degree range.

Buzzing excessively, the Reebee swarm scattered around the green ball of energy. The swarm conquered the force field by absorbing its energy with their stingers.

Without a defense, Jadeleve tried to flee, but before she could move, searing pain invaded her body from a single point. Her frantic cry echoed across the rainforest. However, she knew she could not afford to lose.

Resolve overshadowed the pain. She could feel fresh electrical energy pulsing through her veins and the familiar connection with her ancestral bloodline. She did not flinch as her vision suddenly sharpened, though she got tunnel vision as fury clouded her thoughts. As a swirling green tornado engulfed her body, Jadeleve realized the power of zeal had come to the rescue on its own.

Jadeleve thrust her arms outward in opposite directions, forcing the Reebees back ten feet. Even with the zeal, Jadeleve knew that she could not outfly the Reebees, and she wanted to refrain from killing. After all, *she* was an intruder in *their* home. She would need to incapacitate them somehow so she would have enough time to flee.

While Jadeleve was turning thoughts over in her head, her vision began to blur and she felt a horrifying wave of weakness. The Reebee's poison was starting to take effect. Time was running out.

Jadeleve hastily turned around to face a Reebee that attempted to sting her from behind. After creating a shield of raw energy in her right hand, she blocked the stinger with her palm. Next, she forged the shape of a sword by manipulating raw energy. Roaring emphatically, Jadeleve cut off each and every one of the Reebees' stingers with her energy blade. Having lost their weapons, the swarm buzzed back to where they had come from, fading into the moonlight.

Once the skirmish was over, the zeal's green aura disappeared, leaving Jadeleve to plummet to the ground.

THE WANDERING WARRIOR

IF IT WERE NOT FOR searing pain that invaded Jadeleve's body, she probably would have never woken up. Ironically, it was the pain that let her think clearly. How would she get out of this one? Every time she tried to stand, she found herself right back on the ground. She screamed about Beings who were trying to suck her blood, even though no Beings were in sight. Grandma Bachi, Jadeleve's grandmother, had taught her the ancient ways of survival. However, it wasn't so much the knowledge that Bachi passed on that made the difference. It was the fighting spirit that she instilled within Jadeleve.

Thinking of her grandmother, Jadeleve reached into her pocket where she usually kept the white pendant that Grandma Bachi had given her for her birthday a few years before. She kept the pendant there most of the time to keep it safe, even though her grandmother meant for it to keep *her* safe.

Clutching the silver lace that was attached to the pendant in her hand like a compass, Jadeleve valiantly attempted to move her body upright. However, the young warrior's body rebelled. Again, Jadeleve's muscles contorted, pain erupted from her spine, and the world started spinning. She gasped. Breathing slowly, she managed to regain some of her composure but tried to stay as still as possible.

Instinctively, Jadeleve lifted her grandmother's white pendant up and put it around her neck. Its hot energy grew denser by the second. Soon, the pendant's strength was equivalent to that of Jadeleve's will.

On Jadeleve's tenth birthday, Grandma Bachi had seemed disappointed when the pendant did not react to her strength right away. Today, Jadeleve knew what it all meant. Before Jadeleve had started her journey, she had almost no experience in the outside world, and she paid little mind to the true profundity of the role she played in the survival of her race. Now, even though she understood only a fraction of what was going on, it was enough to ignite the power inside the pendant. The pendant's power was independent of Jadeleve's physical strength, so no matter what her physical condition was, she could always draw power from it.

With the pendant amplifying her strength, Jadeleve was able to move again. She shot upward toward the sky. Once above the misty treetops, she realized it was cloudy and wondered what time it was. She used the treetop she stood on while fighting the Reebees as a reference point so that when she started flying again, she would know she was going in the right direction. Wanting to pick up where she had left off, Jadeleve began to fly north. The faster she was able to get to the nearest town, the faster she would be able to contact her friends.

Since Jadeleve could not recall the events that had happened the few days before she was out cold, it was impossible for her to tell what day it was. As the hallucinations returned, she began to experience muscle fatigue. However, hunger was the main issue. She had not eaten anything but fruit for two days. Water was not much of a problem because she could just extract water from the mist. The trees extending in every direction did not help to ease her mind. Every which way she turned, she hoped to find a sign of sanctuary where she could rest, but none appeared.

Jadeleve flew through the thick silver sky. The clouds sent chills through her body and blocked the sunlight. After what she estimated was ten straight hours of flying, the last of the energy from her pendant was used. Jadeleve was forced to confront a wave of helplessness, a feeling she was not accustomed to. Soon, all she could see was a ghoulish hue of black and blue. Gradually, she began to wheeze and lose altitude. To make matters worse, Jadeleve began to twist uncontrollably in the air.

After coming this far, Jadeleve could not give up. With all the might left in her body, she raised her chin, flattened out her body, and twisted in midair so that her stomach was parallel to the ground. Next, she spread her arms out in an effort to slow down her descent.

Finally, Jadeleve drew energy from the resisting gust that brushed against her body. Without any strength of her own left, she absorbed the wind energy around her until her lungs were filled with enough air to stop the wheezing. Jadeleve had a foolproof plan; she would reenact a technique that she had only used once against Master Dracon to catapult herself into the air. To reduce her descent, she would have to exert a counterforce against gravity. Her mom had taught her about the laws of physics during homeschool when she was younger, seemingly for general knowledge. Now, it seemed that understanding these principles would save her life.

All at once, Jadeleve released the stored energy. She emitted a powerful jet of cool air from her mouth and the palms of her hands. Almost immediately, her descent slowed, but it was not enough.

As the severity of the situation continued to grow, Jadeleve decided that it was all or nothing; she would have to resort to her most powerful technique to provide enough force to slow her plunge and survive the impact.

"Re …!" She slowly started to chant, her adrenaline increasing with her decreasing altitude. "Ca …! Tus!" The brave warrior mustered all her strength in a last-ditch effort to survive and fired an intense beam of purple energy straight at the ground. Her mighty roar echoed throughout the confines of the jungle. Relieved that her blast slowed her descent considerably, the corners of her mouth lifted slightly. However, just as her eyes closed from exhaustion, terror gripped her heart. The heat of her energy blast kindled a fire that set the surrounding trees ablaze in orange light. All the young warrior could do was hope to not be burned alive by morning.

THE SPEED OF LIGHT

BLINDING WHITE LIGHT OBSCURED JADELEVE'S vision as she opened her eyes, and she was almost certain that she had died. However, a millisecond later, searing pain registered on her skin and irritated her nerves. Somehow she had survived her plunge into a fiery oblivion.

But how? She kept asking herself. During her flight the previous day, it had been cloudy the entire time. *Did it really start to rain just before I hit the ground?* It just seemed too perfect. Even so, her theory was backed by logic: the ground was wet, the trees were scorched, and everything around her was blackened by ash.

The more energy put into an energy blast, the faster the molecules that form it move. Being out of energy was what had saved her life in a way; if she had any more power to put into the Recatus, which was her strongest energy attack, the rain would not have been unable to douse the flames in time. Jadeleve had been given another chance to live. She would not waste it.

For about one hour, Jadeleve lay still, her consciousness flickering between worlds of black and white. When she finally gathered the nerve to attempt to move, she was met with staggering pain, but she endured. Too weak to stand, Jadeleve traversed two miles by crawling over the moist terrain. All the while, she swore she could hear her friends' voices and that she was being chased by past enemies. She blacked out several times. Warm blood escaped from the wounds she sustained after falling from the sky and scraping against the rugged tree bark. Worst of all, Jadeleve's pendant was of little help because its power had been drained from constant use.

Finally, one more mile of crawling, Jadeleve heaved for the last time. She lay down on her stomach in the dirt.

I wish everyone was here. I don't know what to do.

A ray of sunlight penetrated the thick mist overhead and landed on her forehead. *Light? Energy ...* Jadeleve racked her brain, not giving it a chance to shut down.

Wait ... Dad. He said ... he said that he used ... sunlight and converted it into ... speed! I'll call it the Solar Speed Technique.

Jadeleve shoved her pendant into her pocket to save its energy and then turned her attention to the task at hand. The solar energy heeded Jadeleve's every whim, forced to bend and twist because of the combined power of her will and her strongest muscle—her eyes. The single ray now moved in front of wherever Jadeleve's eyes darted. With raw tenacity, the young warrior fought through exhaustion and drew the weak energy into her forehead.

Now that Jadeleve had fused her energy with the sun's energy, she could take the form of sunlight and travel through a ray of light. Using this technique, Jadeleve could fly close to the speed of light.

At least that's how I think it works.

Regardless, Jadeleve was Jupiter's only hope for survival. This plan was Jupiter's only hope of survival. She would have to believe in herself and her abilities—or let everyone down.

Jadeleve just wanted to fly to the edge of the rainforest. Hopefully there was an inhabited town nearby where she could recover. From there, she would be able to contact her friends and continue on her journey.

Now that Jadeleve's life force was attached to the rays of light, she let the force flow through the light like water flowing through a straw. Enveloped in solar energy, her body began to levitate and glow, just like a beam of light. Close to the speed of light, Jadeleve sped toward the sky. Now she was free to follow the path of light that would lead her to the forest edge.

Out of the corner of her eye, Jadeleve thought she saw a faint blue light gleaming from an opening in one of her pockets, but she was too focused to pay much attention. The world began to blur as Jadeleve was pushed by the energy of a light beam. Even Jupiter had its limits, as massive as it was, and she knew that she was nearing the forest edge at a rapid pace.

Gradually, the slight tilt of the light beam that Jadeleve was using became more obvious. Soon Jadeleve was taking a nosedive toward the forest edge.

Dang it. Yellow dots began to twirl in front of her vision, washing over all other senses. Like the asteroids in the Asteroid Wars, Jadeleve felt herself lose control over her motion. Her life was now in the cold, unwelcoming hands of fate.

A wave of hopelessness swept over her like a soundless breeze, forcing her to shut her eyes to try to block the sensation. When Jadeleve opened her eyes, all she could see was thick, rotating, white nothingness. After an immeasurable gap in time, Jadeleve was aware that she was being pushed by a mysterious force that was not solar energy. Finally, she was overcome by darkness.

JAIL BREAKERS

"**U**GH," PUPIL MOANED.

"Stop whining, Pupil; we've been through worse," Zephyr whispered. Again Zephyr tried to recall the hazy memory of a recent battle they had lost.

From what Zephyr could remember, they were confronted by an Eyebot and her Being companion. Strangely, the Eyebot's technique could block their ability to draw energy, and their team was easily defeated. The girls could not remember exactly what their enemy looked like, only that she was female. When they woke up in the cell, they realized they had been separated from Jadeleve. After a day, their powers returned, but they experienced several hallucinations. Trying to grasp the faded memory of the battle felt like trying to catch a fish with bare hands; it just kept slipping away.

The Eyebot who had defeated them brought them to this prison. Since the guards had confiscated their transceivers, the girls had no way of contacting Jadeleve. If they had mastered telepathy, this would not be a problem. However, at their level, the girls could only contact people who were in close proximity.

Through careful listening, Zenon deduced that the Eyebots were using them as hostages. In exchange for their lives, the Eyebots wanted either Jadeleve's life or for her to join forces with them. However, Zephyr doubted that stubborn blockhead would hand over her life *or* allow their team to be executed. Jadeleve always had to be the hero and save everyone.

Two years had passed since their group left home in Xaphias. Last week, they finally reached the last of the five See-Through counties: Fantasia. Beyond the Fantasia County, all that separated them from No Man's Land and the Zeal Orb was the Odyssey Ocean. Everything was looking great until this happened. They were so close. If they found a way to escape the prison, they could get to No Man's Land in four months. However, Zephyr knew they could not leave Jadeleve behind, no matter what.

Shoot, but it would be great if we just left her!

Zephyr and the others had spent the first day in the cell unconscious. To keep them from moving once they woke up, the prison guard drugged them by staring into their eyes, causing mist to suddenly appear. It prevented their muscles from working and caused them to see things that were not there. Unlike the energy blockage technique, the repercussions lasted for days.

The mist itself was a hallucination, but it obscured their hearing and made it almost impossible to think clearly. The fraternal twins, Pupil and Iris, who were younger and less tolerant of the attack, suffered the most mental damage. Their usual shining silver eyes were now a dull gray. Their straight, shoulder-length silver hair hung over their faces, and their tan skin was unnaturally pale. Pupil wore the blue version of their team's uniform, which consisted of a blue T-shirt, blue shorts, and blue combat boots, while Iris wore the red version. Although Pupil constantly claimed they were fraternal, they looked almost *exactly* the same. Luckily, Zephyr possessed razor-sharp vision, thanks to her See-Through heritage, and she could always tell them apart, even when they swapped clothes to trick her. However, under the influence of the Eyebots' drug, Zephyr could distinguish them only by the color of their uniforms.

For hours, Zephyr and her identical twin, Zenon, had been contemplating a way to counter the mist's effects. Zephyr had always been glad there were multiple traits that people could use to differentiate between them. For one thing, Zenon had inherited her fiery amber eyes from their father, and Zephyr received her icy blue eyes from their mother. Zenon had always sported the green version of their team's uniform, but Zephyr preferred yellow. Zenon wore her spiky black hair in orderly pigtails, while Zephyr let hers grow out in all directions. Zephyr hated being mistaken for someone else.

Zephyr had a feeling there were other matters, or maybe other prisoners, that the prison guard had to attend to, otherwise he would have been keeping an eye on them 24-7. During the past six days, Zephyr noticed that only *one* prison guard had checked on them, and he checked infrequently. They needed to take advantage of the fact that there was only one security guard, figure out a way to overcome the drug mist, break out of their cell, and find Jadeleve.

Zephyr observed her surroundings, trying to memorize the smallest details of the cell, hoping for a brilliant idea. The walls were a deep peach color. In the cell, there was barely any room to breathe. The perimeter was only about six by seven feet, and the ceiling was a mere six feet tall. The toilet, which the girls avoided, took up too much space in the cell for its worth. Like most See-Through buildings, the room was made of marble, and twelve crystal bars prevented them from escaping the cell.

"I'm hungry!" Pupil squealed.

"Shut up," Zephyr snapped before giving Pupil a hard noogie. As a result of being confined for so long, the slightest complaint was enough get on her nerves.

Nerves, Zephyr thought. *This technique the Eyebots are using to drug us and the technique that girl we fought used … it's the same concept. It's like they're shutting down our brains. If we could stimulate them somehow ….*

"How do you feel?" Zephyr asked Pupil.

"Still hungry," Pupil replied.

"You figured it out, Zephyr. That attack is completely cognitive. It weakens our senses by overpowering our nerves. But nerves allow you to react, remember, move, and do pretty much all the important work in the body. With our current level of understanding of this technique, the only way to regain control of ourselves is stimulate our nerves," Zenon explained.

"Can you stop reading my mind without permission? It's kind of creeping me out." Zephyr glared at Zenon and sighed in frustration. "Anyway, basically, all we have to do is hurt ourselves."

Iris was too weak to move her arms, so Pupil, who had already recovered, hammered her sister on the head. Immediately, Iris jolted upright, wide-eyed. Her irises changed color to reflect her emotions. Now they turned lime green, meaning she was excited and ready for action. Next, Iris elbowed Zephyr in the head, and Zephyr punched Zenon's cheek.

Finally, an excuse to punch Zenon.

I heard that, Zenon eavesdropped.

In less than a few seconds, all four girls were wide awake, but Zenon instructed everyone to stay quiet, as they were about to form their plan of escape.

"We can't just blow down the bars, or we'll get caught," Pupil said.

"No, we don't have to blast through this. Pupil, use your Flashlight Technique to cool the crystal bars," Zenon whispered. Pupil did so without much thought. She drew energy from the water particles in her body, released them into the air through her eyes, and decreased the temperature of the water until it froze. Then she covered the bars with the ice.

After about five minutes, Pupil's job was done. When Zenon gestured for everyone to step back, Zephyr already knew what her sister was going to try. By drawing from heat energy, Zenon heated her hands, creating the cracks in the cooled crystal bars.

Currently, out of the two of them, Zenon was able to access more power from her natural element than Zephyr could. Zenon had practiced using it more in the days before they lost the battle against the Eyebot in Sapolis City because she saw it as another step on the road to ending the war.

Zenon withdrew. It was Zephyr's time to shine. She detected the weakest points in three adjacent bars, and with astonishing speed, she was able destroy all three by striking their vital spots. There was no need to destroy all twelve bars; they already had enough space to slip through.

"Let's go!" Zephyr whispered. However, since they were unconscious when they were brought to the prison, they had no idea where they were or how to escape.

"Wait, Zenon. You should use your Conjunctiva Expansion Technique and go ahead of us. That way, you can warn us telepathically if anything comes up," Zephyr suggested.

"Good thinking. All right, I'm off," Zenon replied, gritting her teeth in anticipation for her conjunctiva to envelop her body in an invisible cloak.

The girls rarely practiced using telepathy because they prioritized physical strength over mental strength. However, it was becoming apparent that they would need to confront their weaknesses, or else the enemy would.

If they attempted to make a loud exit by blasting the prison wall, Zephyr was not sure if they could out-fly the prison guard. On top of that, she was not sure if they would be able to hold their own four against one. Either way, it was likely that they would be captured. With this realization, Zephyr telepathically sent her message to her three trusted companions.

After five minutes of walking through the peach-colored hallway, Zenon suddenly grew anxious and warned the rest to stop following. Next, she deactivated her Conjunctiva Expansion Technique and ran back to the group.

"There are other jail cells … *a lot* of other jail cells, *back there*, and each one has at least one person inside," Zenon explained.

"Who do you think they are," Pupil questioned, her silver eyes alight with apprehensiveness.

"They're all kids, maybe ten to sixteen. We already know this is an Eyebot prison because none of the races attack their own kind. Also, because of the war, there aren't enough adults to protect the kids. Most of the adults who are left aren't fighters, anyway." Throughout their journey, the girls had visited countless towns and cities. Zenon would take polls. On average, there was one adult for every fifty kids under eighteen. Most interim leaders of a town decided to keep all the children in the same area instead of having them scattered, so the outnumbered adults could supervise them. However, keeping them in one place created an easy target. Also, the supervising adults were usually the elderly and were too weak to defend against attacks.

"Some of these kids were captured from towns, some are probably fighters, but some of them must be on their own missions to help end the war. This prison is meant to stop them," Zenon concluded.

"We've got to bust these kids out," Zephyr whispered. The four of them tiptoed forward until they were in the center of the lane of cells on either side of them.

"Hey, who are you?" a dazed, foolish-looking boy shouted. Zephyr turned to him but did not focus on his features, because he was drooling. The guards must have used the Evil Mist Technique, which would make freeing everyone twice as hard.

"Shhh. We're going to try to break you guys out of here," Zephyr calmly assured. Before any of the prisoners could react to Zephyr's words, the girls got to work. Pupil froze three crystal bars from each cell to save time, Zenon heated them with her hands, and Zephyr broke down the bars with her Pinpoint Technique. To make herself useful, Iris did her best to calm the prisoners down.

After the girls broke down the bars and the prisoners stumbled out, Zephyr briefly explained to them the only way to negate the effects of the evil mist. She promised them that it would make sense afterward.

It took ten seconds for the four girls to hit all forty kids on the noggin. Shortly after, they were all speaking in complete sentences.

"Wait, why did you hit all of us?" the drooling boy asked with a slight grin.

"The attack that the Eyebots used on us prevents our brains from operating normally by shutting down our nerves, but pain can stimulate your nerves again," Zenon explained.

"That makes sense." The drooling boy sighed. He seemed to be the only one willing to talk.

"Let's go!" Pupil said. Her spunk seemed to stir most of the kids from their stupor. Soundlessly, they all rose in anticipation for the jail breaking.

"All right!" Zephyr fired two powerful yellow energy blasts, one at the hallway wall so all the kids who couldn't fly could escape, and one at the ceiling for the rest of them.

To avoid being crushed by the rubble that fell from the ceiling after the explosion, Zephyr quickly maneuvered out of the way. She knew that they had ten seconds, tops, to evacuate all the children from the prison. However, there was no need for Zephyr to point out this fact to the others; they were already scrambling for the exit.

"Guys, go on! I have a plan!" Zephyr yelled to Zenon, Pupil, Iris, and the drooling boy, who was the only prisoner to not escape. She would buy two more seconds of escape time by creating a dust storm. With her Zephyr Wind Technique, she spread the smoke from the explosion to give them cover.

After Zephyr had put her plan into play, she escaped outside. The clear, sunny sky greeted her with a warm embrace.

We're free, Zephyr thought. She took in her surroundings, realizing that the prison was on an island off the coast of the mainland. The ocean water was a serene, sparkling turquoise, which starkly contrasted the steel outside the prison. Satisfaction swept over her as Zephyr realized that the main group of prisoners was escaping through the nearby forest, concealing their presence from pursuers. Finally, Zephyr turned her attention to the brilliance of the people she was flying with; these were the future saviors of Jupiter.

Even so, her jubilation was short-lived. Zephyr looked over her shoulder only to see two prison guards in pursuit.

The male guard was youthful, tall, and lean. A mop of long, wavy black hair covered part his pale face and deep blue eyes. He wore a blue silk vest on top of a black combat shirt. On his lower body, he sported black pants and combat boots. He had white gloves over his hands, which was odd in the summer. A strap around his waist connected to a sword's sheath.

The girl looked about the same age as the male guard: twenty. She was pale and of average size. Her flowing reddish-brown hair came down to her elbows, and her piercing black eyes tore through Zephyr's soul. She wore a brown, sleeveless top, gray khaki shorts, and brown boots. Her dragon had purple scales and red eyes that shined faintly. This dragon seemed to be the same species as Aiondraes but looked a little bit older and more mature than him. Aiondraes could not have been much older than two years old (around three and a half in human years, Zenon estimated). The girl and her dragon looked familiar.

Wait … it's them*!*

All Zephyr knew was that she had to fly away faster than the wind. She and the girls were aware of the Eyerobis advantage, so they had to escape, seek refuge, and find Jadeleve.

"Do you know where we are now and the nearest town is?" Zenon asked the drooling boy, who was tagging along with them for some reason. Since the guards confiscated their bags, but they did not want to risk going back for them and getting caught, Zenon did not have her map.

"We're on Ripple Island, and the nearest town would be Pearl Town, which is east of here!" he replied, projecting his voice by drawing energy from the sound waves of the howling breeze.

"You won't escape!" the male guard bellowed.

"Go away!" Pupil retorted. Zephyr became anxious about the girl. Her face felt like a distant memory. Zephyr decided to leave nothing to chance.

"We need to attack all at once! Go!" Zephyr roared. On her command, they each shot an energy beam at the enemy. Before reaching their target, the attacks converged as one. Zephyr already knew that it wouldn't work.

I've got it!

Zephyr realized that since the combined energy beam was a combination of their powers, it was as much hers as it was anyone else's, meaning she could control it. With a split second of preparation, she shifted the beam's course to aim at the prison. Finally, while the two guards' attention was on the shifted direction of the energy blast, Zephyr took advantage of their confusion and fired a second blast, which was meant for them.

As quickly as she could, Zephyr concentrated her energy into the palms of her hands and released her ultimate technique: the Foveno Beam. Both attacks hit their mark. The huge blast detonated the prison and her blast made contact with both Eyebots.

However, Zephyr wasted no time waiting to see if her attack on the Eyebots had any effect.

We have to get out of here! Move, move, move!

Making a sharp, ninety-degree turn, she led her three comrades away from Ripple Island toward Pearl Town, with the boy following close behind. The rest of the kids had escaped into the forest and were hopefully on their way back home.

ENEMY PROFILES

A RED-EYED, PURPLE-SCALED, FEMALE UNCHARTIAN DRAGON hovered calmly in the air with her master sitting on her back in the face of the oncoming blast. When the time was right, the girl, who had auburn hair, caramel skin, and black eyes, deflected the attack with astonishing ease.

"They got away, but it's fine. We did our job." Nyx sighed from atop her companion's back.

"I can't *believe* they escaped." Kerato grinned, feeling admiration for his enemy.

"I know, but I fought her entire group at Sapolis and beat them all. Not to brag or anything. Anyway, this project is over," Nyx said.

"I'm going after them," Kerato decided.

"What's with you and getting excited so easily? Whatever; just make sure you do your job. *I* have to take care of some unfinished business with Chalazia. I'll meet you at Mind Fog Island in October. That's when Cataract predicts we'll be ready," Nyx explained.

"All right then. I'm off." Kerato took off his blue vest to prepare for swift travel, revealing his all-black attire. At the same moment, Nyx jumped onto Chalazia's back and prepared to take flight.

"Don't get carried away again!" Nyx called before she and Chalazia raced away.

Kerato had given his prey a huge head start, but with his unwavering focus, he would soon be on top of them.

THE NEW GUY

"**S**O IT *WAS* THEM," ZENON said after Zephyr informed the group that the girl and her dragon were the ones who defeated them in Sapolis City.

Zenon realized that the forest would work as an advantage and disadvantage. The advantage was that it would be easier to hide from the Eyebots, but the disadvantage was that it prohibited their movement. That was when Zenon thought of another advantage: since the Eyebots were faster than them on flat terrain, the diverse land would even the playing field.

She had not grown up in the forest, jumping from tree to tree like Pupil, Iris, and Jadeleve, but she had her fair share of experience.

Wait, why is he following us? Zenon thought as she turned back to the boy.

"I've just been traveling through the county for a few weeks. I just want to do what I can to help the war effort. I'm an orphan, but that hasn't stopped me yet," the boy explained.

Now Zenon really examined him. The boy had curly black hair and light brown eyes that seemed almost amber. To fight the heat, he sported a white combat shirt. He wore green shorts with yellow and orange sprinting shoes. The boy was very slim, had dark brown skin, and was shorter than Zenon and Zephyr but taller than Pupil and Iris, so Zenon assumed that he was ten or eleven.

"What's your name? Where are you from?" Pupil started with a onslaught of questions. "Whe—" She was stopped dead in her tracks with a death stare from Zephyr.

"I'm from Widria City. It's here in Fantasia. And my name's Kuroski," the boy replied.

"How old are you?" Zenon asked.

"Twelve, turning thirteen on August 21," he replied.

"You're the oldest here by eight months," Zenon mused.

"That's right. So show me some *respect*," Kuroski joked. "What are your names?"

"I'm Zephyr, and this my twin sister, Zenon. And here is Pupil, and her twin, Iris," Zephyr replied.

"Where are you from?" Kuroski asked.

"All four of us are from Xaphias, which is a town on Parabola Island, which is the largest island in the Crescent Straight, which is a largest part of the Celestine County," Pupil responded, showing off her geography skills.

"That's pretty confusing, but it looks like you know your stuff. Hey, do you wear those outfits to tell each other apart?"

Kuroski was referring to their matching, color-coded combat outfits, which consisted of a T-shirt, compression shorts, and combat boats. Zenon's was green, Zephyr's was yellow, Pupil's was blue, Iris's was red, and Jadeleve's was purple. They had stolen the idea from the ancient Power Rangers.

"You totally figured us out." Zenon laughed.

"So you guys are from Celestine? How long have you been traveling?"

"Two years. After we got through Celestine, we went through Laputa, Mononoke, and Nausicaa. We just got here a couple weeks ago," Zenon answered.

"And where are you heading?" he asked.

"We're on a quest to get to No Man's Land and find the Zeal Orb so we can use its power to help stop the war. Mr. Zeal thinks that we need the Zeal Orb to counter transflare and protect Jupiter," Pupil explained.

"Oh yeah! You guys are part of the Original Five, aren't you? I heard so much about you on the news. You guys beat Cocone and Rodney. You've have been in tons of fights. You're famous."

Only members of the royal family, the Castellians, were allowed to provide information to the public.

Wow, Zenon thought. *The Castellians caught the whole battle on camera but didn't even lift a finger to help us.*

"Who's the fifth person in this group again? How did you get separated?" Kuroski asked.

Zenon was quickly adjusting to his inquisitive nature. "Her name is Jadeleve Dawn, but we call her Jadel for short. Her favorite color is purple, so she likes to wear purple clothes, and she has blonde hair with violet eyes. We got separated from her in a battle against the Eyebots a little while ago. But we don't know what happened to her," Zenon explained.

"How long ago was this battle?"

"Last week. I hate to admit it, but I miss that jerk. She's a tough cookie, though, so I know she's fine," Zephyr answered.

"So, are you strong?" Pupil asked Kuroski.

"How do I answer that? I'm from Widria, the City of Dragons. Rainbow-colored dragons were said to live there in ancient times, and they left their scales behind. So once every year, the city picks one hundred of the most talented kids to find a rainbow scale in the forest. The prize is your own dragon. My friend, who's like an older sister to me, was this year's winner. Of course I was happy for her, but it made me think. I realized that I've been living in her shadow my whole life. I decided to run away to find my calling. I've been traveling ever since, until I was captured." Kuroski sighed. "I just felt like I would never accomplish anything *there*. You know what I mean?"

"We feel you, Kuroski." Pupil grinned. The other girls silently agreed.

Zenon realized that their pace had slowed considerably during the conversation, so she urged the others to pick up speed again. She glanced at the blue sky and analyzed the position of the sun. While using the method that Jadeleve had taught her last year, Zenon figured out that it was about four in the afternoon. Zenon realized she could not remember the last time she ate.

Zenon examined the condition of her companions. Ever since the conversation ended, Kuroski had been trailing behind, not having anything to distract him from the effects of physical exertion. Iris's irises had become brown with determination and she struggled to keep up the pace. Pupil, transparent as ever, wore a pained expression. Zephyr seemed to be in the best condition, barely fazed by the task of flying nonstop for hours. Zenon was slightly winded but far from exhausted.

The sun going down did not extinguish her fire. From past experiences, Zenon had always known that it took less effort for her to use heat energy than all the other types. Even though fire was considered destructive, it also had a positive side, just like all the natural elements. Fire could burn and destroy, but it could also light. Lightning might cause forest fires, but it also provided electricity. Water could flood and destroy, but it was the source of all life. Wind might cause tornadoes, but it distributed the seeds for new trees to grow. Zenon noticed that she felt stronger in warmer conditions.

Jadeleve, on the other hand, drew power from solar energy. What was strange was that solar energy was not one of the six main natural elements. They were heat, electricity, earth, water, vegetation, and wind.

This made Zenon curious about what their new ally knew.

"Kuroski. Do you know about natural elements?" she asked him.

"Yeah. A natural element is an element that takes little, almost no energy for you to draw from. You can just draw from it naturally with barely any training. You could also have more than one natural element. I only have one though. Mine's wind."

"Really? Then why don't you push yourself forward with some wind? I do it all the time, and it ends up saving me a ton of energy," Zephyr suggested. Zenon had always suspected that her natural element was wind.

"Oh, I never thought about that," Kuroski said. Zenon felt that they had already taught him so much, and they had only known each other for—what? Four hours?

"How did you figure out your natural element?" Iris asked.

"I just found out through experience. But if you're still unsure, we could go to the Origin Temple in Jazell Town. They teach about stuff like natural elements and mental energy, and they have classes during the regular school year," Kuroski explained.

"I'd love to learn what my native element is!" Pupil beamed.

"Keep it down. First, we've got to lose the prison guard. Then we've got to get out of this forest," Zephyr explained.

"I miss Jadeleve," Pupil said.

"Come on—she's fine," Zenon consoled. She was not just saying that to assure Pupil; Jadeleve just could not die. It would take more than a little breeze to put out *her* fire.

At around six, the sun met the horizon, replacing the blue-orange sky with a black cloak. Jupiter's fourth largest moon, Europa, displayed its mysterious green-brown light over the forest, decorating the forest floor through the tree branches. The serene glow of Europa was intoxicating. Its glistening light soothed them like warm water. *What time is it?* Zenon thought as she yawned.

Suddenly, Zenon heard a loud thump, and she was sure the swordsman from Ripple Island had caught them off guard. However, when she turned around, prepared to attack with all her might, all she saw was Pupil's head lodged in a tree trunk.

Iris flew over and, as gently as she could, dislodged her twin's head from the tree. Pupil rubbed her eyes as if nothing had happened.

"Okay, I think we should call it a night," Zephyr declared.

"How are we going to sleep in this forest?" Kuroski asked in a low voice. He was afraid that the swordsman would be on top of them at any minute. However, Zephyr was confident that a swordsman like him wasn't used to flying for so long; he was accustomed to ground-level, hand-to-hand combat, and he was probably saving up his strength to try to get a head start on the chase the next morning.

"Relax. You've never been camping before?" Zephyr asked.

"Not without supplies," Kuroski replied.

"We're going to cover ourselves with leaves and lay on the grass for camouflage," Zenon explained. She loved finding fresh solutions.

"All right!" Kuroski confirmed their course of action.

There's that spunk again, Zenon thought.

Pupil lightly pushed Iris away and claimed that she was fine. Then she activated her Flashlight Technique so she could see where she was going and help the others find trees with an abundance of leaves. In the back of her mind, Zenon was worried that the night light would attract hostile Beings or the swordsman.

After five minutes, the young See-Throughs had gathered enough leaves to sufficiently blend in with the green background of the forest. At this point, all but two of them dared to talk instead of conserving their energy for the next day: the incredibly hyper Pupil and Zenon, who was too polite to ignore her.

"I'm starving," she whispered, tears streaming down her cheeks. This must have been the longest Pupil had ever gone without eating in her whole life.

"Be strong, Pupil. Jadeleve's fine, and we can make it through this," Zenon reassured. Wanting to end the day on a positive thought, she gazed at Europa in all its majestic beauty one last time and drifted to sleep.

THE DIVERSION

"GUYS, WAKE UP!" ZEPHYR SCREAMED. Kuroski was the first to respond.

"What's going on?" he asked, popping up from under his blanket of leaves like a plume of smoke exploding from a volcano.

"I can sense the swordsman. We have maybe two minutes before he catches us," Zephyr explained hurriedly.

Zenon was the next to rise from her leaf bed. "Pupil, Iris, let's go!" she demanded. She did not wait for the twins to respond and grabbed one hand from each of them. In a flurry of motion, she pulled them from under their leaf pile and sped off. Kuroski and Zephyr followed suit. After much coaxing in midair, the Dawn twins reluctantly opened their eyes to greet what they were sure was going to be a bleak day. They freed themselves from Zenon's protective grip and started to hover on their own. Now, the five weary warriors were able to increase their speed.

"We can outlast him, but he's faster. He'll overtake us." Zephyr shivered. In the short time that Kuroski had known her, this was the first time he saw her lose her composure. He felt that Zephyr was the leader of the pack, and if she was scared, then he knew that the enemy was strong.

With each passing second, Kuroski's heart rate increased until his heart could beat no faster. The wind tousled Pupil and Iris's silver hair, obscuring their faces. Kuroski could only see the back of

Zephyr's head, but he could guess what her expression was like, and Zenon appeared to be intensely concentrating.

Twenty minutes was Kuroski's estimate for how long they spent flying forward at their frantic pace before anyone was able to gather their nerve to speak.

"It's no use; we're just wasting energy. We are going to have to confront him," Zenon said.

That's what she was doing, Kuroski thought. She had been tracking the swordsman's progress by focusing on the position of his bodily energy.

Suddenly, the girls started to decelerate and came to a stop.

"What are you doing? We'll die if we fight that guy! Keep flying!" Kuroski argued.

"Didn't you hear what Zenon said? We can't out-fly him. All we can do is conserve our energy now and fight him," Zephyr concluded with a grave expression. His assumptions had been correct.

"So you guys are going to throw your lives away?" he inquired.

"Someone's got to stand up to the Eyebots or they're going to keep killing," Zephyr replied. "You're the one who said you didn't want to be useless, right? But now you're trying to run away. Only *cowards* run away."

"*Zephyr,*" Zenon seethed. Zephyr simply shrugged and turned away, leaving Kuroski to absorb the blow.

All his life, Kuroski had run away. He had run away from home, run away from his enemies and all the obstacles he had ever faced. That was why no one expected anything from him.

I'm tired of this ... I ... I ... can't let this be my life anymore, he thought.

"I have a plan," Kuroski murmured, gritting his teeth.

"What is it?" Iris asked.

"*I'll* stay behind and fight this guy myself."

"Are you crazy?" Zenon fumed, but Zephyr's mouth twitched in a smile.

"If the Eyebot catches up with us, I doubt he would kill you guys, unless he wanted to be on Jadeleve's hit list for life. They'll probably take you as hostages again," Kuroski explained.

"Good point," Zephyr said. "But the Eyebots have already taken us as hostages once, and we escaped. They would be fools if they think the same tactics will work on us twice. If they were smart, they'd stop underestimating us and kill us already."

"All the more reason for me to stay behind and buy you guys more time. You guys are a very important trump card in the war. You dying could mean the difference between us winning and losing the war. If I save you, I'll be famous," Kuroski concluded.

"Wow. You just want all the glory, don't you?" Zephyr sighed, seeing through his plan. "We've only known you for a day, but I think I can count on you. You're pretty brave." She turned around and flew onward without a second glance.

"Good luck. Don't die," Zenon said. She was not sure how to feel under the circumstances. Not wanting to prolong her inevitable departure, she raced after Zephyr.

"Be careful!" Pupil and Iris cried, and then they rushed in to hug him.

"You bet. I won't go down easily," Kuroski said. The little twins pulled away and then took after the older twins.

As soon as the four girls were out of sight, Kuroski let the tears flow from his eyes, dried them quickly, and prepared to fight. His brain was the most active when he was nervous, and during those few seconds, he had a sudden epiphany. He decided to position himself in a different direction, because the enemy would assume that he was protecting the path that his companions had taken. Even if he was defeated, he would lead the enemy astray, buying even more time for the girls to escape. Where his physical strength lacked, Kuroski made up for it with his tricks. That's how all neglected pranksters got by.

Next, Kuroski concentrated on charging and focusing his energy for the impending battle. Time began to slow down once the Eyebot swordsman finally appeared, hovering in the air. When he drew his sword from its black sheath, the full gravity of Kuroski's situation struck him. He began to quiver but tried desperately to hide it. He would not run away again.

"So where are the others?" The man smiled, surprisingly polite. Kuroski must have looked like he was about to wet his pants.

"Why are you doing this? What do the Eyebots have against the See-Throughs?"

"I'm See-Through, like you," the man replied calmly.

"Wait, really? Then why are *you* doing this?"

"The war is a lot more complicated than you kids think it is. It's not just the Eyebots against the world. The Eyebots think that the See-Throughs, especially, treated them unfairly and stole their land. I was abused by the royal family as a kid, so I agree with the Eyebots' view. See-Throughs are hostile creatures who think they are better than all the other races. They must be stopped."

"There's got to be a nonviolent way to end this war. This has been going on for thousands of years, and violence hasn't worked." Kuroski cried. His parents had been killed by the Eyebots in the war when he was just three years old.

"I agree with you, kid. I would rather not kill. But until someone finds a peaceful solution, this is all we can do. If you're going to get in the way, I'll *have* to use force. Now are you going to move or not?"

"No," Kuroski stated, and he meant it with all his heart. He had conquered his lifelong fear, so whatever the outcome of the battle, he would be satisfied.

"You've got guts. I'm Kerato Yazulon. What's your name?"

"Kuroski," he muttered, deciding against giving his enemy his last name and preparing his fighting stance.

"Kuroski! Give me all you've got!" Kerato roared and drew his sword.

The swordsman flew forth with lightning speed, forcing Kuroski to sharpen his reaction time to the extreme. Even so, he was still too slow. Every one of Kerato's turns and strikes were perfectly executed.

Only one minute into the battle, Kuroski suffered several cuts on his cheeks and on his legs while trying desperately to evade. Kerato was showing the younger fighter no mercy.

Kuroski attempted to fight back. When Kerato drew back to regroup for a second and ceased his assault, Kuroski took the opportunity to fly up and fire an energy blast down at him. As Kuroski expected, Kerato barely looked at the attack and deflected it with his sword, proving that it had no effect. However, it gave Kuroski, even if it just a second, time to catch his breath. In what seemed like slow motion, Kuroski dared to wipe the blood that was collecting on his cheek, which was a big mistake.

Instantly, Kerato disappeared. Before Kuroski was even able to react, let alone turn around, the dark swordsman slashed at his back with one, big furious swipe of his weapon. The weaker warrior cried out with anguish in a high-pitched squeal. Kuroski attempted to whip around, but he fired another energy blast in his panic before he even located Kerato's location. Without any warning, he felt the full brunt of a powerful blow to his cranium, inflicting pain that reverberated throughout his body. When Kuroski urged his body to move, it disobeyed orders. To sum up a triple combo, Kerato dealt Kuroski a hard kick to his stomach, winding him so much that it caused his vision to flicker.

Aware of its physical limits, Kuroski's body began to shut down, but in his mind, Kuroski knew that he couldn't give up no matter what. Surging with one-hit-wonder vigor, Kuroski lifted his head to meet Kerato's arrogant simile. When they had first met, Kerato bore a passive expression, but Kuroski believed that he had now drawn out his true nature: an evil monster. He could care less about what race Kerato was from; they were enemies. With his words and with force, Kerato had asserted his intention to put Jupiter's health in danger, but Kuroski could not allow that.

"Zephyr Wind!" Kuroski roared. Since his native element was wind, he could put more power and speed into the implementation of his attack than people without a wind nature could.

Catching the swordsman off guard, Kuroski was able to blow Kerato away. However, this just seemed to add to his momentum.

If Kerato decided to get serious, Kuroski knew that he was out of luck. Earlier, when Kerato kicked Kuroski in the stomach, he could have just as easily thrust his sword into it. The younger fighter was not sure if he should have been grateful that the more experienced warrior was just playing with him, or angry. Either way, Kuroski was out of techniques, so he had to rely on his wits.

"Shadow Strike!" Kerato raged. Soundlessly, he vanished into thin air a second time.

This time, Kuroski attempted to calm his nerves and try to sense out Kerato's location but to no avail. His blinding speed preceded him again. The skilled fighter sliced through Kuroski's defenses in the form of a shadow, striking him out of the air with the butt of his sword. When Kuroski's body impacted against the ground, his wounds cried out in irritated rebellion. However, the young boy got right back up as fast as he could, battling against the effects of his abrasions.

Kuroski gasped, "If you think you can beat me that easily, you've got another thing coming!"

"Good, but let's see if you can handle *this*."

Giving Kuroski barely any time to think, Kerato focused his energy and then transferred the stored power into his bands. Intense heat surrounded the sword's glistening metal, seemingly protecting it while enhancing its attack power. In midair, mild rapids started to form around him, rustling the leaves of the trees next to him. Kerato's movements had become unpredictable, and he flew toward Kuroski in a zigzag to try to throw his judgment off.

"Zephyr Wind!" Kuroski screamed again in a final attempt to slow Kerato's approach toward him. Out of the corner of his eye, he noticed that Kerato sliced through the gust with the swing of his blade and without much effort.

However, Kuroski's goal wasn't to attack Kerato but to distract. In a split second, he rolled away from the spot where he fell so he would not be in the blade wielder's direct path. Then he exhausted all the speed and power he had left and incorporated it into one final assault. Kuroski teleported behind a momentarily stunned Kerato and released a powerful energy blast that exploded against his back. Showing no mercy, like Kerato had shown him, the young warrior fired a volley of weaker energy blasts around the same spot, constantly adding more pressure.

"Gah!" Kuroski shrieked before he finished the onslaught with another Zephyr Wind, his only named attack. All the while, Kerato only let small grunts of discomfort escape from his larynx, showing no signs that any of Kuroski's attacks had inflicted damage. *Wow!* Kuroski thought; the capacities of both his brain and his body had reached their summits. This guy must be made out of the same metal as his sword!

Faster than even the See-Through eye could follow, Kerato whipped his right arm around, rotating 180 degrees, and slashed Kuroski across the head. If the cut had gone any deeper, it would've killed him in an instant, since Kuroski sensed that Kerato was aiming for the kill. It was either that Kerato's annoyance was starting to work against him or Kuroski was extremely lucky; signs pointed to the latter.

Nevertheless, Kuroski was fading fast. He was losing too much blood from the wound in his back, the fresh cut on his forehead, and the smaller injuries all over his body. The most cumbersome loss was his reflexes; it was the worst possible component of the nervous system to have suppressed when fighting against a speed demon.

At this point, Kerato took control of the one-sided battle, thrashing Kuroski like a punching bag. Despite the excruciating pain, Kuroski could still see light at the end of the tunnel; he was stalling Kerato, whether he was losing or not! He felt the swordsman's attacks getting weaker and sloppier, proving Zephyr's earlier theory about his lack of stamina. Even though Kerato's lagging willpower was prominent, it was not enough to close the gap between their physical conditions. Finally, before the plummet of his power could become too great, Kerato thrust his sword into the side of Kuroski's stomach.

"Agh!" Kuroski howled in anguish. Kerato pulled his blade out and raised it high up in the air, with Kuroski's blood dripping down it.

Suddenly, Kuroski understood. Kerato was sparing his life. Killing him was not his objective.

Kerato sheathed his sword and flew west, in the direction where Kuroski had been standing in front of earlier.

"Ha, *sucker* …" Kuroski laughed faintly. He had played his role perfectly.

RECOVERY

A WOKEN BY A COOL, REFRESHING breeze, Jadeleve's first thought was Zephyr. Her friends had found her.

However, when her vision focused, she realized that she was in some sort of spherical building. Her friends were nowhere in sight. A huge glass dome acted as a ceiling above the pure white, disk-shaped room, so Jadeleve could clearly see Europa. She noticed that there were three windmills stationed an equal distance apart around the dome, so they formed a triangle. They must have been two hundred feet tall, with steel blades for maximum air circulation and thick, steel poles that held them in place. After traveling through a thick, humid jungle for days, Jadeleve was grateful for the cool air. She was captivated by the blue, lustrous ribbons attached to each steel blade. The ribbons sparkled as the moonlight reflected off of them.

She could not help but grin when she learned that her head did not spin when she moved. Even so, her stomach rumbled with ferocity, and she began to feel weak. Finally, Jadeleve took notice of her body. Her purple clothing, which consisted of a T-shirt, combat shorts, black socks, and combat boots, were torn up. She felt the bandages that were wrapped around her stomach under her shirt, as well as around her arms and legs. Her wounds that she had acquired during her adventures through the rainforest had already begun to heal.

"So you're Jadeleve Dawn, the famous Zeal Possessor? Try not to move too much for now," a female voice suggested.

Jadeleve shifted in her bed so she could face the woman, who looked about thirty-five. She had tan skin, wavy black hair, with one side falling over her left eye, and gleaming brown eyes. She wore a white shirt, tan khaki shorts, and white sneakers.

"Thank you for saving me?" Jadeleve bowed her head in thanks.

"Oh! No thanks necessary; this is what I do," the woman replied, embarrassed.

"Where did you find me? I ... I was wandering through this jungle ... I thought I was going to die ..."

"It's *okay*." The woman moved closer to comfort Jadeleve, who was on the verge of tears. After Jadeleve recovered, she was ready to talk.

"You're in Fiome, and this is Fiome Rehabilitation Center. I was on my morning run today when I found you on the ground in the Akapeachi Jungle in critical condition. You were so close to making it here. I've never met someone as young as you who has even *tried* to get through the whole jungle."

So it wasn't all a dream.

"Do you know what happened to my friends?"

"It said on the news that you were defeated in a terrible battle with Eyebots in Sapolis City. A girl and her dragon somehow prevented you from using your energy. Then she hypnotized you and beat you senseless. She tied all of your friends on her dragon's back and rode off with them to ... I don't know. For some reason, she didn't kidnap you," the woman answered to the best of her knowledge.

That's what I thought happened. Now they're using them as hostages.

"Do have any I idea how I went from Sapolis City to the Akapeachi Jungle?"

"The only way to get from Sapolis City to Fiome is through the Akapeachi Jungle. I don't know why you chose to come here, but it's a straight path."

"I was hallucinating in there, so it was lucky that I ended up here. What's your name?"

"Sheenika. It's a pleasure to finally meet you. As you know, the Eyebots have been capturing or killing everyone they can. Since the adults are on Saturn fighting in the war, these kids have to fend for themselves. It's my job to help them. I have a team that helps me heal and a team that does field work, bringing in kids who are too injured to move on their own," she explained.

"So you're like the boss here," Jadeleve smirked.

"Well ... yeah. I founded this place a couple of years ago."

"What are those blue ribbons for?" Jadeleve asked, pointing to the windmill that was directly behind her.

"Well, they are called mistrial ribbons and are enlaced with healing wind energy. The windmills help to distribute the energy across the room. This only works for healing physical or minor injuries. This room is used for that, but in special cases, we use special processes. For example, when we examined you this morning, we noticed that you were experiencing hallucinations, so we entered your mind and cleaned it up. Then we put you in this room to heal your physical injuries."

"You can stop hallucinations?"

"It's a mental energy technique. It's the same type of attack the Eyebots used on you. They took advantage of your lack of experience. Unless you learn how to counter it, you'll be at a disadvantage."

"I didn't know mental attacks could be so powerful. Do you know today's date by any chance?'

"July 19. Your fight was on the tenth," Sheenika replied.

"It's been nine days?" Jadeleve wailed, trying to keep her voice quiet for the sake of the other patients. "We're already behind schedule."

"You mean on your quest to get to the Zeal Orb."

"Yeah. Do you have a map?"

Sheenika's holographic map was the same type that Zenon used. "Thanks."

"Do you know where you're heading next?"

"I guess I'll just keep heading north and try some leads. I know they're all right," Jadeleve assured with a twelve-year-old's conviction. "Those guys would never let me down. Can take a shower?"

"Oh!" Sheenika replied, caught off guard by Jadeleve sudden change in tone. "Of course, honey. I'll show you."

Sheenika led her through the automatic, semicircular door into the shower room. Jadeleve was not expecting the bathroom floor to be made from balsawood, which was not a common material used to make a floor. Jadeleve's house in Xaphias was made from wood—oak tree wood—but her dad had just taken advantage of the trees in the forest. However, the walls and the ceiling were made out the same material as the other room.

There were about twenty-five showers in the room. All the curtains were designed with the same mistral ribbon pattern.

"This side of the shower room is for girls; there are actually fifty showers. To get into a shower, you'll have to take the stairs underground to the changing room and then go up through a stair set that leads to one of the showers. There are toiletries in the changing room. When you're done, you'll find new loose clothes on a bench next to the stairs that led to your shower. Afterward, I'll take you to the eating area. If you feel tired then, I'll show you where you can sleep. I know you want to get back on the road again, but I want to make sure you're healed up, first," Sheenika explained.

"All right," Jadeleve replied, loving how Sheenika treated her like another one of her patients instead of the *Zeal Possessor*.

When she was dry from her shower, Jadeleve glanced behind her and found a gray T-shirt and gray sweatpants. Grateful for clothes that were intact, she eagerly put them on. With her stomach rumbling, Jadeleve sprinted toward the steps that led back up to the shower room entrance and met Sheenika, who was facing away from her.

"Hey, Jadeleve. Come and see this," Sheenika urged.

Jadeleve peered over Sheenika's shoulder to see a man carrying a boy into the rehabilitation room.

"The recovery room has never been so full before. That's Quintell coming back from his mission to rescue a boy who was beaten earlier tonight," Sheenika explained.

"The Eyebots did this. They make me sick. I can't just sit here; I've got to do something."

"Let's get your strength back up first, sweetie. Let's get you something to eat."

BACK IN ACTION

"THIS IS THE SUPPLY ROOM," Sheenika said, the morning of the twenty-first. Jadeleve had spent the twentieth recovering. "Most of our patients are found unconscious by scouts, and they usually have lost all their possessions. We have this just in case a patient needs anything. Feel free to take whatever you like."

"Are you sure? I can take anything for free?"

"Don't get me wrong; take only the things you *need*, but yeah. You kids are the protectors of this land. It's the least we can do." Sheenika beamed.

Thank you!" Jadeleve bowed politely and then went on to explore the contents of the room.

Since Jadeleve wanted to travel light, she took a small purple and black bag with several different compartments. Next, she picked out five combat shirts and shorts, but she also got a few larger clothes that she could grow into. Finally, Jadeleve chose one paper map of the Fantasia County and a world map.

When she was finished, she neatly folded her clothes to save room and put them in her bag instead of shoving them inside. She decided to keep her two maps in her left hand for quick access.

"Do you have any zeal capsules?" Jadeleve asked.

"No, sorry. You can get those in a store at the edge of town. It's called the Travel Atlas. They'll have everything else you need. And don't worry; everything there is free now," Sheenika informed her.

"Okay. Well, thanks so much for everything. If it wasn't for you, I'd still be lost in the jungle, hallucinating," Jadeleve said.

"Oh, sweetie, you've already said thank you. I'm just glad I could do something to help. I'm no fighter, which is why I'm not serving in the war, but healing is what I do. I feel like I'm useful here."

When Jadeleve stepped outside, the beautiful day lifted her spirits. Not one cloud flawed the blue sky. The front lawn of the rehabilitation center was sandy, until about twenty feet outward, where grass flourished. To her left, the immensely tall trees of the Akapeachi Jungle blocked her view.

Sheenika stepped outside to see her off.

"Is there a supermarket where I can get food here?" Jadeleve asked.

"Yep. It's right next to Travel Atlas."

"Okay." Jadeleve hovered off the ground, ready to take off. "I won't let you dow—"

"Wait!" a high-pitched voice called, stalling Jadeleve in midair.

A boy that looked about her age stood in front of the rehabilitation center's entrance. The boy had dark brown skin, light brown eyes, curly black hair, and long arms. He wore a blue combat shirt with green shorts, and yellow and orange running shoes. Jadeleve realized that he was the same boy that Quintell had found. He had recovered as quickly as she had, and he looked prepared to leave with his new backpack.

"Are you Jadeleve Dawn?" the boy asked in awe.

"Who's asking?" Jadeleve questioned.

"My name is Kuroski Weir. I met a group of girls who said they knew you," the boy explained.

"Really? When? Where?"

"Whoa, calm down! I met your friends in a prison on Ripple Island. Last time I checked, they were okay, but this crazy Eyebot swordsman named Kerato was chasing them down. I managed to divert his path so they would have enough time to reach Pearl Town and recoup, but it's only a matter of time before he finds them out," Kuroski clarified.

"So *that's* where they are. Thanks for letting me know. I better get going now." Jadeleve hastily turned to leave.

"Hold up! Can I come with you? I want to help."

"Okay … No one's ever offered us help before. What's your story?" Jadeleve hesitated.

"I've got nowhere else to go. I'm an orphan who just wants to make a difference in the world," Kuroski murmured, giving her the eyes.

Jadeleve sighed and thought it over but ultimately went with her gut feeling. "Pulling the old 'I'm an orphan' trick on me, huh? Fine, you can come."

"Thank you!" Kuroski beamed, flying up to greet her.

"Goodbye, Sheenika! And good luck with the center!" Jadeleve waved.

"Good luck saving the world!" she called back.

Excited for having made progress, Jadeleve raced toward downtown Fiome, expecting Kuroski to be right behind her.

"Wait for me!" he shrieked. However, Jadeleve did not slow down or look back.

This is what you get for baiting me, Jadeleve thought with a smirk.

THE TALE OF THE PENDANT

THE DUO REACHED THE TRAVEL Atlas's iron exterior and automatic doors first.

"They'll have everything we need here," Jadeleve explained.

As soon as Kuroski stepped in, he felt a cold breeze caress his tense muscles. The advanced air-conditioning served as an oasis for Kuroski in the middle of the blazing hot day.

The inside of Travel Atlas was dark blue with white stripes that lined the floor, dividing different products into sectors. All merchandise were stocked on open wooden shelves, except for huge items like fridges and zeal capsules. Zeal capsules were zeal-powered devices that could condense matter and be used for large amounts of storage. They were kept in glass shelves on opposite sides of the store. Jadeleve appeared in front of the zeal capsule section. Kuroski mirrored Jadeleve's movement and snatched about fifteen capsules, but he followed his own path after that, exploring the store at his leisure.

From there, Kuroski went on to select a portable zeal-powered shower, washing machine, and stove. He then transported all his items into zeal capsules. He and Jadeleve met up at the counter once they were done shopping. Kuroski immediately noticed that she carried more than twice as many capsules as he did.

The lady at the counter was petite and elderly with gray eyes and gray hair that came down to her chin. Her skin was pale, as if she had avoided the scorching sun her whole life. She wore the Travel Atlas's employee uniform, which was a dark blue collared shirt and brown khaki shorts.

The price of a zeal capsule was determined by its weight. When a zeal capsule absorbed the molecules of an object into itself, it gained about one-billionth of the object's mass. To measure the price, the zeal capsule was put on a scale, and when the employees found out the mass of the capsule, they multiplied the number by one hundred thousand, which gave the full price. For example, in 10112, an average fridge weighed one hundred pounds. In the Zeal Capsule, it would only weigh one-billionth of that amount, or 0.001, and then multiplied by one hundred thousand, it would cost one hundred dollars. Luckily, everything was free.

The old woman spoke. "Ah. Jadeleve Dawn, my word. It's a pleasure to meet you. The famous Zeal Possessor. I initiated the expedition to carve out the Redundant Dungeon forty years ago for young people to explore and test their abilities. There are loads of traps there. It used to be a mountain, but I sensed large levels of solar energy radiating from it, so I gathered a team to turn it into a cave. It turned out there were crystals that were producing the energy … Ingrain Crystals, we named them. Then I opened up this shop. Around this time, your grandmother came to town."

"W-w-wait. You knew my grandma? What's your name?" Jadeleve asked, startled.

"Jasmine Colbalt, dear."

"That sounds familiar …"

"When she came here, she was about thirteen, around your age. Because she was a Dawn, she was already famous, but she was so modest. She came here for traveling supplies, saying that she wanted to take on the dungeon. She left with an Ingrain Crystal core. It seems that little gem in your pocket is the same one. I don't need to see it. I can sense it from here. Years later, she called me when you were born, saying that you were the Zeal Possessor and that you would come here one day. It must be destiny."

"Wow ... I never knew about this. So my pendant is made from the core of a crystal? Where is the Redundant Dungeon?"

"It's a day's journey outside of town. And it's infested with Beings who lately have been experiencing terrible hallucinations. They have become increasingly difficult to deal with. You and your friend should see it for yourselves ... see if you can get to the bottom of this."

"Okay. What else can you tell me about my pendant?"

"The inner core is made of natural metal that attracts other energy so the energy you store stays inside of it. It can help you tremendously with energy control, and if you practice enough, you could become light itself and travel at the speed of light. If you practice even more, you could travel at the speed of light without the pendant."

"I knew it. I did that somehow in the Akapeachi Jungle, and it's the same technique my dad used to save me once. I'm gonna master it one day. Thanks *so* much for everything."

Jasmine turned to Kuroski.

"I'm Kuroski." Kuroski raised his hand, embarrassed.

"I can see you've made a loyal friend." Jasmine beamed.

Kuroski was left speechless at this.

"Hm. He's all right," Jadeleve smirked.

Later, under the unforgiving sun, the two organized their zeal capsules by labeling each one with the sticky paper Jadeleve snagged from Travel Atlas. Kuroski was confused about why Jadeleve was labeling multiple capsules under the same name, like how she labeled "sleeping bag" on five different ones. Then it hit him: she had picked out supplies for her friends too.

"What's your natural element?" Kuroski asked.

"I'm actually not sure what that is," Jadeleve replied.

"It's basically the type of energy that you can draw from without using your own energy. If you feel stronger around sunlight, maybe your natural element is solar energy."

"I *do* feel more powerful around the sun. I mean, it could be that my native element is solar energy. How would I know for sure?" Jadeleve asked.

"By going to the Origin Temple in—"

"In Jazell Town," she said.

"How did you—"

"Jazell Town is on our way to the north edge of Fantasia County, so we can stop there ... *after* we find the others," Jadeleve stated just as she zipped up her bag. She had organized each of her zeal capsules into a different compartment and put her remaining ones in a separate pocket. As usual, Kuroski had to catch up. Starting today, he would begin working toward changing that.

Next, they stopped by the supermarket quickly to stock up on food and water, making sure to put them in their respective zeal capsules.

"You know that the Redundant Dungeon is just a never-ending maze of repeating patterns, so people tend to get lost there. The worst part is ... Beings. We should just fly over it and get to Pearl Town. Going straight through is just a waste of time."

"Don't tell me what's a waste of time. I could have just *not* brought you along," Jadeleve said. "If there is a chance I can learn more about my pendant and unlock a hidden power, it's worth it. If we can't survive in the dungeon, we have no chance against the Eyebots, even with the Zeal Orb."

Again, these girls had put him in his place. If he wanted to earn their respect, he would have to put his fears behind him.

"I didn't mean to sound harsh, but we can't second-guess ourselves," Jadeleve explained. This time, Kuroski clearly understood where she was coming from. Jadeleve dropped the conversation and focused on the task at hand: getting past the Redundant Dungeon. Now, they were set to leave.

"Goodbye, Fiome!" Kuroski obnoxiously shouted downward after soaring high into the air. Jadeleve flew beside him with an impassive expression on her face. As they advanced through the rest of the town and closed upon the exit gate, Kuroski's excitement grew.

When they arrived at the exit gate, which had black bars that pointed at the stop, a tall man stood in their path. Before Kuroski even stopped flying, he realized that the man had bright, scarlet eyes. His less attention-grabbing features included his dark chestnut hair, his slightly tan skin, and his thick facial hair, which obscured half his face. The big man wore a black suit.

"What can I do for you?" the man asked in a booming voice.

"We're heading into the dungeon. Can you let us pass?" Jadeleve asked politely. As always, she seemed to be focusing hard on something, but it seemed to be something that she just could not grasp. Kuroski was confused by why the man was even there.

Doesn't he know that kids from all over are trying to take action? And shouldn't he be on Saturn fighting against the Eyebots with the rest of the adults? Kuroski thought.

"And proceed on your *quest?*" the guard guessed.

"What do you prefer? Journey? Adventure," Kuroski offered.

"Good luck!" the man roared. Without warning, he fired an energy blast straight at Jadeleve, but she vanished instantaneously.

"*What?*" The guard gasped. Kuroski was also caught off guard, but he instinctively knew what Jadeleve wanted him to do.

Following Jadeleve's lead, Kuroski took advantage of the guard's confusion and broke his jaw with a kick to the chin. Flailing backward, the guard lost his balance, but before he could topple over, Jadeleve reappeared behind him. In one swift move, Jadeleve temporarily paralyzed the man by kicking his spine in the sweet spot.

"What's your *problem?*" Jadeleve said.

"Just you wait. You'll never survive in there." The guard laughed manically through a fit of coughing.

"You must be the one who messed with the Beings," Kuroski said.

"That's right …" The man coughed up blood as he spoke.

"Why? Who are you?" Jadeleve questioned.

"I-I'm just an Eyebot who Cataract ordered to test out a new w-weapon. No one special. I bet you're not brave enough to step into that dungeon."

"We were already going. You don't have to bait me," Jadeleve whispered, then knocked the man out by chopping his neck.

"Let's go," Kuroski said. Finally, they walked beyond the gate where vegetation ruled the land.

Truth be told, Kuroski was feeling a little shaken up from his confrontation with that Eyebot.

"Hey, Kuroski?" Jadeleve asked.

"Yes?"

"How did you know that guy was causing the hallucinations?"

"I just trusted my instincts. Plus he gave some clues."

"You saw right through him," Jadeleve said in awe.

"Well … I've never been that brave, but being cautious can help sometimes. One of the only memories I have of my parents is them telling me where the See-Throughs got their name from."

"Where?"

"'See-Throughs are ones who can *see through* deception,'" he recited.

"Really? Thank you, Kuroski. I have weaknesses; I shouldn't forget that. This experience will help both of us; I can learn to be more cautious, and you can become braver," Jadeleve decided.

"Right," Kuroski moaned. "But you're right; no more running away."

A Home Away from Home

FAMISHED, PUPIL SLOWED THEIR GROUP's pace considerably.
"How much longer?" Pupil whined.

"I don't know. We don't have a map, remember?" Zenon sighed.

Pupil's heart sank. Alarmed, she shook her head in an attempt to regain her bearings, believing that the powerful life energy that she sensed belonged to the swordsman. However, much to her surprise, the power was Zephyr's.

"We're not that far. Come on; we can do this," Zephyr murmured with sheer determination in her eyes. The others nodded, acknowledging her spirit.

As noon approached, Pupil's energy began to return, which was just like how her mom said her dad was when he was young.

When Pupil thought about her dad, she felt calmer, and it was one of the few thoughts that took her mind off food. To her, her dad was the coolest guy in the world, choosing to give up raising his kids in order to protect them.

Pupil's twin stayed silent throughout the whole flight. Pupil had never understood her sister's reticence but loved her unconditionally. She was actually grateful that Iris's personality was the reverse of hers so people could tell them apart.

Pupil thought of Zenon as another older sister. When she needed guidance, she was the first one that Pupil looked to. Although Zenon did not coach her as much as Zephyr did during training, she always gave great advice. It was because of her that Pupil was finally able to stop crying around two that morning.

Pupil was Zephyr's pupil, and she loved Zephyr like family, but Jadeleve was Pupil's role model. Jadeleve was fearless.

After filling her mind with comforting thoughts, all other worries fell away. Where her physical abilities had reached their limit, her mental abilities took over. Pupil knew that if she dwelled on how long it would take to reach Pearl Town, her hunger would return. Finally, she noticed that the number of trees around them was decreasing. Soon, she could see a small grass clearing and beyond it a towering mountain peak that rivaled Xaphias's ranges. As the girls got closer, Pupil had to lift her head to see the summit. The immensity of the mountain was awe-inspiring.

"We're here," Iris murmured. The weary warriors were on edge from their counter with the swordsman, fearing even the slightest sound would give away their location to him.

"What did I tell you?" Zephyr smirked, crossing her arms with pride. After almost two weeks, they had finally reached another town. As stealthily as they could, the girls dove over the hill and then curved up to the sky.

From what Pupil could see up in the air, Pearl Town stood out in stark contrast to the many other towns she had visited through her journey. First of all, vegetation grew on the buildings. Tree branches blanketed the streets, and almost every backyard was a forest. The town was built on a mountain inside of a rocky valley, so the ground was uneven.

After they gained a high enough altitude, the four girls landed in a shady spot in the middle of town, where not a soul seemed to be around.

"Where's our first stop?" Pupil turned toward Zenon.

"Well, we're staying here until we can get a lead on Jadeleve. In the meanwhile, we'll train. We have to find good place on the outskirts of town to set up camp," Zenon replied with a slight grin.

"Yeah! I'm starving!" Pupil hollered.

"Keep *quiet*, Pupil. Wait. Can you use your nose to track down food like they do in cartoons?" Zephyr asked with a serious expression on her face.

"I don't know; maybe. I've never tried it before, but if I can get food faster, I'll do anything," Pupil declared.

Pupil's nose started to work vigorously, twitching and sniffing about like the earth's dog. Thinking solely about food, Pupil let her nose be her guide.

"Do you really know where you're going, Pupil?" Iris squealed. Her irises flashed hot pink in anger and embarrassment.

"Trust me. I can feel it in my bones," Pupil beamed.

After twenty minutes of this, it seemed as if they were just going in circles. Finally, an unexpected voice interrupted Pupil's mischief.

"What are you kids doing here?" a woman from a nearby house asked, peeking out of a slightly cracked door.

"We were just looking for a place to eat. We haven't had anything to eat for days now; we just escaped from a prison on Ripple Island—"

"So you're *criminals*?" the woman asked, her eyes suddenly wide with alarm.

"*No.* The Eyebots have been capturing See-Through children to stop us from interfering with the war. We lost in a fight at Sapolis City, got captured, and got separated from our friend. Yesterday, we escaped and flew from Ripple Island to rest and recuperate here while trying to find any leads on her. While we were in prison, they confiscated our bags, so we don't have food," Zenon explained as calmly as she could.

"Oh my ..." The woman faltered. Suddenly, the fury in her eyes subsided. "I'm so sorry I jumped to conclusions. I just can't bear to lose my son. I've already lost my son and my husband ..."

The girls thought it would be best to stay silent while the woman expressed her emotions. After she recovered, she opened the door wider.

"So you're the ones who lost in that horrible fight. Your friend is Jadeleve Dawn, the Zeal Possessor, right? You guys are protecting this planet already, and you're not even teenagers yet. I hear about you guys on the news all the time. I owe you an apology. I always jump to conclusions. Let me make it up to you. You can stay here, and I'll make you lunch and dinner. We have a summer farmhouse with four beds, which is perfect for you," the lady suggested.

"Thank you. You won't even notice we're here." Zephyr sighed with relief.

Out of the corner of her eye, Pupil saw her twin's eyes flash a mixture of green and yellow, signifying her excitement and curiosity. Iris's irises now sometimes changed into shades that were a fusion of colors because her emotions were becoming more complex as result of her constant exposure to controversial situations like this.

Regardless of the woman's initial hostility, Pupil was grateful for help from anyone. She carried this newfound hope with her as she followed others into the woman's house, leaving the task of exploring Pearl Town for another day. Because she was the last person to enter, she slowly closed the door behind her, trying to savor the moment as she laid eyes on her first meal in days.

THE NEW DISCIPLE

"**I**'M MRS. KAGE," THE WOMAN replied after Iris quietly asked her name.

Mrs. Kage was a woman of average height, with unkempt long, dark brown hair, blue eyes, and fair, apricot-colored skin. In her light green apron with a white undershirt and white slippers, she appeared to be oddly graceful.

The floor in the hallways and in the front entrance was made of polished, brown wooden planks, but the kitchen floor was made of light brown, stone tiles. Beside the kitchen, on the left side of the front door, was a gray carpeted living room with a flat screen TV.

"What are your names?" Mrs. Kage asked.

"Nice to meet you. I'm Zenon, this is Zephyr, that's Pupil and Iris," Zenon introduced swiftly, wanting to get to the food as quickly as possible.

"All right, all right. I'll serve everything soon, but first … can you go talk to my son? Ever since his father and brother died, all he does is sit in his room in front of his computer all day. He won't listen to a single thing I say. Maybe you can knock some sense into him. But let me warn you: he's only eight years old," Mrs. Kage said.

"Sure. It's the least we can do," Zenon agreed.

"Okay. His room is the first door on your right once you get up the steps," Mrs. Kage directed, and then she quietly walked away toward the kitchen.

Zenon led the group up the sixteen wooden steps. The closer they moved to the boy's room, the more on edge Iris felt, though she refrained from showing this uneasiness in her eyes.

Should we knock? Or should we just open the door?

Finally, fed up with waiting, Pupil took action.

"Can we come in and check out your room?"

There was no response.

"*Pupil.* That's rude. Say ... can we *please* come in," Zephyr offered. Again there was no response.

If he's on his computer, shouldn't we be hearing him typing on the keyboard? Iris thought. At first, her explanation seemed too simple to be correct, so she almost disregarded it. Although, she also knew that her perilous journey through Jupiter, which forced her to stretch her mental and physical abilities to their limits, had also caused her to overthink straightforward solutions.

He's not here.

"Hey, guys. I don't think he's in there," Iris explained to her companions.

"I think he's just ignoring us. Where else could he be? Mrs. Kage said that he's always on his computer," Pupil argued. For a second, Iris started to doubt herself again, but she immediately thought better of it.

I can't second-guess myself anymore, Iris thought as her eyes flashed brown with determination.

"Let's knock on the door again. If he doesn't answer, we'll go in and see for ourselves," Iris compromised.

"Fine." Pupil banged against the wooden door three more times but to no avail. Frustrated, Iris stepped forward and flung the door open.

"Are you okay ..." Iris hesitated when she realized that there was no one in the room.

"You were right, Iris. Where could he be?" Zephyr asked as she looked around the room. The gray paint on the walls caused the room to appear dull and lifeless. On the far left side of the room was a disheveled pile of torn-up books. Other than a dirty, unkempt mattress that was positioned parallel to the room's entrance, a small, black, three-drawer wardrobe for clothes, and a desk with a computer, the room was vacant.

Iris observed that the boy's computer was slim, oval shaped, and light as a feather. His computer's monitor checked out as up-to-date as well, and both were in tip-top shape, as if they were the only things in the boy's life that he cared enough about to take care of. However, the boy's monitor was covered with yellow sticky notes, as if he was doing extensive research about something and wanted to refrain from forgetting anything important.

"Maybe there's some clues on these sticky notes," Zephyr suggested.

"We can't just snoop around in here," Zenon muttered.

"Hey, Mrs. Kage wants us to help her son, and we owe her one. We owe Jadeleve and Kuroski. How can we live like this, owing people all the time," Zephyr grumbled.

"I guess we can't ... Yeah, we've got to get even," Zenon agreed. The fiery intensity that was packed into her eyes practically burned through those sticky notes. When her eyes widened, Iris knew that she had found something. The other girls quickly rushed to her side.

"Guys." Zenon held up one sticky note that looked newer than the other ones for everyone to see. "This one says 'to get to secret training zone entrance, press enter on keyboard.'"

"What are we waiting for? Let's do it!" Pupil prompted. She pushed Zenon aside, pressed the button, and vanished into thin air, leaving the others speechless.

"I'm going next," Zephyr declared, followed Pupil's example. She disappeared.

"They *never* think anything through." Zenon sighed.

Iris, naturally, was frozen in place.

Zenon's right. They're so reckless. Who knows where that teleporter sent them.

"But they have the right idea. We can't hesitate," Zenon said, interrupting Iris's negative thoughts. "Let's go, Iris."

Suddenly, Iris was surrounded by darkness. Her body felt weightless like she was falling. Iris gasped as the wind was suddenly knocked out of her. The embrace of solid ground came faster than she expected.

"Uhh," Iris moaned.

Iris somehow found the fortitude to recover from the staggering pain caused by her impact and lifted her head to catch a glimpse of sunlight.

Beyond where her awestruck friends stood, a hilly grass field stretched out for miles. The most distinct features were the jagged brown mountains. Light, soothing wind blew at the girls from behind, improving the ambience.

"I could stare at it for hours," Zephyr muttered.

"How did we get here?" Pupil asked groggily.

"Mrs. Kage's son built a transporting system that transports anyone who touches the 'enter' key from his computer to this fake metal tree. We materialized at the top of the inside of the tree, which is possible because the fake tree is hollow. That's why, for the first few seconds, it feels like you're falling through a bottomless pit. When you reach the bottom, there's a huge exit that you can walk through. This kid has talent if he can build something like this," Zenon explained.

"He's been lying to his mom this whole time. Anyway, we have to go find him. Let's fly," Zephyr declared.

After they were comfortably soaring around an altitude of two hundred feet, Zephyr announced the next phase of the plan.

"I'm gonna try to sense out his energy," she said.

In deep, unyielding concentration, Zephyr closed her eyes. Iris could sense Zephyr's spiritual energy reach out and try to connect with another soul.

"Got 'em. He's not that far away."

After a few minutes, the girls had reached the boy, who looked exhausted. They descended toward him while he looked up at them in awe.

By the time the four famished girls touched ground, the boy had managed to catch his breath and compose himself enough to speak.

"You can *fly?* Who are you guys?" The girls individually introduced themselves. Iris made sure not to stutter when it was her turn to speak.

"Your mom was kind enough to let us stay in your farmhouse while we look for our friend. We want to repay her, so we decided that we'd help you with your training. What's your name?" Zenon inquired softly.

"Wayward," the boy whispered. He mirrored his mother's complexion, with blue eyes and disheveled brown hair that dangled a little over his eyes. Wayward's eyebrows seemed naturally slant upward in a surprised expression, making his demeanor seem innocent. He wore a light green T-shirt and black shorts. Both his socks and his shoes (which were huge for him) were pure white.

"Whaddya doin'?" Pupil asked through a yawn.

"Whaddya think?" Wayward mocked, copying Pupil's accent; suddenly, he became serious. Iris noticed the spark in his eye. "I'm training."

"You call that training? Really? Okay. Come at me then," Zephyr taunted.

"Oh …" Wayward hesitated for second. "All right! You'll be sorry!"

The young fighter bellowed before he recklessly charged at his senior. Iris was astonished by his willingness to try such a risky move. Zephyr effortlessly dodged Wayward's onslaught of punches, teleported behind him, and tripped him with the swift sweep of her leg.

"Ugh … no fair … I was tired," Wayward complained in a muffled voice with his face to the ground.

"You shouldn't have charged." Zephyr smirked.

"Who *are* you people?" Wayward moaned on the ground.

"We were trying to find the Zeal Orb and save the world, but we lost one of our members. We're trying to see if we can find any clues here. It could take days," Zephyr explained.

"By the way, do you know where we are?" Iris whispered.

"We're in the Graze Mountains. It's pretty close to home," Wayward mumbled after he turned to face Iris.

"This place is awesome! Do you come here to train regularly?" Pupil asked, not even fazed by Wayward's earlier attitude. Iris could already tell that he did not like her, but Wayward answered reluctantly.

"I come here a lot."

"That's great, but you shouldn't always train alone. You see that rock over there? I want you to hit it with your strongest energy blast," Zephyr ordered, crossing her arms.

"Okay …" Wayward stood up but was still stunned by Zephyr's power.

Wayward initiated a fighting stance while gathering his energy. Immediately, Iris noticed flaws in Wayward's approach. His energy output was trivial compared to his effort, causing his face to turn purple.

"Agh!" the young warrior gasped as he released the pent-up force. At first, the blast seemed to be successful, erupting in a flash of yellow light from the palms of his hands. However, before the beam hit its target, the light vanished. In exasperation, Wayward fell to the ground once again.

"It looks like you're struggling to gather your energy. You've got to relax when you do it," Zenon explained.

"Because you're using the energy from your own body, it shouldn't take as much effort as when you draw from other energy sources. You would have had a basic understanding of this *if* you actually talked to people," Zephyr said.

"Go away! You don't know anything about me!" Wayward ranted.

"We're just trying to *help*," Iris said. At this, the other girls were startled. Even Wayward, who barely knew them, grimaced with shame.

"Yeah! How do you think we got so strong? We had a bunch of teachers," Pupil pitched in, but this caused Wayward to flush with rage and embarrassment.

"I've only got Mom," He grumbled, clenching his fists and looking down at the ground. At this, the girls sympathized with him.

"We get it. We only had our moms, too," Zenon consoled.

"No, you don't," Wayward insisted.

Iris took a moment to figure out what he meant.

"You mean you wish your dad and brother were with you," Zenon figured out. "I'm telling you. We get it. Our dad was never home, so our older brother didn't have a father figure, either. Now, he bottles up his feelings and acts too serious. I don't want you to turn out like that."

"Oh." Wayward finally looked up.

"Yeah. We'll help with your training. It'll be thanks for letting us stay here," Zephyr offered.

Iris watched as Wayward weighed his options.

"Okay ... but can you carry me back home? I can't fly."

"Can't we use your teleporting device?" Zenon questioned.

"Nope. It's a one-way trip, so I usually walk home," Wayward explained as he stretched out his hands. "But today I want to *fly!*"

MEET THE KAGES

"LUNCH IS ALMOST DONE, KIDS! Maybe twenty minutes! Wayward, show them the farmhouse while you're waiting!" Mrs. Kage called when the kids returned to the house, pretending to have come from upstairs.

"Okay, Mom!" Wayward replied. He directed them outside to the farmhouse.

Wayward's farmhouse was wooden, pentagon-shaped, and freshly planted in dark red. Immediately after they opened the door, a rush of cool, revitalizing air swept over them, negating the extreme heat of the hot summer's sun.

"Perfect. If it wasn't for these fans," Zephyr pointed up at the oak wood ceiling where a circle of twelve fans rotated in a blur, "we'd be baking in here. And it's so lucky that it has four beds."

"Yeah. It used to be one for each of them," Zenon explained, reminding everyone how Wayward lost both his father and brother. Silence fell over the group.

"We definitely have to help Wayward, guys," Pupil exclaimed. The feeling was mutual all around, and Wayward was touched.

Wayward and the girls took turns taking showers in the farmhouse's shower. After taking fifteen minutes to look around the farmhouse, they walked across the lawn and up the porch steps to get back inside Wayward's house. As soon as Zenon slid open the glass porch door, the intoxicating smell of fresh food filled their noses. Pupil pushed past them.

"Slow *down*, Pupil," Zenon pleaded, but driven by food, Pupil did not listen and beat them all to the kitchen.

"Yay! *Finally!*" Pupil screamed. Mrs. Kage, who had just finished washing her hands for the sixth time, turned around and greeted them with a warm smile.

"Dig in. There's plenty for seconds."

The four girls hovered over the mouthwatering banquet laid out before them on a wooden table. Wayward's generous mother had prepared fresh corn and steamed broccoli as side dishes, along with a mountain of lasagna. The lasagna was marinated with fresh parsley, basil, Parmesan cheese, and garlic. Adding to the beauty was the tomato sauce, and for drinks, Mrs. Kage left three water bottles for each of them.

Like a true chef, Mrs. Kage sat back on a marble counter and watched with pride as the girls devoured their food. Zephyr, Zenon, and Iris never thought they would see the day, but halfway through her seventh plate, Pupil finally dropped her fork. She announced that she was full, which she had never done in her entire life.

"You're a *monster*," Wayward snickered.

"You *just* figured that out?" Zephyr laughed.

"That was awesome!" Pupil belched freely and then slapped her stomach. "I feel like a fridge!"

"What is there to do around here, Mrs. Kage?" Zenon changed the subject.

"There's not really much to do besides running and hiking. But since you're new … Wayward, why don't you show them around town? Maybe you can find some leads on Jadeleve while you're at it."

"Okay, Mom," Wayward promised, somewhat reluctantly.

Mrs. Kage withdrew back into the kitchen to wash the dishes while the kids stepped out.

"I'll take you to Public Plaza, which is at the center of town. It'll take us about an hour," Wayward explained.

"Do you go out a lot?" Zephyr asked.

"Nope. Mom never lets me go, but she doesn't want me 'cooped in my room glued to my computer' either." Wayward imitated his mother's voice, causing Iris to giggle softly.

After a small debate between Pupil and Wayward (Pupil won, obviously), the kids agreed to take a dirt road toward Public Plaza.

"Where do you guys live?" Wayward asked.

"We live in Xaphias, which is a huge town on Parabola Island, which is the largest island in the Crescent Straight, which are a strip of islands in southeast Celestine County."

"Well, Pearl Town is the second largest town in Fantasia County," Wayward retorted.

"What's the largest town?" Iris inquired.

"Jazell Town, I think. It's far away, up north. I've never been there before, but I've heard that there's a place called the Origin Temple there."

"Yeah, we were planning to stop by there," Zephyr mentioned.

A long silence followed as the kids daydreamed under the sunny sky. It was Pupil who finally lost the quiet game.

"Do you remember what your brother or your father looked like?" Pupil asked out of the blue, catching everyone off guard.

"I don't really remember my dad. He died fighting in the war when I was one. But I remember my brother. I was three when he was kidnapped. We're not really sure what happened to him ..."

"Then why are you training?" Pupil posed another odd, nosy question. "Do you want revenge? That would be weird because you barely knew them."

"*Pupil.*" Zephyr glared at her. "*Shut up.*"

"Sorry, I just want to know." Pupil raised her hands in surrender.

"It's okay if you ask, guys. No one usually asks me this stuff, but I actually want to talk. I don't really want revenge. I just want to find my brother. We know my dad is gone, but I really want to find my brother," Wayward confessed.

The girls empathized with the boy's feelings.

"What's in the Public Plaza?" Iris changed the subject.

"It has a grocery store, a bank, a train station, a post office, a gym, a church, a couple of restaurants, and a mall. Also, my school is near there; I'm going to third grade next year," Wayward replied.

"It sounds like the whole town thrives on this place!" Pupil threw up her hands in disbelief.

"It's huge, though. Aren't all towns like this?" Wayward asked.

"No. Most of the towns we've seen have at least two plazas. Even our hometown has four big plazas, and it's weird that you have a church in a *plaza*. In other towns, we usually find them in the middle of nowhere. And most don't have train stations," Zenon said.

"I guess that means Pearl Town is special," Zephyr summed up.

After another short silence, Wayward told everyone what was on his mind.

"Why can't I make an energy blast?"

"You have to draw energy from your soul to make an energy blast. So when you try to do it, focus on drawing out the energy that is behind your eyes or at the bottom of your brain. Humans can't do this as easily because they are less aware of their souls. But don't worry; when we train, we'll show you how to find it," Zenon explained.

Wayward decided to take advantage of the long path and enjoy the peaceful walk in comforting silence. With each step, the terrain slowly began to change. The dirt gave way to wood, and then the wood turned into concrete, signaling that they were getting closer to the heart of Pearl Town. Wayward also noticed that Pupil and Iris looked a little winded.

"The air is thinner than what you're used to because we're climbing up Mt. Pearl. That's the mountain that Pearl Town is built on," Wayward explained, and then he became confused about how Zephyr and Zenon were unaffected. "You guys seem fine."

"Xaphias has mountains as big as these. Pupil and Iris live at the base of the mountains, but we lived on top," Zephyr replied. "They're not used to the thin air like we are."

"That makes sense," Wayward said. Immediately after he said this, he saw the girls' expressions turn grim. "What's wrong?"

"Oh, nothing. You just remind us of another clueless boy that we met. His name was Kuroski." Pupil sniffled.

"We got into a tight situation, and he chose to stay behind to protect us. We wouldn't have made it here if it wasn't for him," Zephyr explained.

"Wow," Wayward gasped.

"When Jadeleve was around—" Zephyr started.

"Who's Jadeleve?" Wayward asked. The girls exchanged bewildered looks.

"You've never heard about her? She's always on the news," Zephyr said, somewhat amused.

"I don't watch news; I'm eight."

"Good point. Anyway, she's the newest Zeal Possessor. We're on a quest to find the Zeal Orb," Zephyr said.

"What's that?" Wayward asked. Zenon was at a loss of words.

"Are you a caveman? Have you never read *The Tale of the Zeal Orb*?" Zephyr queried.

"No and no," Wayward responded casually.

"Zeal comes from Neptune. Thousands of years ago, a See-Through scientist flew to Neptune in a spaceship to get the last reserves of zeal, sealed it into an orb, and brought it back to Jupiter. He made it the Zeal Orb. He was our ancestor. We're trying to find the Zeal Orb, which is in No Man's Land, so we can use its power as a weapon to win the war. People who are born with the power of zeal and don't need to take energy from the Zeal Orb to use zeal are called Zeal Possessors," Zephyr explained.

They explained why the Eyebots were declaring war, the state of the royal family, what transflare was, and their own role in the war.

"No way …" Wayward shrank back in disbelief, slowing down the lively pace. He could not absorb all the information at once, so he focused on the most important detail.

"Jadeleve is really cool then. I've got meet her." He beamed. The girls could not help smiling.

The kids walked another thirty minutes until they reached Public Plaza. Finally, Wayward took the lead.

"Come on. I'll show you my favorite place." Wayward ran ahead with the girls close behind.

FAMILY HISTORY

Z EPHYR ASKED AND LOOKED AROUND town, but no one had any ideas about where Jadeleve was. The kids they met at the Public were not afraid of the war and spoke openly about their plans. Some wanted to fight in the war on Saturn. Others wanted to infiltrate the Land of Eyebots for revenge.

Compelled to linger because of the kindness they were shown, the group spent two hours roaming around the plaza. They returned to Wayward's house around seven. Right when they stepped through the door, Zephyr peered into the kitchen and realized that they had arrived just in time, because Mrs. Kage had just finished cooking dinner.

Mrs. Kage greeted them with a warm smile. Zephyr thought back to when they first met earlier that same day. She realized that Mrs. Kage had developed a hostility toward strangers but deeply loved everyone she could trust. They were not so different in that respect.

As they ate, all Zephyr thought about was the next day; they could finally resume their training. Zephyr was not bothered by the lack of activities in Wayward's house. She had become accustomed to passing time in Xaphias by challenging Zenon to board games, taking walks, or doing chores. When was not doing that, she was either training or sleeping. Despite her parents' success in the electronic industry, she spent little time inside with technology. She would thrive here. Even so, something was still bugging her.

"So ... Wayward told us that your husband died fighting in the war and that your son was kidnapped," Zephyr said.

"Yes ... that's true," Mrs. Kage confirmed.

Zephyr motioned with her head for Wayward to talk to his mom.

"Did you ever find his kidnapper?" Wayward interjected.

"No, honey ..."

"And you just let it go? Did you even call the Imperial Knights?" Zephyr exploded, unable to stop herself.

"Who do you think you are? Of course I did!" Mrs. Kage snapped. "But they couldn't help me, and I'm no fighter!"

"That's no excuse. If you really loved him, you'd go after him yourself!" Zephyr shouted.

"Don't you tell me if I really loved my son or not. If I don't stay here and take care of Wayward, no one else can. He's all I have left ..." Mrs. Kage began to cry.

"*Zephyr.* What are you saying?" Zenon reprimanded. Zephyr crossed her arms and looked away. She had no tolerance for cowards.

Everyone sat silently as Mrs. Kage wept, but after a minute, she spoke again.

"It was April 12, 10108, so Rohan was nine. He had been training outside in the backyard for hours. I was watching him from the porch, cradling Wayward in my arms, when I saw a bald man with gray eyes appear out of nowhere and kidnap him. They vanished into thin air without a trace. I tried to call the Imperial Knights, but I had no leads. All I could tell them was the description of the man and my son. They never found them." Mrs. Kage sobbed.

"Well ... I still think you gave up too easily," Zephyr grumbled, earning a smack on the head from her sister.

"Did you see exactly what that man did? Did he say anything to you?" Zenon asked.

"It looked like he stared into Rohan's eyes and put him into a trance. Rohan started acting strange, then the man grabbed him and vanished," Mrs. Kage murmured, not wanting to recall the memory.

"It sounds like what those guys did in that prison," Pupil said. Suddenly Zephyr put two and two together.

"You're right, Pupil. Someone who hypnotizes kids and kidnaps them … it sounds exactly like what happened to us," Zephyr agreed.

"Wait … this happened to you girls, too?" Mrs. Kage gasped.

"Yeah. We had to break out of there. Maybe we ran into your son and didn't even know it." Pupil grinned.

"Here's his picture," Mrs. Kage offered.

Zephyr examined the picture. It looked like Rohan and Wayward were the same person. They both had wavy, tousled, dark brown hair and the same apricot skin. The only difference was that Wayward had blue eyes, while Rohan had deep green eyes.

"So you think … he's alive?" Mrs. Kage asked.

"We never saw this boy at the prison we were at, but there is a good chance that we'll run into him. We broke out of the prison— we weren't freed—so someone is still after us. When he comes for us, we'll make him talk. We promise," Zephyr vowed.

Mrs. Kage started sobbing and wrapped her arms around her son. All the while, Pupil was still eating, helping herself to seconds, thirds, and fourths.

"I'm going, too," Wayward declared after his mother had composed herself.

Zephyr didn't think that Mrs. Kage could look as shocked as she did twice in the same meal, but she equaled her personal best without much effort.

"*No*, you're *not*," Mrs. Kage said as sternly as she could.

"Yes I *am*!"

"You have never trained a day in your life!"

"Yes I have! I go to the mountains to train every day while you *think* I'm in my room."

"*Wayward!* How can you be keeping secrets from me?"

"Because you never let me *do* anything!"

Another long silence filled the room.

"I just don't want to *lose* you, honey. I've lost *everyone* but *you* ..."

"You haven't lost everyone but me, Mom. Rohan is alive, and *we're* gonna find him," Wayward declared.

Mrs. Kage pulled her son into her arms again and wept freely.

"*Please* ... take *care* of him ... I know nothing I say will change his mind, so *please* ... just keep him *safe*."

"Definitely. W-we'll tr-train him ha-hard and make s-sure he's ... oh, man," Zephyr stammered. Feeling nostalgic about when she first left home, she had started to tear up too.

THE REDUNDANT DUNGEON

THE FLIGHT TO THE REDUNDANT Dungeon took longer than expected. Jadeleve and Kuroski ended up getting there at the end of the day.

Because of its stony gray structure, the dungeon reminded Jadeleve of the cave she woke up in when in the Akapeachi Jungle, so it gave her the chills. So far, it was not looking the part of being an inviting place. Jadeleve quickly bounced off the barren patch of grass where she was positioned and caught a glimpse of what lay beyond the dungeon. However, all she saw was more rocky terrain. When the curious warrior landed a second time, she noticed that an extremely thick, brambly, bushy forest lay on either side of the dungeon, making it impossible to travel around it. Jadeleve did not mind, because she wanted to go straight through.

"We'll go in tomorrow." Jadeleve checked the time by taking a hasty glance up at the sun. "It's, like, seven thirty already. Are you hungry?"

Kuroski did not respond. He had already set up a temporary bed beside a stone.

"What? How can you already be asleep?" Jadeleve complained. "Fine," she grumbled. Jadeleve thought she heard Kuroski snicker afterward. *So he's awake! He's just pretending to get me to shut up!*

When the sun rose the next day, Jadeleve woke to the music of the virtually instinct rapping frog, excited to hit the road again. She went into the forest, opened her zeal capsule to take a shower, and got dressed in a purple, short-sleeved combat shirt with black shorts, white socks, and purple combat boots. Next, she started making breakfast.

"Rise and shine!" Jadeleve hollered before she karate-chopped Kuroski's stomach with enough force to knock the wind out of him.

"Ugh ..." Kuroski said. "I think you broke a couple ribs."

"Get *up*, get *ready*. *No* time to waste. I'll make breakfast," Jadeleve informed.

"R-right!" Kuroski gasped. As jumpy as a rabbit, he sprang up and dashed into the woods.

What a goof, Jadeleve thought.

Kuroski was back at their campsite in less than fifteen minutes. Now he was wearing a plain white combat shirt with blue shorts and white socks, though his yellow and orange running shoes remained.

In the time that he was gone, Jadeleve had prepared scrambled eggs with chopped up celery, toast, sliced oranges, bananas, and whole milk.

She had just finished moving two boulders in position for them to sit on when Kuroski reached the table.

Jadeleve looked up with cold, calculating eyes and sighed, making peace with Kuroski's imperfections. If he was going to be her ally, then she had to accept them.

"Eat up."

As they ate, Kuroski started to talk about his life in his home, Widria City. Because Kuroski decided to run away from home, Jadeleve could tell that he did not feel appreciated there. From his brief travels with Jadeleve's companions, Kuroski claimed that he had heard a *little* about Xaphias, so Jadeleve insisted on giving him a detailed description of her hometown from her point of view. Her recount of her residence was the opposite of Kuroski's. She loved the calm environment and being one with the forest, although she wished she could see more of the sun. She explained how regularly she and her sisters used to scale the mountains to get groceries, jump from building to building, literally, and visit their grandmother. Having been content in her home, Jadeleve was somewhat reluctant to leave but excited to see the world after being sheltered for so long.

"What do you do for fun?" Kuroski inquired.

"I like karate, playing the electric drums and the guitar, reading about history, traveling, and cooking," Jadeleve replied before she took a big sip of milk.

"What do you want to be when you grow up?"

"I think I want to be an adventurer, discovering new places, plants, and Beings, like Jasmine did. Like Grandma."

Finally, the two young fighters rose from their stone seats and began to clean up the site of their meal. Before Jadeleve could, Kuroski beat her to the punch by releasing his portable sink to rinse the dishes. To rescue the time they had lost after taking so long to eat, the kids were forced to work together to get their chores out of the way and resume their long adventure.

After storing their traveling supplies in the zeal capsules, Jadeleve put on her bag and slowly shifted her head toward the orange sun. Tints of purple and orange still mixed in with the surrounding blue atmosphere.

"It's a quarter to seven …" Jadeleve whispered, faintly aware of Kuroski's immediate surprise.

"You can tell the exact time just by looking at the sun? *Wow …* Jadel." Kuroski gasped but then hung his head in embarrassment.

"It's fine if you call me that. Do you have a nickname?" Jadeleve asked.

"Well … I only have one friend back home, so …" Kuroski replied honestly.

"What? You've got tons of friends now. You need a solid nickname. It should be short, catchy, and easy to say. How about … Weirwind—your last name and your natural element. Or maybe a short version of your name: Koro?" Jadeleve pondered.

"*Weirwind?* Come on. That sounds like a wolf name," Kuroski said.

"Weirwind it is." Jadeleve laughed mischievously.

"Hey!"

Suddenly, Jadeleve's eyes flashed an illustrious gold shade, signaling that it was time to get serious.

"Are you ready?"

"No."

"Too bad. Let's go."

Jadeleve slowly turned toward the dungeon's entrance. She expected Kuroski to be sulking behind her, contemplating his death, so she was surprised to see him stand up tall and put on a brave face. Jadeleve decided to step aside so they were equally in the center in front of the cave entrance.

It must be the nickname, Jadeleve thought.

Without warning, Kuroski and Jadeleve charged into the uninviting darkness.

At first, the dungeon's inside seemed to perfectly match Jadeleve's imagination. As she expected, the beginning of their trek was marred by darkness. The only thing that was keeping her senses from shutting down was Kuroski's ragged breathing. Their quick footsteps echoed off the walls as they advanced through the cave. Jadeleve gathered that the sound carried much farther than they wanted, so in order to avoid attracting Beings, Jadeleve encouraged Kuroski to tiptoe.

No matter how hard they strained their eyes, all the two See-Throughs could see was black. At one point, Jadeleve activated her aura to provide her own light, but it was too exhausting. Finally, Jadeleve spotted light. At first appearing dim, the turquoise light gained luminosity as Jadeleve and Kuroski crept toward the source. Even though Jadeleve was ecstatic to finally see light within the walls of the dungeon, she was tentative; an enemy could be using light to lure them in. From what the alluring light provided, Jadeleve could see that the cave was treacherous. Redundant Dungeon was a maze of twists, turns, bumps, and curves.

Kuroski stumbled next to Jadeleve into an illuminated circular space. Looking up, Jadeleve saw that the ceiling was even taller than the peak at the front entrance. In contrast to a relatively soft, stone floor, the ceiling was jagged and bumpy, resembling an upside-down mountain range. Hanging down from the tips of these points were lanterns that emitted golden light, unlike the turquoise light that Jadeleve had witnessed before. Confused, she looked around until she found the source of the turquoise light. When she did, she was thunderstruck.

"Kuroski ... look ..." Jadeleve whispered, her voice as distant as the sun from Neptune.

Pentagonal prisms, some measuring forty feet tall, lined the walls of the room, rooted into the stone. No two looked the same. As Jasmine had told them before they left, these crystals grew like trees, drawing energy from the sun. Their cores absorbed this energy.

"Ingrain Crystals," Jadeleve murmured.

"Whoa!" Kuroski gasped. Jadeleve glared at him, not wanting him to yell.

"So my pendant is made out of the core of one of these things."

Straight ahead, Jadeleve spotted two paths. One was unblocked, while the other was blocked by a massive boulder. After analyzing the unnaturally glossy rock, Jadeleve realized that it was a booby trap designed to crush them if they got too close. Even though she could have taken the easy path, Jadeleve was convinced that the blocked path had something worth protecting.

"Recatus!" Jadeleve screamed, firing her signature purple beam at the boulder.

Jadeleve tried to quiet down her inevitable roar, but because of the sheer force used to create, the Recatus forced it out of her. Before the blast collided with rough stone, Jadeleve turned around and covered her head, looking up just in time to see that Kuroski was copying her. A plume of smoke erupted behind them. Smaller, broken rocks fell to the ground.

Whatever. If the Beings are gonna find us, they're gonna find us, Jadeleve thought.

Finally, Jadeleve looked up at her handiwork. She took a deep breath and blew away the smoke. Soundlessly, the cool breeze dispelled the gray haze.

"We're in for it now," Kuroski sighed.

"Yep," Jadeleve agreed.

The young heroine rose to her full height, tightening her backpack against her shoulders, and leaped through the newly opened entrance where the tunnel began. She turned around to face Kuroski, who was taken aback by her ability to jump forward forty feet with as little effort as she did.

"Kuroski, you *coming?*"

The Crystal Map

"What's wrong?" Jadeleve asked, sensing Kuroski's discomfort.

"I … I just don't want to be the one who holds us back," Kuroski confessed. His hands were shaking.

"Who cares? I'm just glad to have company."

"Wait, really?"

"Yeah. I mean when I was hallucinating in the Akapeachi Jungle, and I actually thought I was going to die. All I wanted was for someone to be there with me. Everything else … all the fighting … just seemed unimportant. I used to think it was all about training and getting stronger, but it's not."

"Really? Then what's important?"

"What do *you* think?"

After thinking it over, Kuroski thought he had the answer. It was so obvious that it made Jadeleve's question seem rhetorical.

"Protecting your friends … your family … just everyone you care about," he answered.

"At the end of the day, that's all that really matters to me in life."

During lunch, Kuroski eyed his food with disgust. "Man, I *hate* wheat bread. My loaves are too thick."

"Stop complaining. What, were you rich? We might not have any time to eat again today, so eat up," Jadeleve said.

"Yeah, yeah," Kuroski grumbled and waved her away. Then he stood up, with great effort, and helped Jadeleve clean up the table before the smell could attract unwanted adversaries. Not wanting their muscles to become too cold, Jadeleve decided that it was best to continue right away.

Kuroski noticed fewer ceiling lanterns as they ventured deeper into the cave. Ingrain Crystals took their place.

Why does it seem like it's getting colder every second? Kuroski thought while shivering. Finally, he realized that it was because they were getting farther away from the entrance where the sun baked the air. Now that they were reaching the middle of the dungeon, they were nearing its coldest part. Kuroski's apprehension started to grow.

Finally, a massive gate, outlined by two twin Ingrain Crystal pillars, appeared at the edge of Kuroski's vision. Immediately after the gate was in clear view, an ominous, ghoulish moan drifted through the air. It was as if the voice had a life of its own.

"Did you hear that," Kuroski whispered with wide eyes.

"Let's *move*," Jadeleve declared fearlessly. She ran ahead, flying past him in a blur of purple and gold.

Kuroski was awed by how massive the crystals could grow to be—standing around fifty feet.

Now cautious, Jadeleve led the way toward the towering entryway. Kuroski could not help feeling like they were entering an alternate dimension, where seconds seemed like hours and the gravity multiplied. By the time they stood directly in between the two crystal pillars, a century had passed in Kuroski's mind. However, with a deep breath, he was able to quell his fears, just like he had promised.

Suddenly, the cores of the twin Ingrain Crystals burst into blue flames, shining brighter than anything they had ever seen. Looking for an explanation, he turned to Jadeleve but was horrified to see that her violet eyes were filled with fear. Gasping, the Zeal Possessor crumbled to the ground. Kuroski rushed to help but stopped in his tracks when he realized that she was clutching her white pendant.

She appeared to be trying to stop it from being pulled by an invisible force. Finally, out of breath, Jadeleve was forced to let go of her white pendant, which was now shimmering the same turquoise color as the Ingrain Crystals. Against her will, Jadeleve's pendant dragged her forward, pulling through the crystal pillar gate like a football flying through a goal post at frightening speeds.

"Jadeleve!" Kuroski called, hoping to get through to his friend in time for her to regain her senses. She was speeding toward a stone wall, unable to stop. "Snap *out* of it!"

Driven by desperation, Kuroski sprinted after his possessed companion. He took flight and still was not fast enough. Jadeleve kept getting farther away and closer to her doom. In the end, he could not protect her.

However, the impact never sounded.

W-wait a second, Kuroski thought. *Didn't there used to be a wall in front of us?*

The solid wall that Jadeleve was scheduled to collide with had disappeared.

It's another trap, Kuroski realized.

"Kuroski!" Jadeleve's voice rang off the walls of the elongated cave. "Get over here before the gate closes!"

He left the crystal pillar gate in the dust with his first explosive five steps. At the halfway mark, Kuroski finally understood why Jadeleve was so anxious and why she said, "before the gate closes."

Jadeleve's pendant must have triggered the pillars to open the door. So you can't get through here without an Ingrain Crystal. Wow, that's lucky.

Kuroski sprinted past the wall just as it closed again. However, a new surprise was waiting for him. Jadeleve was levitating twenty feet in the air, and her white pendant was now glowing turquoise, mirroring the shade of the Ingrain Crystals. Jadeleve was also glowing with a turquoise aura.

"Whoa …" Kuroski gasped.

"I just drew from solar energy to get extra power to force myself to stop moving."

"That's the solar energy aura: turquoise," Kuroski said.

"Really. I've drawn from solar energy before, and this has never happened."

"This means your energy control has improved and that solar energy is your natural element. People can draw from any type of energy, but a colorful aura only appears if it's your natural element. And even then it doesn't come unless you have perfect energy control. The aura is a sign that you're starting to master it," Kuroski explained.

"Really?" Jadeleve opened her hands, stretched her fingers, and studied her palms with. Next, she scrutinized her pendant, which was tugging on her neck as if it was eager to proceed with the journey.

Suddenly, Jadeleve's aura disappeared, and her body slammed on the ground, pulled down by the strong attraction between her pendant and the Ingrain Crystals. As she struggled to regain control over herself, she drew from solar energy again and managed to pull away from Kuroski, who she was crushing against the stone floor, and planted herself firmly ten yards away.

"Kuroski! I'm sorry! Are you okay?" Jadeleve exclaimed frantically.

"Y-yeah … I'm good." Kuroski declared after he shrugged off the pain. Since he had been expecting it in the first place, he was able to recover swiftly. "You still need lots of practice. It's really hard to balance your own energy with energy from an outside source. Try taking off your necklace and stop drawing from solar energy."

"All right." Jadeleve sighed, taking off her necklace with its white pendant and cramming it into her left pocket, although she seemed to be losing some confidence. Uncertainly, she reduced her self-induced strain on her energy supply, and once again, the glittering turquoise energy around her vanished.

Almost instantly, her left pocket forced her to move so abruptly that Jadeleve lost her balance and fell to the ground. All the while, her pendant, trying to find a means of escape, dragged her forward toward the unexplored reaches of the Redundant Dungeon, causing her body to skid across the hard floor. Unable to recover in time before her head bashed against another boulder, Kuroski sprinted after her, pinned her arms down, and gave her a chance to draw from solar energy.

Jadeleve rolled over and stood up on all fours as she regained her breath.

"That didn't work. What's next?"

"What can your pendant do?" Kuroski questioned.

"It can store any energy I want to save, repels weaker energy attacks, and recently I used it to convert myself into light and travel at the speed of light," Jadeleve explained with an even tone.

"It's just like Jasmine said. How did you do that?"

"I'm actually not sure."

"We'll talk about that later. I think you just have to deal with this force until we get out of here. Do you know why this is even happening?"

"Jasmine did say the cores of Ingrain Crystals are made from some sort of natural metal. I think they're attracted to the other cores, like a magnet," Jadeleve said, putting two and two together.

"Okay. That makes sense. And this dungeon is made up of several smaller mazes with different tests that challenge our abilities to decipher information and solve problems," Kuroski declared.

"I don't think where the Ingrain Crystals are planted is random. They form a map and act like a guide *through* the dungeon," Jadeleve realized.

"Whoa ... didn't think of *that*," Kuroski murmured.

"My pendant will always be drawn to the larger crystal, meaning that the crystals are getting bigger as we move deeper into this place. Only someone with a core can make it out of here. That's what my grandma realized, too," Jadeleve recognized. "I just kept my pendant in my pocket all the time. Grandma only said that it could deflect minor attacks, so I never used it. I shouldn't have taken her present for granted, no matter how *useful* it was."

Kuroski empathized with Jadeleve's remorse. He often wanted to go back home and start over. Sometimes he felt like he took his foster home for granted. At least he had *something*.

"Well you appreciate it now, right?" Kuroski said. "What's the plan?"

With an impish gleam in her eye, Jadeleve nodded and said, "I think, back where those crystal pillars were, I saw an encryption of the maze. It looks like a bunch of twisted, random pathways designed to confuse travelers. What do you think we should do?"

"Let's keep going."

As they walked onward, toward the next stage of the dungeon, Jadeleve was presented with the chance to practice resisting the compelling tug of her pendant, allowing it to guide them through the cave. Finally, Kuroski and Jadeleve had situated themselves in front of a massive chamber where the tormented cries of unnamed creatures made them shiver.

A LONG ROAD AHEAD

A s soon as they settled into life at Wayward's home, the Dawn and Zeal twins established a meticulous daily training regimen for him to follow. Not wanting to waste any time, Zephyr and Zenon woke him and the younger twins up bright and early. Since the girls had already trained their bodies, their training was more intense but shorter, while his was longer but less strenuous. First, they started off with a ten-mile run while he ran eight miles at a slower pace. Next, they stretched together and loosened their bodies. Afterward, the others meditated while Wayward practiced his energy control. He learned how to focus his energy in different places, mainly his hands. Since he aspired to learn how to fly, he practiced focusing energy into his legs as well. For the rest of session, the young fighters sparred against each other in random order, but most times, Zenon sparred against Zephyr, while Pupil and Iris took turns fighting Wayward. The Zeal twins stressed the maximum four fights per person so they would not be exhausted for the next day.

"Agh!" Wayward cried as he fired an energy blast straight at Pupil, his unruly hair blowing in the wind. In just two days, thanks to Zephyr's galvanized training style, he had mastered using energy beams. Even so, he still had a long way to go.

Showcasing her creative method of defense, Pupil froze his attack dead in its tracks with her Flashlight Technique, teleported behind him, and karate-chopped the back of his neck. Unable to react, Wayward absorbed the full brunt of her attack and crumbled to the ground.

Wayward gasped in a gallant effort to recover. He was able to raise his head high enough to see Pupil drawing from heat energy to melt his energy blast, which was encased inside a block of ice. Before he was able to stand up again, Pupil had appeared beside him with her hands clasped together behind her head. It took a few seconds for his eyes to refocus, because he had almost lost consciousness, but once he did, he was dismayed to see her smiling. She was just toying with him.

"Great job. You almost had me a couple of times." Pupil beamed before she helped him up onto his feet.

"I can't do this anymore," Wayward said.

"Don't give up. Jadeleve destroyed me tons of times before I could even touch her. Mom always says that when you recover from training, you come back stronger. Even if you lose, you still get better," Pupil reassured him.

Nervously, Iris sauntered over from where she was watching the battle. Wayward had come to know her as very shy. She was wearing a plain red combat shirt with black short sleeves, red shorts, white socks, and red sneakers. On the other hand, Pupil was cheerful and wore the same outfit in blue.

They're total opposites, Wayward thought.

"Are you ready for a rematch, Iris?" Wayward asked in an aggressive tone, although he was actually unsure of himself. Iris answered simply by positioning herself in a virtually impenetrable battle stance. Wayward copied her stance, completing the battle ritual.

As Pupil wisely levitated out of harm's way, Iris and Wayward began to inch back from one another to create more room for the battle. With unblinking eyes, Iris's fierce gaze burned through Wayward's soul. Ignoring the odds, which were stacked against him, Wayward returned her stare with one of equal intensity, daring his compatriot to blink. A soft, gentle breeze swept through the grassland. Iris detected which direction the wind was blowing, realized that it was behind her, and used the extra push to add to her speed. She jumped about thirty feet into the air and vanished.

Where is she? Wayward fretted.

With a breath of luck, Wayward recalled the advice that Zenon had given him earlier.

If your opponent vanishes, don't panic; try to sense where they are.

Wayward already knew that his sight would not be the best tool to use in this situation; Iris was moving faster than his untrained eyes could follow. However, the speed of sound was slower. He decided to close his eyes and focus intently on the sound waves created by Iris's constant movement in the air.

Pain exploded on his left cheek. Iris had struck him while his eyes were closed. He simply could not keep up.

"Zonule," Iris bellowed. Two rings of fire, which seemingly blipped into existence, were flying toward him at a breakneck pace.

Wayward just did not understand. They already knew that he was not fast enough to evade or strong enough to counter an attack like this. There had to be a way out.

Convinced that his teachers were testing him, but with only a few seconds before Iris's attacked engulfed him in flames, he racked his brain for a way out. Growing up on the computer, constantly thinking and building things, Wayward had always relied on logic to solve his problems. But if there was no correct answer, what could he do?

Finally, in the nick of time, Wayward knew. Barely having time to think over his plan, he went straight to action. With his life at stake, Wayward willed himself to move faster than he ever had before. He bent down, pulled out a thick chunk of gravel from the ground, and used it as a shield against the approaching rings of fire. For good measure, Wayward flung the shield into the heart of Iris's attack, hoping the dirt would weaken the flames. Next, not even looking up to see what happened, he dove out of the way.

With Wayward barely in control of his movements, Iris teleported in front of him, broke through his fragile defense, and knocked the wind out of him with a hard kick to the stomach. Not giving him any time to recover, she assaulted him with a barrage of lightning-fast punches to the face. He had no hope of winning.

Iris disappeared again. However, Wayward was far from quitting. He anticipated her movements, swung his body around, and stopped her attack from behind with a punch to her forehead. She remained stunned for half a second, her silver hair obscuring the bottom half of her face. However, Wayward faltered at the sight of her eyes flashing blood red. He could do nothing when she retaliated with an elbow strike in the center of his chest.

Wayward clutched his chest with his arms. His vision came up blurry, so he knew he must have been on the verge of unconsciousness.

I've got ... work to do, Wayward thought. Even his thoughts were becoming muddled. He could sense Iris's growing concern for him. She teleported behind him to make sure he did not bang his head against the floor.

When Wayward came to, immense pressure from a source of condensed energy made him feel like the force of gravity had been doubled.

Oh no ... He was afraid to look up at the fighting.

Iris took Wayward's arm and wrapped it around the back of her neck so she could support him while she flew toward her injured mentor. Pupil flew past them to where Zenon was buried deep in the dirt. With a dog's enthusiasm, Pupil dug up Zenon's battered body.

"Zenon and I were sparring. She used her new fire technique on me, and I got carried away," Zephyr explained.

"Can she train tomorrow?" Iris asked.

"I don't think so. We might have to wait until she's healed. *Sorry,* Zenon," Zephyr muttered, crossing her arms and looking away.

"W-wait. Mom grows healing herbs in h-her g-garden. W-we can u-use them, i-if we ask h-her," Wayward offered.

"You h-have healing herbs like M-master Dracon?" Zenon wheezed, making a great effort to speak. Wayward had no idea who that was but was too tried to ask.

"Okay. I'll go ask her," Zephyr declared, wanting to fix her own mess.

A few minutes later, she returned with Wayward's mom, who carried two healing herbs with her. She gave Zephyr one to feed to Zenon, then rushed to her son.

"You better take it easier or I'm calling this training off," Mrs. Kage murmured. She nudged Iris out of the way and cradled her son in her arms as she fed him the green herb.

"If I'm going with them, I've got to be tough, Mom," Wayward insisted.

"Okay, sweetie. Well, be tough some other time. It's time for dinner."

UNDER CONTROL

"**G**ET READY," JADELEVE WHISPERED. KUROSKI was already guarded on all sides. He swallowed hard with trepidation.

Out of the gloom came the massive, lumbering hulk of a Being. She had never encountered this Being before. She took note of the giant's greenish-gray, lumpy skin. Horns covered the middle of its forehead down to its doglike nose. The Being's head was shaped like a rhino's: pointed at the top and curved around the edges. Where its eyes should have been were nothing but two black smudges, rubbed away by its adaption to darkness. The Being had the body of an overgrown elephant, and attached to its rear were three lengthy, slim tails shaped like pointed arrows at the end. Of course, this beast had fangs, which hung down about eight inches below its gigantic jaw line, and claws, which were attached like toenails to its elephant-like feet. Also like the elephant, the Being bore menacing twin tusks that curved outward from its checks, laying just over its jaw.

I think "tuskull" is a good name, Jadeleve thought.

"*Bring* it!" Kuroski blurted rashly and charged forward at full speed.

"Kuroski! We don't know if it wants to fight! Don't be *reckless!*" Jadeleve warned, but he was already in battle mode.

Kuroski leaped, aiming to erase the tuskull's blatant advantage of height. Unexpectedly, the massive creature swiftly whipped out one of its tails from outside of Kuroski's peripheral vision and lashed his cheek. Switching his approach, Kuroski grabbed the tuskull's tail, which was still within range, and twisted it. Next, he released a dense energy sphere from the palm of his hand, destroying one of the tuskull's tails and sending shockwaves into its body. Even though the spark only seemed to annoy it, Kuroski took that opportunity to retreat and prepare for round two.

"You'll waste too much energy if you attack alone. We have to attack together," Jadeleve said.

The earth began to quake beneath them. Before Jadeleve could act, she felt the force of matter colliding into her at the speed of sound. Her body contorted and convulsed with pain when she slammed into stone while crushed crystals fell on her head. From the sound of it, her reckless ally was receiving similar treatment. Despite the unexpected attack, Jadeleve forced her mind to be strong, shrugged off the pain, brushed off the stones piled on top of her, and got right back on her feet. Kuroski was still hurting.

"You want to *prove* yourself? Is that why you keep rushing on ahead? Well that's *dumb*," Jadeleve whispered into his ear after she walked over to where he was buried under rock rumble. "I already told you; you don't need to prove anything. All I need right now is someone who will work with me so we don't *die*."

Kuroski picked himself up with renewed fire in his eyes. This time, Jadeleve hoped that he would use that resolve correctly so they could work as a team.

"If you've got that out of your system, I have a plan," Jadeleve whispered. Just in case this Being could understand their language, she made a point to communicate with Kuroski telepathically.

Jadeleve used her lightning speed to teleport behind the tuskull. Without pause, she activated her After-Image Technique.

"Over here, No-Eyes!" Jadeleve taunted. She plugged her ears with her thumbs and stuck out her tongue. Enraged, the tuskull took the bait by lashing out its arrowed tail at one of Jadeleve's After-Images.

"Sucker! I'm over here!" the cunning heroine hollered, revealing the whereabouts of her second clone. The tuskull allowed itself to be overcome with fury, making it an easier target. This time, it whipped back around and attempted to ram its massive, crescent-shaped tusks into Jadeleve's body. However, the assault only pierced air.

"Groughh!" the green-gray creature barked with confusion.

Now, Kuroski! Jadeleve thought.

On it! he replied. With incredible speed, Kuroski lifted off from the ground to confront the Being again.

Taking advantage of the tuskull's clumsy forward momentum from the monster's previous attack, Kuroski stored as much energy as he could muster to end the scuffle. Gray light began to envelop his body, and power started to surge through him. Harsh winds formed rapidly around him, seemingly from nowhere.

This my natural element aura. Cool. I couldn't do this before, Kuroski thought.

"Here it goes! Soul Twister!" Kuroski bellowed. He released all his stockpiled wind energy from his hands and carved into a twister. With the tuskull unable to dodge, Kuroski's attack found its target with ferocious intensity. The rotating, harsh winds not only swept up the colossal Being, sending it flying, but created thousands of gashes on the Being's skin. Soon, the tuskull was rotating in the same direction of the twister and slammed against an adjacent stone wall. Before its body fell and was buried by rocks, the tuskull was unconscious.

"Nice one, Kuroski! *That's* how you win a battle!" Jadeleve beamed.

"I-I can't believe I just did that," Kuroski gasped in disbelief.

"And when you unlocked your aura, so the wind natural element aura is gray, that was *awesome.* See—this wasn't a waste of time. Now we'll be ready to take down Kerato if he finds out the others are in Pearl Town."

Jadeleve and Kuroski spent another hour jogging on, trusting in the pendant's knowledge to direct them, before they decided to eat dinner, rest, and continue when they woke up.

"Okay, I think this is a good place to—" Jadeleve suddenly stopped.

"What's wrong?" Kuroski whispered with worry.

"I'm sensing another Being. It's the same one as before. I don't mean the same type but the same *exact* one."

"What? We must have covered twelve miles since we last ran into that monster. Maybe he caught up to us," he suggested.

"It couldn't be. I'm sensing its energy coming from ahead, not behind. We'll have to wait and see," Jadeleve said, locking into her signature fighting stance with her elbows bent and fist clenched by her sides.

Within a few minutes, another tuskull appeared from the shadows beyond them. Light from surrounding Ingrain Crystals reflected off the Being's horns and tusks. This tuskull was physically different from the last one but possessed the same consciousness. Jadeleve had never encountered this phenomenon before.

"Cover me. I'm going to try something to figure out what's going on here," Jadeleve said in a low voice to Kuroski, who nodded.

"Graaough!" the tuskull roared, emerging from the gloom.

Mind scan! Jadeleve thought.

Jadeleve used her mind's eye to see inside the tuskull's mind. Immediately, she recognized the Being's mind was being tampered with. It was being forced to fight with a mental technique that she had never seen before.

The man at the gate did this. The Eyebots did this, Jadeleve thought with rising anger. *They probably took them from their natural habitat and put them here to test technique.*

"I know what's happening here. Eyebots are controlling these Beings with a mass hallucination. Both these Beings are experiencing the same hallucination, which is why I thought they were the same one when I tried to sense them," Jadeleve solemnly explained.

"It's kind of like what they did to us at Ripple Island, but I think they created individual hallucinations. They just looked into our eyes, and it made me feel lightheaded. I could barely hear and couldn't think straight, but we still had free will," Kuroski said.

"Yeah. That has to be what they did to me at Sapolis too."

"Grough!" the tuskull roared again.

"Okay! Since they're all hallucinating, these Beings don't have control over themselves. We have to knock out every one we see," Jadeleve declared. "Got it?"

BREAKTHROUGH

Aᴀ ᴄʟᴏʙʙᴇʀɪɴɢ ᴅᴏᴢᴇɴs ᴏғ ᴛᴜsᴋᴜʟʟ and other unknown species, the two young fighters were exhausted. As the hours passed, their pace slowed to the point where they were practically dragging their feet across the stone floor. Despite this, Jadeleve's pendant continued to tug on her neck.

Jadeleve huffed. "We should take a break and—"

Out of nowhere, a piercing, high-pitched screech invaded her ears. Terrified, she looked over to see Kuroski's ears starting to bleed. He was gradually losing consciousness.

Come on, Kuroski! she screamed into his mind before she ran over to cover his ears, thus sacrificing her own.

With great effort, Jadeleve looked up to meet the face of their attacker. This Being was an astonishing bat-like creature, carrying a five-foot frame and an eight-foot wingspan. It had shaggy brown fur on the top of its head, around its back, and covering the top of its scythe-shaped wings. On the inside, the Being's wings were purple, but the center of its body was gray and oval shaped. Just like the tuskull, the creature's eyes were just smudges shaped in curved lines, giving the impression that it was squeezing them shut. It possessed a nose like a pig's. Luckily, the bat-like animal lacked a massive jaw and was equipped with small fangs that curved down from the top of its small mouth. Strangely the bat-like, pig-nosed Being had ostrich legs—pink, long, and with two sharp toes on each foot. Jadeleve could not yet think of a name for the mutated creature.

"Kiisssyyyeee!" The monster shrieked a second before it set a direct course for them with the aid of its powerful wings.

Still covering Kuroski's ears, Jadeleve miraculously found resolve to defend.

"Energy Force Field!" she screamed.

Instantaneously, a ten-foot-tall, lime-green orb of energy enveloped their bodies. Even so, the Being shattered the shield by slashing its left wing against it as it flew past. Next, the Being emitted visible sound waves from its mouth.

When Jadeleve realized that the attack was not aimed at them and instead bounced off the stone walls, she knew that the creature was intelligent. It called its friends for help, and two more identical foes appeared.

Jadeleve stood.

"Kuroski, we've *got* to stay calm. You ready?"

Kuroski stood up and nodded.

"If we're going to make it out alive, we've got to use all the power we've got!" Jadeleve roared.

The three bat creatures cried in unison, giving Jadeleve and Kuroski the green light to attack. Kuroski resourcefully created a wind tunnel to counter the sound waves, while Jadeleve dodged with the After-Image Technique. After she was out of harm's way, Jadeleve quickly rebounded and landed between Kuroski and the three beasts.

In awe, Jadeleve observed the trio's split second of panic, as if they thought their opponents had vanished. Immediately afterward, however, their leader launched another sonic wave. Having no other choice but to cover their ears, the two young fighters were helpless to defend themselves as the two other Beings sliced their bodies with their wings. Fresh, sharp cuts formed on both Jadeleve and Kuroski's right oblique as the two beasts whizzed by. Jadeleve was flung backward five feet and fell on her back, gripping her right side with her left hand. When she recovered enough to move, her hand came away from the wound with warm blood. Getting back up and putting weight on her right leg was an agonizing effort. However, to her surprise, Jadeleve looked over and saw Kuroski levitating, not unfazed from the assault but gritting his teeth. When their eyes met, Jadeleve remembered the crucial information that would let them win.

Kuroski, these guys are just like bats. The only way they can see us is by emitting special sound waves at us so they know where we are. We have to damage their ears!

Okay!

Improvising, Jadeleve jumped twenty feet into the air.

"Hey! Give me a boost!" Jadeleve called to Kuroski. Quickly catching wind of her scheme, he produced a powerful air current that pushed Jadeleve forward. While riding the wind, Jadeleve activated her spherical Energy Force Field. Her electrical energy was carried to one of the Beings by the breeze, electrocuting it. While inside the force field, Jadeleve added rotation to it and rammed into the beast. The Being was burnt to a crisp before it hurdled toward the ground, unconscious.

The distinct frequency of the fallen Being's cry told the remaining pair of narbats (her name for them) all they needed to know. Enraged, they advanced toward the See-Through warriors with less graceful movements than before. Wanting to quickly end this miserable fight, Jadeleve activated her Slow Motion Technique on the narbats and signaled Kuroski to finish the combo.

"Soul Twister!" Kuroski roared. A dense, swirling mass of fierce winds formed inside his palms and then smoothly morphed into a funnel. The combined culmination of the cyclone's compelling control and its aggressive accuracy ripped the narbats' skin apart as the same channel pushed them away. Finally, the twin beasts bashed their heads against a rocky wall and fell in a dazed heap next to their friend. Jadeleve let loose a sigh of relief and deactivated her force field.

"I hate the Eyebots," Kuroski scowled as he floated by back down to ground level.

"Yeah, but why are they doing this? Why are they going so far? I thought I knew, but … I'm not sure anymore." Jadeleve sighed. "All we can do for now is protect our friends."

"You're right. And we're getting out of this dungeon today, whatever day it is," Kuroski whispered.

"Hm." Jadeleve giggled.

"What's so funny? I don't care how many more monsters find us. It's today."

"That's the spirit. I have a feeling that we're almost out."

Jadeleve ran on ahead with higher spirits.

However, as they proceeded deeper into the dungeon, they encountered more monsters than before. Soon, Jadeleve's mind could not keep up with her body. Feeling extremely lightheaded, the next thing Jadeleve knew, Kuroski was bumping into the stone walls as if he was going blind.

Every time either of them suggested taking a break, the Beings would unexpectedly attack. It was almost as if they were stalking them and waiting until their guard was down before they struck. Only sheer willpower was keeping them on their feet now. Never in her life had Jadeleve been so disgusted by the thought of combat, but the constant exposure to bloodshed on both sides began to make her rethink her favorite hobby. Hallucinations finally started overpowering Jadeleve's mind, making it impossible for her to distinguish fantasy from reality. When Kuroski fainted, Jadeleve picked him up and kept going as if nothing had happened. She was turning into a zombie.

Suddenly, light began to pour into Jadeleve's eyes more intensely than ever before. This had to mean they were nearing the outside world again.

Fueled by excitement, Jadeleve activated the zeal with Kuroski still enveloped protectively within her arms. Potent lime-green electrical energy coated her skin. Jadeleve was mentally aware of the concentration of lipochrome within her irises, turning them from violet to amber. Her power was soaring, leaving her troubled thoughts in the dust.

Silently, Jadeleve flew onward, gradually reaching her top speed. Combining the pulsating electric current of the zeal and her Energy Force Field, she had an unstoppable offense and defense on her side. Every time she glanced down at her friend who was cradled in her arms, it rekindled her fire.

Finally, right when Jadeleve believed their journey through the Redundant Dungeon was near its end, she realized that what she was approaching was not sunlight. Jadeleve stopped in her tracks about fifty feet from the giant rainbow-shaped exit. As carefully as possible, she laid Kuroski down a good distance away from where she wanted to stand and walked back to the spot so she could better assess the situation.

It feels like sunlight ... but it's summer; it should be boiling in here, Jadeleve mused. She studied the color of the bright light before her. It was divided into unnaturally equal beams of light, and they were tinged blue instead of the golden color of sunlight. Suddenly, she noticed a detail she would have instantly seen if she was fresh: the exit was sealed shut by a bush of Ingrain Crystals. Most likely, every time someone blasted their way out of the Redundant Dungeon to eagerly embrace freedom, the crystals just grew over the hole again.

Even with the zeal's power, the combined magnetic force of the Ingrain Crystal wall dragged her forward. Little by little, despair worked its way around Jadeleve's system, making it increasingly tough to fight the intoxicating pull of the strange plants. She had to figure out how to blast out of there before losing all her energy.

I can focus zeal energy into my pendant. That way I won't be dragged in and have more control over my solar powers.

"All right! We're busting out!" Jadeleve bellowed as she focused zeal energy into her pendant. It began to glow the color of the deep sea.

Jadeleve quickly glanced at Kuroski, double-checking to see if he was in a safe position before she fired her strongest attack. She knew that she would need the rest of her power to break through the crystal wall.

"Re ... ca ... tas!" Jadeleve screamed as she felt the strain from releasing the energy. Within a second, the violet beam collided against its target in a flashy explosion. The blast incinerated the center of the barrier, carving out a large, circular chunk.

Instead of rejoicing, Jadeleve silently but roughly grabbed Kuroski by the back of his shirt collar and dragged him along as she ran through the opening. Swiftly, because she knew she had little time before she lost consciousness, she ran as far as she could from the dungeon's exit and found a quaint spot between too bushes. She decided that this was the perfect place to rest, so she set Kuroski down, swung off her backpack, got out the zeal capsule labeled Tent, and threw it down. A second later, Jadeleve fainted, not knowing if they were surrounded by the protective structure of the steel tent or if she had fainted a little too early.

A CHANGE OF HEART

"THOSE KIDS!" KERATO SEETHED, FINALLY realizing that his foes had tricked him into taking the wrong path after two and a half days of continuous pursuit. The journey had brought him to the Graze Mountains in the north. Miles of uninhabited land stretched in all directions, and the cool breeze casted a feeling of serenity over the landscape. However, it did little to quell Kerato's rage.

He covered for them! That kid tricked me! I can't believe I let them get away. I knew I was being too nice!

Kerato was born and raised in Ionize Town by South Celestial Beach. Yohan, Kerato's older brother by six years, was convinced that the only way to protect his race was to form a guild. At sixteen, Yohan left the house and travelled through all five counties to form a guild that could defend against Eyebots who were invading the land. Their parents had always sought peace among the races. They decided that they would protest peacefully on the Saturn Front. However, they waited until Kerato had found his own path before they left.

On his thirteenth birthday, Kerato packed his bags and took a submarine train to the royal family's castle on Coreicean Island to begin training as a knight. Meanwhile, his parents left for Saturn. Since he was exceptional with his sword, Kerato was promoted to Imperial Knight status with only one year of training. Imperial

Knights guarded the castle from guilds and organizations that tried to negotiate with the king. In other words, they executed them on sight, mercilessly. These knights were trained to have hearts of stone and believed that everything they did was for the protection of their race.

However, Kerato, being as young as he was, did not understand the killing policy. He hated how the king ordered the See-Through knights to slaughter everyone who rebelled against the land division system, even members from his own race.

Kerato began to seek the power that would allow him to change the world so all races could coexist peacefully, and for that to happen, he needed to train. The young warrior trained diligently for hours each day, improving his skills and moving up the ranks.

However, one morning during his third year at Coreicean, Kerato woke up late after a tough day of training the day before and missed the beginning of a routine guild invasion. He hated to participate in the killings, or even watch them. After the fight was over and he was helping the other knights collect the bodies, Kerato stopped dead in his tracks when he saw one face. It was a face he had not seen in eight years. The face of his now twenty-two-year-old brother. Terror, shock, and bottomless rage gripped his heart as Kerato finally confirmed the face as his loving older brother.

"Y-Yohan?" Kerato stammered.

"K-Kerato ... I n-never ... wanted th-this to happen. I-I asked Dad to ma-make y-you join ... b-but th-this wa-was something I-I ha-had to d-do ... I-I lo-ove y-you a-always ... F-f-ight ... f-for wh-what is right ..." Yohan gasped, adamantly believing in his parents' beliefs to the very end. Blood seeped profusely from a stab wound in the center of his chest. There was no way he could be saved.

In rage, Kerato cruelly executed all the guards who had fought in the recent battle, just as they had done to so many others. Before reinforcements could arrive, Kerato stealthily slipped into a submarine train and traveled to mainland Fantasia through the Savior Ocean, signifying a new beginning. He was determined, as his parents and his brother before him, to fight for what he believed was right. He would join or form a group with the sole objective of assassinating the king and destroying everyone left in the Land of See-Throughs. In reality, he needed to fill the gaping hole in his heart, which had been increasing ever since his brother was killed. His parents died in the war two months later.

No one sheltered me from the world. No one showed me *mercy. There's no way I'm showing these kids any mercy, either.*

DOUBLE ASSAULT

"**A**RE YOU GUYS READY?" ZENON asked the posse.

"Yeah! I can't wait to beat Wayward up again!" Pupil cheered. Wayward tried to ignore her.

"We're here to build his confidence, Pupil." Zephyr sighed.

Mrs. Kage walked onto the porch where the fighters had assembled in preparation for meticulous training. By now, they had accumulated enough information about each other to develop a schedule to maximize their progress.

"I'm gonna start dinner early today so you guys can eat early and go to bed early. If you want to be better fighters, you need rest," she said with her sweet voice. Everyone nodded in response, except Iris, who was nervously biting her fingernails and looking off into the vastness of the Kages' backyard. Her eyes were orange with worry.

"What's wrong?" Zenon whispered.

"We still haven't found any clues on Jadel. I'm worried," she mumbled, on the verge of tears. "And Kuroski …"

"Come on, Iris. We've got to think *positive*. Jadeleve wouldn't want us to worry," Zenon consoled.

"You're right." Iris sniffled. She wiped her damp eyes and stood up tall.

Mrs. Kage smiled. However, her expression became grave once she turned back toward the house.

"It's breaking news. Kids, come inside to see this."

Everyone rushed into the living room, their eyes glued to the screen.

"We've received reports of a man with a sword terrorizing the Public Plaza in Pearl Town," the anchorwoman said. "He's been killing the citizens in search of five children. Pearl Town is expecting reinforcements shortly, since its current division of Imperial Knights is no match for this man. Until the murderer is brought to justice, all outdoor activities are prohibited. I'm Colbalt Christie from Fantasia News."

"It's Kerato! I think that's his name; we heard that name circling around the prison sometimes. He was chasing us after we escaped from Ripple Island. I thought we lost Kerato, but I guess Kuroski didn't make it," Zephyr explained with a shaky voice. "No more running away, guys. This is our fault. It's our problem."

"Agreed," Zenon added.

"I'm coming too," Wayward whispered. Everyone, even Pupil, became silent.

"Wait," Mrs. Kage interrupted. She knelt down to Wayward's height and wrapped her arms around her son. After she pulled away, her eyes began to sparkle.

"A week ago, I didn't even want you to go to the backyard on your own when you asked me, even though I knew you did it behind my back all the time. But you've grown up, Wayward. I trust you. Just be safe. I love you."

"I love you too, Mom, and I promise I won't die," Wayward whispered before he buried his face into his mother's flowing brown hair.

Wayward slowly pulled away. He gave her one last intense look that broadcasted all his emotions. Finally, he turned away and swiftly exited the room. In a blur, he fled his house and took flight. The girls appeared behind him, willing to protect him if it meant their lives.

"Sorry, Wayward," Iris murmured.

"Why?"

"Kerato's here because of us, she means," Pupil said.

"I'm not blaming you guys. If it wasn't for you, I would have never made up with Mom," Wayward assured them.

The tension in the group seemed to lighten ever so slightly, allowing them to accelerate toward their foe.

New to proper energy control, Wayward could faintly sense the growth of hostile energy emanating from a certain point inside the vicinity of the Public Plaza. The signal grew stronger as they got closer.

Flying at about ninety miles per hour, what normally took them an hour to walk to took them only two minutes to fly to, but to Wayward, it seemed like an eternity. A piercing scream sliced through the air, and Wayward was horrified by the possibility that the swordsman had claimed yet another civilian. Shockingly, though, as soon as the quintet flew over the shopping market, the swordsman was in view. Around him was a circular battlefield, outlined by the eight dead bodies of the Imperial Knights. Now, the killer was preparing to do away with a terrified little girl. By the looks of it, in a surge of adrenalin, she tried to attack the black-dressed warrior and was now about to pay the ultimate price.

"How dare you!" Zephyr bellowed in fury, charging straight for the swordsman.

Faster than Wayward's eye could follow, Zephyr rammed her leg into Kerato's face. However, she did not waste any time. The graceful warrior swiped the little girl, who was maybe six years old, off the ground. Wayward, Pupil, Iris, and Zenon, who had stayed behind waiting until the right moment, took that chance to join Zephyr and the child on the ground.

"Dad ..." the girl repeated between sobs.

"Where do you live?" Zenon queried.

"Ruby Lane ... P-please ... b-beat him!" the girl wailed.

"That's a promise," Zephyr said. She vanished along with the girl, probably meaning to take her home. In less than five seconds, she returned empty-handed and ready for battle.

The swordsman took much longer to recover than Wayward had expected. Either he was weakened from fighting all of the Imperial Knights, or Zephyr was strong. He staggered in the face of Zephyr's surprise attack. He was able to crane his neck and cock his head back so he was directly facing the young warriors again. Wayward had never seen a man stare down at him with such hatred in his eyes. On top of that, the villain's sky-blue eyes did not seem to suit him.

"I looked for days without stopping for food or *anything* until I found out. I thought you guys were funny, so I was gonna let you live. But no one tricks me. I'll make you suffer," Kerato seethed.

Regardless of the swordsman's threats, Zephyr and Zenon were unfazed. They just stood there, frozen in time within their fighting stances, burning through their opponent with a fiery gaze of unmatched intensity. Having been in countless fights had steeled them.

"Why'd you kill them if they didn't know we were here?" Zenon asked calmly.

"Believe it or not, I used to be a knight. These guys would kill guilds like you to keep you in one place if they had the chance. They killed my brother. I'm just being a good guy and killing them before they can kill anyone else," Kerato seethed. Then he screamed and began his ferocious assault.

"Shadow Strike!" His attack was launched directly at Iris, who had no time to dodge.

"Ack!" Iris made an uncomfortable noise as the dark wave of energy made contact with her right shoulder. She skidded backward and toppled over from the sheer force. Frozen with fear, Wayward did not react.

Sensing his distress, Pupil responded.

"Wayward! Snap out of it! Go help Iris up, and we'll start taking this guy down a notch." Pupil rushed off into the fight.

As Wayward sought to help Iris, he kept tabs on how the battle was progressing from afar. His astonishment only grew. The three fearless fighters had the crazed knight surrounded and took advantage of their superior teamwork to frustrate him further. Pupil baited him by pretending she was about to throw a punch and then teleporting away. While the Kerato's guard was up in the wrong place, Zenon elbowed him in the center of his back, pushing him into Zephyr's fierce attack, a dropkick to the head. Not allowing him to rest, the girls cornered him even while he lay with ragged breaths on the ground. Kerato attempted to catch the trio by sweeping his sword in a perfect circle around himself, but all three were able to evade. Before he could make it to his feet, Pupil landed on the flat of his silver sword, wrenching it from his reach. Finally, she sprang back up like a kangaroo and sent an uppercut to his chin. Dazed, Kerato stumbled backward.

Putting aside his fear, Wayward flew in from behind, clasped his hands together, and rammed them against Kerato's head. Kerato's eyes rolled up. Wayward retreated, leaving the knight to crumble in a heap on the dirt floor.

"He's moving. There's no time to lose," Zenon decided.

"Right." Zephyr sighed as they slowly trudged toward their slack enemy. Iris was now standing strong again next to Wayward and Pupil. Pressing apprehension wrinkled all three faces, only Iris could not hide her feelings, because her irises changed to a gloomy shade of orange.

I want to go home, Wayward thought.

The identical Zeal twins were just inches away from where the swordsman was huddled on the floor, preparing to strike. Wayward inhaled slowly and efficiently, making sure that air was getting into his lungs. He tuned into his surrounds. Thin rivulets of water streamed down from Iris's eyes and fell off her face from her chin. Pupil was clutching her belly, either feeling sick to her stomach or hungry. The Zeal twins were biding their time and storing their energy for their impending final attack. Pearl Town remained silent.

Without warning, Kerato stabbed Zephyr in the thigh with his sword and vanished.

Zenon kept her composure and was able to remove the sword that was lodged in her sister's leg. Zephyr did not scream during the whole transaction but was left astonished. Without hesitation, Zenon fired an energy beam to destroy the sword. Unexpectedly, black energy was released from the metal and revealed the swordsman's location by traveling back to him. The knight had been busy battling the younger fighters, who were scrambling to put up a formidable defense. Iris, in a rare fit of fury, jump-kicked Kerato's face, giving him a bloody nose.

Taking advantage of Kerato's undefended position, Iris drew from electric energy.

"Thunder Bash!" A crackling sonic boom created from her explosive energy propelled her forward as a rotating field of electricity engulfed her. Like the name suggests, Iris bashed her skull into Kerato's stomach, sending him hurdling fifteen meters away. Even so, he recovered and regained his footing swiftly.

Unexpectedly, Kerato jumped up and extended his right hand in Zenon's direction. Instead of firing an energy blast like Wayward thought he would, Wayward witnessed the knight's sword, which Zenon had just demolished, reassemble right before his eyes. The sword moved on its own and slashed Zenon's left arm.

Zenon yowled in anguish and tried to cover up her arm. The sword whizzed back to its owner as he landed in the center of his enemies' divided force. Out of nowhere, Wayward felt the force of a mallet slamming against his skull. Somehow, he found the power not to fall, but yellow dots danced across his eyes. Kerato had infiltrated their defenses and slammed the hilt of his sword into Wayward's head.

Wayward felt like he was moving through air made of sludge and wet cement. He could barely hear, but what he did hear were the muffled cries of Pupil and Iris who were fighting off the beast as best they could.

A-are … are we gonna die? he thought.

"N-no," Wayward gasped. He was recovering a little of his strength every second. The young fighter tripped, fell, regained his footing, and stumbled again, but he finally found his bearings. Next, his vision and hearing returned. When it did, he saw the Dawn twins valiantly fighting Kerato. They were wearing him down but were clearly struggling. Even if Wayward could do nothing but cheer them on, he had to do something. He would not just stand by while this villain destroyed his hometown.

As if he were a puppet, Wayward's legs moved on their own toward the raging battle. As if they knew of his intentions, the Dawn twins parted when he flew up to confront the knight, making way. With all his might focused into the attack, and with the beast it was meant for caught totally off guard, Wayward struck a devastating punch against his cheek.

Kerato swung around and kicked Wayward in the head, opposite of the spot where he attacked before. Showing no mercy, the monster prepared to cut off his head with his sword. Luckily, Pupil grabbed Wayward's hands and pulled him out of range of the attack. Next, she released Wayward into Iris's arms, did a front flip to get up close, and kicked Kerato dead in the forehead.

"Ah!" Kerato cried in distress. Before Pupil could react, Kerato slashed her across her forehead. Next, Kerato yanked her silver hair and punched her in the center of her stomach, knocking her out cold. Finally, he threw her to the ground where she collided with Iris and Wayward.

"Uhhh," Pupil moaned.

"Pupil!" Iris exclaimed. She looked sharply into Wayward's eyes, no doubt mentally preparing herself for a rash act of justice. A terrified Wayward noticed that Iris's irises morphed into a passionate indigo shade. Her eyes held hints of other colors, too: gray, which represented sorrow, and pink, which was compassion.

What're we gonna do, Iris? Wayward was in the midst of fighting the toughest inner battle in his life. It was with panic, and the panic was starting to overwhelm him.

Iris was not one for words, and this moment brought no exception. She simply turned back toward her enemy, who looked like a floating statue with a subtle degree of lively chaos in its eyes. Courageously, Iris teleported behind him, placed a hand on his broad back, and fired a red beam of electricity straight through. Then she muttered, "How'd you do it? How'd you fix your sword after Zenon destroyed it?"

"Heh ... It's mixed w-with my energy. W-when it br-breaks ... all the energy is released, but a-all I h-have to do is use my en-energy ... like g-glue, to r-repair it," Kerato stuttered weakly. Blood dripped from his mouth due to the huge wound in his upper back and chest. His bright blue eyes started to dull.

Iris nodded. Iris tried to swing around and end the fight with another powerful blast through his body, but Kerato was one step ahead.

"It's n-not like I'd tell y-you anything ... if you could use it against me!" Kerato laughed hysterically.

"Zonule!" Iris bellowed as she launched two scarlet disks from her irises. They grew massive but held their shape and flew straight toward the former knight. The first one made contact with his shoulder, but he managed to deflect the second ring with his energy-guarded sword.

When Kerato's blue eyes suddenly twinkled with wrath, Wayward could sense that the tide of the battle was about to change for the worse. With Zenon and Zephyr in pain, he had to do something but remained where he was next to Pupil. A quiet, chilling breeze swept over him as he stared at the ground, desperately trying to gather all his resolve into one point. Though it seemed pointless, Wayward, finally realizing that he did not have the will to fight, decided to cheer on a friend who did.

"Watch out, Iris! He's going all out!"

With a look of disdain, Kerato turned toward the sound of the young warrior's voice for a split second. Wayward's warning morphed into the perfect diversion for Iris to attack.

"Corona Barrage!" she roared defiantly. Before Wayward could blink twice, Iris's eyes had begun to glow an intensely bright yellow, and the energy seemed to flow from her eyes around her whole body. Iris fired two disks from her eyes with her Zonule technique, only these were neon yellow and left a trail of light in their wake. However, the experienced knight blew away both attacks with one stroke of his supernatural sword and directed them right back at Iris. Anxiously scrambling to evade being caught in her own attack, she descended about fifteen feet in the sky. She fell right into Kerato's trap. The swordsman was already behind Iris. By the time she realized, it was too late. With one powerful stroke to the back of her skull with the hilt of his sword, the fiend knocked Iris out cold. The knight, suddenly uninterested, allowed Iris to fall to the ground in a comatose state, intending for her to land hard on her head.

"No!" Wayward wailed as he ran toward his friend's falling body, leaping just in time to catch her. Shuddering, he slowly sat her up and dragged her over to where Pupil lay facing a similar fate. He did not dare run over to where Zenon and Zephyr were bunched up together, because he would be crossing the enemy's path.

"W-Wayward! Run away! Get out of here!" Zenon screamed from about seventy meters away.

"Shut up," Kerato fumed, giving Zenon the death stare.

"No ..." Wayward murmured.

"Wayward ... please ... I know exactly how you feel, but we couldn't prepare you for this. It's our fault that he's here in the first place," Zephyr begged, struggling to stand up without putting weight on her bleeding, injured leg. Zenon, who had received a less severe injury, looked poised for another attack beside her twin.

The next thing Wayward knew, Kerato was behind the Zeal twins, leaving them both aghast with disbelief.

"Look out!" Wayward cried, but his plea was useless.

The swordsman snickered over the twins' shoulders. A few brief moments of dreaded silence passed over the battlefield before something more astonishing occurred.

"You know … you're a real idiot," Zenon said. Her long, black, dagger-shaped bangs almost covered her face, leaving her expression indecipherable.

"You think we were sitting here just doing nothing?" Zephyr chimed in, looking far from pleased.

Suddenly, Kerato was propelled fifty meters to the left by a powerful gust of wind. The swordsman recovered almost instantly. However, he started moving in slow motion. Next, his weapon vanished into thin air, and a huge explosion appeared ten feet above his head. Finally, he was pushed forward about six feet, by a second gust of wind, into an inescapable energy blast. An orb of violet light popped into existence next to the center of his stomach and exploded. When the smoke from the bomb cleared, Kerato was doubled over, coughing out blood.

Iris stirred beside Wayward, but her eyes remained closed.

"Jadel," she whispered.

A tanned girl with flowing, golden blonde hair, violet eyes, and in an all purple combat suit calmly descended to ground level. A boy with curly black hair and brown skin, wearing a blue combat suit and orange shoes, followed her lead, landing between Kerato and their comrades.

"What'd you d-do to me?" Kerato smoldered.

"After Iris got you to talk, Zenon told me about your powers. We can use telepathy, you know," Jadeleve explained. Wayward realized that the girl's hair wasn't flowing because of the wind but because rich lime-green energy was rotating around her like a mini-twister.

"Jadeleve vaporized your sword, so you can't fix it anymore," the curly-haired boy explained. Wayward was so focused on Jadeleve's rising anger that he had not even noticed when the boy went over to check on Zephyr and Zenon.

"I'll kill you all," Kerato started.

"You've changed, Kerato. At least you spared me before. What happened to you?" the curly-haired boy said.

"That was before you tricked me."

"I had to protect them."

"What're you talking about? They used you as a diversion to get away. Nobody cares about you."

"Shut up. I chose to do that. They were the ones telling me not to go, but I went on my own free will. Don't talk like you know me."

"Well don't talk like you know me. None of you know what I've been through."

"Then stop killing people and enlighten us!" Jadeleve exploded.

THE MASTER OF ILLUSIONS

"**K**UROSKI! YOU'RE *ALIVE!*" ZEPHYR EXCLAIMED.

"Yep." Kuroski grinned, kneeling next to her and Zenon.

"What happened?" Zenon queried. Once he gathered his thoughts, Kuroski told his story, about how he was rescued and treated at Fiome's rehabilitation center.

"That's where I met Jadeleve. We got new supplies, went through Redundant Dungeon for training, and here we are," Kuroski finished.

"Anything major?" Zenon asked, recovering more strength with each passing second.

"Yeah. We learned that Jadeleve's pendant is made from Ingrain Crystals and she can use it to store solar energy. Also—"

"What?" Zephyr rose to her feet, forgetting about the huge wound in her leg.

"The Eyebots are using this technique that causes hallucinations and controls minds. When Jadeleve and I were fighting in the Redundant Dungeon, we found a bunch of Beings who were possessed by the same attack. They used it on Jadeleve during your battle in Sapolis and forced her into the Akapeachi Jungle. She barely made it out," Kuroski explained.

"Why are you even fighting? Just stop," Jadeleve demanded as she loomed over Kerato, who she had pummeled into the ground. Kerato remained silent for a while, avoiding her gaze. When he finally did reply, he ignored her question.

"You're are real lost c-cause, a-aren't you?"

After shouldering a short silence, Jadeleve lifted a shaky hand in Kerato's direction. Zephyr ran around about twenty feet to confirm her suspicions: Jadeleve was crying. Having known her for years, Zephyr knew that all Jadeleve wanted was to get along with everyone. She could not accept the fact that some people never change.

Zephyr was about to intervene when a man materialized out of thin air in front of Kerato, shielding him from Jadeleve's halfhearted attack.

"Kerato, you got carried away. We are already done with the testing phase; you have a new job to do. Do not step out of line again," the man reprimanded with raspy voice that sounded like it was wrought with years of smoking, though he looked around forty. He wore a black cloak that covered his entire body, expect for his head and his navy combat boots. He was tall, bald, and had lifeless gray eyes. He then turned to Jadeleve. "So you're the Zeal Possessor."

Jadeleve deactivated the zeal.

"Who are you?" she demanded.

"Cataract, leader of the Eyebots' Jupiter Base Squadron."

"You're Cataract? A man from Fiome who was testing out your hallucination weapon mentioned your name," Jadeleve gasped. Zephyr turned to Kuroski and saw his eyes widen as he recalled the event.

"Good. You know me, and I know you," Cataract replied.

Suddenly, Zephyr realized that she, Zenon, and Kuroski should make their way over to their younger comrades in case they needed help. She passed on her idea to the two in a low voice, and both agreed. While Jadeleve was distracting Kerato and Cataract, they slowly traversed the distance that separated their allied forces.

When Zephyr, Zenon, and Kuroski reunited with Pupil, Iris, and Wayward, Iris, surprisingly, was the first to greet them.

"Are you guys okay? What's going on?" Iris seemed more hopeful than distressed. Enticingly, her eyes light up in a brilliant blue, signifying bravery and hopefulness.

Zenon embraced Iris.

"If we have to fight, be ready," Zenon warned the youngsters.

"All right! Keep on your toes, Wayward," Pupil warned.

"O-okay," Wayward muttered. Finally, the six tense warriors turned their attention back to the unfolding argument between Jadeleve and the enemy.

"So you sent Cocone and Rodney. You probably sent all the people we've ever fought," Jadeleve said.

"Yes."

"Jupiter is our home too. Stop acting like you own it."

"We were here first, you little fool. The See-Throughs betrayed everyone and took over the land. We were here first. It's like a child using its mother. You're the real tyrants."

Jadeleve had succeeded in confirming everyone's uncertainties: they could not persuade the enemy through talking. She looked over and gave Zephyr a grave look. Effortlessly, Zephyr translated the Jadeleve's unspoken plea in her head.

Cataract's just testing us. They only way to scare him is with a combined attack. Zephyr turned and conferred the message to the others.

As if Cataract had already caught wind of their scheme, he snickered, cocking his head. This only fueled Zephyr's resolve. Unexpectedly, however, Jadeleve released 100 percent of her dormant power, a sight Zephyr had only witnessed when they fought each other or against Eyebots. Inside the protective walls of her superheated green aura, tears slid from Jadeleve's eyes and rose up along the rising current of energy. Almost instantly, the tears vaporized and morphed into small pockets of steam, like a kettle. Rocks broke off in chunks from the ground and floated around her.

"Choroid Gun!" Zenon roared at the top of her lungs, liberating a thin beam of light from her palms that matched the color of Jadeleve's zeal.

"Argh!" Pupil screamed, firing her brilliant blue Sclera Beam. Next, Zephyr fired a Foveno Beam, a powerful golden burst of energy. Iris jumped twenty feet into the air before she discharged her red Rings of Fire.

"Soul Twister!" Kuroski said before he pushed a tornado outward from his hands at Kerato and Cataract.

"Recatus!" Jadeleve bellowed defiantly and fired her purple attack.

"Take this!" Wayward screeched, firing his first successful orange energy blast.

About ten feet away from their target, the spectrum of beams, propelled by Kuroski's wind, merged into a super, white beam. Zephyr studied their opponents to see how they would react. Kerato seemed petrified at first, but Cataract was unimpressed.

It won't be enough, Zephyr thought.

Nevertheless, the super beam collided with *something* and triggered one of the biggest explosions Zephyr had ever seen. Clear apprehensiveness settled over the young group as they waited to see the result of their efforts. When the smoke cleared, the Eyebots were nowhere to be found. In their place was a massive crater, which was definitely the largest Zephyr had ever seen in person.

"They escaped," Wayward murmured with defeat in his voice.

"I know," Zephyr said. "But it was the best we could do."

Zephyr glanced over at Jadeleve, who was still staring at the crater.

"I knew we couldn't beat them this time, so our only option was to scare them off. Cataract only came here to get Kerato and check us out." Jadeleve had to yell to be heard by the other six, since she was still seventy meters away from them.

"Great job, Wayward. Even though you didn't hear the plan, you still did great." Pupil grinned.

"Whaddya mean?"

"When I asked you to run away, it was just a diversion so Kerato wouldn't detect Jadeleve's energy. We knew you could handle it," Zenon explained.

"Really? I did it?" Wayward gasped. Zenon giggled and rustled his already unruly hair.

"I'm starving! Let's go!" Pupil sang as she levitated off the ground and zoomed back to Mrs. Kage's house for dinner.

"Pupil hasn't changed at all." Jadeleve laughed, having made it over.

"Neither have you, golden girl!" Zephyr chuckled before she tackled Jadeleve in a hug. Before Jadeleve could react, all the others, excluding Pupil and Wayward, had piled on top of her.

"Whoa! It's great to see you guys, but you're crushing me!" Jadeleve wheezed. When Zephyr, Zenon, Iris, and Kuroski finally returned her free will, Jadeleve sat crisscross-apple-sauce and was directly facing Wayward. This was her first time noticing him.

"What's up? What's your name?" Jadeleve asked.

"Wayward. Nice to meet you, Jadeleve," Wayward said as politely as possible, wanting to make a good impression.

"You're so shy. You can call me Jadel if you want. Are you coming with us?"

"Yeah, I am. But … I'm not that strong," Wayward said.

"You seem pretty strong to me. I have a feeling that one day you'll be super strong," Jadeleve claimed.

"Really?" Wayward's eyes lit up. "Then let's go home right away so I can train!"

"Hey, if you don't take a break, you'll be a train wreck," Zephyr lectured.

"H-hold on. W-what sh-should we d-do about the bodies?" Iris stammered, killing the mood.

"Yeah … you're right, Iris. I hadn't even thought of that," Wayward said as grief washed over them.

Kuroski looked around at the used battlefield and seemed startled to find the defeated soldiers of Pearl Town scattered around them. "I didn't even notice them …"

"One of the reasons I wanted to make this pit was to bury them," Jadeleve explained. Most See-Through provinces did not have graveyards but buried the bodies of the deceased near where they had died.

Somberly, the warriors collected the eight Imperial Knights who lay around the site of their latest battle and gently placed them all in the crater, where there was enough room for all of them. Silently, the team covered the crater with the same gravel that was displaced by the force of their super beam. When it was all over, Zephyr broke the silence.

"I never want to see this again. *This* is why I fight."

RETURN

"**W**OW ... OKAY ... THAT'S WHY YOU didn't answer the last couple weeks. Okay. We'll keep that in mind. Keep it up, guys. Bye." Xaphias finished talking with his sisters on his transceiver. Since they lost all their things on Ripple Island, Zenon and Zephyr had to call him using the new transceiver that Jadeleve had gotten from the Travel Atlas.

Things are getting complicated, Xaphias thought.

"Let's head out, guys. We're almost at Widria," Xaphias declared.

"Fine. Lead the way," Maelin grumbled.

"Time for more training, right?" Teresa muttered.

Xaphias, not meaning to sound so demanding, sulked. With pain from their long travels showing in his every step, he trudged over to the edge of the cliff and stood beside the girls. Gato soon followed.

Finally, something broke the silence. It was the cry of a young Unchartian dragon. Within seconds after hearing his cry, Aiondraes came into view amid a clear blue sky. For a fraction of a second, he looked like a dot above the horizon, but incredible speed carried him into full view before Xaphias could blink twice. Aiondraes had returned from his brief mission scouting the area for trouble before their group continued on.

"Aiiii!" Aiondraes greeted. He flapped his wings, creating air resistance to slow his descent. Then he majestically lowered himself on the grassy hill beside them.

"Is it safe, Aiondraes?" Teresa asked excitedly. Aiondraes nodded in response, so she tackled him in a hug, actually knocking the thirty-foot dragon over. His blue scales had grown harder, and his silver tail spikes had grown sharper, and the horn that grew out of his forehead had stretched out in the last two years. His pencil-thin red eyes were more alert than ever, and Xaphias was grateful for that.

Due to the Eyebots' latest attacks, Xaphias and his group decided to postpone their infiltration of the Land of Eyebots and stay in the Land of See-Throughs to fight the enemy. Since Widria had a reputation as the City of Dragons, they thought it would be the perfect place for them to train. Xaphias wanted to make sure Aiondraes was at his best.

"If it's safe, then let's go," Maelin urged. Without another word, the group took flight and continued onward toward Widria.

THE AVENGER

"I DON'T THINK TRAINING AGAINST DRAGONS in Widria will make a difference." Gato sighed. Xaphias had no idea why he had even agreed to come on their quest in the first place. Gato did not care in the slightest about how he looked. He was sloppy with dirty blond hair, brown eyes, and tanned skin. He liked to wear overalls and rolled-up collared shirts with his brown sneakers and dark pants. Before he joined their team, he was a farmer.

"Maybe Gato's right. We need to be training mentally, not physically," Maelin piped up. She had very long brown hair with natural red streaks at its tips (that she tried to pull back into a ponytail, but the rest was still shoulder length). Her bangs draped over her right eye, and they were big and blue. Today, she wore a sleeveless, pink tunic with brown shorts and black leggings. Her sneakers were bright red.

Teresa nodded, but she remained quiet, which was unusual. She was the opposite of Iris: talkative, outgoing, and perky. Even her golden eyes and red hair were opposite Iris's; Teresa's hair stood out on all sides in a spiky, ruffled mess. She wore a neon T-shirt and orange shorts with her white sneakers.

Xaphias chose them out of all the kids he had met for their unique skills. Maelin excelled at hand-to-hand combat and handling weapons. She used her agility, abnormal flexibility, and strength to take down unsuspecting opponents. Her weapon of choice was a dagger. Two years before, after separating from the Original Five and Celestine in the Celestine County, Xaphias traveled east to Navel Town. Navel Town was famous for producing top-notch blacksmiths, and because Xaphias was in need of a sword, it was the perfect place to go. After watching how Maelin crafted a sword with such astonishing ease in her workshop, Xaphias knew she would be a helpful companion on his quest. To win over Maelin's trust and become the creator of his own weapon, he used Aiondraes's flames to heat the iron that made his sword.

Gato was another story. Xaphias, Maelin, and Aiondraes had met him in Ionize Town on his farm in the middle of fighting off a serpent-like Being with his strategy alone. Impressed, they asked him if he would be interested in coming, but he could not make up his mind. Fed up, Maelin decided that if Gato was not serious that he should not come. However, there were Imperial Knights blocking all passages to the Laputa County, which was their next stop. The trio attempted to go around, but they were intercepted by Cocone and Rodney. Xaphias convinced Maelin to run for cover, so if anything happened to him or Aiondraes, she would take the enemy by surprise. After being severely beaten, their only hope was to use the play-dead technique and trick the Eyebot twins into thinking they had killed them. Maelin stayed hidden when she heard the Original Five's approach because she did not recognize them as friend or foe, but luckily, Jadeleve had brought healing herbs to heal Xaphias and Aiondraes.

After they were healed and said farewell to their healers, Xaphias met back up with Maelin. They ventured east, back toward Ionize Town so they could figure out another way to get past the guards. Luckily, when they had returned, half of the Imperial Knights were in a daze, groveling on the ground. Gato had defeated them all, giving them room to escape. It was his way of saying that he wanted to come along after all, and so the four of them raced across the Celestial Ocean toward Laputa. They had been traveling together ever since.

Gato specialized in using tactics to fight and protected himself with an iron staff. Teresa possessed a separate skill from the rest. She used special goggles that had X-ray vision and could fire laser beams using her energy. She usually kept them wrapped around her head like a headband, but when they were in a pinch, she never hesitated to use them. Xaphias and the others had met Teresa while they were wandering through the Akapeachi Jungle. They were about to eat fruit that was poisoned by Reebees, but Teresa detected the poison by seeing through them with her special goggles. Their team was well balanced and good-natured.

Aiondraes whimpered, dragging Xaphias back to the present; it was time for lunch. During lunch, Maelin sat next to Xaphias, which he found uncomfortable, especially since no one was talking. Xaphias tried to inch away from her, slowly, so she did not notice. Maelin was not having any of it though, because she scooted next to him again without a word. Xaphias did not mean to hurt her feelings; he was just an antisocial person.

"What? Don't want cooties?" Maelin finally asked.

"No. I just …" Xaphias stammered awkwardly.

"We never talk about anything except the war or our next move. Is this our life?"

Xaphias looked up to the sky and pretended to be reminiscing, but really he was trying to end the conversation and regain his composure.

"Do you not like us?" Teresa prompted.

"Of course I like you. I like all of you. Why else would I choose you guys to help us?" Xaphias motioned toward Aiondraes. Aiondraes rumbled in response to being recognized.

"I left home when I was eight. I really never had friends before, so I don't know how to act." Xaphias sighed. It felt good to get that off his chest.

"Fair enough," Maelin said, and gentleness returned to her face. "We should get to know each other. I'll start. I was born—"

"I can tell this won't be ending anytime soon," Teresa said, forcing laughs from Xaphias and Gato.

"Do you have any better ideas?" Maelin fumed.

"Why don't you let Xaphias tell a quick story? He needs practice talking to people." Teresa giggled.

"Yeah. All right …" Xaphias agreed. It only took him a few seconds before he decided what story he wanted to tell. Next, he got comfortable. "I'll tell you how I broke my sisters out of jail. Well, the first time they were in jail."

After a great lunch that was prolonged by storytelling, the Secondary Five (Xaphias's new name for his group) set off on the path to Widria City again. Clear blue skies and warm weather were perfect conditions to make their long trek feel like nothing. It turned all the silence into serenity. Aiondraes decided to walk with them on the ground rather than fly so he could build up the muscles in his arms and legs, and every so often, he rumbled with effort. As the sun dipped to touch the horizon, Xaphias became more alert. His senses sharpened to compensate for his loss of vision. His body was preparing itself for the vulnerability of night.

"I think it's time we set up camp for the night." Gato yawned, not waiting for a response before he plopped down on the ground.

"Good idea," Teresa agreed.

"You guys are so lazy. You didn't even get out your sleeping stuff." Maelin sighed as she rummaged through her bag.

"Fine, guys. But we're going to have to make up extra ground tomorrow," Xaphias said, and suddenly he felt a powerful surge of energy.

"What was that?" Gato jolted up from his nap in the grass. The group's attention shifted to the sky. Unmistakably, a battle was raging just ahead, and sparks of potent energy lit up the night. From the language of the energy signals, this melee was nothing like friendly sparring. One side was growing weak at an alarming rate. Something was wrong.

"Come on, guys. Let's see what's happening," Xaphias beckoned. As quickly as they could, the others gathered up camp and followed. They were practically sprinting down the grassy hills toward the disturbance. As they grew closer, they could hear screaming.

Xaphias knew he had to fly if he wanted to make it in time to break up the fight. He smoothly lifted off the ground and picked up the pace in his flying. Even when they were met with the small forest that was blocking their view from the fight and the branches of healthy trees bombarded them, Xaphias did not slow down.

Finally, the Secondary Five entered the forest, but Xaphias had not expected what he saw in the split second of confusion. A young boy clutched an older girl's shirt collar with shaking, unstable hands. There was fierce rage in his eyes. Blood stained her arms. Her pants were torn, and her hair was a mess. The boy's hostility vibrated all around him in the form of a golden aura.

When Xaphias's group landed on the grass in succession, the boy instantly noticed. They boy also seemed to notice Aiondraes, who was circling high above. There were several unconscious people on the ground, none dead. All of them were kids.

Xaphias's head began to pound with unbearable pain.

Kill each other, Xaphias thought. The order just seemed to pop into existence.

Suddenly, Xaphias's peripheral vision disappeared, replaced by a black background, and he could only see what was directly in front of him. He involuntarily turned toward Gato, prepared to kill him. Gato stared back at him with a deadly expression, seemingly prepared to kill him.

Wh-what's happening to us? Why can't I c-control my body? That kid!

Suddenly, the boy who Xaphias believed was controlling all of their minds was knocked back by the girl he was just restraining.

I'm freeing you. You're the strongest here. Can you destroy that machine? A high-pitched voice spoke in Xaphias's mind. He quickly realized that it was the girl and located the machine she was talking about. At the edge of the forest stood a twenty-five-foot-tall, parabolic, silver-colored, aluminum satellite dish. Its feed horn was thin and cylinder shaped, growing narrower as it extended outward from its center until it ended at a sphere.

Without giving it a second thought, Xaphias fired the strongest energy blast he could muster to destroy the machine. After the explosion, everyone returned to normal.

"Wh-what happened?" Maelin muttered once she regained her bearings.

"I think that kid was using the machine to control us. Am I right?" Xaphias seethed, turning his attention toward the boy.

"You guessed it." The boy snickered, before catching the girl off guard and punching her to the ground next to the other defeated victims.

"Hey!" Xaphias barked. The boy jumped out of reach.

"What're you doing?" Xaphias demanded.

"Just testing out a weapon."

"Why? Who are you working for?"

"Like I'd tell you."

Distract him so I can infiltrate his mind and get his information, the girl's voice rang in his head again.

"Ground Shredder!" Xaphias roared. He unsheathed his sword, absorbed the surrounding earth energy, making it weaker, and stabbed the ground. The shockwave split open the ground and forced the boy off balance.

"So you're working for an Eyebot named Cataract. You're a See-Through and your name's Rohan," Xaphias smirked. Shocked that he was found out, the boy lost his cool. He drew his sword and teleported in front of Xaphias. They clashed with their swords.

"If you're a See-Through, why are you working for the Eyebots? You're not even being hypnotized. We'll just read your mind if you don't answer," Xaphias threatened.

"They kidnapped me four years ago and threatened to kill my family if I didn't help them," Rohan seethed.

Xaphias paused for a moment. "But what're you planning?"

"We're going to control everyone who's left in the Land of See-Throughs with our new machine and kill everyone."

"What? That's insane!" Maelin gasped.

"So you would chose your family over your race?" Xaphias asked in the midst of their sword fight.

"Wouldn't anyone?"

"You remind me of one of my close friends. She used to think just like you. She thought she had to do everything alone and that she had to betray her race to save her family, but she found a way to protect her family and her race," Xaphias said, thinking of Celestine, who was working hard to improve relations between the royal family and the other races on Coreicean Island. "Do you think your mom and brother would be happy to find out what choices you made?"

"How do you ... Stop reading my mind!" Rohan raged.

"I'm not doing it. That girl you beat up is and relaying the messages to me. You could've beaten us with comrades, but I guess you don't have any."

"I do!"

"What? The Eyebots? Where are they now? They're just using you to get the job done. I bet after you help, they won't even spare your family. You're making the wrong choice. You could've gotten help, but you're too scared to make a move."

"Shut up!" Rohan bellowed. Pain exploded all over Xaphias's body.

"Xaphias!" Maelin gasped. Xaphias came to at the sound of her voice.

"What happened?" Xaphias murmured. He was laying on the ground.

"That levitated a bunch of boulders and hit you from close range," Teresa recounted.

"Agh. Feels like it." Xaphias groaned.

Maelin took out her first-aid kits and gave Gato and Teresa one for the injured. The only one Xaphias had noticed who was not taken care of was the girl who had helped him. Her arm was badly scorched, but she tried to make it seem like it was no big deal. Without conversation, Gato threw Xaphias a special salve to rub on his body. Xaphias snatched it out of the air without looking and applied it to himself. Then he slowly walked over and gave it to the girl to apply.

After thirty minutes of making sure everyone was on the road to recovery, the girl from before, who was obviously the leader of the Widria Warriors, called for a debriefing. Standing in the center of their eleven-person line, (now with bandages her right arm) the girl seemed to be the oldest among their ranks. She looked about seventeen or eighteen, with dark tan skin, brown hair, and hazel eyes.

"That's a cute name ... the Widria Warriors. Never thought of that." The girl giggled despite her situation.

"Stop," Xaphias grumbled, annoyed.

"Sorry. Habit. You have to know how to read minds to understand your dragon. Come out; we don't bite," the girl cooed. Slowly but surely, Aiondraes crept out of the brushes as quietly as any thirty-foot dragon could, his ruby eyes glinting with suspicion. His tension eased after he extended his long neck so the girl could pet his head. Aiondraes rumbled with pleasure.

"Who are you?" the girl asked without looking up from grooming Aiondraes. In order, Xaphias, Maelin, Teresa, and Gato introduced themselves.

"You could've just read our minds," Gato complained.

"Yeah, but I like the suspense. Ever since the war started and the elders left, we decided to stay behind and protect the ancient relics of our city. Most of the See-Throughs on Jupiter are headed toward the Land of Eyerobis for infiltration, to give them a taste of their own medicine. But we have an endangered species of Beings, which we call Aqua dragons. There are said to only be three clans left of them in the whole world, including ours. We raise the same kind as Aiondraes here in our temple. The Eyebots have tried to steal our dragons before, and some have succeeded, which is why we are so picky about who enters and exits our home," the girl explained, calming Aiondraes, who perked up at the sound of his name with the soft touch of her hands.

"Oh ... I've been to all three clans then. I found Aiondraes a couple years ago in an uncharted land near Greenland ... northwest of Celestine City. Since the place didn't have a name, I just referred to it as the Uncharted Valley. He shot out of the lake without his mother, which was weird because he was an infant. Also, my sisters, our friends, and I were crossing Earth's Sea, and we found five of his kind again. They seemed to be the only Beings there. It seems Beings like Aiondraes only live in the least inhabited bodies of water in the world. That's why we call them Unchartian dragons," Xaphias replied.

"Wow. That's an awesome name ... the Unchartian dragons." The girl took a second to marvel at the new word. "Speaking of names ... mine is Sophfronia. I think from now on, we'll call them Unchartian dragons. By the way, it's nice to meet you guys. What can we do for you?"

"We'd like you to train us. We've got to be prepared when the Eyebots try their attack on us," Maelin declared.

"Okay then. Come on. We start tomorrow," Sophfronia said simply. The platinum gates of the city slowly creaked open, and the young group trudged inside.

RESUMING THE QUEST

JADELEVE FLINCHED UPON WAKING TO the brightness of the sun. For a second, she studied the other girls who were littered around the room ... her friends and family. After spending so long away from them, even after taking a week to catch up, it still seemed surreal that they were together again.

The young warrior crept further out of bed and stretched and yawned. Next, she gazed around the wooden farmhouse that Mrs. Kage had let them sleep in for the past week while their injuries healed (Mrs. Kage had run out of healing herbs). The girls promised they would protect Wayward at all costs during their trip to return the Kage family's kindness.

"Wake up, everybody!" Pupil's voice blared through the room. Startled, Jadeleve jerked and fell off her bed, face-first.

"What the heck, Pupil?" Zephyr raged. She got up and smacked the younger girl on the head, much to Jadeleve's amusement.

"Today's the day. Besides ... Jadel was already awake," Pupil moaned, trying to shift attention away from herself, but Zephyr did not take the bait.

Jadeleve levitated. She then touched her index finger to her lips and whispered, "I'm a morning person; this is nothing for me."

"Anyway ... Zephyr, when are we leaving then?" Pupil asked anxiously.

"How should I know? I'm not the leader," Zephyr replied.

"Come on, guys." Zenon moaned from under her covers. Her hair was a mangled mess, which was rare for her. When Iris got up, her eyes flashed red with anger, but at least she was quiet.

"Sorry we woke you up," Jadeleve apologized.

"No, it's okay. Thanks, actually. We have a big day ahead of us, so we should get an early start," Zenon said.

"Okay, let's get ready," Jadeleve agreed. The Original Five was back.

Once the girls had taken showers and gotten dressed, they strolled across Mrs. Kage's grassy backyard and made their way to the porch. Zephyr opened the door, and everyone rushed in, leaving Iris to close it. Guided by their noses, the girls walked down the short hallway that led to the Kitchen of Stone Tiles where Mrs. Kage was rustling up breakfast. The mother smiled warmly at the sight of them but then turned back to what she was cooking.

"The boys are still sleeping in Wayward's room. Would you mind waking them up?" Mrs. Kage requested without looking their way, which Jadeleve took as a sign of trust.

"Not at all, Mrs. K!" Pupil replied in her usual chipper tone. "In fact … *I'll* do it!"

"That's sweet of you, dear, but do it quick. I don't want their food to get cold." Mrs. Kage smiled again.

With Mrs. Kage's approval, Pupil raced up the stairs and barged into Wayward's room. Jadeleve braced herself for one of her little sister's shrill, wake-up cries with only a second to spare. The precaution was well worth it.

"Wake up, you guys!" Pupil shrieked. The snoring persisted. It amazed Jadeleve how the boys could sleep through that when it had woken her up so many times before. Well, she was a pretty light sleeper, but Jadeleve would not have been surprised if people living a mile away heard that.

"Fine! I didn't wanna have to do this!" Pupil declared. Suddenly, Pupil created a laser, which stretched down the stairs and into the other girls' faces. It was Pupil's Flashlight Technique. Jadeleve could only imagine how painful it would be to look directly into Pupil's eyes while she was doing that.

"Ugh! All right, All right! We're awake! You don't have to blind us!" Wayward complained.

"Good. Another job well done," Pupil said as she cleared all the steps on the way down with a single jump and tackled Zephyr with a hug.

Jadeleve picked up on the sound of someone stumbling out of the room. Before she could react, Kuroski had tumbled down the stairs and landed head first on the ground.

"Kuroski!" Jadeleve gasped. She ran to the foot of the steps to help. The battered boy lifted his head just enough to project a weak voice.

"Uhhh ... n-next time ... just use an alarm clock."

"Sorry. Next time we'll be on the road, so you won't fall down the stairs at least," Pupil said, not turning to face Kuroski.

"Oh ... good." Kuroski sighed.

Following that incident, Wayward and Kuroski got ready for the day. Afterward, everyone met in the kitchen for breakfast. While there, Zenon, with her vast knowledge of traveling, helped Wayward pick out what he would bring with him on their journey. Since the group had all the necessities between them, Wayward only had to bring his clothes and toiletries. Jadeleve noticed that he mostly brought clothes for combat, like his wristbands and sneakers. What really caught her attention was the fact that he brought a compass.

"Where'd you get that, Wayward?" Jadeleve asked kindly so he wouldn't think she was nosey.

"My great-great-grandpa gave it to me for my birthday the year he passed away. He said it would help 'show me the way.'"

"Interesting. Well, do you think you have everything you need now?"

"Yeah. I'm ready," Wayward said with finality, making him seem four years older for a second.

Finally, once their food was digested, it was around eleven o'clock and the kids were ready to embark on the second leg of their quest. Now reunited with her friends, Jadeleve felt more confident than ever.

Mrs. Kage met the seven warriors outside the front door to see them off for the final time, and Jadeleve was not surprised to see tears in her eyes.

"Stay safe. All of you. And Wayward ... honey ... just come back in one piece." Mrs. Kage wept. Her bright blue eyes shined with so much love that it made Jadeleve homesick for her own mother. Mrs. Kage placed her right hand over her chest as if her heart was about to burst.

"Well ... see you later, Mama Kage. I love you!"

As Zephyr, Zenon, Iris, and Kuroski said their goodbyes, Jadeleve turned toward Wayward, who seemed frozen in his tracks. Fear and uncertainty tainted his expression. Jadeleve could see that he was having second thoughts about leaving home, but there was no turning back. There was no time for indecision. Maybe Jadeleve could not prevent the inevitable from happening, which meant parting ways with love ones, but she could make something happen. It was something that she did with her mom to ensure that their bond would never break, even if their bones did.

Without warning, Jadeleve picked Wayward up and threw him into his mother's arms. It was as if Wayward had found the missing piece to the puzzle. He broke down and cried alongside his mother, buried in her blouse. Jadeleve had just created a golden moment.

"I l-l-love you, M-Mom," Wayward stammered.

"Same here, sweetie. Come back when you find your brother. School can wait," Mrs. Kage replied. She kissed her son on his forehead and squeezed him tight for another minute before finally letting him go.

OLD BONDS

*T*HERE'S THE TELEPATHY SATELLITE, JUST *like Rohan said,* Nyx thought as she surveyed her hometown, Widria, while riding on Chalazia's purple back. The two quickly swooped down so Chalazia could pick up the remains in her jaws. Nyx put the remains in a zeal capsule for later use, and they kept flying.

"Other than you, there was nothing good about this place." Nyx beamed and scratched Chalazia's left check where she liked it. Chalazia rumbled with joy.

"They kept us cooped up. It was so crowded. We needed to stretch our wings. That's why we moved here."

By the time Nyx finished talking, they had reached Culloqui. Other than the Martial Arts Academy, Nyx loved the architectural design of Culloqui's houses. With friendly-looking houses made from only red bricks or wood, plenty of playgrounds for kids, and government buildings that were distinguished by being made of marble, it was a very organized town. There was barely any crime, so the mayor never found the need to hire Imperial Knights. Nyx was so comfortable there she dreaded the day she left.

Nyx was See-Through, but her parents were not. Her father was an Eyebot, and her mother was human. Both of them, her mother from the Land of Humans and her father from the Land of Eyebots, had fled to the Land of See-Throughs by submarine in search of a better life. They were illegal immigrants.

Financially, it made more sense to start off in the city, so they chose Widria. From a young age, Nyx had been taught the history and culture of all three races, so she excelled at the subject in school. But the main reason her parents stressed that area of knowledge so much was that when she was older, Nyx could fit in wherever she decided to live.

When she was eight, she and her parents snuck away to the Land of Humans for vacation, using her mother's submarine. There, Nyx met her maternal grandparents, aunts and uncles, and cousins. They were all human and welcomed them warmly. However, it was there that Nyx realized that interracial relationships were illegal in many towns and were frowned upon in others. It was the same situation when they traveled to the Land of Eyebots the following summer to meet her father's family after sidestepping the Imperial Knights and illegally traveling to another land with her father's rusty, blood-red submarine.

"If they can't even stop us, what gives them the right to say that we can't go?" her father teased during the long journey of underwater travel.

Upon their second return to Fantasia County, the Imperial Knights had been anticipating their arrival after receiving several reports of them missing. The guards had already given them a criminal codename: the Stowaways. After several consecutive torture sessions, her parents finally confessed about their submarines, which the guards confiscated and destroyed. Afterward, Nyx's parents were sent to the local prison and sentenced for life while she was condemned to live in a foster home. There was no more traveling.

At the orphanage, the other kids ridiculed and bullied her. She was fine with that, but when they started criticizing her parents, she drew the line. Why was it illegal to travel to other lands? Why were all races so racist?

"There is a long history of conflict between the three races. The Eyebots think of themselves as the superior race and wanted to control everything, but the See-Throughs and humans rebelled, giving birth to the land division system. Not only is it illegal for people of different races to come to this land, but it's looked down upon for them to marry," Nyx's father explained during visiting day. From that day on, Nyx swore that she would end the eternal divide between races and break her parents out of jail.

At sixteen, after winning the annual Dragon Scale Contest and receiving Chalazia's egg, Nyx decided to run away from home. She moved to Culloqui. There, she worked at the local elementary school as a mental energy education teacher, having excelled at using mental energy growing up. She discovered an especially hardworking student named Lila. Lila wanted to do something about the corrupted racial system, having grown up at the forefront of the problem. Nyx saw herself in the girl.

When Nyx turned seventeen, Chalazia had just hatched. When Cataract sought her out, Nyx discovered her ticket to ending the conflict between the See-Throughs and Eyebots. Cataract had accepted her, Kerato, and Rohan even though they were See-Throughs. The Eyebots recognized that something was wrong with the way the See-Throughs treated other races and were actively doing something to stop it. She had been deeply compelled by that idea and felt that in carrying out the plan, she would be protecting her parents' ideals.

However, after the war became more serious, to the point where much of the planet was evacuated, Culloqui was abandoned. It was not the place that Nyx once knew. She wanted to tear it down so that it did not remind her of her past.

Once Nyx and Chalazia were ten feet above the tallest building, Nyx leaped from Chalazia's neck. In order to gain momentum, she performed a triple backflip before firing a volley of energy blasts at the town below. When it seemed as though Nyx's deadly energy beams would destroy the town, a spark of bright blue light flashed across their path, sending them bouncing back up. She and Chalazia, flabbergasted, barely evaded them.

"What? A force field?" Nyx gasped.

Leave, or you'll regret it ... Nyx heard a female voice in her head. At first, she chose to ignore it, but the voice was very familiar. It had been years since she heard it last, so it sounded a bit more mature, but Nyx was sure she had heard it before. It was the voice of the same person who pleaded for her to stop when she ran away from home three years prior. It was the same girl she had trained at their martial arts school.

Why did you leave? Why are you kidnapping and manipulating people? I heard about what you've been doing on the news. It isn't right.

Lila? Is that you? You're still here? Nyx replied in her mind, shocked.

Just answer me! Lila fumed.

This is the only way to set things straight, Lila. See-Throughs have acted like the dominant race for thousands of years. We need to be put in our place.

You're only going to make things worse.

Don't tell me what works and what doesn't if you don't have a plan. Lila did not respond.

That's what I thought. Now get out of here. I'm tearing this place down.

No way.

I don't want to hurt you. Now move!

But you'll hurt thousands of kids that you've never met before?

Last chance!

Never! I don't even know you anymore!

You just don't get it ...

Nyx repositioned herself on top of Chalazia's neck, and the two focused their minds with the goal of harnessing their shared mental energy. First, they had to make sure they were providing an equal amount of their power, so Nyx scanned Chalazia's mind, and Chalazia analyzed Nyx's. Once that process was complete, their minds merged, as well as their separate mental abilities. Now they had the aptitude to overwhelm countless weaker adversaries by using thoughts alone.

"Nullification!" Nyx cried at last. With Chalazia's added mental power, she emitted a silver supersonic wave straight at the invisible force field. The noise being generated by the ring of pure mental energy was deafening for everyone who heard it besides Nyx and Chalazia. Lila's force field was shattered, along with her defensive strategy. The girl clutched her ears and crumpled to the ground, doing anything she could to escape the devastating raucous surrounding her.

"Okay, Chalazia! Let's do it!" Nyx encouraged. Chalazia roared with what Nyx assumed was pleasure, so she was confused when Chalazia shook her head.

"What's the matter, girl? You don't feel well?" Nyx asked, concerned. Chalazia hummed and nodded.

"Fine, then. Take it easy. I can take her on myself," Nyx whispered as she carefully unhooked herself from her partner's neck, not wanting to make matters worse by being rough. Since she had no natural element, it took excess energy to draw power from anywhere other than her own reserves, so Nyx fired another volley of energy blasts. With the force field shattered, the blasts ventured even closer to the ground in the center of town in Lila's direction. However, at the last second, her attacks vanished again.

"What? You shouldn't be able to do anything. Nullification makes it so you can't move for twenty-four hours," Nyx said.

"Y-you d-don't have t-to move ... to use your head," Lila strained to speak. Even so, she stood strong even as Nyx continued to press, repelling everything that was thrown her way. She had not changed since Nyx left home.

"Guess I taught you a little *too* well." Nyx grimaced.

"Don't flatter yourself. You abandoned me, yourself, and Culloqui!" Lila roared with strength that caught Nyx off guard. Anxious, Nyx whipped around to see if Chalazia wanted to help, her auburn hair obscuring her vision for an instant. Searing pain laced through her back; Lila had fired an energy beam at her when her guard was down. Obviously, Lila did not plan on giving her old teacher time to recover, because almost immediately, Nyx experienced the same type of pain in the back of her head. It seemed as though Lila had successfully infiltrated Nyx's mind with the purpose of tearing it apart.

I swear … if you don't leave … I'm going to rip your brain in half! Lila topped her previous threat.

You're bluffing, Nyx taunted, despite the fact her brain felt like it had been used for a punching bag. *Why don't you put your money where—*

Nyx's thoughts were sharply cut off when she suddenly felt a terrible headache. She screamed in agony, trying to shake the unbearable pain out of her head, but it only seemed to make it worse.

Why do y-you think I'm d-doing this? I'm tr-trying to fix the world! Nyx thought defiantly to Lila, but even her thoughts had become labored. Just when she thought the younger fighter would gain the upper hand, Nyx felt her pure black eyes light up with an idea.

Nyx called upon her hidden reserves of energy and released it all like a dying star, surprising her opponent. As Nyx had planned, Lila, not yet skilled enough to use multiple techniques at once, had to switch from pinning down Nyx's mind to protecting herself from Nyx's attack with a force field. After her mind was released but before Lila could activate her force field, Nyx took control of Lila's mind. This immobilized Lila enough to prevent her from using her energy. All that was left to do was to watch as Nyx's third volley of energy blasts collided with Lila's vulnerable body. *Boom!* When the smoke cleared, Nyx's former student lay on the dirt floor, unmoving.

Slowly but with purpose, Nyx hovered next to her defeated foe to gloat.

"Wake up! If you want to change the world for the better, you have to make sacrifices!" Nyx scanned Lila's energy supply, and her senses told her it had diminished completely, confirming the fact that she was truly beaten.

"You don't have to sacrifice lives, though!" Lila screamed.

Nyx kicked Lila in the ribs, sending her skidding across the ground to slam against a huge oak tree, unconscious.

"Stop acting naïve, Lila, or else this won't end," Nyx murmured, turning back toward her companion.

"Gaaaaaaiiii!" Chalazia bellowed.

"Yeah, it's time to move on. Destroying this place would be a waste of energy anyway," Nyx claimed as she mounted Chalazia's neck. Chalazia flapped her wings against the ground three times to get comfortable. Then she pushed off the ground with one mighty leap from her powerful legs.

First, it's off to plant the weapons. Then, Mind Fog.

WAVES WILL CRASH

ROHAN SAT QUIETLY ON THE shore of the Shoapin Bay as the waves crashed. Summer was winding down, so the night air was cool, but the water was still warm. As he recuperated from his battle with Xaphias, he reflected on his mistakes.

"I heard your mission was successful. Now that we know the telepathy satellites work, all that is left is for Kerato and Nyx to distribute them to each county," Cataract whispered from behind in his raspy voice.

"Yeah," Rohan said without even turning around. Cataract blended into the night with his black cloak, so Rohan could barely see him anyway. He had grown so used to Cataract popping out of nowhere. It was the same way that Cataract managed to kidnap him.

"We need to make sure you're ready. We're going to Mind Fog Island now to start training," Cataract explained emotionlessly.

"Okay," Rohan replied with an empty expression, still looking out to see.

Maybe Xaphias was right. I'm sick of being used. There has to be another way to save them without killing everyone else, Rohan thought.

Cataract infiltrated his thoughts.

"Remember. I won't hesitate to kill your family if you betray me. There is no other way. Do *not* waver."

"Yes," Rohan murmured. From the very day he was captured, Rohan knew that he was destined to crash. Defeated, Rohan placed his right hand on Cataract's broad shoulder, and the two silently disappeared.

STRAINING TO SEE

O N THE MORNING OF AUGUST 6, Maelin's team woke up early to start their training routine. Having allowed them to stay at her house during their time in Widria, Sophfronia expected results. After breakfast, their group was walking toward the training site when Teresa spoke up.

"Can't wait, guys!"

"Same here," Xaphias smirked, rubbing Aiondraes under the chin where he liked it. "I bet it's twice as hard as training with Master Dracon, but we can handle this."

Streets in Widria were mainly purple or blue colored concrete. Most houses had mystical dragon designs painted over them. Unlike most Fantasia towns, the architects of Widria put more emphasis on the width of the buildings rather than the height. The terrain was bumpy in some places, rocky in others, with large ponds littered everywhere. Sophfronia had a pond in her backyard.

"This training will strengthen your mind enough to stand up to basic mental attacks. You have to keep practicing on your own if you want to become masters," Sophfronia explained, her hazel eyes flashing with expectation.

After twenty minutes of walking, they had finally reached the training site, which was breathtaking. The building was five hundred feet tall, made of steel, and carved in the shape of an Unchartian dragon. The base of tower was like a box, but the dragon's long, jetlike body spiraled up, ending at the top with its large open snout. This made it seem like the dragon was about to breathe fire. With light of the orange sunrise glinting off the steel dragon, it almost looked like the dragon itself was on fire.

"Before you guys came here, this place was just called the Training Grounds, but Xaphias has inspired me to rename it. Now, we'll call it the Unchartian Tower!" Sophfronia beamed. Aiondraes roared with a sudden burst of enthusiasm.

"You excited, Aiondraes?" Xaphias asked his partner. Aiondraes nodded excitedly. Sometimes it amazed Maelin how childish he acted.

"Let's go," Sophfronia encouraged.

The six of them climbed each cement step toward the foot of the steel tower where there was a huge iron door. Maelin anticipated that they needed a password to enter, but Sophfronia simply said they all had to push together. Sophfronia counted up to three, and all six of them heaved. It was awkward for Aiondraes at first because he was using his arms. However, when he switched to pushing the door with his hind legs, Maelin could tell he was much more comfortable. Also, he had more muscle in his legs. With his extra effort, the door started to push back and lifted up. Sophfronia, who was familiar with her surroundings, walked in without hesitating, but the rest of them entered more cautiously.

Immediately, Maelin's ears rung from the loud echoes of dragons' voices. The steel interior of the building was lit by daylight, and the space around her took her breath away.

"Welcome to where you'll be training for the next three weeks." Sophfronia spread her arms out wide. The floor of the Unchartian Tower was soft and blue.

"The outside is made from a mix of marble and steel, which protects outside. But this is made of turf," Sophfronia explained.

"Why is it so big?" Maelin gasped, trying to soak it all in.

"We'll be training with the dragons. Unchartian dragons get pretty big. The males can grow to seventy feet long, and the females get to sixty feet. They need space." Sophfronia beamed again. "How old is Aiondraes?"

"Maybe three or four. We weren't there when he hatched," Xaphias offered.

"You don't have to guess. You can tell by the tail spikes. An Unchartian dragon gets a new spike on its tail every two years. Since he has six spikes, he's three years old in See-Through years, but he's almost five in dragon years. He looks around thirty feet. That's taller than average for his age. They age a little faster than See-Throughs but slower than humans and can live to around one hundred. You were pretty close."

"Interesting." Xaphias grinned.

"So ... how are we going to train, exactly?" Maelin got to the point, pulling out her dagger.

"Yeah! Are we going to learn some new moves?" Teresa added.

"You can use telepathy, right? Well, that's just like being able to talk; it's beginner level. I'm going to teach you how to block people from reading your mind and penetrate other people's mind even when they try to block you. I'm going to push your minds to their limits. You'll be able to see through *anything.*" Sophfronia smiled. Then, as if she were a hologram, she disappeared.

Suddenly, Maelin felt a great headache, like her thoughts were being intruded upon, so she desperately tried to shield it. However, the compelling force was so strong it was gaining the upper hand. Her dagger slipped out of her hands and fell to the ground.

"G-guys ... th-this is our first test! J-just fight it!" Xaphias roared in agony. A familiar voice in the background gave them advice.

"Physical energy comes from your soul. Mental energy comes from the mind. You have to train *both* or else you can never beat the Eyebots!" Sophfronia declared.

"Argh!" Maelin cried from the intense strain. Now Maelin was starting understand; the Eyebots were taking advantage of their inexperience. She could not let them rule her anymore.

With a burst of effort, Maelin pulled back her mind from Sophfronia's stronghold. She and Xaphias were the only ones who managed to free themselves; Gato and Teresa were still struggling.

"Nice job, Maelin! I knew you had it in you," Sophfronia praised.

"Me too," Xaphias agreed.

"Thanks." Maelin turned a little red with embarrassment. Succeeding on the first day of training was a big accomplishment. Even as the others managed to slip out of Sophfronia's grasp, Maelin steeled herself and picked her dagger off the ground. Although she managed to complete this task, she knew that what lay ahead would be an even greater challenge—facing those dragons.

THE RESCUE MISSION

THE GROUP HAD BEEN TRAVELING on Crossway 300 for three days on their way through Culloqui. It was a scenic and silent route, with only a few small Beings lurking here and there. None attacked. The Graze Mountains, tall and majestic, could still be seen east of Pearl Town. A dense forest was split in two by the dirt road. Also, the lakes and streams that were littered along the way were perfect from cooling off.

First thing the fourth morning, Pupil could hear a voice in her head.

Please … come save me, a weak female voice said.

Alarmed, Pupil replied, *Who are you?*

My name's Lila. I was defeated by an Eyerobi yesterday in Culloqui, and I've been buried under rubble ever since. I'm losing too much blood from my head, and I can't move. Please help me …

Without thinking anything through, Pupil promised that she would save the girl. *I'm on my way!*

Pupil set off on her own toward Culloqui. She lifted off into flight and stretched both arms out in front of her with clenched fists so she could have better control against the harsh winds. Low on energy from not having eaten breakfast, she was struggling to stay awake.

Silver clouds the color of her hair started blocking her view of the sky like closing gates. Knowing what was about to happen, she tried to hurry toward Culloqui, but it was unavoidable. Heavy rain droplets started to pelt her back, pushing her down inch by inch. However, with a streak of perseverance coursing through her veins, Pupil made it to Culloqui in thirty minutes.

The forest curved around the town, forming a circle. The place looked like all the other places she had been to—abandoned.

Pupil flew over the middle of the town for the largest field of vision. She thought that would be her best bet to find Lila in one swoop. After about another ten minutes of meticulous searching, near the end of town, which continued on with another Crossway, Pupil spotted the pile of rubble Lila had described. Pupil, with heart pounding, made a dive toward the heap. She sensed a very weak life energy, a force that was growing weaker by the second, near the bottom of the pile. Lila seemed to be buried under several feet of marble from a nearby building. Pupil frantically clawed the marble blocks away. At last, when Pupil had uncovered Lila's head, Lila inhaled sharply, trying to get as much air into her lungs as possible. Quickly but carefully, Pupil dug up the rest of Lila's body.

When Lila was free, Pupil helped her out of her tomb and led her to sit beside a nearby tree. As Pupil gazed up at Lila, she finally grasped the severity of the situation. There were streaks of red dripping down the teenage girl's blonde hair, which was tied in a ponytail that hung over a black headband. She was bruised and scratched in several places. Pupil's most heartbreaking realization was that the girl's legs were broken from having been crushed under all that marble.

Who would do something like this?

"I-I'll t-tell y-you about it l-later. D-do … you … h-have any … medicine or … f-food?" Lila asked desperately. Pupil realized she had forgotten her backpack at camp. Luckily, she did carry around a small reservoir of food in case of emergencies. Pupil nodded and pulled out a zeal capsule labeled Snack Tank. Watching Lila eat made Pupil hungry, but she realized that Lila probably needed the food a lot more than she did, and seeing the older girl regain strength with every bite made Pupil feel helpful for once.

Thank you so much. You saved my life, Lila thought.

No problem, Pupil replied.

"By the way," Pupil began. "My name's Pupil. I'm on a quest to find the Zeal Orb and save the other races from the Eyebots."

"Wow. I tried to p-protect this place … b-but I … couldn't. I have to destroy that creep," Lila declared.

Pupil was confused. "Who—"

"Pupil! *There* you are!" Jadeleve called. Pupil jerked her head in the direction of the sound to see Jadeleve, Iris, Zephyr, and the others hovering down toward them with worry clear on all their faces.

"Why did you run off?" Jadeleve demanded, her voice quickly changing from relief to worry.

"I heard Lila's voice in my head and came to help her."

"What if it had been an enemy trying to trick you? You just ran off to the first voice you heard?" Zenon scowled.

"Yeah." Pupil beamed. The thought that her actions could have been dangerous never crossed her mind.

"Wake us up *first* next time," Jadeleve reprimanded.

"Oh no. Are you okay?" Zenon gasped, and suddenly she was at Lila's side. "What happened?"

"It'll be e-easier if we u-use telepathy," Lila said.

From there, Lila shared her whole story in thought. She told them about how she had lived in Culloqui her whole life. Her mom had left to fight in the war and died before Lila had a chance to remember what she looked like. Her dad took up the responsibility of raising her until she was old enough for school before joining her mother to rest on Saturn. At the academy, Lila learned about mental energy from her teacher, despite not initially having excelled in that area. She explained how four years ago, her teacher, Nyx, with her dragon, had abandoned her and joined the Eyebots' mission. Lila had continued her training in her teacher's absence, dreaming of singlehandedly ending the war. She stayed while all the other kids left to try to infiltrate the Eyebots' land. Whenever Lila felt hopeless, Nyx's latest crimes inspired her to keep training.

Lila had to stop to think about what she would say next, not realizing she had caught the others off guard.

And then—

"Wait! We fought them before. That lady used to be your teacher?" Pupil said.

Lila managed a smile. *Nyx is the master and Chalazia is the dragon. Her dragon was not my teacher.*

"After she beat us, she took us to this prison on Ripple Island to rot with a bunch of other kids she and her friend were keeping hostage," Zephyr said.

"And they made us hallucinate," Iris added.

"And during our fight, she cut off our energy supply with this weird technique," Jadeleve stated, still wanting a rematch.

Yeah. That's called the Nullification Technique. It's a mental energy attack where she enters your mind and stops you from being able to draw energy. You can only block it if your mental energy control is good enough. She's heading to Mind Fog Island. We need to stop her.

"Why don't you come with us, then? We're heading to the Origin Temple to train," Zenon offered.

"Yeah. All we have to do is take Crossway 313 straight there," Kuroski said.

You would really let me come? You guys are … famous.

"Don't worry; we have a bunch of medicine. Wayward and I can alternate between carrying you, unless Wayward chickens out." Pupil giggled.

"Hey!" Wayward whined, drawing laughs from everyone.

Guys … I promise I'll make the difference, Lila declared, with spirit burning in her blue eyes.

"I'm sure you will, Lila." Jadeleve smiled and scooped Lila off the ground.

"Let's go!" Pupil pointed forward, but Zenon pulled her back with a whisper.

"I hoped you learned your lesson. We need you *alive*."

Pupil nodded, showing her understanding. She tried to walk on but immediately clutched her stomach in hunger. "Have you guys eaten breakfast yet?"

"We'd never eat without you, Piggy," Wayward sneered.

"Oh, shut up, Pipsqueak," Pupil retorted, drawing laughter once again from the group.

"*That's* why we need you," Zenon smirked.

As the eight children slowly made their way out of Culloqui, toward the start of Crossway 313, Pupil finally felt needed by the group—and in more ways than one.

THE KEY TO SUCCESS

MAELIN'S SUDDEN DETERMINATION TO IMPROVE inspired Teresa to do the same. Xaphias's fortitude had affected everybody, but none more so than the two girls. As the days passed, Teresa felt like her mind was becoming stronger. She had learned more about herself in a week than she ever had in her life.

Finally, on the morning of August 13, while the five of them were meditating, Maelin was about to erupt. Maelin, who had grown closer to Teresa in these passing days, opened one eye and peered curiously at her friend, sensing that something was off.

"What's wrong, Teresa?"

"I figured it out! We have to know more about ourselves if we want to master this," Teresa announced.

Out of nowhere, Sophfronia materialized.

"That's right, Teresa. I've been waiting for you guys to catch on. When it comes to mental energy, it's not brute force that wins. It's about willpower, and only people who know who they are have willpower. You can only infiltrate someone's mind if your will is stronger than theirs," Sophfronia explained.

"So ... if we learn more about ourselves ... we can beat the Eyebots?" Gato summarized.

"Not exactly. In order to beat them, you'll need to be able to shield your mind, analyze your enemy's mind, and attack. This training is designed to improve your willpower by testing you against all kinds of things. Remember when I had you spar against each other while dodging fire breath and trying to block your mind from being infiltrated? That's what you need to do in a real fight. But you have to keep practicing. When we finish in two weeks, you'll have to continue at the Origin Temple," Sophfronia said.

"Why can't we stay for more than three weeks?" Maelin moaned.

"I have other students. You guys are a special because you saved us last week and you're trying to stop the Eyebots from killing all the See-Throughs left on Jupiter. It would be a crime if I didn't help."

"So the Origin Temple is our best option?" Maelin gasped.

"It's your *only* option," Sophfronia assured.

"That's where the others said they were going to train. This is perfect; I haven't seen them for two years. We'll head out to Jazell Town after we're finished," Xaphias said.

"All right, so what are we waiting for?" Teresa asked with excitement. Her fire spread to Aiondraes, Gato, and Maelin. Xaphias's amber eyes glinted, proud of his choice of allies.

"You've got it," Sophfronia agreed. "Let's keep going."

A SPECIAL BIRTHDAY

"**R**ISE AND SHINE, BIRTHDAY BOY!" Pupil giggled, causing Kuroski to stir from his pleasant sleep inside the steel tent. Even when he opened his eyes, it was still dark, since the natural light from only the top window reached inside. He could barely make out the small forms of Pupil and Iris hovering over him.

"Come on. We got you a *present*," Iris wheedled.

"W-what? Y-you remembered my birthday?" Kuroski's eyes lit up, but he was slightly embarrassed.

"Of course we did! Now come on; we can't eat breakfast until you open your present!" Pupil snickered excitedly. Instead of waiting for him to get dressed and take a shower, they yanked him out of bed and led him outside, where everyone else was already gathered.

"Happy birthday!" the gang yelled. Wayward started clapping, and Lila threw confetti up in the air. Zenon and Zephyr smiled warmly at him and returned to what they'd been doing: preparing a feast. Kuroski was so surprised that he did not notice Jadeleve standing right in front of him, holding a small orange package.

"I told the twins to wake you up, but on second thought, you should take a shower. You stink." Jadeleve giggled. Since they were the same age, he could feel his body temperature skyrocket as he rushed to take Jadeleve's advice.

When Kuroski returned, Zephyr and Zenon had finished cooking breakfast. Someone had set a long wooden table for all the food. The girls had prepared eggs, bacon, and pancakes. They had also poured a glass of milk for everyone. Kuroski, not used to seeing such a feast, marveled at the sight. These were people who cared about him.

Soon, the eight warriors in Kuroski's ever-growing friend group gathered around to eat. Throughout the meal, Pupil kept singing the birthday song, which had been passed down to them by humans, with her mouth full of food. That kind of ruined his appetite. Even so, as he gazed around at his comrades, waiting for them to finish eating, he thought that there was no place on Jupiter that he would rather be.

"Thanks so much, you guys. You're awesome—" Kuroski started, sniffling after the meal was over.

"If it hadn't been for you, we wouldn't have made it this far," Jadeleve said. "So we pooled all our ideas and decided that my present was the best. For all the times you helped me out on our travels. Here."

Jadeleve shoved the orange box in front of him. Kuroski reached out for it, overcome with emotion. Once Kuroski had the box in his possession, he knew why Jadeleve was clutching it so tightly. It was as if the north wind was trapped inside and trying to escape. After he opened the package, he realized that his guess of what was inside had not been that far off. Inside were two orange wristbands made from the finest silk he had ever seen. Maybe it was his imagination, but Kuroski noticed that the material sparkled as the sunlight shone through it. It seemed to produce a gentle and refreshing breeze that also sparkled as it came in contact with the morning light. Kuroski could feel power rushing through them. It was only when he took a closer look that he realized that attached to each wristband were rhombus-shaped sapphires. Awed, Kuroski carefully turned the band over in his band, watching as the pair of sapphires deflected the sun's light. The white light created such pure brilliance that it almost left him at a loss for words.

"J-Jadeleve … h-how …"

"I made them using the mistral ribbons that Sheenika let me keep when I was recovering in Fiome. I got one ribbon for each color of the rainbow, and I know orange is your favorite color, so I used the orange ribbon. Also, Fiome Rehabilitation Center is where we met, so I thought it would be symbolic," Jadeleve explained, seeming slightly embarrassed as well.

"And your natural element is wind, so the ribbons make your wind power stronger. You can use it to heal or to fight. It'll come in handy," Zephyr, who was also a wind elementalist, said.

"Try it, Kuroski. I wanna to see it," Pupil said.

Shaking with glee, Kuroski put on his thirteenth birthday present. Instantly, he felt like he had better control over his energy than ever before. He threw a concentrated ring of air. The ring traveled to a nearby boulder and smashed it.

Iris's eyes turned a brilliant shade of yellow, signifying her joy and curiosity.

"Now we're even." Jadeleve laughed.

"Thanks so much!" Kuroski jumped with joy. He did not know what else to say, but he could not contain himself, so he tackled Jadeleve with a big hug. Jadeleve hugged him back.

After Kuroski's birthday breakfast, the group packed up camp and proceeded toward Jazell Town. Having heard so much about the Origin Temple growing up in Widria, he could not wait to take on the training regimen himself. However, he settled for tuning in to the conversation of the group. Everyone was talking about life before the war.

Pupil and Iris told tall tales about how they won the most medals in Grandma Bachi's tai chi tournaments and beat their older sister at her own game: roof leaping. Jadeleve dove into her stories with much more depth. She expressed how she basically grew up in the forest at the foot of the mountains, playing tag with Beings. Jadeleve said she had grown up knowing she was the Zeal Possessor and always felt special for it. However, she was a celebrity and an outcast at school. She also had trouble controlling her powers when other kids teased her. At six, Jadeleve was pulled out. Pupil and Iris were pulled out when they were six for being related to her. The same year that Jadeleve dropped out of school, Jadeleve met Zephyr and Zenon for the first time when her mom wanted to visit their mom. Zephyr picked a fight with her, and they fought for hours before Jadeleve was too tired to move. Jadeleve used the loss to train harder. She often came home from fighting in the dojo or the woods bloodied and bruised. Her mom had to use her healing powers all the time.

Next, Zephyr plunged into the story of her life as a pampered rich kid. Her mom had to take care of all the business aspects of life since their dad was at war. Xaphias, a prodigy, left on a quest when he was eight. To pass time, Zenon went to the library or played chess with other kids while Zephyr liked to do more physical activities. They tried not to spend too much time at home, where their servants would bug them. The clean mountain air and the occasional visit to Moonbeam Falls were the only things that could entertain them. However, at the time Xaphias was preparing to leave for his second quest, Zephyr admitted that she had made life interesting. Jadeleve had been bragging that she was the Zeal Possessor and the strongest six-year-old fighter in the world. Zephyr could not resist teaching her a lesson. That was when their rivalry was born.

Zenon had chosen to take the first shift carrying Lila, so she positioned herself so Lila could project her voice more easily. Lila was an only child, just like Kuroski was. However, Kuroski could barely remember his parents, so his grief could not compare to hers. To take her mind off things, Lila turned to training, as her father once did. She decided that she would not only avenge her parents one day but help to erase all the evil that poisoned her world. Kuroski knew the rest of her story, having been informed just a few days prior.

Kuroski shared his story with Pupil, Iris, Zephyr, and Zenon before when they were rushing through a forest, but this was mostly new news for Jadeleve, Wayward, and Lila. The young warrior never got to know his parents before they were killed. His first memories were of being bullied in the orphanage by older kids, even when he was one of the youngest kids there. The only upside was his older friend named Sophfronia. She always stuck up for him when he was being bullied and was constantly bullied herself for it. Sophfronia had never met her parents either, but she had a great attitude. During training, she never gave up. No matter what anyone threw at her, nothing seemed to get her down. Despite that all, her most remarkable trait was her ability to stay relaxed in any situation. One time, they were walking through the woods late at night and got lost. They were just about to call it quits when they were backed into a tight space by a dragon. Kuroski almost wet his pants, but amazingly, the nine-year-old Sophfronia managed to stay calm. She scratched its cheek in just the right spot. The dragon calmed down and was happy to give them a ride home. From that day on, Kuroski wanted to become strong just like her.

A year later, when Sophfronia was old enough to enter the Dragon Scale Contest, she won on her first try. For the next eight years, she talked about how she could start her own training camp with dragons as helpers. Kuroski wanted to be part of this dream and win his own dragon, but he could not win the contest. He ran away from home earlier this year.

Once Kuroski had finished, silence fell among the kids. Since Wayward was the youngest of them, no one anticipated that he wanted to share, and he did not. Storytelling was over, and now Kuroski felt like he knew his teammates better than before, but he could find nothing else to talk about. Thankfully, Jadeleve decided to break the silence.

"Guys, my perfect internal clock tells me that it's half past noon. Should we stop for lunch?" She raised her eyebrows at Pupil in a teasing manner.

"You know it! Let's start cooking … *there* … by that water!" Pupil pointed excitedly. To their right, Kuroski became aware of bright sand and crashing waves. It was a beach that he had not noticed up until now, since he was immersed in his storytelling.

Out of the corner of his eye, Kuroski noticed how Zenon was fumbling through her pocket while Lila was on her back. He turned toward her just in time to see her take out her new holographic map.

"That body of water is called Shoapin Bay. It stretches from Widria City to Jazell Town."

Zenon slowly set Lila down by a large boulder to lie against. While Zephyr and Zenon were cooking, Kuroski could sense that the moods of the other campers were going in the wrong direction. Somewhere in the midst of his thoughts, Kuroski realized that most of their stories were sad. He was about to suggest something to lift everyone's spirits when Jadeleve stood up and stole the show.

"Zephyr. We've both taken a break from training lately to heal; you must be at full strength now. And it's been a while since we fought, so ... how about a battle?" Jadeleve smirked, her violet eyes twinkling playfully.

Zephyr's bright blue eyes widened in shock but also started to glint with excitement. Much to Zenon's initial dismay, Zephyr left her post to get ready to fight. However, once everyone realized what was happening, Kuroski could feel the excitement in his heart spreading around to everybody. Zenon stopped cooking to hear her twin's response to the challenge.

"You're on!"

"Great. But I'm gonna mop the floor with you, Zephyr!" Jadeleve warned.

"We'll just see about that, golden girl!" Zephyr retorted. The spectators moved about fifty meters away from the fighters to avoid getting hurt. Zenon had to relocate Lila to a safer position because she knew how catastrophic a fight between the Zeal Possessor and her sister could become.

Ignoring the sound of the crashing waves against the shore, each fighter assumed her respective stance. Jadeleve reared back on one leg with that leg bent, which kept her backside defended, but protected her front side with both arms, so she could attack easily. On the other hand, Zenon put all her weight on her front leg and leaned forward so she could attack and defend her front easily. The contrast between their signature stances was striking. Kuroski did not think he could find a pair more polarized if he searched the whole universe.

Under unspoken consent, Zenon would be the referee of the match. She stood up tall but with much apprehension. Finally, she raised her hand and got ready to signal the start of the fight. "Ready? Go!"

Almost instantly, both girls vanished, creating tidal waves on the nearby water from their kinetic energy. Kuroski looked to the skies where, sure enough, they had taken the brawl.

"Zephyr Wind!" Zephyr bellowed. She created a powerful gust of wind from the sweep of her hand directed straight at Jadeleve. Jadeleve was able to block it with her Energy Force Field, splitting the gust in two. Even so, Zephyr seemed to be one step ahead. She used her Pinpoint Technique and found the force field's weak point. Next, she flew up to Jadeleve, who was still struggling to resist the wind, and shattered her green force field with a Power Punch. After the Power Punch beat Jadeleve's shield, it beat Jadeleve as well. Zephyr switched from using her right hand to her left hand and caught Jadeleve off guard, squaring her on the cheek. The force of the blow sent Jadeleve plummeting toward the sand. Despite the small victory, Zephyr knew it would take much more than that to defeat her rival.

"Wow," Lila gasped. "You guys … are on another level."

"Yeah. They're prodigies," Kuroski explained.

Zephyr had levitated back down to the beach to conserve energy, and Jadeleve was back on her feet but was shaking with fatigue.

"Take this!" Jadeleve roared. Zephyr, using a split second to read what her opponent was about to do, protected herself in the most creative way possible. As Jadeleve fired her Slow Motion Technique, Zephyr engulfed herself in a swirling sand tornado so she would not make eye contact with Jadeleve. When the sand fell back on the beach, Zephyr was nowhere to be found. Instead of panicking, Jadeleve concentrated on sensing Zephyr's energy, so when Zephyr attacked from behind, Jadeleve was able to sidestep and counter with a kick to Zephyr's chin.

When Jadeleve tried to continue her assault with another blow, Zephyr evaded the attack by using the After-Image. She reappeared in the same place she was when the battle began, and the two girls reset their stances. They moved so fast it left Kuroski in a daze.

"Foveno Beam!" Zephyr roared, firing her golden energy attack straight at Jadeleve. Before the blast could reach its target, Jadeleve shielded herself with her Energy Force Field, dividing the Foveno Beam into two smaller beams. Believing that she had thwarted her adversary, Jadeleve let down her guard and deactivated the force field, but trouble was brewing right behind her.

"Connection Cannon!" Zephyr screamed, faster than Jadeleve could react. The divided blasts joined together again and found their target: Jadeleve's back. After the collision, Jadeleve's purple combat shirt was smoking, and she began to fall. Unconvinced that Jadeleve would be beat so easily, Zephyr rushed her rival a second time. Jadeleve confirmed Zephyr's doubt by evading her oncoming punch with the After-Image Technique. She rematerialized above the beach, and before Zephyr could recover, she fired her own attack.

"Recatus!" Jadeleve screamed. Opposite in color to Zephyr's golden blast, the young warrior's brilliant purple attack was a sight to behold. The attack collided with Zephyr's back, evening the score. The force of the blast pushed Zephyr facedown into the sand, heaving with exhaustion. Now it was Jadeleve's turn to be cautious.

Zephyr picked her head up and turned to face her challenger with strong resolve in her blue eyes.

"No holding back now."

At that moment, the sun peaked out of clouds. It had been gloomy the whole day, but now the sunlight flooded their view.

"I decided to only use the zeal … in case of emergencies," Jadeleve murmured. Kuroski could see the obvious strain on both girls' faces after such a great battle. "So … *this* is my full strength without zeal."

"Really? So *this* is the best you've got? Zephyr Ice!" Zephyr declared. She called forth a great gust of icy wind with the stroke of her hand. Before Jadeleve realized what was happening, she had been blown forty feet away. Not giving her enemy a chance to counter, Zephyr attacked while Jadeleve was still on the ground. Zephyr punched and kicked, but her desperation was starting to work against her. Jadeleve started blocking the attacks with her elbows. As Zephyr tired, Jadeleve gained the advantage. Jadeleve knocked Zephyr off balance with a low kick, allowing her to stand up again.

Even so, Zephyr did not let up. Before Jadeleve could gain any ground, Zephyr resorted to hand-to-hand combat. She threw a right, which Jadeleve sidestepped, and then a left, which Jadeleve blocked. Zephyr kept pressing, and Kuroski realized how much he admired her stamina. When the persistent fighter finally did break through Jadeleve's seemingly flawless defense, she elbowed her in the nose. Jadeleve, not expecting such an old trick, was stunned. Even so, Zephyr continued to improvise. She kicked Jadeleve repeatedly in between her legs and karate-chopped her left shoulder. Both these moves were designed to stun the receiver, and the damage was adding up. Jadeleve was in hot water.

At last, Jadeleve snapped. She knew Zephyr was getting tired, so she had to counterattack. Jadeleve quickly dodged Zephyr's next punch by ducking under it, and then, while her front was exposed, Jadeleve jump-kicked her stomach. With the wind knocked out of her, Zephyr fell flat on her back, giving Jadeleve another chance to strike back. In that moment of triumph, Jadeleve draped her birthday pendant over her neck. The white pendant lit up in brilliant blue light, just as it did when during their trek through the Redundant Dungeon. Zephyr kept her cool and quickly found a strategy. With one last burst of effort, Zephyr clouded Jadeleve's vision by blowing sand in the way. Zephyr circled around with incredible speed and then kicked Jadeleve in the back. Preparing to launch another attack, Zephyr reset her fighting stance, but Jadeleve was not having any of that. Jadeleve recovered from the attack in midair, twisted around, and slapped Zephyr across the face. Kuroski had a feeling that was the most effective move Jadeleve could have done, because it not only did damage but left Zephyr in a daze. Jadeleve was a true fighter.

Finally, free to carry out her plan, Jadeleve released the solar energy that she stored in her pendant with a blinding explosion of turquoise light. Similar to what occurred in the Redundant Dungeon, the light engulfed her body with the same turquoise light. Soon, all that Kuroski could make out of Jadeleve was unstable radiance, like the shape of her body had been carved out of a star. She had transformed her body into pure solar energy. Suddenly, with a flash of light, Jadeleve disappeared into the sky. She reappeared in the blink of an eye, tackling the earth with tremendous force. Shock waves rattled the beach and created a small sandstorm. The force of the blow was too great for Zephyr to withstand, so it sent her flying. Her wails were drowned out by Jadeleve's earthquake. Kuroski heard a loud plop—the sound of Zephyr falling into the bay. Jadeleve had won.

After the battle and the search party had fished Zephyr out of the water, the team decided to set up the camp right there on the beach. Nobody wanted to walk another step. They ate dinner around six thirty while watching the beautiful sunset. As the orange sun dipped into the horizon, it seemed to be bleeding, tainting the blue sky until it turned purple. Kuroski loved the sunset, because orange was his favorite color. When he watched, he felt like he was sharing what he loved with the whole world. It gave him such a warm feeling. It filled him with hope that maybe the lands really could be united again. It motivated him to do whatever it took to achieve that dream. And that night, right before he went to sleep, he realized that seeing that sunset sealed the deal.

That was the best birthday ever.

THE TEMPLE TEST

"Yeah. And Xaphias called yesterday. He said that the Eyebots were testing their new weapons outside of Widria. First they have to distribute them across the lands. That should take at least a month, even by hovercraft, so we have time," Zenon explained.

"Was anyone hurt?" Kuroski asked, startled.

"He said there was a scuffle, but everyone's fine now. Also, he said to train hard so we'll be prepared for anything," Zenon replied.

Following her recent loss to her rival, Zephyr trained harder than ever before they arrived at Jazell Town. She was more than ready to make the transition into training at the Origin Temple. Zenon had repeatedly warned her to not overdo it. Zephyr hated to admit it, but without her sister's warnings, she probably *would* have. It was just that Jadeleve seemed stronger than ever, and Zephyr would do whatever it took to keep up.

Finally, a week after Kuroski's birthday, the group reached the end of Crossway 313. It came to an abrupt halt, with large boulders framing the entrance to Jazell Town. Like so many other towns and cities they had visited, the forest parted both ways to make room.

"We're here!" Pupil cheered.

"Yep. Now we've just gotta find the temple," Jadeleve confirmed.

"How long are we gonna stay here?" Kuroski asked.

"About a month. The Eyebots can't teleport to places they've been before like Dad and I can. With the fastest ship today, it should take them a month to plant weapons in all five counties," Jadeleve estimated, referencing Xaphias's news from last week.

As the group drew nearer to the town, Zephyr could feel the unmistakable presence of youthful energy surrounding them. The streets were made from a mix of plain old dirt and shiny steel. There were few buildings to be seen. Zephyr also noticed that this was one of the few towns she had visited where the forest blocked the roads. Others included Gravity Falls in the Celestine County. It was as if this forest had been planted by people. From an aerial view, Jadeleve reported that the forest formed a perfect circle around an open clearing with most of the town in the center.

"Why are these trees so tall?" Pupil pondered.

"Why are you so short?" Zephyr teased.

"I read that people planted these trees hundreds of years ago to create a natural barrier to the town," Zenon explained.

"Well ... let's go," Wayward prompted, putting on a brave face. The crew followed his lead.

Their leisurely stroll was interrupted by a harsh buzzing sound. Zephyr clamped her hands over her ears and shut her eyes. It sounded like a million bees were surrounding them, trying to destroy their eardrums.

"Reebees!" Jadeleve and Zenon yelled over the current of noise. Jadeleve prepared to attack. Zephyr steeled herself, set Lila down, and prepared to fight.

"Calm down! These guys are cool! Thanks!" a young male voice assured. At his command, the Reebees flew off as abruptly as they had appeared. Shaken, Zephyr's shoulders slumped.

"What *was* that?" Pupil whispered. All eyes turned to the approaching person.

The voice belonged to a boy who looked sixteen years old, the same age as Lila. He had dirty blond hair and eyes almost as silver as Pupil and Iris's. Whoever the kid was, Zephyr felt a calming presence about him.

"They're security around here. The Reebees sound the alarm when anybody comes. If the people aren't hostile, I call them off, but if they're threats, I just let them attack." The boy smiled.

"How can you tell?" Jadeleve asked suspiciously.

"Reebees can't use mental energy, but they can sense aura. We've trained our Reebees to sense your inner aura. They give us a special signal, the buzzing, depending on your intentions," the boy put simply.

"Wow. It's awesome that you could train them to do that," Jadeleve complimented. Next, everyone introduced themselves.

"I'm Jax Jazell. And, Lila, we'll get you fixed up at the temple so you'll be ready to go. My sister can heal," the boy explained.

"Thanks so much," Lila said with a twinkle in her eyes and snapped her headband against her forehead.

"So this is the way to the Origin Temple. Who runs the place anyway?" Kuroski asked nonchalantly.

"My sister and I. Our great-grandparents founded this town and built the Origin Temple for kids to train. We're running it while our parents are fighting in the war," the boy replied.

"Wow. Really? Are you strong?" Pupil asked, suddenly excited.

"I have a few tricks. Come on; I'll show you where all the action is," Jax offered.

Jax led their troops onward and further into his territory. After walking twenty minutes through the dense forest with an apprehensive companion on her back, Zephyr finally got a view of what was in the heart of town. Kids of all ages and backgrounds were sparring, sharing stories, and learning. The Origin Temple was made of stone and stood in the center of the complex. Eight stone steps led up to a large rectangular platform made of stone tiles. On either end of the platform were identical buildings with a hexagonal prism as a base and a hexagonal pyramid as a roof. At the far edge of the platform was the main part of the Origin Temple. This colossal building had a rectangular prism shape. The building possessed no front wall but had six stone pillars instead, so the inside could be seen. Attached to each corner of the building were cylinder-shaped stone towers measuring up to two hundred feet, more than twice the height of the main structure. Built on the center of the roof were two much thinner towers. At the crest of one tower was a magenta-colored orb, and on the other was a lime-green orb. They glinted in the sunlight. It was a sight to behold.

"Whoa ... so I'm guessing *that's* the Origin Temple. But what are all these kids doing outside?" Zephyr shifted under Lila's weight.

"They're training. You know how a lot of kids are going to the Land of Eyebots, right? Well, they stop here to pick some pointers or form guilds." Jax explained. "What's your story?"

At that question, Zephyr, along with the other six, turned toward Jadeleve. Although she hated to admit it, they recognized Jadeleve as their distinct leader.

"I'm the Zeal Possessor and we're going to get the Zeal Orb. We've just been sidetracked lately by the Eyebots," Jadeleve explained.

"Oh. You're Jadeleve Dawn? Whoa."

"Who else do you know named Jadeleve?" Zephyr snickered.

"I didn't put two and two together. Anyway, we're not giving you special treatment here," Jax warned.

"We wouldn't want you too," Jadeleve retorted.

"Good. I have some something to tell you about the Zeal Orb," Jax said. Suddenly, a lump formed in Zephyr's throat.

"What?" Jadeleve demanded, alarmed. The others tensed up too.

"You'll have to pass before I tell you," Jax smirked.

A young woman who was barely taller than Jax strolled toward them to join the gathering. She had hair a little darker than Jax's, so it was more brown than dirty blond. Even so, this girl had the same eyes as Jax, so Zephyr could tell almost she was his sister.

"Hey," the girl greeted.

"Yeah. Guys, this is Retina. She's my older sister," Jax said, triggering another round of introductions. After only a few minutes of conversation, Retina seemed even more astonished than her brother.

"I can't believe you guys would come to *us* for help. We'll put you through our month program. A month with us and you'll be beasts," Retina promised.

"We'll give you the tour of the temple today. But first, Retina? Lila's legs are broken. Could you heal her?" Jax asked politely.

"Sure. Set her down by that tree, Zephyr." Retina pointed out the spot to Zephyr. Zephyr did as she was told, and the rest of the group crowded around Lila to watch Retina do her work. With a brief, dim glow of energy, Lila was healed. To Zephyr, it felt so weird to see her on her feet, but Lila looked tall, strong, and proud. Lila gave Retina a hug, showing her thanks.

"Perfect. *Now* we can give you the tour!" Jax hollered.

That's gonna get annoying, Zephyr thought.

GRAND TOUR

JAX AND RETINA LED THE group of young fighters straight into the main, rectangular building of the Origin Temple, passing the two smaller octagonal buildings without a second glance. Once they passed in between the pillars, it was like stepping into a whole new world. The inside looked like an old cathedral. Beautiful multicolored windows lined the walls. The room only used the natural light of the sun. More stone pillars supported the Origin Temple from the side as well, stretching as high as eighty feet to connect with the roof. The entire room had a length of 120 feet and a width of 100 feet. Jadeleve liked how the stone tiles from the platform continued to be used as the floor for the inside. A grand piano, an organ, a harp, guitars and an assortment of woodwind instruments were lined against the wall opposite of the entrance. On that same wall were doors that led into hallways and into other rooms. There were six curved doors that extended deeper into the Origin Temple like them, each about ten feet tall. In the center of the room stood the bases of those two towers with the orbs that they saw on the outside. Also, unsurprisingly, a door stood at each of the four corners of the room, leading to the other towers, completing the pattern.

"Why does everything come in groups of six?" Zenon asked.

"Great observation, Zenon. The number of sides on those two buildings outside, the number of stone towers, and the number of doors here are all six. It's a symbol that there are six different types of energy that we can draw from: heat, electricity, earth, water, plants, and wind. Every technique that's ever been used is made from drawing from one or a combination of those," Retina explained.

"Yeah. And everyone's different. Your natural element depends on genetic and environmental factors, just like your personality or your talents," Jax added.

"Wow! But how do we figure ours out?" Pupil asked with wide eyes.

"Don't worry, Pupil. We'll show you in a minute." Jax flashed a smile.

"Much better!" Pupil nodded vigorously.

"Good. So let's continue," Retina decided.

The older warriors led them to the far wall where all the instruments were. Jadeleve, who could not help herself, asked if she could strum a few tunes on the guitar before they went on, and Jazell seemed fine with it. After getting that out of her system, she returned her attention to the tour.

"These rooms are training chambers designed to make the most of your individual fighting talents. After we figure out what your natural elements are, you guys can choose which rooms you want to train in. While you're at a certain room, you'll have a master. If you're not compatible with an element, don't worry. We have masters that can help with close combat, your mental capacity, using weapons, map reading, strategizing, and more. There's plenty of things to do here." Jax beamed again.

"Hey … I thought you said you ran this place by yourself," Zephyr sneered.

"Come on; I'm sixteen, and she's eighteen. You really think we can run this entire place alone?" Jax chuckled.

"We do help out here a lot, but the masters are in charge. They're adults who decided to help train kids at home rather than fighting in the war. It's thanks to them that all this is possible. It's actually kind of run like a school; the fall training session starts September 1. You're right on time," Retina said.

"My school started today. I'm going to third grade, but I guess this is fine, too," Wayward said shyly.

"Aw, really? Well, I'm glad you're here. If you work hard, eat right, and get plenty of rest, you'll get stronger. It's that simple. Anyway, you guys can start training in five days when classes start. Tomorrow, we'll let you get more familiar with the place. We'll show you the ropes. Also, we'll give you all a schedule. But right now, we've got to find out what your natural elements are. Follow me back outside," Retina instructed. Nobody argued.

Their group of ten marched back outside, through the stone pillars and onto the now familiar stone platform. Next to the far corners, before the steps, stood those two octagonal buildings right where they had left them.

"These are Natural Element Compatibility Chambers, or the NECCs. You're about to find out how they reveal your natural element," Jax said. Then he walked toward the chamber on the left and opened the door.

Inside the NECC were all the six elements. They were preserved inside their own specially crafted glass containers, which provided the right environment for each of them.

"Each of these is called a repository. We have a water, vegetation, earth, heat, wind, and electricity repository," Jax explained. The first container held a gallon of water. The next one displayed a plant and some grass growing on a thick layer of soil. To the right of those two was a container that only had soil and a couple of rocks. After that, Jadeleve inspected one that did not look like it had anything inside; it was just foggy. The fifth one had a small fan inside of it that was blowing cool air, and the sixth container held two magnets that were producing an electrical current. All the main elements were accounted for.

"Let's go outside. We need go over how to create your regular aura," Retina beckoned. When everybody was outside, she began her lesson. "To show your regular aura, all you have to do is concentrate your bodily energy inside your soul and then disperse it throughout your body. You've probably never noticed before, but when you draw from your own energy, you create an aura; it's just clear. It's almost invisible. All it does is warm you up, like starting an engine. It uses up energy but lets you access more power."

After warming up for a good ten minutes, Jadeleve realized that all their auras were clear. She knew the auras were there because of the heat distortion that was being produced from their bodies. Humans, because of their poorer eyesight, would not be able to see this; that's how subtle the aura was. Wayward, unsurprisingly, was struggling with the task. He could not get his to show.

"It's okay, Wayward. If you want to work on this during class, you can. The reason I had you do this is so you would recognize the change in your auras when you started drawing from different energy sources. You saw how all of your auras were clear? Well, depending on the type of energy you draw from, your aura will change into a certain color, which you know," Retina continued.

"Yeah. Let's go back inside so you can see the difference. People who know their natural element, show the others how it's done," Jax suggested. Once inside, Jadeleve could feel the tension in the room rising; no one wanted to be the one to demonstrate and fail in front of everyone else.

Jadeleve was about to volunteer when Zenon beat her to it.

"I think my natural element is heat. Let me try," she bravely volunteered. Silence enveloped the room as Retina opened the heat repository and stepped aside. Steam seeped from the open container and slowly dissipated. Suddenly, the room felt thirty degrees warmer, which was very unpleasant in the summer. Even so, Zenon had stepped forward. She took a deep breath. Next she stretched out her hands. Jadeleve could see her straining to absorb as much of the energy from the warmth as possible. As soon as she had reached her limit, Jadeleve watched in wonder as Zenon infused the heat energy with her soul energy, just as Retina had instructed. Finally, Zenon dispensed the latent energy throughout her body. With a flash of light, Zenon had created a dazzling orange aura.

"Amazing, Zenon. You did it on your first try," Retina applauded.

"So you can create an aura by drawing from *any* type of energy?" Jadeleve asked.

"Yeah. Heat is a type of energy just like zeal. If you can use the power of zeal, then you should be able to draw individually from electrical energy and solar energy, since they are the closest to zeal energy. Give it a try," Jax encouraged. Zenon went over to stand in between the twins, who were admiring her shinning aura. However, Zenon let it fade, much to their displeasure.

Jadeleve inched closer to the electricity repository. Retina, who seemed amused and considerate of Jadeleve's cautious behavior, opened the container for her. Jadeleve, like Zenon, had never tried this before. Drawing for zeal was second nature for her since it was a part of her. However, when it came to drawing from outside sources, which was supposed to be the See-Throughs' gift, Jadeleve was as clueless as her peers.

Wait a second, Jadeleve thought to herself. *I can do this.*

Brimming with renewed enthusiasm and confidence, Jadeleve stepped forward with the same anticipation as Zenon did. She closed her eyes and focused on seizing the electric energy for her to use. At first, the electricity shocked, like it usually did, but Jadeleve did not break her concentration. She allowed the current to pass through her body so she could absorb it into her soul. Soon, the energy that was working against her was now hers to use. When Jadeleve finally experienced the familiar sensation of electrical liveliness surging through her veins, she knew she had succeeded. At that point, Jadeleve opened her eyes to see nine young faces gapping at her. Her aura was bright yellow.

"Wow, Jadel! I thought you met your match, but you did it!" Pupil gave a thumbs-up.

"Thanks for having faith," Jadeleve snickered sarcastically.

"Okay, Jadeleve. Now I want you to draw from solar energy," Retina instructed.

"Okay," Jadeleve agreed.

In less than thirty seconds, a radiant turquoise aura appeared around her.

"What's your point, Jax?" Jadeleve pried. "It's pretty, but ..."

"The reason that electric energy and solar energy are yellow and turquoise is because they split from the zeal. Zeal is the origin of all energy in the universe. It's the energy that keeps the endless cycles of new universes going. In *this* cycle, the first types of energy that zeal split into were solar and electric energy. That's why Jadeleve can already draw from them," Retina explained.

"What? If zeal is the origin of all the energy in the universe, then why isn't there more of it?" Zenon inquired.

"Zeal is everywhere, but it can only exist in one concentrated spot in the universe at a time. Right now, that's Jadeleve," Retina replied.

"No way. So there's more than meets the eye here ... isn't there?" Kuroski said with a weak smile.

"Yep. But don't worry; we all have a lot of training to do before we get into that. Let's finish up with this then." Jax smiled. He walked back into the NECC without looking back. If he had, he would have noticed how Jadeleve was frozen in place.

Something doesn't add up. If zeal can only exist in one concentrated place at a time in the universe, what about the Zeal Orb? she thought.

"Are you okay, Jadel?" Iris whispered in her older sister's ear. She hugged her softly and then scampered after Jax and the rest of their group. Jadeleve joined the others inside the NECC just in time to see Zephyr successfully draw energy from the wind repository. Her aura changed from its normal clear color to gray, as did Kuroski's. They could not draw from any other energy source, so Jadeleve was convinced. Lila was unsuccessful, however. She could not draw from any of the elements. Pupil and Iris, who Jadeleve had seen draw from other elements while they were sparring, could not concentrate long enough to draw from any of the elements either. Iris seemed especially troubled by it, leaving Jadeleve to watch with worry as her sister's beautiful silver eyes turned the color of bricks. Wayward, who had failed to make even his normal aura show, refrained from trying.

"So half of you figured it out. That's okay. Some people, about 30 percent of the See-Through population, don't have a natural element. *You* three are probably too young to know for sure." Retina motioned toward Pupil, Iris, and Wayward. "This is just to see where you're at. For now, we'll show you guys to the cafeteria and then to where you guys will be sleeping. Tomorrow, you'll choose your schedule, and in four days, you'll start training. It'll give you time to get used to life here. Is everyone ready to go?" Retina called.

Zephyr, the girl at the front of the pack, nodded. The rest of them followed Jax and Retina toward what would be a filling meal. The cafeteria was a wide, dome-shaped room that had a door that opened outside where kids were sparring. Several students had already gathered to eat and chat. Jadeleve and the others quickly ordered their meals. Anxious to see where they would be sleeping for the next month or so, they scarfed down their food in twenty minutes and joined Jax and Lila back in the shady instrument room.

"Your rooms are on the eighth floor of that tower. We'll show you." Jax pointed to the door at the far right corner. They climbed up seven flights of spiral steps. Conveniently, there was a small window every six steps, so Pupil and Iris peaked outside every so often to see how high up they were. At the end of each flight was a small hallway comprised of six rooms. The lighting was so dim it was hard for even a See-Through to see. That's when Jadeleve noticed that the whole temple used natural light.

"Do you guys not have electricity or something?" Pupil blurted.

"We save all our electricity for the training rooms. It's okay though; we get by just fine. When the sun goes down, we use good old-fashioned candles."

"How do you get by without air-conditioning?" Pupil gasped.

"*Guts.* Pure guts," Jax chuckled.

After a few more steps, Retina finally said, "Here we are. Girls, this is your room. Room 44. And, boys, you're room 47."

As Jax walked the boys to their rooms at the end of the hall, Retina pushed the dust-covered door into the girls' room. Immediately, something stood out to Jadeleve. It was not the fact that the room had only one window or that the floor was covered with dust, or even that there was no fan; there were six girls and two beds.

"Shoot. I'm so sorry. We'll have your room cleaned up before dinner tonight. You can leave your bags here if you want," Retina whispered. Jadeleve could tell that she was trying hard not to laugh.

"I think we'll pass," Jadeleve snickered.

"Okay! I want to see the training rooms!" Pupil demanded.

"Then the training rooms it is!" Jax declared, rejoining the group with Wayward and Kuroski in tow.

Each of the training rooms was a chamber. In order to reach them, the group had to go through the curved doors at the end of the music room and down the hall. The wind chamber was the first room they visited. At the end of the hall was its curved door. It was a massive, gray-colored, dome-shaped room with six wooden fans attached to the ceiling. Students could move freely on the flat ground, which was made of turf, or fake grass. At the two ends of the large turf field were goal posts. A row of wide windows draped the far top of the far wall, opening their view to the outside world.

"This place is *awesome*," Kuroski beamed.

"You said it," Zephyr agreed.

Out of the corner of her eye, Jadeleve noticed how Retina was walking back toward the entrance. She flicked on a switch near the door, and suddenly, the ceiling fans came to life. As the speed of the wooden blades increased, so did their power. In only seconds, it was like they were trapped under a tornado.

"That's powerful," Kuroski yelled over the roar of the wind.

"Yep. Since we use all the power for the training rooms, we can make them rotate even faster! But for now, let's move," Retina advised.

The earth chamber was next. Spaces in the hallway walls connected each chamber's individual hallway so they did not have to walk all the way back out and through another hallway.

"This is the earth chamber. Being able to draw from earth energy is pretty rare. It was hard to find teachers. Too bad you don't have anyone in your group who draws from it," Retina said.

The earth chamber's landscape was rocky, bumpy, and jagged, like a Xaphias mountain face flattened on the ground. This chamber was filled with boulders, bushes, and even a couple of high-up caves. It was enough to make a hiker feel at home. Jadeleve observed that the shape, size, and color of the room were all pretty much the same as in the wind chamber, including the placement of the windows. She figured that aspect of the training rooms would stay constant throughout and only the landscapes would change.

She was correct. The next room, the heat chamber, followed the same patterns as the other ones. However, it was scorching in that room! Immediately, Jadeleve could see why. Most of the land was dirt and rough sand. Dead grass and weeds covered this soil. But a thirty-foot artificial volcano was right in the center of the desolate room. Bubbles from the sizzling soup rose, popped, and reformed. Steam clouds drifted high above, fogging the windows and distributing the heat. Strangely, Jadeleve could see small sparks of electricity spark inside those smoky steam clouds. *What a dangerous training room.*

"This is one of the toughest training rooms to use ... and drawing power from heat is one of the toughest elements to draw from. Zenon, you'll need a lot of practice to improve. But don't worry; you've got us and the masters to help you out," Jax encouraged.

"'Okay," Zenon murmured. It was rare to see her out of her comfort zone, and Jadeleve could tell she was having doubts. Iris's irises turned pink, and Jadeleve knew that meant she was nervous about something. She was probably thinking, *If Zenon is nervous, how should I feel?* Jadeleve tried to comfort her little sister.

"Don't worry, Iris. Just try your best and you can't go wrong," Jadeleve promised.

The fourth room their tour brought them to was the vegetation room. It was exactly how Jadeleve imagined it would be: a floor with real grass, a small forest, and a large garden. The windows were even larger in this room than the ones in the other rooms.

"Vegetation is my favorite element to study. So few people can draw from it. When you draw from vegetation, you're basically killing the plant, draining its energy. Reverse vegetation energy allows you to grow your own plants, but you need to be able to draw from solar and aqua energy simultaneously, which is extremely difficult, even if they're your natural elements." Retina warned.

"Can you draw from vegetation in the winter?" Pupil asked.

"Good question. Yes. But the trees have even less energy. You could kill it in one go if you're not careful," Retina repeated her warning.

Moving on, the next chamber was the aqua chamber. It was a pretty serious name for something that looked like an indoor swimming pool.

"All you really need to draw from water is … water," Jax laughed.

Finally, they arrived at the electric chamber. Manmade thunderclouds flashed, creating the ear-splitting sounds of thunder. With nowhere to go, the sound waves were trapped in the room, intensifying the sound. The flooring was made up of silver-colored rubber. At either end of this rubber field stood two massive copper magnets. They created such a harsh magnetic field, Jadeleve almost felt dizzy.

"All I can say is that this place will either turn you into an even better fighter … or tear you apart. It's all up to you guys," Retina whispered. Jadeleve could see the solemnity in her eyes. She was worried.

"Yeah. I've seen worse," Jadeleve said tenaciously.

"Great—then we shouldn't have a problem," Retina smirked, her eyes lighting up. "Want to check on your new rooms?"

What Retina promised earlier was true: their rooms were altered by the time they returned. Jadeleve and the other girls' room was sparkling clean. There were four beds instead of two, which was much more manageable in terms of sleeping arrangements.

"Thanks, Retina. This is a lot better," Jadeleve said.

"No problem, Jadeleve. If you're all going to take this huge challenge and train here, then the least we can do is make sure you get plenty of rest. Meet us in the music room tomorrow so we can help plan your schedules," Retina replied.

After that, their posse headed down to the cafeteria for dinner, where they ate meagerly. Everyone was thinking about how tough the training would be, and that did not help create an appetite. They went back to their rooms with sullen faces. Jadeleve, Pupil, and Iris slept on the first bed, and everyone else got a bed for themselves.

"Jadel, I'm scared about training here. I'm … not even sure what my natural element is," Iris whispered in her big sister's ear.

"Yeah. This place is kind of weird. The food is weird, the training rooms are weird, the sleeping rooms are weird, and there isn't enough light. How are we going to make it through here?" Pupil inquired.

"Iris, it's okay to be nervous. We're all going through this together. And, Pupil, it's going to take time to get used to this place and the training regiment, but we'll get used to it, and we'll keep moving. That's all we can do."

SCHOOL FOR WARRIORS

"RISE AND SHINE, EVERYONE! IT's seven thirty!" Jax called right at sunrise. He had informed the girls the night before that he was assigned to do wake-up duty in this tower every day at this time, and Iris was glad to hear it. This was one thing about her life that did not change: waking up early. She was used to it from spending years with her overactive twin and early-bird sister. Jadeleve could never stay asleep for long. She always claimed the sunrise filled her with energy; now they knew it actually did.

Jadeleve, of course, had woken up at least half an hour before the Jax alarm. She was nowhere to be found in the room and most likely had taken a shower, gotten dressed, and was exercising outside already. Iris was about to slip out of bed and follow her sister's example when she realized that everyone else was gone except for her and Pupil. Even Pupil was already wide awake.

"They all left already," Pupil whispered, "even before we woke up. They're stepping up their game, Iris. We've got to keep up." Fear started to creep into Iris's heart.

After picking up the shower and toiletry zeal capsules from the communal desk where Jadeleve must have left them, the young twins took turns grooming. All the while, Iris found herself stuck in a clash between solemn contemplation and grudging disbelief.

Jadeleve and Zenon didn't wake me up because they wanted me to get rest. They're taking it easy on me! They don't think I can handle it, but they're wrong … aren't they? In the end, Iris was left feeling more hesitant than ever.

Pupil and Iris followed the crowd of kids heading downstairs for breakfast. They walked down eight floors, and not a word passed between them. Both of them were in their own worlds. Jadeleve would have been saddened by their attitudes, but at the moment, she was absent. *She abandoned us!* Iris thought darkly, just as they entered the cafeteria. Iris, having known her sister for so many years, immediately guessed where she was sitting—at the table farthest possible from the entrance. Pupil disappeared to go get food, but Iris immediately marched over to Jadeleve, who was eating with all of their friends. With all the rage that was building inside her, Iris was sure that she would have the courage to tell Jadeleve off right there in front of everyone. There was nothing stopping her from screaming it to the world, but *something* stopped her. It was the love that shown in her sister's violet eyes that stopped her. It was the overwhelming feeling of admiration, faith, and hope that protruded from them that triggered Iris's change of heart. Jadeleve had absolute confidence that Iris could take care of herself, and once she realized that, all the rage melted away.

"Good morning, Iris. You ready to make your schedule today?" Jadeleve asked. Zenon, Zephyr, Kuroski, Lila, and Wayward all looked ecstatic to see her. Pupil walked up behind her, completing the circle. She plopped her tray of breakfast foods down on the steel table and hooked her arm around Iris's shoulder.

"I'm ready," Pupil beamed. Having a shared bond with both sisters, Iris could see the same confidence that Pupil had for her in her eyes. Finally, the last layer of doubt crumbled away.

"Me too."

By the time everyone was done eating, it was eight thirty, though Iris could hardly believe she had only been up for an hour; she had already been through so much. Confident or not, she could tell that it would be a long day.

Their group left the cafeteria and entered the grand music room where Retina had told them to meet her last night. Retina was there with Jax, and they were easy to find because they were standing right in the middle of the room.

"I'm glad you all made it on time; you'll probably need at least half the day to figure out these schedules. *That* is the schedule board," Retina said as she pointed to a large chalkboard on the east wall. "Jax will explain the whole thing to you."

"It's pretty self-explanatory," Jax said as their group of ten walked over to the schedule board. Having been encouraged by Jax's words, Iris decided to examine the board for herself.

Everyone's schedule was divided into seven periods. A period's number was signified by the letter *P*, followed by a number, except for the following events: wake-up at 7:30 a.m. and bedtime at 8:30 p.m. Period 1, or P1, was breakfast, from 7:40 to 8:20 a.m. P4 was lunch, from 12:00 to 12:40 p.m., and P7, dinner, spanned from 6:00 to 6:40 p.m. Pupil noticed that meals were every three periods and that each was forty minutes long, but Iris noticed something that was even more interesting; the rest of the periods had multiple events.

"Everyone has to go to bed, wake up, and eat at the same time, but you decide how you want to spend the rest of your time. You can choose your P2, P3, P5, and P6 activities. But in most cases, you can only choose one per period, so choose wisely," Jax explained. Iris was overwhelmed by the sheer number of options of activities that she could take for a period.

"Here's a helpful hint: each period offers a certain type of class," Retina explained. "P2 classes are more relaxing and are designed to help get your mind and body ready for the day. P3 provides how-to classes, introductory class, level 1 classes, that sort of thing. P5 has some repeated classes from P3 in case there are two classes you want to take that were in the same period. On top of that, it has extra activities. And P6 classes have all the advanced classes, and fun activities for the younger kids."

"Here the list of classes." Jax reclaimed the spotlight. "For example, these are all the classes available during P2: Music Class, Eyesight Stretching Class, Muscle Stretching Class, Sparring Session, Recess, or Meditation Class," He pointed to the class options next to the P2 row. "This sheet will give you a thorough description of each class. You'll start all your classes tomorrow, so get plenty of sleep tonight. Take your time choosing; we've got to go help other people out!"

After that, they were on their own, and Iris was afraid that the overwhelming sensation she felt before was coming back. Luckily, Jadeleve and Zenon were there to reassure her. "Here's an idea, Iris. Choose classes that will help with skills you need to develop more, and then you can cross out skills you've already mastered. Like, Flying 101; you already know how to fly, so you shouldn't take that class," Zenon explained.

"*I* need to take Flying 101, though," Lila admitted. She circled that as one of her options.

"Same here. I can fly a little but not for long, so I should practice," Wayward agreed. He copied Lila's strategy and organized his schedule. It was cool how giving a little suggestion could go such a long way.

"I need to work on hand-to-hand combat. Close Combat Training Level 2 is at the same time as Natural Element Training during P6, so I'll take level 1 during P3," Zenon declared, giving her young pupil a hint.

"Iris, since you're young, you shouldn't be taking training so seriously yet. Why don't you take recess with Pupil during P3?" Jadeleve suggested with a sweet tone.

"Okay ..." Iris responded, circling Recess on the option sheet. She also chose Emotion Training Class, which was during P5, 12:40–1:55 p.m., and Exploring Class during P6, from 2:00 to 5:55 p.m. Iris chose Exploring Class because it was a great opportunity for her to become familiar with Jazell Town outside of the Origin Temple and interact with kids her age, since it was for children age seven to ten. She convinced Pupil to join, who immediately expressed her excitement upfront, like she did with everything. Now she only had one period left to fill.

Around eleven, everyone was reading their schedule aloud and revising with pickiness. Jadeleve was first one to complete hers, and no one was surprised with the classes she chose.

"I'm taking Music Class for P2, Mental Training Level 1 for P3, Speed Training for P5, and Natural Element Training Level 2 for P6. I love music, and I think I could stand to get a little faster and stronger," Jadeleve expressed.

"That's cool. I think my aim could use some improvement, so I'm taking Eyesight Stretching Class for P2 and Target Practice for P3. Also, I need to get better at making plans, so I'm taking Strategy Scenario Class for P5, and obviously, Natural Element Training for P6," Zephyr informed.

"I'm taking Strategy Scenario Class and Natural Element Training as well. Also, I need to work on my fighting skills in case we are in a bind, so I'm taking Muscle Training for P2 and Close Combat Level 1 for P3," Zenon added.

"I need to work on fighting too, but I still want to challenge my mental powers … I think I'll take Sparring Session for P2, Close Combat Level 1 with Zenon for P3 and Mental Training Level 2 for P6. Flying 101 is during P5, so I'm set." Lila smiled, happily snapping her headband against her forehead.

"I'm taking Sparring Session and Close Combat Level 1 too. But I'm also taking Speed Training and Natural Element Training Level 2," Kuroski mumbled.

"Don't you think that's piling it on the physical stuff?" Jadeleve asked.

"Why don't you take Mental Training Level 1 for P5 instead of Speed Training? You'll get faster naturally from Close Combat. You can do both, since they offer some of the same classes for P3 and P5," Zenon lectured.

"Yeah, but Mental Training is so hard," Kuroski whined.

"Don't be lazy. Besides, if you do too many physical classes, you'll be breaking yourself down more than building yourself up," Zephyr countered.

"Fine; I'll take it, I'll take it." Kuroski sighed and then wrote himself a note on his sheet.

"I helped Wayward figure out his schedule. He's taking Recess for P2, Energy Control 101 for P3, and Flying 101 with me during P5, and Exploration Class. Exploration is basically just a class where the masters take the younger kids on field trips around town and do a bunch of different sports outside," Lila explained.

"That's perfect," Jadeleve beamed, remembering how her mother treated her when she first started training. Their mom had always believed that slow and steady won the race. "How about you guys? Are you done?"

"Well … Iris and I know that we're taking Recess and Exploration Class with Wayward. Iris is taking Emotion Training Level 1, and I'm taking Mental Training Level 1 during P5 … but we don't know what we should take during P3," Pupil explained.

"I … have something to say," Iris started nervously. Everyone knew how hard it was for her to speak up, so they all tried to look supportive. But once she said what she wanted, their expressions turned to shock. "I think we should take Natural Element Training Level 1 for P3."

"Wait, what? Neither of you knows what your natural element is because you couldn't get your aura to show," Kuroski protested.

"That's true, Iris. Are you sure about this?" Jadeleve looked concerned, as did everyone else. This was not just about what classes they would take for a month; the ones they chose could mean the difference between life and death in the future if they were ever unprepared for a battle.

"Yes … I'm sure. Natural Element Training Level 1 is a class that helps you figure out your natural element. In Natural Element Training 2, you already know your natural element for sure, and you want to focus on improving your skills with it, which is what *you're* doing," Iris responded, pointing at Jadeleve.

"Yeah, but Jax said that some people, like me, don't have a natural element," Lila replied glumly.

"But I know I have one! I've drawn energy from heat to use Zonule, electricity to use Thunder Bash, and solar power to use the Corona Barrage. If anything, I have three natural elements. I just want to see if I can use it when I fight." Iris's irises turned from their usual bright silver to dark brown, which signaled her determination.

"Yeah! Maybe it has to do with your personality that decides for natural elements," Pupil added cheerfully, "Since Iris has so many mood swings—"

"Hey," Iris complained.

"It would make sense that she has three different natural elements. I think I can draw from electricity because I can use the Flashlight Technique."

"Do you guys really think you can handle this? You've only been training seriously for five years ..." Jadeleve trailed off.

"That's why we want do this. Jadel, I'm not afraid anymore. We can do this," Iris persisted. Suddenly, her eyes changed colors again, this time from deep brown to light blue. Iris's eyes sparkled with the perfect picture of hope. Pupil remained the same as always, bubbly, cheerful, and forthright. It always surprised Jadeleve how different they were from each other when their goals were always the same.

"All right. If you're sure," Jadeleve conceded.

As soon as they had finished making their schedules, it was time for lunch. Zenon reminded the group that they had to find Retina or Jax to give them their schedules so they could enter it in the master schedule. However, since that was their last task on their to-do list, the rest of the day just flew by for Iris. Everyone wandered around the Origin Temple, just like Iris and her sisters used to around their house when there was nothing to do. It was such a relaxing environment despite the bustle of people. Iris was with Pupil and Jadeleve, who tinkered around with instruments in the music room.

Zenon had discovered a small observatory in one of the towers and rushed off to see it, dragging Zephyr along. Lila got permission from Retina to take Kuroski and Wayward sightseeing in downtown, which Iris was dying to see, but she was afraid that if she stepped out of the Origin Temple, all of her resolve would dissolve. She decided that she would save her sightseeing for Exploration Class, which Pupil had coaxed her into.

Instead, she and Pupil decided to go outside through the back cafeteria doors where a bunch of kids their age were playing capture the flag, an ancient game passed down from human ancestors. They decided to be on opposing teams. During her brief time in the school system at home in Xaphias, Iris had never been able to enjoy recess. She and Pupil had always been picked on for being related to Jadeleve, the girl who'd been kicked out of school. Now, Iris was getting a taste of what recess free from bullies was like: a paradise. Iris's team won, which was satisfying because Pupil normally beat her. She took it as a good sign for things to come.

Their posse reunited at dinner, where Iris did not have much of an appetite again, but this time it was because she was excited. Finally, they trudged up the eight flights of stairs to their rooms to call it a night. That night, she fell asleep with an air of certainty, knowing her team was there for her every step of the way.

AN ILLUSION REVEALED

THE ENDLESS FOG, THICKER THAN the mist that hovered over the Akapeachi Jungle, made travelers extremely disoriented. After the war started, people evacuated Mind Fog. It became desolate and uninhabited, the perfect place for the Eyebots to build their base.

"This training makes no sense," Rohan complained after another hard day. "Why do I have to fight these guys when you could easily beat them yourself? I planted my share of the transceivers. Now can you let me find my family and spare us?"

"You'll do what I tell you to," Cataract reprimanded.

Finally, Rohan snapped.

"No! Okay? I'm done putting up with this!"

Without flinching, Cataract remarked, "Fine. You've done your job. I'll just erase you along with everyone else."

"What? Why? You kidnapped me, and I did everything you told me to for four years. Why can't you do one thing for me?" Rohan exploded.

"You are very stupid, boy. You really do not get how this works, do you? We are not equals. You were too afraid to fight me. That's why you are still here." Cataract laughed, which sounded something like a dying crow. "Have you forgotten your own race, boy? The death of all See-Throughs includes you."

"I'm gonna kill you!" Rohan declared before he charged, his sword fully drawn. A moment before Rohan could sever Cataract's head, Cataract vanished from thin air, reappeared behind Rohan, and kneed him in the gut. With the boy's back exposed, Cataract brutally elbowed his spine. Rohan's body slammed to the ground.

"Learn your place, boy. You are a slave. You are no match for me, and I have allies that are many times stronger than you. You will fail every time," Cataract scoffed.

"You … traitor," Rohan whispered.

"That is true, but you are the fool who believed me. I would never spare your family. I could teleport to your house any time. You will serve me until I see fit. Defy me again and I will kill your family on the spot."

"You're a psychopath. You kill for no reason? What's wrong with you?" Rohan sobbed. At this comment, Cataract was dead silent for a moment.

"You are not worth killing, you trash. Get out of my sight right now or I will destroy the planet."

"You're bluffing! If you could do it, then you would have done it already!"

"I would rather not kill the Eyebots who still live here, but I will if I have to. Now leave."

Not waiting for Rohan to move, Cataract teleported him away with the touch of his hand.

Rohan appeared in the middle of the Jazell desert.

Why didn't he kill me? I wanted him to kill me, Rohan thought, sobbing into his hands.

After twenty minutes of sobbing, Rohan ran blindly into the sandstorm with no clear path.

SOAR

"CONGRATULATIONS. YOU'VE COMPLETED YOUR TRAINING," Sophfronia applauded as she and the Secondary Five stood outside of her front yard.

They had struggled through resisting their minds from being infiltrated, learning how to break free from hallucinations, and mastering their energy control for three weeks. On the morning of August 27, they were finally free to apply their knowledge to the outside world.

"Really? We're done? There's no final test?" Teresa asked hopefully.

"If you are looking for a final test, look for it after you've gone the Origin Temple. Your final test will be facing the Eyebots. Hold nothing back," Sophfronia reminded everyone.

In the past three weeks, Gato had learned how to store his energy in his staff to get more power out of his attacks. Maelin now started incorporating strategy into her fighting style to help win battles where strength could not. Teresa could aim her lasers better and learned how to fly faster with Sophfronia's speed training program. Still, although Gato hated to admit this, Xaphias discovered something about himself that no else's improvements could compare to. He had discovered his natural element.

"This has been an awesome experience, Sophfronia. Thank you so much!" Maelin said, bowing her head.

"At first I only did it to repay you guys for saving us and to pitch in to help save the race, but you guys aren't half had. Come back anytime you want to learn something new. I can lead you in the right direction. Will you visit, Aiondraes?" Sophfronia giggled, scratching Aiondraes on his sweet spot. The young dragon rumbled with delight.

"Yeah. Of course," Teresa beamed. Gato hoped they could keep their promise.

"We will. Let's head out, guys," Xaphias advised.

They were allowed one more glimpse of the pond in her backyard before they met at the entrance gate, the place they had first met. There, the only things to greet them were trees whose leaves were starting to change color. Before them, cutting through the thicket of trees, was a single dirt road. Gato suspected this was the road they were taking to the Origin Temple.

"Sophfronia! You're more than our teacher! You're our friend!" Teresa cried. She continued to weep as she wrapped the older girl in a hug.

"Yeah. We would have been lost without you … literally," Maelin chimed in, unable to hide her sadness. She joined Teresa in a group hug. Even Xaphias joined them. Gato was uncomfortable, but Aiondraes pushed him forward, rumbling with encouragement. He found that his embarrassment melted away once he felt the warmth in the huddle.

When the six of them finally drew way from each other, Gato felt like he had fulfilled something. He was better satisfied and more prepared to leave. He could tell that everyone else was too.

"Do you know the numbers of the Crossways you're taking?" Sophfronia asked.

"Yeah. We're taking 298 to get out of the forest, 300 to go through Culloqui Town, and 313 to get to Jazell Town. It'll be easy," Maelin assured.

"Guys! Aiondraes is big enough for all of us to fly on him now! How about it? Do you mind leading the way, buddy?" Teresa laughed into Aiondraes's tiny ear. The little dragon rumbled with a high pitch, meaning he was okay with it.

"I guess we're starting out going on Aiondraes's back then." Gato shivered. No one knew this, but he was kind of afraid of dragons. It just made his training at the Unchartian Tower that much tougher.

"Anyway, safe travels. And, Xaphias, make sure to master your element. It'll be so useful. Oh, and if you ever meet my friend Kuroski Weir, tell him I said hi," Sophfronia pleaded.

Xaphias was silent for a moment, reflecting upon Sophfronia's words as if he wanted to remember them forever.

"You've got it. Later, Sophfronia."

Finally, Xaphias, Gato, Teresa, and Maelin mounted Aiondraes's back. With one mighty roar, Aiondraes used the power in his legs to leap off the ground into the air. He soared up toward the sky. Once out of the forest, he started to flap his wings, using the power of the wind.

THE GRIND

*A*NOTHER DAY, ANOTHER DOLLAR. JADELEVE sprang to life and jumped out from under her covers. She, along with her seven companions, had been training at the Origin Temple for almost a week. The young warrior thought the Origin Temple was every bit the place she dreamt it would be. Music Class was awesome. She got to show off every day when she did her amazing guitar solos in front of everyone. Mental Training was somewhat challenging; they had to play board games while trying to protect their minds from being infiltrated and infiltrate other people's minds while *their* minds were fully focused, but Jadeleve knew she would get her head around that eventually. Even so, she was barely able to get used to Natural Element Training. The drills were so rigorous it took most of her energy to keep from fainting. The only reason she could keep going back was because of all the eating and resting that Retina forced her to do.

"I know you're not used to it, but you'll be surprised by how much better you feel after a meal and a good night's sleep," Retina had lectured. Pupil and Iris were also a big help. Their support provided Jadeleve with just enough encouragement to get through another session.

"It'll be really cool when you master it, Jadel!" Pupil would say when they had returned to their room after a long day. Iris would back up her sister and nod in that shy, quiet way of hers. Since she was not taking any of the same classes as them, Jadeleve saw her sisters first thing in the morning, during meals, and right before bed, so she cherished the moments they were together. Jadeleve had spent her whole life with her little sisters.

Jadeleve had to get ready. She swiped her bag off the communal desk and headed out the door toward the bathroom at the end of the hall so she could take a shower. Jadeleve used her own shower from her zeal capsule instead of using the community stalls to save room for other kids. After a long and refreshing shower, she got dressed in her new clothes from Fiome. Instead of wearing her usual all-purple outfit, she mixed it up by putting on a gold shirt, silver shorts, and purple combat boots with black wristbands. She was going all out again today.

An hour later, Jadeleve had completed her morning stretches and eaten breakfast and was on her way to P2, Music Class. Around eight twenty-five, the trombone bell sounded, signaling the start of the period. During this class, the instructor, Mr. Vibrado, gave each student sheet music to read. Jadeleve's piece was called "Jupiter," a very old, powerful song created by the first humans who found interest in the planet. The class was given twenty minutes to figure out their pieces. When the majority of students had got the music down, Mr. Vibrado allowed kids who were interested to play for the whole class. Jadeleve was the first to raise her hand and the first to get picked. She confidently deciphered the notes on her sheet and translated them into a flawless tune. Her classmates applauded.

After Music Class, Jadeleve traveled down a hall and into Master Dayson's class for Mental Training from nine to eleven fifty-five. Master Dayson was a short woman with short, dark hair and big brains. Inside this classroom, the constantly distracting atmosphere caused Jadeleve to sweat from the strain of trying to concentrate on whatever she was doing. The class always started with a short session of quiet meditation but quickly morphed into a madhouse. Later in the period, Jadeleve was trying to figure out a way to put her opponent into checkmate during a game, but Ms. Dayson's blaring music kept her from doing so. She ended up losing the game, which only strengthened her dislike for the class.

"There are many distractions in life. One of the goals of this class is to train you to ignore them!" Master Dayson screamed over the boisterous music. As usual, Jadeleve left the class with a pounding headache.

Luckily, lunch followed Mental Training, which gave Jadeleve a chance to replenish her energy before Speed Training, P5. At lunch, Jadeleve returned to her group's usual table and sat in her spot between Pupil and Iris. She asked the boys about their day first (she preferred to talk to the boys during their meals because she barely got to see them at any other time, whereas she could talk with the girls in their room). Jadeleve saw the happiness in Wayward's eyes as he proudly claimed that he loved all his classes, particularly Exploring Class. He had finally been able to make some new friends his age. Kuroski complained about his day being so exhausting, since he had to combat with sparring session, CCC (Close Combat Class), and he was not looking forward to Mental Training for P5. However, when Zenon suggested that he switch classes, he adamantly said that he was not going to give up. Lila was taking the same classes as him for P2 and P3, although unlike him, she wasn't taking another hard class like Natural Element Training on top of that. Zenon also had CCC, but at least she took Muscle Stretching Class beforehand to avoid injuring herself. Jadeleve sometimes worried that Kuroski might be pushing himself too hard, but if he said that he wasn't throwing in the towel, the best thing she could do was support him.

After lunch, Jadeleve walked outside through the Origin Temple's front entrance for her P5 class, Speed Training. It had to be Jadeleve's second least favorite class, seated right in front of Mental Training. This was ironic, since the two classes focused on enhancing opposite aspects of fighting. Even so, in Speed Training, Master Menona drilled them way too much on, well, speed! Jadeleve thought they would be doing drills to sharpen their agility, recovery rates, and efficiency of attacks, all the things that went hand and hand with raw speed. What good was raw speed in a fight? You're not racing your opponent. A fighter will waste more energy using raw speed to fight than making sure each strike is on target.

Master Menona must have read Jadeleve's mind, because today, the class went differently than she was used to. Menona usually made her students race against each other in pairs based on the initial speed of the student. In these races, Jadeleve normally lost to a sixteen-year-old girl named Veeaira, and it was far from interesting. But today, Master Menona changed everything. She set up stations that were designed to improve all the subdivisions of speed that Jadeleve had thought of and more. The first station that Jadeleve visited was set up a little deeper in the forest. Now that the climate was getting cooler and the leaves were dying, not as many Reebees were around, so the kids did not feel as rushed. In this station, Master Menona told the kids to form lines and time each other running to the top of a thirty-foot hill and back down the other side. This way, they could start to become more explosive, because they needed powerful legs to climb up the hill, and they could become more stable, because they needed to gain control over their bodies to swiftly but safely run down the other side. Jadeleve finally had a way to interact with her classmates and work as a team to get through workouts.

Of course the schedule organizers saved Jadeleve's toughest class for last: Natural Element Training. P6 was everyone's longest class, so Jadeleve had to contend with this grueling training for nearly four hours every day. It was a harsher atmosphere than anything she had ever experienced before. There were only six kids in her class; all of them were exceptional for their age. Even, so drills were just as intense for them. Their master, Master Arion, was a strict, well-built man in his fifties who fought as if he was at the peak of his powers. He taught them to draw the power of the electricity around them in many different ways. His favorite way was through sheer spirit, and his least favorite was by concentrating. Both were strenuous, vein-popping tasks that daunted Jadeleve every day. She had to resist the pull of two-hundred-pound magnets every day by creating an electric charge that repelled the force. She had to absorb the lightning bolts that Arion threw at her, harness their energy, and use them to destroy boulders the size of elephants. It was not fun. Yet Jadeleve endured.

CROSSING PATHS

MUSCLE STRETCHING CLASS WAS ZENON's first class, and as the name implied, it was also the easiest. All she did was stretch her muscles. It prepared her for the strenuous training to come, because from then on, it only got harder.

Zenon's P2 class was CCC, and so many other students outclassed her. However, her pride took the biggest hit. When she realized her weakness, naturally she strove to work twice as hard as anyone else. Even when she was knocked out before she could land a single blow or beaten before the fight began, she managed to keep going.

As resourceful as ever, Zenon used skills that she learned from her two remaining classes, Strategy Scenario Class and NE Training to advance in CCC. In Strategy Scenario, she learned to make effective strategies on her toes, in the middle of fighting off a foe. She learned to draw upon heat energy from her own body heat in the matter of seconds and turn into fire. Now, she was in the midst of working on a new attack that she called the Fire Typhoon. In using this fierce attack, Zenon morphed heat energy into an immense, swirling mass of fire and hurled it at her enemy. It was *exactly* how it sounded.

Zenon was in the same Close Combat Class as Lila and Kuroski, so every now and then, they would challenge each other to evaluate their progress. She relished their company in fighting.

Both of them had such different styles of fighting; Zenon had to use her powers and her head to subdue them. Lila tended to rely mostly on strategy, luring Zenon into traps that were difficult to avoid or escape. Kuroski was much more unpredictable. Sometimes he seemed focused on dodging Zenon's attacks to avoid damage, and other times, he attacked her head-on. Also, Kuroski could call upon the winds, which complemented Zenon's fire power. Every time, fighting one of them held promise of a new kind of test.

But as mid-September drew near, Zenon's feeble sense of security at the Origin Temple was shattered. The urgency in Jax's voice reminded her that she could never live in peace until this war between races was over. No one was safe.

"It's the Reebees' signal. We have new students. Retina and I will get them," Jax announced to everyone in the cafeteria during lunchtime. Zenon did not worry about this new information and concentrated on her training like it was a normal day.

But at Strategy Scenario Class, Zenon could hardly think. Her master kept on yelling at her, snapping her back to focus for a few seconds, but she just zoned out again. A deep sense of apprehension flooded her thoughts. It was not necessarily a bad feeling but overwhelming. Zephyr, who was in her class, immediately picked up on her mood.

"What's wrong? Is SS Class too hard for you?" she teased at first, but when Zenon did not respond, Zephyr turned serious. "What's wrong?"

"I don't know. I just don't feel right today." Zenon sighed.

"Seriously, though. Are your classes too much?"

"No … I guess I'm just homesick. For a minute, the Origin Temple felt like home. We were living normal lives, going to school, eating cafeteria food, with a room and a soft bed. Then I remembered that we're in the middle of the worst war in history."

Zephyr agreed with her. "Yeah, I'm homesick, too ... now that I think about it. I miss Mom, Xaphias ... even Dad. But that's why we're doing this. We want to get strong to protect them."

During NE Training, Zenon almost passed out. Their master pushed them to the brink, over the edge, and beyond. All Zenon could do was hold out until their month was up.

At dinner, Zenon expressed everything that was stressing her out. First came the tantrum, and then she broke down in front of everyone. She had never felt so helpless, tired, or weak in her life. Lila had called Jax and Retina to take her away to the nurse and unravel. From there, with Retina by her side while Jax went to run more errands, Zenon let it all spill out.

Zenon had no idea when she fell asleep, but the next time she opened her eyes, fresh sunlight poured into them. With a start, she recalled the events of last night. At first, she almost decided to crawl back under the covers, but then she thought better of it. It was better to face her problems than run from them, like her mom always said. After overcoming that, she yawned and stretched. Her eyes still had some crust in them, so she hadn't really digested her surroundings yet. When she did open her eyes completely, what she saw in front of her was the *last* thing she had expected to see.

Eleven pairs of eager eyes were all focused intently upon her. Three of them Zenon had never seen before, seven of them she knew very well, and one she thought she might never see in person again. A twelfth pair, belonging to a royal-blue dragon, snaked its way toward her through the small door. The door to the nurse's room was not even close to being wide enough to accommodate his enormous thirty-two-foot wingspan, but his neck was just long enough to reach her.

"Aiiiyyyyy!" the dragon shrieked. He recognized her. This was someone he had known since he was an infant. Aiondraes arched his neck and fondly started rubbing his head against Zenon's cheek. As

Zenon began to rub her hand against his cheek to return the love, she almost felt tears return to her eyes as well.

Without looking up, Zenon could feel another pair of eyes focused on her. These were ones that she recognized instantly, and they were the same amber shade as her own.

"Hey, Zeezy," Xaphias smirked.

"Hey, Xaph," Zenon stammered, letting her tears fall.

THE ORIGIN OF ZEAL

"YEAH! LET'S GET THIS SHOW on the road!" Pupil hollered as their growing group of fifteen walked through the Origin Temple's front entrance for the last time.

"I'm with you," Xaphias agreed.

"I know you're in a rush, guys, but this is important. We promised we'd tell you about the true origins of zeal once you completed your training. This is it," Retina announced. For once, Pupil knew that this was no time to joke around. Everyone else must have known, too, because the chatter quieted down.

"What do you mean?" Jadeleve asked.

"*The Legend of the Zeal Orb*, that book that your parents read to you hundred times when you were a kid, is a myth. It was written by the royal family. The Zeal Orb is not real, and zeal isn't only found on Neptune. Zeal energy was the catalyst for the Big Bang. It exists everywhere in nature. However, it's sparsely concentrated. A tiny percentage of zeal exists within all the elements, but the concentration is too small for anyone to draw from. Zeal is the most concentrated in stars, but even the sun, the closest star to us, is too far away to draw zeal from. Zeal can only exist in one highly concentrated place at a time, which is usually a star. These stars are called zealots by the science community. The zeal accumulates in the star as it ages. At the end of the star's life, it becomes overzealous and explodes as supernova. The energy disperses and is eventually used to create a new star. Then the cycle continues," Retina explained.

"Do our parents know about this?" Jadeleve demanded.

"I don't know, but they knew you were going to be the Zeal Possessor before you were born, right? After doing the ultrasound test?"

"Yeah, I guess so."

"If I were them, I would get a little curious after finding out my soon-to-be-born daughter was going to be the Zeal Possessor. I would set out confirm if the legends were true," Retina replied before she turned to Xaphias, Zenon, and Zephyr. "It's true that your ancestor, Kochin Zeal, discovered zeal. It was named after him. He found small deposits of it on Neptune and sealed it away in an orb. He built a shrine on No Man's Land to honor it, but the orb has probably broken down by now. It was thousands of years ago. That's the truth," Retina explained.

"Wait, so you're saying the Zeal Orb doesn't exist?" Zephyr inquired.

"Yes. At least not how you thought of it. Jadeleve is the current place of concentration. Like I said before, zeal is usually concentrated in massive stars. Small deposits may end up on planets after stars explode, but it's extremely rare. Stars last for millions of years, so … Jadeleve is the only living creature to possess zeal in all of recorded history."

"What? Why did no one tell us?" Jadeleve said.

"Your parents were trying to protect you. They probably think that if you can't even make it to No Man's Land, then you're not ready. A war is no joke. There are people there who've been fighting on Saturn for ten years. Billions have died. Billions. What difference do you think you guys can make if you went right now?" Retina replied.

At this, their group was silent.

"Eyebots want to blow Jupiter up from the outside and colonize Saturn," Jax continued.

"So why should we believe anything you just said?" Zephyr interrupted.

"Hey." Zenon gave Zephyr a death stare. Zephyr crossed her arms and looked away. "How do you know all this?"

"We don't know everything. All we're saying is that you should be aware that you're being lied to. Our great-grandparents were scholars who were interested in the true origin of the universe. That's why they started up this school, to help teach the next generation."

"Can you tell us everything else you know?" Zenon asked, eager to learn more.

"Sure. Let's recap first. Zeal is the energy that created the universe. The universe has a life cycle and zeal acts like the growth hormone. The universe is born, grows, expands, slows down, and then collapses in on itself. When it collapses, a new universe is born, and the cycle starts again. Zeal is the origin everything. Also, all other zealots have been stars. It's actually kind of impossible how you can contain so much energy in your body. You're basically a living star."

Silence again swept over the group.

"We'll only know for sure by going to No Man's Land ourselves. I'm sorry, guys, but we've come this far. We've got to see for ourselves," Jadeleve decided.

"We understand. I'd feel the same way if a couple people I barely knew said what I'd believed my entire life wasn't true. Who knows; our folks could have had the wrong story. They didn't know everything. We actually hope we're wrong." Jax smirked.

"Thank you. We'll keep what you said in mind," Zenon assured.

Aiondraes circled above them and then perched on top of the Origin Temple and let out a halfhearted roar. Pupil felt like he was reluctant to leave but knew he had to.

Finally, Lila broke the silence and embraced Jax with a hug. Lila, as if her brain finally caught up with her actions, quickly pulled away, snapped her headband in embarrassment, and blushed.

After getting over his initial shock, Jax had returned the hug. Luckily, Wayward beat the awkwardness by calling for a group hug. Pupil felt up to it. Somehow, the group hug rejuvenated her drive to keep going.

"Should we go now?" Pupil asked.

"Yeah ... we should go. Off to Mind Fog," Jadeleve answered.

"That's about right," Zenon confirmed as she pulled her holographic map from her backpack. "First we have to pass over Crossway 334 and a valley. Then we'll be close enough to the sea to fly east over Shoapin Bay to Mind Fog. Does that sound like a plan?"

"Yeah. Thanks for everything, guys." Jadeleve waved at Jax and Retina, igniting a conflagration of farewells.

Once everyone had gotten a turn saying goodbye, Xaphias called Aiondraes down from the top of the Origin Temple. The young dragon immediately, landing on the dying grass below. His red eyes were wide with apprehension.

"It's time to go, bud. I want to you to lead the way. Zenon, show him the map," Xaphias instructed both of them. After one quick glance at the computerized map, Aiondraes propelled himself into the air and glided toward the right. They were on their way.

Ten strides into their race to follow Aiondraes's trail, Pupil called back to their friends one last time. "Hey, Retina! Jax! Next time we visit, I'll be a master!"

"You better be, Pupil!" Jax called back.

"Good luck, you guys! And, Iris, don't hold back!" Retina shouted.

THE BIRTH OF RIVALS

I N THAT LAST FEW WEEKS, Iris's trust in her companions, old and new alike, had flourished through their adventures and the shared stories, food, and laughs. Encounters with new, undiscovered Beings were frequent because they traversed such diverse terrain. Fueled by ambition, their team of youngsters had hiked mountains, crossed rivers, and navigated through dense forests. Crossway 334 was by far the most remote region that had ventured through so far and the most abundant in terms of challenges, but they endured. The spirit of fall compelled the leaves of the forest to turn scarlet and gold, which enticed her in a familiar, thrilling way. It reminded her of the forest she was born and raised in.

Now that their group had grown from the Original Five to the Fantastic Thirteen, Iris felt like they could conquer the world. With their oldest member, Lila, at fifteen, and their youngest, Wayward, at eight, they had a solid seven-year age range. Also, a larger group meant variety of sparing partners to choose from, so it kept everyone on their toes. Nobody was left out, except Aiondraes sometimes.

On October 3, Zenon announced they were within a day's journey of Battle Valley. This reminded Iris that they were still on a mission to save the world.

One night when they were extremely close to Battle Valley, Zenon decided to set up camp beside a majestic river under the stars. The moons were shining so bright that Teresa suggested they ought to observe them. She set up a small observatory from a zeal capsule to study the sky. This meant they wouldn't be using the tents.

They could see the four main moons, Lo, Europa, Gamyede, and Callisto, right off the bat, but Teresa claimed that the constellations were much more fascinating. It seemed as if time stood still while their eyes were glued to that sky, even though their environment seemed so restless. Cool air sent chills down their spines, and the dying leaves rustled in the wind. Everything seemed right with the world. The noise of the natural world finally managed to lull Iris to sleep.

"Let's move out," Xaphias commanded with an impatient voice. Iris timidly opened her left eye. When she saw that the sun was not up, she went back under her covers.

"Aiiiaaaa!" Aiondraes roared, coming to Xaphias's aid. If he was Iris's alarm clock, she would never sleep in again. This time, Xaphias's strategy worked, and Iris was aware of the others starting to stir, though with much irritation.

"Give us a break, Xaphias!" Maelin whined with a muffled voice from under her blanket. The others chimed in immediately. Even Teresa was in a bad mood.

"I'm *serious*," Xaphias responded.

"You're *always* serious!" Pupil protested.

"I can sense something …" he murmured, as if he was drifting off into an intense bout of concentration.

Iris opened her eyes fully and was surprised to see how much the sky had brightened in such a short time. She sat up, stretched her back, and went over to where Xaphias and his loyal companion were. She was startled to see how far away they were from their camp. Xaphias sat with his legs crossed and hands folded, with Aiondraes by his side at the edge of a rock plateau. The rock formation was about twenty feet higher in elevation than where they had set up camp and was easily accessible. Iris decided to climb the cliff side instead of flying so she could get some exercise. She hauled herself over the edge and snuck up behind them.

"I know you're there, Iris," Xaphias whispered without looking up. Ever since their training at the Origin Temple, he did that frequently. Iris did not respond and quietly sat down next to him.

When she finally looked in front of her, the scene stole her breath. She was overlooking the center of an immense valley. On either side of a majestic lake, which emptied out toward the eastern side, colossal rock formations rose hundreds of feet above the earth. Carved from the rock of both formations, protruding from their center, were statues of men. They radiated power.

"Hey, Xaphias ... what is this place called? Zenon didn't say its name," Iris wondered out loud.

"That's because it doesn't have an official name, but Mom calls it the Battle Valley. Those two statues on opposite sides represent how the Eyebots and See-Throughs are constantly fighting," Xaphias explained.

"Is that what you were excited about before?"

"Kind of. I'm expecting someone, someone I have unfinished business with," Xaphias replied simply. When he opened his eyes, they gleamed against the reflection of the sun.

"Really?" Jadeleve interrupted. She was so stealthy, Iris jumped in surprise at the sight of her. "Is he strong?"

"The last time we fought, we were about even. But I know what he looks like," Xaphias snickered. "He's probably become a lot stronger by now."

"But we've gotten stronger too. Let me guess ... you want to fight him alone," Jadeleve mused.

"You got me." Xaphias shrugged.

"Then just make sure you use your new powers. We'll keep watch in case you need backup. Right, Iris?" Jadeleve said.

Iris was certain that her sister half-expected her to quietly submit, but Iris was stubborn.

"Don't you think we should be taking this a little more seriously? Why don't we outnumber him and make sure we beat him?"

"If the enemy knows that he's outnumbered, he'll retreat, forcing us to use even more energy to catch him. But if only I fight him, then the others can save energy to defeat him if I lose," Xaphias explained.

"Plus, we need to get a feel for his intentions. Heck, this guy may be a good guy. If so, he could join our team and help us fight the Eyebots on Mind Fog Island," Jadeleve suggested optimistically.

In a split second, that all changed. Xaphias's eyes went wide with fear.

"Iris! Jadeleve! Get down!" He screamed. Before Iris could react, he had pushed them off the cliff side and sent them rolling back to the campground. A split second later, the sound of an ear-splitting explosion suspended Iris's hearing. She landed awkwardly on the ground and took a second to recover. Jadeleve's voice ripped through the air, shouting Xaphias's name. The blast must have woken every else up, because they were all alert and ready for a fight.

Iris, who was propped back up by her twin's rough hand, was shocked to see that the spot she was sitting on just moments before was demolished now. Rocks crumbled. Smoke swiftly surrounded the site.

This time, Iris registered a powerful beam of light approaching her at an astonishing speed, but she was able to warn her closest teammates in time to avoid the impact. After she was a safe distance away from the rubble, Iris ran over to her mentor, Zenon, for advice on a defense strategy.

"We need to map our surroundings. Let's fly," Zenon commanded. Everyone except Zephyr, who stubbornly refused, and Jadeleve, who wanted to help Xaphias, followed her orders. As for Iris, she hastily surveyed her surroundings after climbing to a secure altitude of eighty feet. Almost immediately, she spotted their ruthless opponent.

The unrelenting culprit was a boy who looked Xaphias's age. He had green eyes, but with his dark, unkempt hair, he was the spitting image of Wayward. The colder weather must have prompted him to start wearing warmer clothes, because he was sporting black combat pants, a purple shirt, and thick, dirty white bandages around his arms. He also wore big brown and black combat boots. The boy wielded a sword that looked just as long and reliable as Xaphias's, only the hilt was purple instead of blue. There was something much more unruly about him though. It went deeper than appearance. Iris could tell by the look in his eyes that he was confused and frustrated.

In the blink of an eye, the enemy was struck out of the sky by a powerful energy blast produced from Xaphias's right hand. Crying in agony, he plunged into the lake, creating a massive splash, and started drifting toward the bottom. From afar, Iris witnessed Xaphias reassuring her older sister and following the enemy's path. Since he knew more about the enemy than the rest of them, it made the most sense that he should go to fight him. Cautiously, Xaphias hovered over the center of the valley's river, right above the spot where his opponent was submerged. Meanwhile, everyone followed Zenon, who found a good spot on the ground to take cover from the impending battle.

"Maelin, Gato, Teresa," Jadeleve whispered, suddenly next to Iris and the others behind the huge boulder that Zenon had chosen as their hiding spot, "were you with Xaphias when he fought this guy for the first time?"

After a second of confusion about who would talk, Teresa decided to speak up. "Yeah. We were with him. It was scary, because that kid beat a bunch of other kids before we got there. Xaphias managed to fight him off, but that fight really got to him."

"Honestly, I don't know what Xaphias sees in him. He wasn't that tough," Gato grumbled and crossed his arms, as he so often did.

"Jealous?" Maelin snickered, receiving an annoyed shove in response.

"Let's just wait, then," Jadeleve suggested.

"Why do you have so much faith in Xaphias's decisions?" Zephyr inquired, causing Jadeleve's cheeks to redden.

"I trust him. What good is teamwork if you don't trust your teammates?" Jadeleve replied, but she seemed uncomfortable with her response.

"Naw. You're just head over heels for him, aren't you?" Kuroski deduced.

"Wait! Jadeleve, really?" Pupil interrupted. "You have a—"

"I don't think this is the right time for that, Pupil." Zenon sighed, saving the day for Jadeleve and then turning her attention on the battle. "Look."

Xaphias's opponent surfaced from his watery grave with the speed and force of a missile and soared until he equaled Xaphias's altitude, although Xaphias remained unfazed. He and his rival drifted silently in the sky, orbiting each other, while Aiondraes surveyed the area. By shrieking, the young dragon was gathering information about his surroundings, learning how far away the rock formations were from him and how deep the water was below. His mighty wings carried him speedily through the air. All the while, Xaphias glared at his adversary, who was eight feet away from him. His sword was clutched tightly in both hands and pointed directly at his opponent's nose. He began to draw energy from the all the elements that were infused inside the Jupiter's crust. A powerful crimson aura exuded from his body. Oddly enough, his enemy was able to copy him. Iris thought back to her time at the Origin Temple, about how Retina and Jax educated their team about the auras of natural elements. Finally, she found the missing piece in the puzzle. Iris realized that both Xaphias and his rival both had earth natural elements, canceling each other out. This would fall under the most brutal type of battle. It would be a battle of wills.

"So you've learned how to use your natural element, too," the enemy said with a smirk. Xaphias did not respond. Instead he asked his own questions.

"So you came. Why?"

"I want an alliance. Cataract's gonna pay."

"So you finally woke up, huh? You couldn't just take my word for it? You had to wait until he betrayed you."

"Hey, I couldn't risk him killing my family. Now do we have an alliance or not?"

"If you want an alliance, why were you trying to kill us?" Xaphias scowled, skeptical.

"There's no way I'm gonna team up with a bunch of weaklings. I'll test you out first." The boy smirked again.

"Hmph. Don't underestimate us, Rohan," Xaphias said.

This guy used to work for Cataract? And he said his name was Rohan. Is he … He's guy in the picture! Iris thought, remembering when Mrs. Kage showed them a picture of her older son. She cautiously turned to her teammates, who were all handling this sudden news the same way. When she looked at Wayward, her heart sank. He was kneeling right next to her and held his head in his hands, sobbing.

"You have to tell us everything you know about Cataract, his team, and his plans before we trust you," Xaphias demanded.

"You'll have to beat me before I do!" Rohan bellowed.

Xaphias transitioned into his midair fighting stance and flared his crimson aura.

Rohan's green eyes turned dark as he steeled himself for battle. He drew back his elbows and clenched both fists, counteracting Xaphias's attack stance almost perfectly. Finally, it seemed as though they were both ready to have a long conversation by exchanging fists.

Moments before the impending clash, Wayward gathered enough courage to speak up.

"So Xaphias and my big brother are gonna fight?"

"Yeah, they are. But it's more of a brotherly fight. They're just testing each other," Jadeleve assured.

The moment she finished her sentence, a massive explosion rattled their ears and pushed them back twenty feet. In the background came Aiondraes's signature battle cry. The battle was on.

THE EARTHLY BRAWL

A POWERFUL THUNDERSTORM BOOMED IN THE background at the dawn of their battle. Rohan and Xaphias charged at each other and attacked with bone-shattering force: Rohan with his left knee and Xaphias with his right elbow. Rohan absorbed the blow and then struck with his sword. Xaphias dodged by teleporting behind him, but Rohan had already turned around. The two then began a ferocious bout of clashing with their respective blades. Due to their close proximity to each other, their auras seemed to fuse, creating a single aura of deep crimson.

Rohan must have realized that it would take too much energy for him to continually block Xaphias's more skilled strikes, so he decided to break the stalemate. Before Xaphias could attack with an exceptional powerful blow, Rohan dodged and landed on Xaphias's sword, trying to balance like he was on a surfboard. Xaphias, who had been clutching his sword with both hands, was shocked to realize that he could not use either of his arms for a moment because he was carrying Rohan's weight. Leaving no time for his opponent to recover, Rohan slammed his right leg into Xaphias's cheek and sent him flying. In order to recoup and slow his movement, Xaphias preformed a double backflip. He regained his original stance and stared Rohan down while he analyzed what had just occurred in his head.

He seems calmer ... using tactics and strength. And he has all of my extra abilities. He can use a sword and his natural element. How do I counter someone who mirrors all my attacks? Xaphias thought. *Well ... I'll just have to use some of my new tricks ...*

His thoughts were abruptly interrupted when Rohan changed tactics and charged at Xaphias, almost catching him off guard. Xaphias managed to evade his punch and used Rohan's momentum to his advantage. Xaphias slipped under the strike and elbowed Rohan in the stomach. Next he followed up with a roundhouse kick, which seemed to dissuade Rohan, even if only a little bit.

"All right. Enough clowning around. Sandstorm!" Rohan declared. He stretched hands up toward the sky. Xaphias could tell that his foe was calling upon the earth for more strength, because his crimson aura flared dramatically once again. This time, however, it grew massive. As Rohan had promised, sand started to circle all around him, enveloping him like a tornado. At his command, the sand took the form of a funnel. It began to rotate faster. All the while, the storm overhead grew worse, increasing Xaphias's sense of impending doom. He had to act fast, before it was too late.

"Take this!" Rohan hollered. Time was up, and he thrust the condensed sandstorm at Xaphias.

"Reflection!" Xaphias replied, creating, a sandstorm of equal magnitude that collided with Rohan's storm. The rapids clashed and canceled each other out, resulting in a powerful of energy from the collision point. Gusts of powerful wind forced them in opposite directions. Eventually, they each collided with the rock formations on opposite sides of the lake.

"Not bad," Xaphias gasped while buried under a pile of rocks. By revving up his power with a quick burst of energy, Xaphias created the force to destroy the rocks that had entombed him. However, there was no time for respite. Rohan had recovered and was about to launch another attack.

"Earthquake!" Rohan shouted. He flew to Xaphias's rocky island and then descended swiftly and pounded the earth with both fists.

A powerful shockwave tore its way from Rohan's bloody fists toward Xaphias at a breakneck pace, leaving Xaphias only a second to react. He had been cornered by behind a boulder on higher ground. A cascade of rocks rained down on him faster than he could dodge them. The rocks battered the young warrior like cannonballs and pinned him to the ground, crushing his torso.

Without warning, Rohan commenced another attack. It was a technique that Xaphias had heard of at the Origin Temple but had never witnessed.

"Elemental Barrage!" Crimson aura surrounded Rohan's body. Pure energy from the elements buried deep beneath the earth rose to the surface and added to his growing power. Finally, crimson energy blasts in the form of missiles separated from the aura aimed directly at Xaphias. With their long red tails, the blasts resembled comets, but Xaphias did not have time to admire them.

In his position, Xaphias could not dodge, so he decided to do something crazy. He used the Eyebots' strongest technique to defend himself and absorbed the energy from Rohan's blasts. Immediately, his energy supply was replenished. Thinking quickly, Xaphias decided to use the extra energy to launch a deadly counterattack.

Xaphias leaped into the air and propelled himself forward by pushing off the side of the cliff with his feet in order to get a better attack range.

"Reflection!" Xaphias shouted and was able to perfectly mirror Rohan's previous attack, the Elemental Barrage, with his own technique. The same red aura appeared around Xaphias as he began to focus the energy that was required for such a concentrated attack. Lastly, he released the earth energy through a series of six comet-shaped blasts, leaving Rohan to squirm under the approaching onslaught. However, with sheer force, Rohan managed to break a huge mound of rock from the earth and use it as a shield against the counterattack. The earthly energy collided with the earth, causing the smoke from the explosions to become infused with dirt.

After the collision, Xaphias decided to stay floating in midair. In order to get rid of the dirt-saturated clouds that were masking Rohan from his sight, Xaphias used his Reflection Technique again to copy Rohan's sandstorm and blow the clouds away. When the clouds had disappeared, Xaphias had seconds to react. Rohan was on top of him and about to swing his sword.

Acting on instinct, Xaphias was able to block Rohan's slash with a right-handed parry. In frustration, Rohan began to focus all of his power into his arms. He wanted to gain the upper hand. Xaphias would not let that happen. He copied his adversary's actions. Gritting his teeth, Xaphias took the struggle one step further and concentrated the energy from his natural element into his sword. He combined the force from his own body and his natural element into his sword with the sole intention of winning the battle. Although the strain on his body was great, Xaphias did not care. The prospect of victory far outweighed the idea of self-preservation.

Catching Xaphias off guard, Rohan pushed off their stalemated swords with one hand to propel himself over Xaphias's head. Then he elbowed Xaphias in the middle of the head, stunning him.

"I won't miss again! Elemental Barrage!" Rohan bellowed.

"We'll see about *that!* Energy Force Field!" Xaphias replied. A large spherical shape enveloped his body and protected him from the barrage by reflecting all the blasts with incredibly fast rotation. Now it was Rohan's turn to be stunned.

"Where did you learn that?" he gasped.

"I know a lot more than you think!" Xaphias declared and then charged at Rohan with all his might. He propelled himself with earth energy and tackled Rohan. Next, he grabbed him around his waist and flew straight toward the ground with Rohan in his arms. At the last moment before colliding with the ground, he released Rohan, causing him to crash into the rocky terrain. Xaphias had trapped Rohan under a couple of boulders. Finally, he flew back up toward the sky, leaving behind a trail of crimson energy in the shape of an upside arc over the width of the rocky island.

"It's time to wrap this up!" Xaphias roared. He raised his right hand toward the sky, clutching his sword, and let it absorb his crimson aura. "Ground Shredder!"

Xaphias raced back toward the earth with such speed his clothes were starting to tear apart. It was too bad that Jadeleve wasn't there to see what he was about to do. She would have been so jealous. When he reached ground level, he combined the massive momentum he gained from his speedy descent and the energy in his sword to stab the ground with all his might. The impact caused a huge shockwave that rapidly gained mass as it tore through the earth, charging straight toward Rohan.

Even though he was trapped inside the ground, there was no way Xaphias expected Rohan to just stay there, waiting to be attacked. He was too ambitious to be defeated so easily. Rohan confirmed Xaphias's suspicions with his next move. The tenacious young warrior deflected the crushing blow by causing an earthquake and weakening the shockwaves power. Simultaneously, he weakened the rock around him, causing it crumble, freeing him.

Anticipating a counterattack, Xaphias broke a chunk of rock out of the ground and used it as a shield. The earth shield managed to block Rohan's onslaught of energy blasts, but it was destroyed in the process, leaving Xaphias vulnerable once again.

"This fight is just getting started! Elemental Barrage!" Rohan howled once again.

"Don't you have any other moves? This one won't work on me again!" Xaphias boosted and dodged the blasts with ease, stepping from one rock to another to avoid them.

But when the barrage ended, Xaphias barely had time to prepare for Rohan's next attack. He caught him by surprise.

"How's *this* for a new move? Earth slash!" Rohan had enveloped his sword with the familiar earthly energy. He used his sword to cut through the air, and in doing so released the latent earthly energy. It was shaped like a crescent moon and left ghostly wisps of crimson energy in its wake. There was no way Xaphias could dodge to the left or right, because the wave was about fifty feet long, nor could he fly up, because there was no telling if Rohan would launch a subsequent attack. Xaphias decided to take the safest route—down.

Xaphias focused all his energy into his hands and used that force to push a mound of weakened earth deeper into the ground, essentially creating a small tunnel. An instant later, Rohan's Earth Slash Technique collided with the nearby earth and caused a cascade of boulders to seal Xaphias's escape route. Xaphias activated his natural element and kept pushing through earth with his hands as quickly as he could.

Every attack strategy he had used in this battle, except for the Mirror Technique, had been developed during those training regimens in the Unchartian Tower and the Origin Temple. He referred to the method that he was using now as the Burrow Maneuver. All he did was gather earth energy into his arms and push the earth wherever he wanted. The by-products were perfectly shaped tunnels that allowed him to maneuver underground. Xaphias could even see where was going, because the light from his crimson aura illuminated a path and was even brighter than it usually was above ground because he was closer to the energy source.

Finally, Xaphias penetrated the surface, pushed the mound dirt that eagerly embraced his face aside, and breathed in fresh air. Despite his efforts to evade his opponent, Rohan was already on top of him. He must have been tracking Xaphias's movements the whole time, waiting for the perfect moment to strike. As expected, he did not give Xaphias time to react and exuberantly launched a second Earth Slash.

This time, Xaphias knew he had no time to dodge. His body was still partially inside the ground, prohibiting his leg movement. Now, he was in the same predicament as before, only he could not move. There was only one option: block. Xaphias focused the maximum amount of crimson energy into his sword and steeled it for its toughest block yet. At the moment of impact, Xaphias left like he was a rocket in the liftoff stage, moving faster than the speed of sound toward outer space, only he was going the opposite direction, descending deeper into the dark depths of the earth. Jupiter was swallowing him whole, absorbing him, and crushing him under its immense weight. There was no escaping this brutal fate. It was best to just give up right there and submit.

Suddenly, Xaphias could hear his parents' voices ringing loud and clear in his head. Somehow, he had managed to unlock a hidden memory. They were the last words his dad had said to him before he left to investigate the Eyebots ten years prior. Xaphias was only three at the time, so it was hard to distinguish if this was a memory or if he was pulling these thoughts from thin air, but a clear picture of his dad consoling him appeared in his mind. The battered warrior settled down so he could calmly analyze the traumatic recollection.

"Listen, son. I'm leaving for a while and you might not see me for a while ... if you ever see me again, that is," his dad had said.

"Where you going, Dad?" Xaphias had not been paying much attention until he heard that last part. Afterward, his ears perked up. Luckily, his father was not the type to butter things up; he explained his most important plans to a three-year-old. That day changed him forever.

"I'm going to a faraway land to find out about trouble," his dad replied.

"Why do you have to go?" Xaphias was starting to throw a fit.

"All the adults will have to take the trip sooner or later. I just happen to be going now because I don't think I can go on doing nothing when a fight is about to start. It's an adult's duty to protect their loved ones, right? You and your sisters are way too young, so your mother decided to stay behind and look after you until you're old enough to take care of yourselves. Keep each other safe, will you?"

"But you just said you want to protect us. Don't go!" Xaphias had pleaded. But no matter how much Xaphias cried, he could not change his father's mind.

"Son, you have to always remember that no matter what, you can never give up fighting for what's important to you." Then he turned away with his sword and backpack and flew away.

Six months later, around his fourth birthday, Xaphias decided that he would stop crying and do something about the war. He developed a colder personality and isolated himself by training alone every day. His ultimate goal was to get strong enough so that one day he could fight by his father's side.

As the years passed, he grew increasingly impatient with his progress. Xaphias would rather spend time with his sisters and help his mother around the house than train all day. Each time he asked himself, "Why am I doing this?" the answer took longer to remember. Finally, around his seventh birthday, he convinced himself that the only way to get stronger was to stop focusing on family and start focusing more on training. He distanced himself from everyone he loved, for the sole purpose of improving his skills. Soon, he began bringing up the subject of why his father left them, which ignited countless fights between him, his mom, and even his little sisters who had nothing to do with it. From these disputes, he finally learned that the Eyebots had a weapon that were going to use to exterminate all the other races, and his father had left to try to gather information about how to stop them.

After gaining this knowledge, Xaphias had come to terms with his father's decision and even started to respect him. He found that he felt the same way and could not just sit there while he knew what they were planning. Finally, around his eighth birthday, Xaphias snapped. He decided that he would venture out into the world alone to hone his skills so that one day he could gain enough strength to stop the Eyebots.

The day of his departure, Zephyr and Zenon had tried to change his mind, similar to how Xaphias had approached his father that day. It had a similar effect: it broke his heart, but there was no way he could change his mind.

His mom stepped up to him with a sad grin and put a hand on his left shoulder.

"Xaphias," she said, "I want you to remember something. I want you to remember that it doesn't matter how strong you are, okay? All that matters is what you do with that power. Remember what you're doing this for, okay? Don't forget." She was losing him. He was already walking away like the arrogant, reckless fool he was. "We love you!" she called. That was the last thing Xaphias remembered hearing from her.

Throughout his travels, he became lonely. He had made a few friends here and there, like Master Dracon, but made no meaningful connections with anyone. He had forgotten who and what he was fighting for.

But then when he reunited with his sisters and met Jadeleve, Pupil, and Iris, they helped him remember the reason he was on this quest. They helped him see the truth again. After he teamed up with them, it seemed as though one good thing after another started happening. He met Aiondraes, became friends with Celestine, got stronger, gained experience, and saw so many places he had never seen before.

All the while, there was still a huge piece of his old self in hiding under the surface. He still felt alone, rushing into battle with all those Imperial Knights at Celestine City and charging ahead to battle the Eyebot twins by himself. In both instances, he failed, and his friends came to the rescue. On the inside, all he kept thinking was that he needed to get stronger.

Jadeleve always pulled through. As the Zeal Possessor, she developed a desire to prove herself to everyone she met and never gave up, even when the odds were stacked against her. It was what allowed her to come this far and not lose hope. It was what let her surpass Zephyr and beat Master Dracon and the Eyebot twins. She believed in Xaphias. She believed in his judgment and his decisions, even when they were to fight alone.

I always screw up, so why does anyone respect me? Xaphias racked his brain for an answer until he found it. *I'm not afraid. I'm not afraid to go out alone and fail. That's what sets me apart.*

First, Xaphias located his opponent's whereabouts by sensing the area for a high concentration of earth energy. Luckily, Rohan was kneeling on the ground. He was probably too exhausted to waste energy levitating. This was Xaphias's chance. With all the energy he could muster, he called upon his strongest attack to help him end the battle once and for all.

"Plate Boundary Divergence!" Xaphias roared. He absorbed as much earth energy into his body as he could and used it to pry the earth apart with his bare hands. Slowly but surely, the earth around him split apart, similar to how the movement of plate boundaries caused earthquakes that created cracks in the earth. Xaphias knew that the lava would start bubbling to the surface at any minute, so he had to get out of there as fast he could. Using his legs to propel himself, Xaphias flew out of the freshly made chasm with only a second to spare.

When Xaphias reached the surface, fell to the ground beside the abyss, and looked back, a think wall of lava erupted from the earth. The lava and smoke acted as cover from Rohan while Xaphias contemplated how to deliver the final blow. Once he figured out a winning strategy, Xaphias flew to the right around the chasm and directly toward an unsuspecting opponent. Rohan was so focused on staying clear of the lava that he did not notice Xaphias's approach. Xaphias took the opportunity to elbow his neck, turn around, kick him in the most vulnerable part of his back, grab his arm, and then flip him over on it. Blood flew from Rohan's mouth once he collided with cold, hard, unforgiving ground.

Rohan was not finished yet. He recklessly tried to trip Xaphias with a fast sweep from his legs, but Xaphias evaded the futile attack with a backflip. When Xaphias landed, he taunted Rohan with a land gesture, finally making him crack. Rohan charged recklessly again, this time with his purple sword. One final time, they engaged in a brutal brawl of clashing swords. Rohan jabbed and jabbed, but Xaphias blocked and dodged, allowing his rival to waste his energy. Xaphias sidestepped Rohan's last attack, got behind him, and confiscated his sword with a quick swipe-and-grab tactic. Then he tripped Rohan with a harsh sweeping quick, causing him to fall forward, and jabbed him right in the stomach with the hilt of his own sword, knocking the wind out of him.

Finally, Xaphias proceeded to incapacitate Rohan with repeated punches from all directions. After he felt like he had done a good job, Xaphias feinted him, causing him to open himself up completely. Then he kicked Rohan in the stomach with such force that it sent him flying into the nearest boulder. Not taking any time for reprieve, Xaphias took to the skies and focused his energy for his final attack.

"I've been saving this one for the end! You haven't had the chance to develop a counter strategy for it yet! It's over!" Xaphias declared with finality. With tremendous effort, Xaphias pried six boulders out of the earth, forcing them to levitate up toward him with the power of earth. In order to end the struggle once and for all, he sent them straight toward Rohan at one hundred miles per hour. "Meteor Shower!"

"This isn't over! Not yet! Elemental Barrage!" Out of tricks and out of energy, Rohan resorted to one last counterattack and forced six blasts of earthly energy from his aura straight at each of the boulders.

A huge explosion sounded when the two concluding attacks collided. The boulders were vaporized, leaving dusty, brown smoke. Wind pushed the smokescreen toward Rohan. Not only was he exhausted and partially trapped against a cliff face, but he was blinded. He was more exhausted than he had ever been in a battle and momentarily forgot what the whole point of this was in the first place. He realized he hadn't eaten for days. All he could feel was pain.

Rohan had not realized how much time had passed before he opened his eyes again, but when he did, the smoke had cleared. He nearly had a heart attack when he saw the predicament he was in though. His arms and legs were buried inside the cliff face that he had been kicked into, and Xaphias had both his sword and Rohan's sword pointed at his neck. Rohan had lost.

"This battle is over. Tell me everything you know. Now," Xaphias demanded.

Rohan finally gave in.

"You're brutal. We'd make a good team. Fine. You win. I'll tell you everything."

WRATH

THUNDER BOOMED, AND THE DOWNPOUR continued. After Rohan explained everything, their group left the Battle Valley for Mind Fog Island. It took them two days to reach the island. They slept near the shore on the night of the fourth. The next morning, they flew in waves; the Original Five, Kuroski, and Wayward flew in the first wave. The Secondary Five, Lila, and Aiondraes flew in the second wave. The second wave would defend against surprise attacks while the first would actively look for Cataract's base.

Rohan slept in and said that he would catch up with them. He warned that Kerato and Nyx were supposed to be done distributing the telepathy satellites by the next day. That only gave them one day to find the base and disable the telepathy satellites' control source: the death transmitter. Cataract could kill everyone left in the Land of See-Throughs with one attack using it. No one waited for Rohan to catch up. There was not a second to lose.

During the afternoon of the fifth, the impenetrable mist, which had Rohan described as a distinct characteristic of Cataract's base, appeared on the horizon. Once they had reached this point, Jadeleve periodically used her Mind Scan Technique to see if Kerato and Nyx had returned yet. So far, she could only sense Cataract's life energy.

"We need to get rid of this fog," Jadeleve complained as they were flying, hopefully closer to a landing spot.

"We're on it," Zephyr said. Zephyr drew from the surrounding wind energy and created the most powerful gust of wind she could to dispel the fog. Kuroski followed Zephyr's example. He pumped both arms out in front of him, using the power of his wristbands to create two condensed rings of air. With the added influence of his power, the two wind warriors tore thorough through the fog as easily as a pair scissors cutting through a piece of paper. Rapidly, Zephyr's field of view expanded.

Hundreds of limp bodies were littered along the island. None of them were bloody because all were killed by Cataract's mental attack. They were all people who had tried to stop him. These were people who would rather die fighting than wait to die.

"I don't know if you guys know exactly what you're getting yourselves into." Zephyr recalled what Rohan had told them before they left. "Cataract can regenerate by using his own energy like glue for his cells. He can use telekinesis and doesn't feel pain. And his plan? He's going to focus his strongest mental attack into the death transmitter. The telepathy satellites that Kerato and Nyx scattered all over the land pick up his signal and give him a huge range. He could take us all over at the same time. And after he takes you over, he can kill you instantly by splitting your mind from your body. It's painless, at least."

"Rohan," Zephyr had warned, "if you're lying to try and scare us …"

"Trust me," Rohan had replied, not at all offended, "I'm not the one you should be worrying about."

"Jadeleve. Use your Mind Scan Technique again. Let's see if Nyx and Kerato are here yet," Zenon commanded her old teammate.

"You've got it," she replied. Immediately, strain from intense concentration became clear on her face. All the while, they continued to dive toward the ground.

"I sense three auras on the way, coming fast!" Jadeleve reported finally, seconds away from landing. She and the others dropped their bags on the ground.

227

"There's only three? We can take 'em!" Pupil hollered.

"That means Nyx, her dragon, and Kerato are coming, Pupil. Remember? It's the girl who beat all five of us at once and the guy who took on seven of us," Zenon reminded her younger teammate.

"Oh, yeah ... but we're *a lot* stronger now."

"It's gonna take a lot more than strength and numbers to beat all three of them, Pupil. We have to find Cataract before Kerato and Nyx find us," Zephyr lectured.

"Lila and I will find them," Jadeleve declared as the second wave landed behind them. Aiondraes's roar, which sounded deeper each time he did it, ripped through the rain and gray clouds. Their team of thirteen had been reunited in style.

As soon as the second wave landed, Jadeleve told everyone the plan and pulled Lila aside with her. Just like she had promised, Jadeleve and Lila immediately got to work and put their brains together to find the enemies' location. With the combined effort of Jadeleve's Mind Scan Technique and Lila's Mental Assault Technique, they did it.

"We found them! Ten o'clock, five miles away," Lila reported.

"Let's go!" Zephyr proclaimed. Zephyr was done letting Zenon be the leader when she clearly had better leadership skills.

"I better take the lead. I'll—watch out!" Xaphias shrieked. Before Zephyr could react, his head had already been cut clean off. Rich scarlet blood showered the ground, and Xaphias's headless body fell lifelessly on top of it. Her beloved brother had been killed by the enemy in an instant.

"Xaphias!" Zephyr felt herself losing her grip on reality.

"Snap out of it, Zephyr! You were hallucinating," Xaphias explained. He kept shaking her until she could see clearly.

"It was a hallucination. I had to cancel it out," Lila further explained. "They're already here."

"You guys never quit, do you?" Nyx seethed. Then her eyes grew dark with rage and irritation. Even though she did not possess a wind natural element, with the quick sweep of her arms, all the fog within a mile radius receded from view. Now, the whole landscape revealed itself. Not only was Zephyr still stunned, but the terrain was even more treacherous than she anticipated. Thick tropical forests mixed with the jagged land and rivers cutting thorough them covered the area. To top it off, now everyone could see thousands of bodies littered everywhere. They were mainly men and women who had decided not to fight in the war on Saturn, so they were not warriors. Instead, they fought to protect their children and their homes.

Chalazia appeared overhead with Kerato on her back. Kerato effortlessly maneuvered off of the dragon's back and executed a quadruple backflip before landing lightly on the ground with his sword. He looked even more lethal than he did the last time they met. Chalazia swooped down and retrieved her real master in one swift, clean motion. The two cautiously began surveying the area from a safe distance above ground, leaving Kerato to fend for himself.

"This time, we'll finish you for good," Kerato sneered.

"It's three against thirteen. How can you win?" Gato said. He was one who did not like to be taken lightly. With his long, blond hair drenched with sweat, it stuck to his forehead, covered his left eye, and made him look dangerous.

"Just *watch!* Infinite Replication!" Kerato chanted just as he pointed his navy blue sword toward the sky. An explosion of smoke engulfed his body, momentarily masking the contents of his grand technique. However, once the smoke dissipated, it revealed yet another terrible scene. Thousands of Kerato clones had surrounded them and occupied the landscape as far as any of them could see. They all stood in the same victorious position as the original previously did, with their swords pointing up. Only now did Zephyr realize that it was a taunting tactic. Now, it was too late to attack or locate the real one.

"Prepare to die!" the Kerato Army chanted in unison. Counting their battle cry, they began to charge. Since they had surrounded their enemies, there was nowhere for Zephyr and her team to run.

Kerato was too fast for them to try to escape with flight. This was the end for them.

"We're doomed!" Maelin cried. Overwhelmed, the young warrior lost all composure and fell to the ground on her knees, sobbing.

"Get a hold of yourself, Maelin!" Zenon snapped, shocking her teammate. Afterward, a look of guilt crept over Zenon's face when she saw that her anger only made things worse, but she was too proud to apologize.

Maelin's closest friend in the group, Teresa, walked over to her distressed teammate and placed a hand on her shoulder.

"Zenon's right, Maelin. We're all scared, but we can't give up. We can't afford to lose here. We have to use everything we've learned win. Remember what Sophfronia told us on our first day of training in the Unchartian Tower?" Teresa paused, wanting Maelin to actually respond to her words.

Maelin took a moment to wipe her eyes and sniffle before answering. "What? I-I don't remember specifically ..."

"She told us that we'd learn to see through anything." Teresa smiled. Her plain words summoned a wave of silence within their group. The world around them seemed to slow down, as if the approaching thousand-man army with killing intent did not matter anymore.

"Yeah. We can't let these guys walk over us," Zephyr added.

"That's what we've been training to fight this whole time; these hallucinations ... them messing with our minds. We have to overcome this," Jadeleve summarized.

After dramatically shifting her goggles from their usual inactive spot on her forehead to their rightful spot in front of her eyes, she howled, "Exactly. And if we can't even recognize that this is just another one of his tricks, how can we ever beat him? X-Ray Vision!" Two spiraling beams of light, one yellow and one purple, rocketed from her goggles and enveloped the entire field in its radiant brilliance. All but one of the soldiers in Kerato's army refrained from becoming translucent after Teresa launched her technique. The army finally collided with their group, and the transparent soldiers passed right through them like gusts of wind. Zephyr spotted the real Kerato instantly, but he was about one hundred meters away.

"He's *there!* Quick! Someone use your fastest technique!" Zephyr urged. She knew her own techniques could not reach him in time, but someone else's could.

"Argh!" Pupil struggled as she gathered up as much electrical energy as she could. With her training in the Origin Temple, she had gained control over her natural element but had trouble gathering enough energy.

"Pupil, here; take some of my power," Jadeleve offered. She grabbed a hold of her little sister's hand and let Pupil draw from the electric energy in her body, leaving Jadeleve exhausted. Jadeleve kneeled down to regain her strength, compelling Iris to comfort her. However, Pupil, knowing what needed to be done, focused on the task at hand.

"Thunder Clap!" She extended her little arms as far as they could and released all the electrical energy from her body in one motion. The horizontal bolt of lightning seemed way too fast for Kerato to evade. Surely, it would hit its target. Unfortunately, Nyx would not have it.

"Nullification!" Nyx yelled. Once again, their foe had released a silver, supersonic wave straight at the lightning bolt in order to counteract it. Pupil's assault had failed. Chalazia roared triumphantly, and Nyx taunted them. "What now, you little brats?"

Not wasting a second, Zenon motioned for everyone to huddle around her to talk about their next move. Aiondraes stopped gliding overhead and settled down next to his partner, Xaphias.

"What's up?" Kuroski questioned, but he seemed more excited than scared.

"Listen, guys. They're going to stall and keep us from searching the island for the death transmitter until Cataract finishes distributing the telepathy satellites around all five counties and arrives to activate it, just like Rohan told us. If that happens, they'll be able to take over the minds of everyone living in the Land of See-Throughs and kill us in an instant. We have to figure out where they are hiding that transmitter and destroy it," Zenon whispered.

"We need to locate where the death transmitter is. Rohan said that it was around twenty-five feet tall. He also said that it was hidden between two rocky cliffs in the center of the island, beside a large stone pillar. Now that the fog is gone, with all our visual powers, we should be able to find it once we get past the enemy. Teresa, I want to scan every inch of this area with your X-Ray Vision Technique. We can't escape to look anywhere else unless we beat them, and we might not even be able to destroy it if we can find it, but it's essential that we know where the target is so we don't waste energy," Zenon carefully explained.

"Okay," Teresa agreed and quickly followed her orders.

"Lila, you weaken their minds with your Mental Assault Technique and that new illusion technique that you learned at the Origin Temple. Provide defense with your Compulsion Shield when you can," Zenon continued barking orders.

"Got it," Lila consented.

"Xaphias and Aiondraes, you two can take the skies and provide aerial support. Attack from above. If something goes wrong, Xaphias can drop and use the terrain to take advantage of his natural element to add to the attack force."

"No problem. Come, Aiondraes! Let's go!" Within a second after being commanded to, Xaphias and his partner were already climbing into the air.

"Everyone, Split up into groups of five to attack each person; Teresa, Lila, Pupil, Iris, and Zephyr will focus on Nyx while Jadeleve, Kuroski, Wayward, Gato, and Maelin focus on Kerato. I'll give backup to anyone who needs it or offer extra strategic advice! And, Teresa, make sure you report back to me when you find the target. That is all! You are dismissed!" Zenon concluded, and everyone readily followed her command. Everyone except her twin sister.

"You must have gotten a lot more out of Strategy Scenario Class than I did, didn't you?" Zephyr said jokingly.

"We have to use every resource we can get to win. We won't have a chance if we don't," Zenon responded with a monotone voice.

"Is that why you made Teresa fight while searching for the death transmitter instead of staying behind with you?" Zephyr asked testily.

"Yes. We have to use all the cards in the deck."

"I know that. And there's no way we're going to lose," Zephyr declared, finally accepting her sister's wishes and joining her comrades on the battlefield.

ATONEMENT

"GUYS! NO HOLDING BACK!" ZENON encouraged from the rear.
That's a load off my shoulders, Lila thought. This was the
perfect time to test out the extent of her powers and exact revenge
against her master's betrayal.

Lila thought back to her days at Culloqui Martial Arts Academy.
At ten, she had entered four years later than the average child because
she had suffered from mental retardation since birth. Her parents,
before they left to fight in the war, spent the four years she was
supposed to have spent at the school preparing to live on her own.
By the time she was ten, she was still below average intellectually,
but this only made her want to work harder to improve. Instead of
focusing on improving her combat abilities, she worked on increasing
her mental capabilities at the academy, under Nyx's tutelage. Her
master's abandonment had been a big blow, but after hearing of her
many exploits with the Eyebots, Lila had slowly come to terms with
the fact that Nyx was a traitor and it was okay to be angry. Lila swore
that today would be the day Nyx finally atoned for her crimes.

"Everyone, I have got a strategy too. I didn't take Strategy
Scenario Class for nothing. We'll attack in waves; that way, Nyx
won't have a chance to recover in between, and we have time to move
freely on our own," Zephyr explained.

"Okay. I'll attack first then," Lila said. She stepped forward and was rearing to go, snapping her black headband furiously against her forehead.

"A wave means that a couple of fighters go to attack at once, not just one," Pupil intervened, making a valid point. "Iris and I want to fight first with you!"

Lila wrestled with her emotions before responding, but she finally realized that they would have a better chance if they did what Pupil suggested. She gave the younger fighter a curt nod, signifying the official start of what would be a brutal brawl.

"It seems like a good approach to me. Do your best, and I'll keep searching for that death transmitter," Teresa declared and activated her x-ray vision goggles once again.

"And I've got everyone's back, of course, until Teresa finds that thing," Zephyr announced quietly.

"And what makes you think you can defeat us?" Nyx sneered. Somehow, she had sneaked up on them while they were talking and was only twenty meters away.

"Take this!" Lila cried as she fired a volley of yellow energy blasts straight at Nyx and Chalazia. However, maneuvering as if they were one, the two partners evaded her attack effortlessly.

"Is that all you've got! I thought if you had learned to fly that you had become a little smarter!" Nyx taunted.

"Then you were right! Mental Assault!" Lila linked her mind to Nyx's and focused all her mental energy into it.

"Are you serious? I taught you that move! Compulsion Sheild!" Nyx scoffed, ceasing the flow of Lila's energy into her mind with little effort. "Get serious! This isn't—ugh!"

Pupil and Iris had fired a round of energy blasts from behind, making direct contact with both Nyx and her partner. It had almost no effect on them, but it still filled Lila with pride. Her teamwork with her allies was improving.

"You're the one who needs to get serious. I won't give you another chance to escape," Lila sneered, quieting her old master's boasts. A look of silent hatred washed over Nyx's face, turning her expression stone cold. Even her partner's eyes seemed to become glassy and unfocused as if they were both possessed by an outside force. Once more, Lila reflected upon her past. She definitely would not be where she was today without her old master, which was exactly why it was her duty to stop her. The young mental energy user put all those memories behind her and steeled herself to embrace the darkness that lay ahead of her. She could feel that Nyx had done the same. This was the final chapter of their relationship, so there was no holding back. Right then, Lila resolved to push the sight of her master and her as friends out of her mind. Nyx had taken too many lives during her alliance with the Eyebots. The old Nyx had died long ago.

Lila decisively snapped her headband against her forehead, which had been a gift from her parents before they left to fight in the war. Her father had said to her, "Honey, just give it a snap if you're feeling confused. It'll help you think clearly." So far, his method had worked for its intended purpose. Her teammates hardly seemed to notice it, but to her, the headband was her savior. Whenever she was feeling troubled or did not know what to do, she stretched it as far as it could go and let it strike her forehead, giving her a jolt of insight. Over the years, however, it just became a habit. Now she did it when she was happy, excited, and even embarrassed. Not only was it part of her appearance, but it shaped her personality. Anyone who knew her well knew that whenever she did that, she meant business. When Nyx grimaced in response to the action, Lila felt a twinge of satisfaction.

Lila was not surprised to see that her old teacher was trying to hold back tears. Nyx must have invaded the privacy of her old student's mind and read her thoughts. Like Lila, she too was questioning past decisions and struggling to justify the path she had chosen. It seemed that Nyx had come to a similar resolution to Lila: it was too late to reverse the past. Lila's old master wiped away the tears, and two black holes waiting to swallow everything in their path remained.

"You're right. It's time to settle this!" Nyx bellowed, giving her final verdict.

"Aiiiiooo!" Chalazia shrieked alongside her master, a cry that was a slightly higher pitch than Aiondraes's. Carrying out her master's will, she drifted closer until she loomed over Lila's team like a storm cloud, giving warning signs of a downpour, then released a bright shower of flames at them. The all-girls team took advantage of their flexibility and danced around the fire with basic evasive maneuvers. However, when Lila evaded the line of fire and turned her attention back to her opponents, she was terrified to realize that Nyx had disappeared and Chalazia was preparing for another attack.

"Everyone! Protect each other!" Zephyr warned. She was forming a force field around herself and Teresa, who was the closest to her, not having time to get to the others.

"Orraaaeeeee!" the young dragon thundered. With her wings and arms outstretched and straining, Chalazia called upon a massive typhoon by drawing energy from the surrounding ocean. Heading to Chalazia's call, the surrounding ocean enveloped Lila's team before she could blink twice. All the while, Lila stood frozen in place, awed by the awesome spectacle of a Being manipulating energy on its own as the Dawn twins hastily tried to invent a counterstrategy. *What amazing power ... What I am I doing? I have to stop her!*

Lila entered a state of introspective serenity and thought of an excellent solution. She circled around until she was in the right position and gazed directly into Chalazia's red eyes with fiery intensity.

"Delirium," Lila whispered, and it sounded as if it was coming from another person. A beam of light shot straight from Lila's eyes into Chalazia's. Almost immediately, confusion overwhelmed the young dragon, and she began to break down. With her mind tormented by Lila's illusions, which depicted the dragon's worst fears, she could not concentrate enough to keep the attack together. Struggling against the hallucinations, Chalazia plunged to the ground. Her screeches rang with fear and defiance. Lila was used to being the one who was being persecuted, but persecuted others felt even worse. The approach of the water that Chalazia had called upon lost momentum and receded back into the surrounding Shoapin Bay. Lila saw that her friends were okay and breathed a sigh of relief. It was too late to notice that Nyx was still nowhere in sight.

"Lila! Behind you!" Zephyr cried. She was silenced and swatted from behind by Chalazia's tail, who had already recovered from Lila's metal onslaught.

"You have a *lot* left to learn, Lila," Nyx scoffed. Lila had let down her guard and let her enemy get behind her, which was a strategy that Nyx had always wanted her to remember.

When Lila sensed that her mind was being invaded, she constructed a wall.

"You know that doesn't work on me!" Lila seethed as she countered Nyx's Mental Assault Technique with her Compulsion Shield. Meanwhile, Pupil, Iris, and Zephyr fought Chalazia. Teresa still searched diligently for the death transmitter.

"Oh, I know. But this will! Telekinesis!" Nyx hollered, and instantly, Lila felt like her body was being ripped apart. She had lost control of all her physical movements and was levitating.

"S-so th-the Mental Assault was ju-just a dis-distraction? Bu-but wh-when di-did you learn this technique?" Lila stuttered, struggling to regain her willpower.

"Cataract taught me. You'll have the pleasure of facing his much stronger version of the technique—if, that is, you manage to defeat me. And the Mental Assault Technique wasn't just a distraction. I'm still attacking your mind," Nyx said smugly. Lila was facing away from her, but she imagined a disgusting sneer played across her foe's face.

"H-how c-can you do two men-mental at-attacks at once?" Lila demanded. Tears threatened to spill from her eyes from the strain of struggling against the great invisible force.

"Can't you sense it? Telekinesis is a physical attack. I'm controlling your bodily energy and attacking your mind simultaneously. The moment you let your mental guard down to attack my mind, I already had my attack ready. Trying a physical attack is also impossible because I have control over your body. In other words, you're powerless."

"Ugh!" The combined weight of the excruciating pain from the attack and being shocked by its consequences left Lila speechless.

"That's what you think! Foveno Beam!" Zephyr roared in outrage. Having been caught off guard, the golden beam of light collided with Nyx head-on, pushing her fifty meters to the left. With the sudden loss of the force that was keeping her afloat, Lila almost fell to the ground. However, Zephyr caught her in midair and set her down gently.

"You okay?" she asked Lila quietly once she was safely on the ground.

"I …" Lila began. Her bands began to tremble. Before she could break down, however, Zephyr snapped her out of it by snapping Lila's headband herself.

"It's not over! Get it together, Lila!" she chided.

Lila nodded, then muttered something about where the twins were. Zephyr simply nodded in their direction, and what the fifteen-year-old saw was something she would never forget. Pupil and Iris were working in perfect harmony to fight off Chalazia. While Iris created an attack, Pupil found Chalazia's blind spot and used her Thunder Clap Technique to barbecue her wings. Then the twins followed up with a simultaneous attack; Iris fired her Rings of Fire attack from the front while her twin released her bright blue sclera beam attack from behind. Chalazia evaded both attacks, whipped around, cut Pupil with her left wing, and slammed her onto the ground with her tail. The force of collision created cracks in the earth and buried the young girl under a pile of rocks. She broke free of her prison, only to be scorched by Chalazia's golden flames. Pupil landed on the ground next to her sister.

"Pupil!" Iris squealed, wanting to tend to her sister's wounds like their mother used to but lacking the skills. She was about to waste all those grueling hours of emotion training at the Origin Temple right then and cry.

"W-what's wi-with that look, Iris? You-you ... sh-should feel ha-happy. It's fi-finally time f-for you to sh-show your stuff," Pupil stammered, acting tough in front of her twin like always. Suddenly, Lila sensed great power begin to surge through Iris. From that point on, Iris would never be quite the same. Lila felt that Iris felt a similar obligation to her friends to not give up or let their sacrifices be in vain. If that was the source of her power, then it was a power to be reckoned with.

"Do-don't worry. I'll b-be f-fine on-once y-you s-start!" Pupil promised, before fainting. Teresa decided to take Pupil to a safe place on higher ground before continuing to look for the death transmitter. Once Iris knew that her twin was at least out of harm's way for a little while, she acknowledged her promise and began marching toward her opponent, Chalazia. Teresa continued searching from where she was.

In the face of Chalazia's vehement howls, Iris stood expressionless. She seemed to be focusing her mind for a decisive assault. Deciding to take her sister's advice, she sought to utilize her emotion and natural element training. Iris closed her eyelids for a moment and entered a state of deeper meditation. The next time she opened them, they shined with all seven colors in the rainbow, like an Immortal Seer. Once the spectacle faded, Iris was left with a red aura and brown eyes.

Using what she had learned from Emotion Training Class and Natural Element Training Level 1, Iris, with a flash of brilliance, realized that she could draw from any element by changing her eye color. It was a groundbreaking discovery that made the news.

She figured out the combinations: brown eyes and earth energy, yellow eyes and electricity, indigo eyes and water, gray eyes and wind, red eyes and heat, and green with vegetation. If she was lucky, she could draw from solar energy with blue eyes. So far, she could only unlock those seven elements. Since each eye color corresponded with one element, Jadeleve decided to call Iris's attack the Element Emotion Correspondence Technique.

Both her teachers were astonished by the breakthrough. If Iris was not a special case and this was a technique that could be taught to other people, it would rewrite everything that was known about the science of energy manipulation. Jax, Retina, and her teachers clearly stated that the potential for Iris's technique was unknown. Iris did not know how many eye colors she had or how she gained the ability to change it at will. So far, she had noticed eleven different colors, about twice as many as there were natural elements. However, even without the attack used at its full potential, whatever that potential might be, it was definitely something to be reckoned with.

Without warning, a cluster of boulders separated from their earthly tether, shot up from the ground, and pelted Chalazia like a meteor shower colliding with the moon. Chalazia wailed in agony, emitting an earsplitting cry that ripped through the battlefield. Battered, Chalazia began to plummet at a high speed. However, at the last second, she regained her composure by extending both wings. Using a similar floating mechanism to a parachute, she slowed her descent. Obviously, the battle was far from over. Chalazia would continue to struggle as long as Nyx did. At that moment, Lila knew that in order to win, she would have to beat her old master first. She would have to put her personal opinions to rest and become a cold-blooded warrior.

"You stole the thoughts from my mind," Nyx whispered in Lila's ear. Impossibly, Lila had been deceived again. A shiver ran down her spine when she dared to peer over her shoulder. Nyx had cast her telekinesis technique on Zephyr, pinning her to the ground. Zephyr showed no weakness, but Lila knew that on the inside she was hurting. Her body was shaking, struggling against an invisible force. From the look in her startled eyes, the message was clear: do whatever it takes to win.

"It ends here," Lila finally declared before teleporting behind Nyx and brutally punishing her with a dropkick to her shoulder. By disrupting Nyx's concentration, Lila gave Zephyr just enough time to retreat. With her out of harm's way, Nyx had no more crutches to lean back on.

"So you've finally made up your mind," Nyx seethed as she looked over her shoulder at Lila. She was prepared to kill or be killed.

"You'll get what you deserve," Lila sneered, then spat in Nyx's direction.

"Fine then."

Nyx fired a pair of purple energy blasts straight at Lila, but Lila diverted their path with her mind, causing them to bend around her and collide with the surrounding rock. The smoke from the collisions masked Nyx's approach, temporarily startling Lila. However, Lila regained her composure quickly and decided to focus strictly on defense.

The instant Nyx revealed herself from her smoke mask, Lila released a barrage of blasts of her own, which were yellow in color. As she expected, Nyx dodged all of them effortlessly with teleportation and tried to reuse her telekinesis from close range, but Lila cleverly countered this as well with her Delirium Technique. Since they both were applying force on the other, the stronger force would decide the winner. With a genius, Lila concocted a strategy to prevent Nyx's telekinesis from working simply by anticipating her attack, and the fight turned into a battle of wills.

Ever conscious of conserving energy because she was outnumbered, Nyx ceased her attack and tried to fall back, but it was too late. Lila could read her movements like a book. Unlike Nyx, she actually paid attention to her partner's habits during their time together. Part of that was attributed to the fact that Lila was the student and wanted to soak up as much information as possible. Now, all the skills she learned were coming in handy. If there was any message that she wanted to pass on to her kids one day, it was "stay in school; you're not just learning useless junk!" At this point, Lila began to exploit not only everything she had learned under Nyx's tutelage but the techniques she had picked up at the Origin

Temple. The maturing warrior teleported behind her opponent, who had been trying to move away but was now within attacking range, and rammed an elbow into her spine. Lila took advantage of Nyx's stunned state of exposure and assaulted her mind with her Delirium attack once more. This time, Lila would not let go. Before Nyx could react, Lila mercilessly fired an energy blast that penetrated her body. Knowing well that it would take more than that to kill her old master, Lila swiftly released a second attack. However, Nyx reflected the blast right back into Lila's face with a perfectly timed Nullification attack.

Lila was pushed back a couple of meters with her feet skidding on top of the gravel, but she did not lose her footing. The young fighter's last attack had noticeably stunned her adversary, resulting in a meager attack that barely had an effect. Thick crimson liquid dripped from the core of her body. Her body shook on top of an unsteady stance, but it was obvious that Nyx would not go down without a fight.

"You think it's over?" Nyx taunted and began to charge. A taciturn calm swept through Lila's spirit as her crazed, former mentor sprinted toward her. She assumed her signature fighting stance, which had been burned into her mind by her close combat teacher from the Origin Temple.

Nyx's first strike contained a lethal amount of force, but Lila stood her ground, caught Nyx's fist in her palm, and curled her fingers around it. With a short display of acrobatics, Nyx flipped over Lila's body in order to slip out of her grasp and attempted a heel kick to the side of the head. To her misfortune, Lila's suddenly heightened reflexes allowed her to duck in the nick of time. With the front of Nyx's body facing away from her, it was easy for Lila to strike Nyx's back with a powerful punch, upsetting the wound she had created earlier. Not wanting to waste any opportunities, Lila followed up with a fierce onslaught of punches. Pretending for a second that her opponent was a volleyball, like her teacher had instructed for this attack, Lila set Nyx up for a spike by forcing her into the air with a ruthless uppercut to her chin. Finally, the moment before she fell back to the ground, Lila finished the move with an energy blast, sending her old master skidding against the ground toward the outskirts of the battlefield.

"That's something that *I* have that *you* don't. It's something that *you* never taught me … how to *fight*," Lila dissed Nyx again.

Suddenly, Teresa's voice rang through the battlefield.

"Found it!" she bellowed triumphantly.

"Great! Now keep pushing Nyx toward the transmitter!" Zephyr ordered.

"You've got it!" Teresa assured, leaving her post beside the unconscious Pupil to take a more offensive position.

Lila let her guard down for a split second, and it proved to be a fatal mistake. The image of an injured Nyx in a heap on the ground in front of her vanished from view. Somehow, Lila had been tricked into an illusion. Protected by muscle memory and guided by instinct, Lila was able to block Nyx's sidekick from behind just in time with an arm thrust. Encouraged, she grabbed Nyx's ankle with her bare hands and flung her into the middle of the fray, forcing her to contend with three opponents at once. The revenge-hungry warrior had now been satisfied and was ready to share the rest of her feast with comrades.

With their combined might, they were able to overwhelm the enemy and, led by Teresa, push her back toward the death transmitter. First, Zephyr unsettled Nyx with a powerful gust of wind, making it difficult to pinpoint the source of the next attack. Then Lila took control of her mind with her Mental Assault Technique, giving Teresa an easy target to fire her Laser Beam attack at.

This continued for another half hour. Although she was outclassed, Nyx sporadically produced flashes of combat brilliance. During these flickers of ingenuity, she would execute her tactics perfectly, like possessing Zephyr's mind and forcing her to attack her allies, or tricking Lila into punching Teresa. Nyx's tenacity slowed their progress, but slowly and surely, the girls were able to penetrate her defenses. Sensing her intent, her teammates got out of the way as Lila leapt forward for one final blow.

In that single second, Lila contemplated, as she so often did, her entire life. Lila did not like to remember much of her life before she had met Nyx. She had been an outcast, a dimwitted kid with no prospects of a bright future. When she met Nyx, she felt like she finally had someone to look up to. Nyx had made her feel that maybe, just maybe, she could have a bright future. That's why, even after Nyx left Culloqui, Lila had trained and trained in hope that one day it would make a difference in her life. That was why she had decided to endure all the hardships of life. So when she finally found out that Nyx had joined the enemy, Lila was forced to question her whole reason for living. What was the point of living for a dream that could never come true? Why keep fighting when people you thought were your friends turn their backs on you?

A dream doesn't end when someone dies ... or gives up ... or changes ... as long as someone else can carry on their legacy. You always used to tell me how you wanted to break your parents out of jail ... how our society is so corrupt and it isn't fair. That's why you fought, but now ... you've become the problem yourself. I choose to fight for your old dream, even if you've given up on it.

Finally, Nyx's weak voice suddenly entered her mind. *You can think for yourself ... I gave in, Lila. It was too late for me to turn back. But you and your friends can be the change. Please, take care of Chalazia for me ...*

Nyx ... Lila was on the verge of tears, despite her earlier resolve. *We'll succeed where you failed. We'll set them free.*

"Skull Crusher!" Lila roared. With an explosion of intensity that she did not know she had, Lila combined all her mental and physical energy to penetrate Nyx's skull and destroy her brain. One punch sent Nyx three hundred meters away and crashing into a cliff side. Lila had never been surer about anything than she was right then: she had finally beaten her old master.

"Nice job, Lila. Take it easy for now." Zenon patted her on the back.

"But … Chalazia …" Lila stammered as her body erupted in pain from extreme exertion.

"Don't worry. Unchartian dragons won't fight without reason. Now that Nyx is gone, Chalazia will stop. Look," Zephyr said, pointing back to where Iris had been fighting hard just a few minutes before. Now, the scene had changed. Iris was petting Chalazia gently on the nose, just like she would with Aiondraes.

She really wanted to take care of Chalazia, Lila thought, tearing up.

"These dragons are pretty gentle. Come on; let's go get everyone."

When Teresa went to retrieve her, Pupil woke up with a start and accidently poked her in the eye.

"I'm awake!" Pupil declared.

"It's all right, Pupil. All that's left is Kerato," Teresa solemnly informed.

Lila glanced back at Iris, who seemed to be enjoying Chalazia's company. She was glad, too; they would need all the help they could get.

"So," Lila started, "what's next?"

"Everybody, *listen* up!" Zephyr demanded. "Since we beat Nyx, we can destroy the death transmitter. Kerato is too busy to fight us. Teresa, lead the way!"

"Okay," Teresa obeyed and bolted in the direction of where she had spotted the weapon of mass destruction.

"Everyone else, climb on Chalazia. It'll save energy," Zephyr ordered.

Without hesitation, the three other girls did as they were told. It was crucial that no one argued or complained; time was of the essence.

"Aiiiiiiooo!" Chalazia screeched and extended both wings in preparation for flight. Either it was wishful thinking on Lila's part, or the female dragon was much happier with her new company than she had been with Nyx. With one powerful pounce of her hind legs, they were off to save the world.

THE PRODUCT OF REVENGE

HAVING RECEIVED THE UNSPOKEN MESSAGE that their other team had beaten the enemy and was now on its way to destroy the target, Wayward felt elated. They might actually be able to win this thing!

"Keep your head out of the clouds, Wayward! We've still got a battle to win!" Jadeleve warned the youngest member of their team before charging at Kerato. Kuroski followed her lead; the two decided to from a tag team. Wayward, Maelin, and Gato stayed back so they could be the next line of attack, just as Zenon had instructed them to do.

"You two think you can take me on alone? Seven of you couldn't take me on before. What makes you think anything's changed?" Kerato snickered.

"You idiot. There are thirteen of us now, and we're all stronger than last time. Get over yourself," Jadeleve barked.

"You couldn't even beat Nyx!" Kerato erupted with laughter.

"Think again," Kuroski smirked.

"What?" Kerato jerked his head to the left. His eyes met the sight of smoke billowing from the side of a rock formation that was indeed his teammate's tomb. It was the perfect opening; he had let his guard down.

"Never underestimate us again!" Jadeleve bellowed as she charged at Kerato again. He tried to strike with a wild swing from his sword, only to be met with empty air and shoved backward by powerful air. Jadeleve had dodged Kerato's sword with her After-Image Technique while Kuroski scored an air punch, a new move, using his mistral wind wristbands.

The two young warriors smoothly transitioned into the next combination, not wanting to miss a beat. Before Kerato could recover from their first assault, Jadeleve decelerated his movements with her Slow Motion Technique, giving Kuroski the perfect opportunity to deal some damage. Kuroski punched, kicked, and elbowed, channeling all his frustration into each attack. Finally, Jadeleve teleported behind her foe and blasted straight through his body with her Recatus technique, sending him flying in the same direction. All their training over the past couple years made dealing with enemies like Nyx and Kerato, who they had struggled to defeat so much in the past, child's play.

"I-I d-don't get it. Why don't you just die?" Kerato demanded as he coughed up blood, using his dying breath to ask a question he had probably wanted the answer to long before he met them.

"We're fighting for something big … bigger than ourselves. We'll unite the land again. That is how the world was meant to be," Jadeleve said.

"Idiots. The lands were never really united. The races could never get along from day one. That's life, and we can't do anything about it … no matter what we try," Kerato muttered.

"What do you mean?" Wayward intruded, suddenly outraged. "You've been a bad guy from the start! You killed all those people in Pearl Town and—"

"Shut up! What do you know about it, kid? You … you've probably been protected your whole life. You don't know that the world is really like. We … we can never really accept each other," Kerato seethed, struggling to speak.

"Hey," Gato said. "You're in our way."

"That's right," Maelin chimed in. "We haven't given up. We're doing something to try to stop this war. If you wanted to help, why are you in our way?"

"You d-don't get it. Nothing you do will work. You're fi-fighting f-for what y-you think is ri-right ... and so am I. But our ideas of h-how to achieve peace ... aren't the same. That's wh-why we're fighting," Kerato explained.

Throughout Kerato's dreadful speech, Wayward's eyes were glued on Jadeleve. Even though Zenon usually called the shots, he looked to Jadeleve first and foremost for guidance, so he was eager to hear her rebuttal. However, throughout their enemy's spiel, she remained silent and listened intently to what he had to say.

"And I think eliminating your r-race is the only way."

"Why?" Kuroski asked.

"I-I used t-to be ju-just like you ... wanting the lands to be united again. That all changed the day I watched my brother get killed right in front of me!" Kerato screamed, bursting with tears.

"We didn't know ... Well, our lives haven't exactly been perfect, either. I never even had parents ... or a brother. I was bullied. All I had was one friend growing up, but she meant the world to me. I hung in there, and now I have these guys," Kuroski replied with pride.

"And my parents died in the war two months later!" Kerato continued wailing. "It's pointless to fight for unity. The lands have never, can never and will never be united!"

"*Never, never, never*; you sound like a broken record," Lila scowled. She suddenly dropped out of the sky and landed next to Jadeleve. Overhead, Pupil, Iris, and Zephyr piloted the evil woman's purple dragon toward the northern rock formations. They were led by Teresa, meaning she had discovered the whereabouts of the death transmitter and the girls had defeated their evil enemy.

"My parents died in the war too. And I didn't have any friends growing up. All I had was my teacher. Then she gave up on me and left. Then I had to fight her to the death."

Suddenly, Kerato's intensity diminished, and he became pale with grief. "Y-you … y-you're t-talking about Nyx, are-aren't you?"

"Gee, what gave it away?" Lila sneered.

Finally, Jadeleve stepped forward.

"I've never had anyone close to me die before … not yet, at least. I don't know what that's like. But I do know that if someone I love died, they'd want me to be happy and keep living. They'd want me to carry on for them because that's the type of people *my* loved ones are."

"You're living in a *fantasy!*" Kerato screamed. "If *I* was your loved one and *I* died, *I'd* want you to suffer for the rest of your life! And you think I'm the only one? *No* one wants life to go on without them. And you … you're absolutely *foolish* to say that you could carry on! You'll drown in despair just like I did! Don't think you're special! In war, *everyone* eventually becomes—"

Xaphias suddenly fell from the sky, as Aiondraes went to follow Chalazia and impaled the center of Kerato's body with his steel sword, ending his life. Rich red blood began to seep from Kerato's final wound and cover the surrounding earth. The frailty of a life astounded Wayward. It could be taken in an instant.

"Don't listen to him," Xaphias advised as he pulled his sword out of his victim's back.

"Xaphias!" Jadeleve exploded with anger. Wayward was shocked as well, but the fact that Jadeleve was disturbed about the death of a hated enemy confused him greatly.

"This is *war*, Jadeleve. Sometimes, you have to go against your moral code," Xaphias replied.

"But you didn't even flinch," Jadeleve pressed on. "When did you become so coldhearted?"

"I'll do whatever it takes to protect my friends," Xaphias said.

"Xaphias …" Jadeleve gasped.

"Come on, guys; we're done here. Teresa's found the death transmitter, so we need to destroy before it's too late," Lila urged.

Without another word, the rest of their group followed her lead, leaving the bloody battlefield behind.

At last they had located the death transmitter. It was much smaller and a lot less complex than Wayward had imagined it to be. The so-called transmitter of death was a simple parabolic structure made of aluminum and consisting of two feed horns. There was nothing menacing about it; it resembled a standard satellite dish from Earth during ancient times. Wayward was familiar with them due to his mother's interest in the devices.

"It looks harmless, but if Cataract uses his technique on it, this thing could kill us all," Zenon warned, as if she could read Wayward's mind. "We need to destroy it."

"I got this one," Jadeleve declared. She began drawing from the dormant solar energy inside of her pendant, causing it to glow with brilliant turquoise light.

"Re … ca … tus!" Jadeleve chanted. A violet beam of light skyrocketed from the palms of her hands at the death transmitter.

The moment Jadeleve released that light from her hands, Wayward gave a sigh of relief. However, a second later, his unrest returned. About five meters from making contact with the sixty-foot transmitter, Jadeleve's attack split in two, as if the death transmitter was cutting through it. The divided attack was forced off to either side of its target, counting on its path to destruction and eventually colliding with the nearest rocks.

"A force field?" Xaphias sighed, frustrated.

"Let's all attack together! Aim your strongest attacks at one point!" Kuroski attempted to rally the group, succeeding with everyone except Zephyr.

"Since when do I take orders from—"

"Now isn't the time, Zephyr!" Jadeleve screamed. "Recatus!"

"Fine! Foveno Beam!" Zephyr hollered as she released a brilliant golden blast from her hands.

"Choroid Gun!" Zenon chimed in, emitting a powerful lime-green attack from her hands.

"All right!" Pupil chanted before firing her blue beam. "Sclera Beam!"

"Zonule!" Iris yelled. In the process, her irises turned a deep red to match her clothes. Finally, two super-hot red rings of energy soared from her eyes at the death transmitter.

"Soul Twister!" Kuroski roared, contributing a blustery vortex of wind at the target.

"Aiiiiaaa!" Aiondraes rumbled before using his best attack, the Ember Orb.

"Aiiiii!" Chalazia screeched, discharging a cascade of flames from her mouth.

"Gahhh! Laser Beam!" Teresa wailed.

Xaphias, Maelin, Wayward, Lila, and Gato each fired regular blasts. But despite everyone's help and despite using their maximum efforts, their combined attack was effortlessly repelled by the barrier. It was hopeless.

"Come on, guys! Think outside the box. Maybe it only repels energy attacks but can't block physical attacks," Maelin suggested. She was eager to finally contribute to the team.

"Good idea, Maelin. Come on, Gato; let's try the physical attack first," Xaphias directed, drawing his sword again.

"Gato nodded and readied his iron staff. Following Maelin's theory, he and Xaphias did not integrate their bodily energy into their weapons on the chance that it would get repelled. Xaphias stabbed with his sword, Maelin struck with her dagger, and Gato swung with his staff, but all three attacks had no effect.

"Guess not." Maelin sulked.

"Better luck next time?" Xaphias suggested.

"There might not be a next time," Gato said.

"Not helping!" Maelin blurted, ending the conversation.

"Chalazia! I think you should fly away to someplace face, girl. Cataract might target you for going against him. I don't want you to get hurt. I'll call you when I need you," Lila instructed her new partner. Chalazia stared back at her for moment, then obeyed her new master's wishes and flew off.

"Let me give my mental attacks a try," Lila proposed. "Mental Assault!"

Seconds later, Lila clutched her head in pain, meaning that her attack was reflected instead of repelled like the other attacks.

"Are you all right, Lila?" Iris rushed to her aid.

"Yeah … I'm fine."

"Hey, why was Lila's attack reflected instead of repelled like the other attacks?" Kuroski pondered.

"It must be a barrier created by Cataract's mind. Mental barriers counter mental attacks and absorb energy blasts and physical attacks," Zenon explained, obviously perturbed by this fact.

"So … is there anything we can do to break it?" Pupil murmured.

Zenon was about to respond, but someone else beat her to it.

"Nothing. Only I can dissolve this barrier," a raspy voice enlightened the young group.

"Cataract," Wayward gasped. Despair began to overwhelm him as he saw Cataract's bald figure with his cloak flowing in the distance.

"If you insist on getting in my way, I will just have to annihilate you."

"I would be careful if I were you. We just defeated your comrades," Zenon said.

"Those weakling were not my comrades. They were the trash I used to get the job done. I did not care about them in the slightest. Now enough talk."

Suddenly, Lila stood up straight with wide eyes and began to scream her mental message.

Everyone, he's planning to release the barrier so he can use that technique! We need to figure out a way to destroy it before he uses it!

Oh no! Think! Think! Silent agony enveloped the group as each person (and two dragons) thought over the countless possibilities.

At last, a spark flashed in Jadeleve's eyes.

"It's risky, but it's the only thing that will work." Suddenly, everyone's eyes turned to her. "Pupil, quick: start generating electricity for your Thunder Clap technique. Release when I say so!"

"Roger!" Pupil replied. Trusting her sister, Pupil did as she was instructed and began concentrating electrical energy in her arms. But time was of the essence.

"Release!" Cataract cried. The barrier was deforming.

"Not yet," Jadeleve advised.

"Get ready to die!" Cataract raved.

"Not yet!" Jadeleve repeated, her heart racing.

"Argh!" The strain of concentrating so much electricity in one place was a heavy burden for anyone. Pupil had reached her limit.

"Fire it at the sky!"

"Hiya!"

Finally, Pupil released all of her latent power at the sky. Wayward was perplexed. She had missed the target.

"Fool! Now all the See-Throughs on Jupiter will perish! You have squandered your only chance!" Cataract roared with triumph. "Evil Mist Dis—"

"Telebolt!" Jadeleve bellowed defiantly. Her voice seemed to echo around the whole island and beyond. Zeal began to envelop her body, and with eyes of pure gold, she gazed up at the cloudy sky. A bolt of lightning lit up the sky, streaking through the air until it had reached its target: Jadeleve. In a flash of light, too fast for anyone to follow, Jadeleve disappeared. A second later, there was an explosion. Smoke was billowing from the remains of the death transmitter, and Jadeleve reappeared beside her sister.

"Whoa." Kuroski gasped in amazement. "How'd you do that?"

"It's just like when I turn into sunlight; I can turn into electricity too," she replied.

"So you drew the maximum amount of electrical energy into your body and converted yourself into electricity, allowing you to attack at the speed of light." Zenon admired the science behind Jadeleve's attack.

"Do you have any idea what you have done?" Cataract rasped.

"She's saved us!" Pupil yipped.

"Just the opposite. Maybe I cannot kill all the See-Throughs on the planet at once, but nothing is stopping me from destroying your minds right now!" Cataract fumed. Eighty-mile-an-hour winds began to encircle them. Waves crashed harder against the shore. Lighting danced freely in the sky like serpents ready to bite at any moment. "I kill you all!"

"Everyone! Steel your minds! He can attack multiple people at once," Lila warned.

"Evil Mist Dispers—"

Cataract was suddenly on the ground. Rohan had returned.

"Rohan," Wayward gasped. He immediately rushed into his older brother's arms.

"Right on time," Xaphias smirked forlornly. He was already exhausted. "You here to help?"

"Yeah. But on one condition: after this is all over, you let me join your group. I've been working for this creep for four years because he said he would spare my family from his plan, but now I know he doesn't plan to keep any of his promises. I'm done with him. I'll protect my family my own way." Rohan grinned. He stood up from his crouched position with his arms around Wayward and unsheathed his purple sword. Then he matched Xaphias's stance. Wayward knew that this was the start of a lifelong rivalry.

"Deal. Just make sure you don't get in our way, loser," Xaphias smirked.

"There's nothing you sniveling See-Throughs can produce that could possibly counter my best attack! Nothing!" Cataract boomed.

"Someone with decent mental control could block your so-called ultimate attack if they saw it coming. But your planned revolved around taking people by surprise. You're not as strong as you act," Rohan sneered.

"Perfect. Time to beat you up." Kuroski rolled up his sleeves.

Cataract remained silent for a long while. He let that silence fill the air, eating away at his opponents' vitality. Somehow, Wayward felt hopeless again. In his heart, he desperately wanted to believe in Pupil and Kuroski, that they could win this battle no problem. But Cataract's silence dashed those hopes as fast as Jadeleve dashed his death transmitter.

"Stay back; he is still the strongest opponent you have ever faced … and me too," Rohan grumbled.

"Who do you imps think you are? Huh?" Cataract's voice reverberated across the whole island. His intent to kill tainted the air like a poisonous gas. Nobody was safe in his presence. "Impenetrable Force Field!"

When nothing happened, Wayward grew impatient and charged ahead, but an invisible wall shoved him back again.

"What is this?" Wayward uttered.

"It's the same attack he used to protect the death transmitter. He can't attack us, but we can't attack him either," Zenon explained.

"You are a perceptive one. Then you should know why I used the attack on all of you and left Rohan out: I kill him first! Watch and be helpless to stop me!" Cataract laughed manically.

"Go get him, Rohan!" Wayward cheered his brother on despite being trapped inside the force field.

"Bring it on," Rohan taunted before disappearing.

"Mind Resonance!" Cataract rasped. Immediately, reappeared behind Cataract and was swatted away like a fly by Cataract's arm.

Rohan rubbed the fresh, bloody wound. But as he stood up from the ground once again, Wayward was astounded to see a hidden amusement in his eyes. Maybe he was overjoyed by the prospect of reliving his glory days, which were full of battles and bloodshed.

"I sent a ripple through the atmosphere with my mind that travels in every direction until it finds another mind. When the signal reaches someone, it confuses their brain into doing exactly what I want it to do. In this case, it was to interrupt your teleportation." Cataract chuckled.

"Why are you still fighting? We beat you," Rohan demanded, starting to tire.

"I live to kill."

"Well ... I live to protect the people I care about from creeps like you!" Rohan boomed, preparing himself for another charge.

"None of your attacks work on me because of a mental barrier I have built over my mind. I do not feel pain, and I can regenerate my cells with the surrounding energy of the atmosphere. I have plenty of attacks to choose from to destroy you," Cataract rasped. He levitated and began to float around Rohan, like a planet orbiting its star, in order to taunt him. When Rohan tried to attack with an energy beam, Cataract simply disappeared and reappeared in a new location. Clearly, he was only toying. Cataract could kill Rohan at any minute, but first he wanted the satisfaction of Rohan succumbing to despair.

Rohan was right, Wayward thought.

"Stop it right now!" Wayward began to wail again, pounding on Cataract's Impenetrable Force Field with futility.

"Calm down. Instead of getting worked up, we should try to figure out a way to get out of here," Xaphias advised, placing a reassuring hand on his younger comrade. All the while, Cataract was pummeling Rohan. Wayward watched in horror as Cataract repeatedly took over Rohan's mind, clasped his hand around Rohan's neck, and squeezed. The battle was one-sided. If they did not find a way to counterattack, they would be too late to save him.

"I'll burrow underground," Xaphias decided. He was gone before Wayward could even turn around, leaving a hole in the ground, which was about ten feet in diameter, in the middle of where they all stood. Ten seconds later, he appeared on the other side of the invisible wall. Aiondraes followed suit, squeezed through the tunnel, and took to the skies. Anything but unaware, Cataract caught wind of Xaphias's maneuver and fired a massive black energy blast right at him. With only a second to react, Xaphias barely dodged the attack by leaping about fifty feet into the air. Soon, Xaphias was fleeing from Cataract's black energy blasts just like a pesky fly fleeing from a swatter. He dodged and darted, evading the powerful attacks by mere inches.

Finally, when Xaphias had half a second of reprieve from the onslaught, he took one look back at his comrades who were still stuck gaping inside the invisible shield. The blur of action that took place in the following few minutes was almost too fast for Wayward to keep up with. Xaphias had succeeded in distracting Cataract. Taking full advantage of the opening, Rohan tackled Cataract's cloaked body with all his might, body slamming him, knowing full well that Cataract felt no pain. Even so, Rohan succeeded in pinning him down and bought more time for his comrades' escape.

The remaining warriors that were still trapped inside Cataract's barrier began to escape through Xaphias's underground barrier. Pupil illuminated the way with her Flashlight Technique.

"What should we do?" Wayward inquired.

"Fight. We've got to find some way to beat him," Zephyr declared.

Once the group reached the end of the tunnel and found daylight, Zenon ordered the group to surround Cataract. Wayward stood frozen on the outside of the circle while Xaphias and Aiondraes hovered overhead and Rohan kept Cataract busy. Xaphias had decided to rest on Aiondraes's back to conserve energy as he so often did. Even though no one said it, it was clear that they were entering a new phase in the battle. At this stage, there was no turning back.

"It would seem that I cannot use the Impenetrable Force Field on you anymore. You are too spread apart," Cataract mused in his raspy voice, but he seemed anything but worried.

"We'll wipe that smile from your face," Rohan scowled.

"I will just have to kill you first," Cataract retorted.

A dozen boulders began to until they reached his altitude and surrounded him. Then, abruptly, they surged down, straight at Cataract.

"Meteor Shower!" Xaphias roared.

"Aiiioooo! Eoiyyyy!" Aiondraes released his Lightning Wave attack from the tips of his three silver-colored claws to electrify Xaphias's meteors.

The electrified meteors were the perfect distraction. Rohan joined the circle that surrounded Cataract as the rest of Xaphias's Meteor Shower did its job. For a second, the group relaxed.

"Never let your guard down in my presence!" Cataract bellowed. Abruptly, Rohan flew back and slammed into a boulder. Following the impact, Rohan fell down and tasted dirt. Cataract was far from finished. He lifted his right hand, showing signs of strain in that arm, forcing Rohan to levitate. Wayward watched in horror as his brother began convulsing violently. His arms and legs began to twist and bend at impossible angles. Then Cataract formed another force field around them.

"Rohan!" Wayward squealed and ran toward his brother. Xaphias jumped down from Aiondraes's back and started digging underground.

"Wayward …" Rohan struggled to speak. His face contorted in his effort to talk. "St-stay back!"

Cataract turned his body so his cold, gray eyes faced Wayward, but his right arm was still controlling his brother's every move. Wayward was enraged by the amusement in his voice.

"How perfect. Now your brother has a front-row seat to watch you die."

"I'll b-be just f-fine." Rohan chuckled under his breath. For all his talk, however, he was battered and bruised. Blood began to drip from his mouth, and he closed his green eyes. One more blow, and he was done for.

"You fool! This is what happens you defy me! When you betray me!" Cataract began concentrating a massive amount of pitch-black energy into his left hand.

"No! Don't do it! Stop!" Wayward wailed. "Let him go!"

"Die, scum! Purging Light!" Cataract boomed. He clenched his fist, trapping all the dark energy inside it, and struck the center of Rohan's body. The collision of matter and energy created an explosion. When the smoke cleared, Rohan was nowhere to be found. Blood stained the ground.

He ... he blew him up, Wayward thought, horrified.

At last, Wayward had lost control.

"Arghhhhh!" he screamed, which was fueled by a bitter mixture of anger and sadness. Rage had consumed him.

"You'll pay!" Wayward continued. Rich, potent energy began to pulsate through his veins. The whole world began to blur around him into one red image. Without realizing it, Wayward had discovered how Jadeleve felt whenever she drew power from zeal. The power to crush his enemies and to make them feel the pain he felt dominated his thoughts. Now that Rohan was gone, he was alone. There was no one left to save him now. As he thought this, he did not register Pupil and Iris, who were by his side and trying to calm him down. He pushed them away.

Finally, Wayward released all his energy in one attack, a massive red beam with a thinner, purple energy beam spiraling around it. The attack disregarded the Impenetrable Force Field and engulfed Cataract in its dazzling red and purple light. The explosion that followed surpassed Cataract's earlier attack by tenfold.

"Wayward, it's okay. Rohan is okay. He's fine. Look," Jadeleve whispered into his ear, placing a calming hand on his heaving back. Then she pointed over to where Xaphias was recovering from their near-death experience.

"How?" Wayward inquired, shaking.

"Xaphias stabbed Cataract in the arm to shift the direction of the blast. He got them out just in time. What you just did was amazing too. You used two blasts to weaken the force field; the first one was to weaken it. Genius, Wayward," Zenon complimented. Then she gathered Wayward up in a hug.

Cataract laughed manically as he rose from the ashes of his own blast. Wayward should have known that his effort was in vain. Cataract could regenerate.

"Why don't you just die?" Jadeleve rose to her full height in a menacing fighting stance. "Wayward, stay back!"

"No! You hurt Rohan! I'll make you pay!" Wayward ranted, slipping out of Jadeleve's reach like the agile youngster he was and charging his head once again.

"Time to meet your end!" Cataract hollered, preparing to launch another attack.

"Not if I can help it!" Rohan declared. Rohan disregarded his own injuries, swooped in from behind, and sliced through Cataract's torso. Knowing full well that his foe would regenerate, Rohan took that second to grab his brother and fly as far away as possible.

"Put me down! I wanna fight!" Wayward exclaimed. He flailed in the arms of his brother.

"Don't go charging in there like a bull!" Rohan reprimanded in midair and silenced his little brother. "We have to learn from our mistakes. Do you hear me?"

Wayward was stunned. After he closed his mouth, he started to think clearly. Finally, he realized that his brother was right. The worst thing they could possibly do was keep trying the same strategy.

By the time Rohan thought he was far enough away to drop Wayward off, Cataract was finished regenerating and ready for the next round. He stood triumphantly in front of their group of fourteen fighters who, in contrast, wearily got into their respective battle stances. Jadeleve was at the front of the pack with Xaphias and Maelin slightly farther back. Further away from Cataract were the Dawn twins with Kuroski right beside them. The Zeal twins stood in the middle, then Lila, while Gato and Teresa stood the closest to where Rohan and Wayward landed. Aiondraes still hovered anxiously in the skies above.

"Who is next? It is one against fourteen," Cataract rasped.

"The real fight starts now, monster!" Jadeleve roared. "Guys, let's take him down together!"

Rallied by their leader's war cry, eleven of the young warriors raced toward their toughest opponent yet as Aiondraes dove down.

Rohan turned expectantly toward his brother, obviously waiting for a reply to his earlier question. At that moment, Wayward realized that his brother was struggling to hold back tears. His eyes glistened despite the absence of the sun's light, and they were marked in a reddish hue. Rohan felt just as much anguish, yet he still chose to fight. Wayward came to his final decision: he would never run away again, no matter what happened.

"I hear you," Wayward finally replied. And with that statement, the two siblings sprinted toward the action.

SACRIFICE

"GUYS, WE NEED TO FIGURE out how to beat him or we'll end up fighting him forever. Since he can regenerate, he's pretty much immortal," Kuroski said.

"It's kind of hard to fight for your life and think at the same time!" Lila replied.

"Then some people fight and some people figure out we're gonna survive!" Kuroski suggested again.

Zenon, Lila, and Xaphias, the three brightest minds on the team, formed a hasty brainstorming group to think of a surefire way to beat Cataract. The plan had to account for his power of regeneration and his other abilities. It was no small task and required some hard thinking. It was the job of Kuroski and the other fighters to keep Cataract busy while they brainstormed.

"Take this," Gato bellowed and drew his iron staff. He swung with a left and then a right, relentlessly striking his opponent.

"I cannot feel pain," Cataract rasped, before picking up Gato by his staff and ramming them both into the ground. Next, he stomped on Gato stomach.

"Get off him!" Maelin thundered, trying unsuccessfully to tackle her foe. Cataract teleported away, slipping out of her grasp. When he reappeared behind her, she was pushed twenty feet away, seemingly by an invisible force, but it was Cataract's telekinesis. She landed on her back but got up quickly.

Finally, Lila screamed to break up the pointless struggle.

"Stop, guys. Physical attacks won't work, remember? He doesn't feel pain, and he can regenerate! We can only tire him out! Delirium!"

Cataract knelt down and clutched his head in agony.

"You're right, Lila. Slow Motion Technique!" Jadeleve screamed. Jadeleve multiplied the amount of time Cataract had to endure Lila's gruesome illusions.

Clever, Kuroski thought.

"Okay, guys! You've got time to catch your breath. Brainstorm," Zenon encouraged from the sidelines.

"All right … I think Jadeleve's Slow Motion attack and one of Lila's illusions should be in the plan," Zephyr suggested, huffing from exhaustion.

"Yeah," Pupil agreed. "Lila's illusion could catch him off guard."

"While Jadeleve's Slow Motion Technique gives us more time to do what we want with him," Iris finished her twin's thought with a shaky attempt at a firm voice. However, Iris's irises fluctuated between a deep crimson and bright orange, meaning that her mood was shifting from rage to fear.

"Eventually, Jadeleve's attack will wear off. What do we do after that?" Zephyr inquired while dodging an energy blast.

While that question hung in the air, Gato attempted for the second time to attack Cataract to buy time. Having been the closest in their group to him, Rohan, Teresa, and Maelin rushed to his aid. Gato was usually unwilling to fight, but today he was giving it his all. It gave Kuroski an odd feeling.

"I'm not done," Gato cried and swung his staff back like he was preparing to hit a home run. His staff seemed to vibrate as the heat distortion created by his intense aura began to surround it. "Energy Wave Barrage."

Once Gato revealed the name of his attack, he began swinging his staff with such force and speed that it looked like a blur. With each swing of the staff, Gato created a wave of golden light that resembled a crescent moon. It only took a few of the golden waves to demolish Cataract, as their team had done so many times before, but Gato fired one hundred waves so he could stall Cataract's regeneration process. The smoke from the continual blasts masked Cataract's presence.

"I always thought you were lazy, but you learned a new move at the Origin Temple. You're stronger than you let on." Maelin smirked at Gato and nudged him in the arm.

"You didn't even need our help," Teresa complimented. If Gato was flattered, he did not show it.

"I think I just found a way to slow Cataract down even more with my sword," Rohan began.

"I will be taking that!" Cataract hollered. Suddenly, Rohan's sword began to levitate from his right hand. It maneuvered quickly through the air, and before anyone could react, it had pierced Gato's chest.

"No!" Teresa shrieked.

"Gato!" Maelin exclaimed. The girls' high-pitched cries were like an explosion of sound in the silence.

Kuroski watched in horror from afar as Gato's body stilled and his deep brown eyes lost their light. Blood slowly seeped through the top of his white shirt where Rohan's sword penetrated. Kuroski quickly lurched his head in the other direction as Cataract ruthlessly yanked Rohan's blade out of Gato's chest with no regard for Gato's body. Gato's iron staff, which Gato had been clutching defiantly to the very end, stopped rippling and fell to the ground with a soft clang. Gato, like his staff, also fell to the ground. Unable to say any last words, Gato was gone, just like that.

As everyone mourned, an all too familiar silence hung suspended in the air. Cataract laughed in the background.

"I hesitated … *again*," Rohan murmured. He solemnly picked up his bloodied sword and flew back to talk to the strategists. Finally, Teresa snapped and recklessly rushed Cataract. Everyone else was too stunned to move.

"Foolish girl! Come meet your demise!" Cataract rasped. Dark light began to flow from his left hand. Now he was going to kill Teresa. He was going to pick them off one by one.

"No! Teresa! Stop!" Kuroski pleaded, forcing his legs to move. It felt like trying to run at the bottom of the ocean with a thousand pound weights tied to each leg. The world seemed to move in slow motion around him. If he did not sacrifice himself and find the will to fight, even more of his comrades would die.

At the same time, Cataract dramatically raised his left hand. The dark energy's concentration reached its maximum, and he was prepared to continue his killing spree.

"Argh!" Kuroski grated his teeth in frustration, desperately trying to pick up speed so he could stop Teresa from running to her death. He took flight and then looked back at Xaphias, Lila, and Zenon, who were frantically trying to piece their new strategy together. "You better come up with something quick!"

"You are too late, boy! Purging Light!" Cataract bellowed, releasing his powerful black beam of light straight at Teresa, who was only about one hundred meters away.

"Ahhh!" Teresa squealed. Since she had not mastered the Energy Force Field Technique, all she could do was protect her face.

"Super Air Punch!" Kuroski screamed. Using the combined power of both mistral wind wristbands and drawing wind energy from the surrounding environment, Kuroski created a super-powerful gust of wind to counter Cataract's attack. Rohan flew by and got Teresa out of the way before she could be pushed too. Miraculously, Kuroski's blast overpowered Cataract's attack and pushed it right back at him. The beam exploded after colliding with Cataract's body, and he was vaporized again. The smoke had hidden the fiend from view. With a stroke of luck, their team had time to recover.

Kuroski and the other fighters anxiously sprinted away from where Cataract's body was reforming behind a veil of smoke and toward the three strategists.

"Anything? Anything at all?" Maelin asked on her knees in between sobs.

"We ... we'll have Rohan keep cutting Cataract into a million pieces," Zenon responded shakily.

"Yeah ... and I can keep him from reforming with my telekinesis," Lila added, trying her best to put up a strong front and not cry in front of the younger warriors.

"Cataract, I'll bury you!" Xaphias erupted in rage. He clenched his fists, and his amber eyes flashed. Kuroski had never been so angry before. This also unsettled him.

"Come on, bud! Let's go!" Xaphias beckoned his partner to fight with him.

"Ayyyyyiii!" Aiondraes whimpered, reluctant to fight.

"Come on, Aiondraes! We have to avenge him. We have to avenge Gato!" Xaphias urged. He tried to force his companion to move, but Aiondraes stood his ground defiantly. Halfway through watching this spectacle, Kuroski realized how wrongly he read Aiondraes. Aiondraes was not scared to fight, but he was scared to face the consequences of disobeying his master's orders. He must have thought it was the better option if Xaphias continued strategizing with Lila and Zenon. That was the best thing that Xaphias could do right now. Kuroski told Xaphias what he thought Aiondraes was trying to say.

"Don't worry, Xaphias. I'll go. I've got your backs," Kuroski assured.

"It might be risky for us to attack him again. I think he's pretty angry now," Jadeleve warned.

"That's why I'll go alone. I'm the one who attacked. This is our last chance to stall him. All of you should help them plan, and I'll distract him," Kuroski declared, becoming surer of his decision with every passing second.

"Wait at a second. Don't sacrifice yourself again. We need you here," Jadeleve pleaded.

"My choices are the only things I've had control over in my life. I chose to run away from home, join your team, and protect you from Kerato. That was me. No one can take that away from me." Kuroski had already made up his mind. There was no going back. "I'll avenge Gato for you, Xaphias."

"Not again! You could get killed this time!" Iris cried, running over to hug his waist.

"Yeah! There's no way to beat that monster!" Pupil mimicked her sister and also went to hug Kuroski. Kuroski knelt down so they could be at eye level.

"I'm going. You guys help the others come up with a plan. I just don't want anyone else to get killed," Kuroski explained, but as he did, he became less calm. Harsh gusts of wind began to sweep through the battlefield, moving the slate-gray clouds above.

"How heroic," a familiar raspy voice mocked. "But in the end, you're scum."

Kuroski had never felt so overwhelmed by such powerful emotions before. Rage, fear, and desperation circled through his mind. Even so, in the end, nothing could change his mind. If sacrificing himself could buy his friends at least a little time to save the world, then it was worth it.

"With my friends here, nothing you say can touch me," Kuroski declared with decisiveness that echoed throughout the battlefield and beyond. "Mistral Soul Twister!"

As Kuroski stockpiled wind energy, the blue sapphires attached to his orange wristbands began to glow ominously. This was it. He was putting everything on the line. Wind, pure and pulsating, began to swirl around him at an incredible speed. It was like nothing he had ever felt before. Gradually, a vortex began to form around him. He harnessed its power and moved it to the tips of his fingers. Lastly, the power of the mistral wind began to feed the vortex, making it more massive. Bright blue sparks of light began to encircle the tornado like fireflies dancing in the wind.

"Go ahead, boy! Take your best shot!" Cataract taunted. However, he looked like he was preparing to evade.

"Kuroski, wait!" Zenon stalled at the last second. "We just want to give Cataract a little present."

"Yeah. We think new moves that we learned at the Origin Temple can help give the Soul Twister some pizzazz!" Zephyr added.

Nothing at that moment could have made Kuroski happier. His friends supported him and had his back.

"I've been wanting to do this for a while anyway!" Zenon boasted. Suddenly, a thick orange aura began to envelop her body. Kuroski could see the air simmering around her, influenced by the intense heat. Flames exploded from the palms of her hands, illuminating her face and causing her amber eyes to glow. Next, the flames began to lengthen and twirl upward. At this point, they looked like two fiery snakes performing a sacred snake ritual. Finally, the two thin, swirling streams of fire had grown to the same height as Kuroski's Soul Twister, about eighty feet. Zenon had created a fire twister.

Following her twins' example, Zephyr drew from the power of the wind. At her feet, wind began to circle around her in the shape of a tornado. Its funnel was about thirty feet in diameter, much wider than Kuroski's tornado. Zephyr's tornado did not go above three feet, so the circle of dusty wind resembled a tire that was turned on its side. Even so, the speed of her tornado's rotation was at least twice as fast as Kuroski's, maybe 200 miles per hour, and was almost comparable to the wind speeds of the legendary Great Red Spot.

"Now ... let's combine them," Zenon instructed.

"Fools!" Cataract mocked. "No matter what you do, I will come back! I will keep coming back until every last one of you is dead!" Even so, their team was unfazed. Kuroski lifted his vortex up to give the twins a clear shot at it.

"Okay! Here we go! Fire Typhoon!" Zenon roared, flinging her attack right at Kuroski's Soul Twister.

"Shadow Circle!" Zephyr bellowed, throwing her attack like a Frisbee that skidded across the ground, right at the bottom of the Mistral Soul Twister.

At the moment of collision, the twins' new attacks caused Kuroski's original tornado to burst into flames.

"There's no stopping this, Cataract!" Kuroski said with confidence that he did not know he had. "Here's our original attack ... called ... Shadow Flames! Argh!"

"Ahhhgggack!" Cataract shrieked as he was incinerated. After the fiery twister consumed its target, it continued on its quest toward an inevitable destruction. The explosion was massive and lit up the sky like the sunset, leaving an equally massive crater in its wake. But when the smoke cleared, Cataract's reforming remains were nowhere to be found.

"Hey! Where is he?" Pupil said.

Kuroski tensed up and squinted his eyes, straining to see if his opponent was hiding in the shadows far away. After five minutes, out of nowhere, a stabbing pain began in Kuroski's head that felt like someone was trying to rip his brain out. Kuroski clutched his skull in agony. He was forced to his knees and cried out in agony. His friends' cries of distress in response to his distress became somewhat muffled to him.

The Original Five tried to console him while Aiondraes went off to search for their missing adversary. Wayward, Teresa, and Maelin knelt in front of Lila, Xaphias, and Rohan, who were still trying to finalize their strategy to take Cataract down once and for all.

"Kuroski!" Pupil exclaimed. "What's wrong?"

Kuroski could not understand his own speech. It sounded like incomprehensible mush. Luckily, his team understood what he meant by his actions.

"Cataract's infiltrating his mind," Zenon quickly deduced.

"I'll make sure," Jadeleve suggested. She took a look inside Kuroski's head with her Mind Scan Technique and confirmed

Zenon's hypothesis. "Pupil, Iris! Help Aiondraes find Cataract! He's still around here somewhere!"

"Okay!" Pupil obeyed her sister. Iris nodded before her more energetic twin dragged her along.

"Lila, can you battle Cataract's mind out of Kuroski's?" Jadeleve asked desperately.

"Hold on. You guys keep thinking," Lila said and then turned to Jadeleve. "Yeah. It'll hurt him, but I can try."

"Hurry! I feel like he's trying to tear my brain apart!" Kuroski moaned.

"All right!" Lila agreed with some reluctance, not wanting to hurt her friend in any way. However, Lila knew better than anyone that it was the only way. "Mental Assault!"

Kuroski's screams doubled in volume. Two people were using his mind as a battlefield.

After a long, five-minute tug-of-war struggle, Lila finally gave in. She was sweating profusely and gasping for air even.

"I ... I couldn't do it. He's just too strong," she admitted.

After nearly a minute of Cataract's mental torture, Kuroski felt like his mind would give out soon too.

"We found him!" Pupil finally announced. She and Iris stood at the edge of the chasm that had been created by Shadow Flames. Aiondraes hovered above the center of the crater and dipped his head down below his shoulders and wings so he could face his nemesis directly.

"How many times must I say it? It is futile!" Cataract rasped from the bottom of the crater. "I will kill the rest of you slowly, one at a time, starting with him!"

"That's what you think, monster!" Iris screamed with red eyes.

"We'll teach you a lesson! Come on; let's attack together!" Pupil ordered. "Thunder Clap!"

Pupil charged all the electricity in her body into her palms and discharged it with one powerful clap of her hands.

"Aiyyyyaaaa!" Aiondraes released boiling water from his mouth.

"Rings of Fire!" Iris, fueled by anger, threw two sizzling-hot red discs of energy straight at her foe.

"Now I will not stop until he dies! Impenetrable Force Field!" Cataract bellowed. Before any of the attacks could reach their target, Cataract's force field absorbed them and trapped Kuroski inside. Cataract continued to infiltrate Kuroski's mind, intending to destroy it. Pupil, Iris, and Aiondraes flew back to where their teammates were to pass on the message. Kuroski's moans grew weaker by the second.

"Wayward, you're the only one who can destroy that barrier. Come with me!" Jadeleve urged, snatching Wayward's hand. She figured that she could get him there a lot faster than he could himself. Even so, when they arrived at their destination, Wayward froze.

"I am waiting for your attack, *hero*," Cataract taunted.

"Wayward, what are you doing?" Jadeleve prompted. "Attack! Come on!"

"I ... I can't ..." Wayward said. He was shaking worse than Jadeleve had ever seen him shake before. Tears dripped down his face.

"Why not? Wayward, Kuroski is going to die!" Jadeleve pushed even harder.

Wayward sobbed.

"Listen, Wayward. The moment you stepped out of the house, I promised to protect you at all costs. I never break my promises. Never. As long as I'm around, I won't let Cataract hurt you. So go ahead. Just let him have it!"

"Jadeleve ... I ... I want all this to end! Reversal Beam!" Wayward wailed at the top of his lungs. The potency of his own power overwhelmed him once again, and Wayward lost almost all control over what he was doing. His emotions took over and filled in the gaps in his reasoning.

Now with a name, Wayward's combined big red and small, spiraling purple beam attack soared out of his hands and destroyed

Cataract's Impenetrable Force Field again. Just like Kuroski's mind, Cataract's force field could not handle two simultaneous attacks. The Reversal Beam continued streaming beyond the Impenetrable Force Field's original boundaries and exploded as it collided with the bottom of the crater and created an even deeper crater. When the smoke cleared, Cataract was nowhere to be found again.

Cataract used telepathy to talk to every one of his opponents. It was like listening to a voice from the sky, since they could not see or interact with the owner.

He said, "I can do this all day, but your friend cannot."

"Stop it, Cataract! Just stop it!" Jadeleve protested. It was the first time that Wayward, who was exhausted by this point, had ever heard her voice crack before.

"Did you ever stop when you killed my comrades?" Cataract laughed manically.

"You said you didn't even think of them as comrades! Why are you doing this?" Jadeleve shrieked, but this time, Cataract did not even bother to respond.

"Jadeleve ..." Kuroski called weakly. Jadeleve turned around to see his head resting on Zenon's lap. He had reached the end of his rope. Not knowing what else she could do, Jadeleve quickly rushed to her dying friend's side.

"Kuroski ... I'm here," Jadeleve whispered as she knelt down next to him.

"I ... did it ... I stalemated him. He's using too much energy on me, so he can't attack you guys ... My plan worked ..." Kuroski chuckled weakly.

"You wanted this to happen? You're insane," Zenon gasped.

"Yep ..."

"Hey, guys!" Rohan hollered from behind where he, Xaphias, and Lila were still planning and Maelin and Teresa were still sobbing. "We're almost done! Just two more steps to figure it out!"

"That's good news ..." Kuroski speech became slurred. He could feel his consciousness slowly slipping away. His mind grew colder. Everything was getting dark.

"Cataract! Come out and fight!" Jadeleve yelled up at the heavens. No response.

She was about to try again when Kuroski's cold hand brushed against hers. "Thank you ... for everything ... everyone," Kuroski began, but soon it became a struggle for him just to speak. "Traveling around w-with you w-was th-the best thing that's ever h-happened to me. I f-felt ... free ... like a hero ..."

Jadeleve grabbed his right hand with both of hers.

"Don't say that now! You're gonna make it through this ... just like always. You've gotta fight it!"

"I'm fighting ... I-I'm just losing ... but st-stalling hi-him f-for as l-long as possible w-was part of my pl-plan." Kuroski chortled weakly.

"Kuroski," Iris whimpered. He had never seen her eyes become that color before, dark gray like the storm clouds above. Pupil closed her eyes, bit her lips and cried silently to herself. As if influenced by the tears, the storm clouds, which had been inactive all day, began to cry.

Unable to keep fighting, Kuroski's mind grew cold, and his body followed suit. His friends' laments became distant. Darkness began to cloud his vision. He knew without a doubt that this was the end. With his dying breath, he whispered, "Bummer ... things were just starting to make a little sense ..."

SEE THROUGH DECEPTION

"COME ON ... THINK. HOW DO we seal him away?" Xaphias seethed with frustration. He, Lila, and Rohan had racked their brains and still had not come up with anything. They knew that the only way to stop Cataract once and for all was to seal him away since he could regenerate, but how would they do it? Where would they seal him?

Suddenly, a powerful shockwave stole Xaphias's attention. Xaphias was shocked to find that Kuroski was limp in Zenon's arms, the Dawn twins were sobbing, and Zephyr was trying not to cry. She took his wristbands off his wrists and treated them as if they were sacred. Faced with unfathomable anguish, Jadeleve activated the zeal. Wayward stood somberly in the background with his head hung low. Kuroski had just died.

"Cataract. That was the last straw. I'll never forgive you for this," Jadeleve declared, overtaken by rage. Xaphias wanted to stop her before she did something reckless. As if the heavens themselves had heard his plea, Lila finally figured something out.

"We don't have to trick Cataract into our trap. Once Rohan cuts him up into a million pieces and Jadeleve slows down his regeneration with her technique, I can force him to go wherever I want with telekinesis," she explained.

"Yeah, but how do we trap him?" Rohan asked. Lila had no answer.

Suddenly, Xaphias experienced an epiphany of his own. Once he realized what he could do, it seemed so simple.

"I can literally bury him! I can create a chasm, Lila can force him inside, and I can seal him up. I could dig a hole so deep that we drown him in magma. The magma will constantly burn his cells, making it impossible for him to reform."

"That could work. That could work! Let's do this!" Lila agreed.

"I'll tell everyone. Hey, guys! We have the plan!"

Everyone turned toward Xaphias with a hint of hope replacing the tears in their eyes. Everyone except Jadeleve. She turned away from him, staunch in her position. Instead of running down her face, Jadeleve's tears floated up with the current of the zeal's vibrant, lime-green aura. Kuroski's death had caused her to snap. She wanted revenge more than anything and focused intently on sensing Cataract's spirit so she could find his body.

"Jadeleve! Did you hear me? We have a plan!" Xaphias called again, louder this time, but her overwhelming rage blocked out his voice. She continued to try to find his location.

"Over here!" Cataract taunted. Before Jadeleve could react, she was blasted in the back. Jadeleve fell onto her side and skidded back about twenty feet.

"Still think you can defeat me?" Cataract rasped.

Jadeleve answered by teleporting off the ground, reappearing behind Cataract, and delivering a mighty blow to his stomach. Not giving a chance for him to recover, Jadeleve went on a rampage and attacked Cataract with a barrage of lightning-fast punches. At the end of the onslaught, Jadeleve rammed Cataract's stomach with a power kick that sent him flying. He landed one hundred meters away but teleported away.

"Jadeleve! Are you satisfied now? Come on! Snap out of it!" Xaphias urged his friend to break free from her anger-induced trance. Her sisters and everyone started yelling and trying to stop her as well, but it was no use.

"Listen to your friends, Jadeleve. You are too weak to beat me!" Cataract laughed. As he entered everyone's mind again, it seemed as though his voice resonated throughout the battlefield. This made Jadeleve even angrier. It was like trying to swat a fly that kept slipping out of reach and just wouldn't go away. "Let us see how you deal with *this!*"

Suddenly, Jadeleve felt Cataract's presence weighing down and pushing against her mind. She knew he had infiltrated it. For a second, Jadeleve felt overwhelmed, unable to pinpoint her own consciousness while being attacked by Cataract's supermassive consciousness. Somehow, however, she stumbled upon a moment of concentration, was able to recall her mental training at the Origin Temple, and was able to battle him out of her mind.

"Mind Resonance!" Cataract voice rasped from the sky once again. His body was nowhere in sight.

Jadeleve knew if she got out of the way, her friends would get attacked, since the Mind Resonance attack hit the first mind that the mental wave came in contact with. She easily defended herself with a mental shield.

"Hmmm. So it seems you are in control of your mind. Funny— for most youngsters, that is their weak point," Cataract mused. Then he reappeared inches away from Jadeleve's face. "Regardless, let's see how you do when I take control of your body. Telekinesis!"

Before she could blink, Jadeleve's body was frozen in place. No matter how much she struggled, it would not move. Cataract started beating her with every one of his power-packed blows. He delivered a left and then a right, repeatedly. He kicked and elbowed and kneed. In one combo, he swept his leg under Jadeleve's feet, causing her to fall over. Before she hit the ground, he kicked her back up, clasped both hands together, and slammed them into her stomach. When she crashed into the ground, she coughed up blood. Now she was battered, rough, and running out of energy fast.

"All you See-Throughs are the same. Soft, weak, and, worst of all, terrible liars. You crowed about protecting your friends, but look what is happening. You weak, spineless fool. The only thing your race is good for is dying!" Cataract spat. He stepped on Jadeleve's stomach and pushed her deeper into the ground.

"Just shut up!" Jadeleve screeched at the top of her lungs and was burdened by a new wave of tears. Chunks of rock all around battlefield began to break off from Jupiter's crust. Compelled by Jadeleve's incredible force, they levitated, defying gravity, and started orbiting around her. Once again, Jadeleve's pendant shined a brilliant turquoise light. She pushed Cataract back with the sheer force of her energy. Turbulent, electrical winds began to blow in all directions from where she was. As Jadeleve rose from where she was beaten down. Her aura had increased to twice its original size and was a darker shade of green. With her long, unruly hair blowing in the wind and a permanent death stare on her face, Jadeleve looked like a monster. Jadeleve had broken free of Cataract's telekinesis with pure will and was ready to exact her revenge.

"Beast! Are you even part human? Just stay down!" Cataract ordered. It was the first time Xaphias had ever heard a hint of fear enter his voice. Jadeleve had successfully countered almost all of his attacks. Xaphias was not sure whether he should be happy that Cataract was finally getting a taste of his own medicine or worried for Jadeleve's well-being.

"Hard to tell *what* race I am, isn't it? Humans, See-Throughs, Eyebots ... it makes no difference; we all look the same! What you're doing makes no sense and I won't just stand here and let you get away with killing my friends!" Jadeleve declared.

"Then you do not stand. Die!" Cataract roared, at last releasing his strongest attack, Purging Light. A black beam of energy, representing all the evil in the hearts of all men, flew from his palms.

"Recatus!" Jadeleve bellowed. She fired her purple energy beam right at the Purging Light. Xaphias had never seen it so big before, but with her drawing from both extra solar and electrical energy, the Recatus was the strongest it had ever been. Even so, the moment those two attacks collided, the battle took a turn for the worse. The

Purging Light extinguished Jadeleve's blast and continued on its quest for devastation. Exhausted, Jadeleve deactivated the zeal and stopped using energy from her pendant. Without any energy, she could not even use Slow Motion in time to slow Purging Light. Xaphias realized that she had lost her will to fight. He was by Jadeleve's side before he even knew what he was doing. He wrapped his arms around her and teleported them back to his original spot seconds before the blast exploded. Cataract vanished once again, giving their shrinking team time to recoup.

Feeling slightly awkward, Xaphias tried to release his grip from around Jadeleve's waist and give her room, but she held his arms in place.

"Thanks … Xaphias," Jadeleve said and started sobbing into his shoulder.

"Don't mention it," he replied. By then, everyone, even Aiondraes, crowded around them. Zenon and the others laid Kuroski on ground where he had died, with his hands folded peacefully. They also performed a similar ritual with Gato. He made a mental note that they would give them both a hero's burial, after they won the battle.

"You calm, now?" Xaphias said, softly this time. He was more comfortable putting Jadeleve's feelings before his own.

"Yeah … I …" Jadeleve faltered. "I just …"

"You wanted revenge," Xaphias summed up.

"I've never felt like that before. It was like I couldn't control myself," Jadeleve confessed. She looked up at him and everyone else for a second but then buried her face in his shirt.

"You're not alone." Xaphias's simple words were enough to grab her attention. "You have us. And we have a strategy. We can beat Cataract together."

Jadeleve finally wiped her eyes with a bruised hand and stood up straight.

"I let you guys down."

"Don't say that!" Pupil scolded, her cheeks still wet and her eyes still red from sobbing. "You were awesome! You taught that creep a lesson!"

"Hmph." Zephyr sighed. "She was all right."

"She's right, you know," Zenon agreed, pointing at Pupil. "You took everything he threw at you and got in a few hits. Just think about what we could do together."

"Our plan will definitely work," Lila confirmed.

"But we need everyone's help," Rohan restated, looking at Maelin and Teresa, who were still sobbing quietly.

"Maelin, Teresa, we've got to keep fighting. Gato hated when people pushed him around, and, he would hate how Cataract is pushing us around right now," Xaphias said. Sure enough, the motivation helped, and the girls stood up too. The only one left was Wayward, who Rohan wanted to talk to.

"Wayward, everything I did was to protect you. I was only helping Cataract so he would leave you and Mom alone. I shouldn't have tried to do everything alone—"

Wayward interrupted his brother's speech with a great big hug. "I forgive you. All I want now is to get this guy."

"Aiiyyyyy!" Aiondraes roared with joy.

With the apologies and confessions over and done with, it was time to refocus their attention on the battle. Cataract was nowhere to be found, but they were used to that.

"Okay, so here's the plan," Xaphias began and proceeded to tell everyone their final course of action.

Without warning, Cataract's Purging Light appeared from the sky. At the speed it was moving, the blast would vaporize them in seconds. Xaphias knew that they could not counter the attack with another beam, as the Purging Light would absorb it. They also could not risk trying to block it with a force field, because they had no idea if the black beam vaporized shields too. Their only option was to evade, but how could they get twelve fatigued bodies out of range in under ten seconds? Luckily, Jadeleve was on top of things.

"Grab hands and stand in a line! Someone grab Aiondraes's horn!" Jadeleve commanded, startling everyone to rush into position as fast as they could. Jadeleve stood in front of the pack and held Iris's hand in her left hand. She wasted no time after the last person grabbed onto someone else to give her next order.

"Pupil! Fire the Thunder Clap in front of me!" Jadeleve ordered, pointing at a random spot on the field that was far enough away from the blast. Without stopping to think, Pupil followed her sister's orders. She released a powerful electrical current with the clap of her hands. The path of electric stream formed a T with the positioning of their line. Jadeleve reached her right hand into the pure stream of electricity and converted her body into pure electricity as well. Using her body as a bridge, Jadeleve converted everyone else's body into pure electricity, following the principle that when they all held hands, the electrons flowing through her would continue to flow to the last person in line. Once all of them were converted into electricity, they were pulled into the electrical current. Riding on that stream of electricity, all twelve of them were able to get from point A to point B at the speed of light, evading the blast by a fraction of a second. Jadeleve, through quick thinking, and the use of her Telebolt Technique, was able to save all of their lives.

The only downside to the plan was that they could not stop moving until they collided with a cliff face, and moving at the speed of light, it hurt. They crashed and fell to the ground in a heap, triggering a small rockslide, but it was better than dying. Once they recovered, another chance to beat Cataract presented itself.

"Argh," Lila moaned, physically and mentally exhausted. "Okay, guys. We didn't plan for this, but I think I know how we can draw Cataract out and distract him long enough to execute the plan."

"How?" Pupil asked.

"I'll tell you how." Lila smirked with a glint in her eye. "Chalazia!"

"What? Traitor!" Cataract seethed. Losing interest in his stealth tactic, he finally reappeared, floating eighty feet above ground.

So that's where he was, Xaphias thought angrily.

Chalazia came out of hiding and raced toward Cataract. Not needing to be told what to do, she provided the perfect distraction for their team and shot her fiery breath at him.

"Come on, guys! You know what to do! Bring him down to earth!" Zenon prompted. Pupil, Iris, Maelin, and Teresa took to the cloudy skies. Zenon followed from behind. Their final assault was on its way.

When those four left to start things off, Xaphias tried to make sure things were in order. "So, Rohan, once they get him on the ground, you know what to do, right? Then, Jadeleve, you—"

"We know, Xaphias," Jadeleve confirmed. Finally, Jadeleve, Rohan, Zephyr, and Xaphias followed the first wave's example. Aiondraes and Xaphias flew side by side.

Pupil and Iris confused Cataract by flying around him at incredible speeds and, utilizing their striking resemblance, tricked him into seeing quadruple with the After-Image Technique. Teresa forced Cataract to dodge in midair into Maelin's attack by firing a laser beam straight at him. At last, Maelin landed a dropkick that sent Cataract plummeting to the ground.

"Now!" Zenon shouted from the skies.

"Mental Assault!" Lila yelled from above. She infiltrated Cataract's mind and forced him to be still. "Go, Rohan! Now's your chance!"

Rohan did not need to be told twice. He dove down and met his foe with murderous intent clearly on his face.

"Fool! Even if you destroy me, how is this different from any other time! I will just reform!" Cataract warned one more time.

"Not this time!" Rohan declared upon landing in front of his enemy. "Die, you monster! Argh!" Rohan shouted a battle cry and drew his sword by its purple hilt. He ripped Cataract's body and his cloak into shreds with furious swing after furious swing, until the pieces were too small to slash anymore. Once their work was done, Rohan teleported away and Lila released her grip on Cataract's mind, giving Jadeleve room to do her part.

"Slow Motion!" Jadeleve bellowed. By twisting time with the energy in her eyes, Jadeleve slowed down the pace of Cataract's reformation, giving Xaphias plenty of time for the next phase.

In midair, Xaphias situated himself on Aiondraes's back, and together they ascended to one hundred feet.

"Right there, bud," Xaphias ordered, pointing to a spot out of harm's way to everyone on his team and far enough from Cataract that it did not interfere with Jadeleve's Slow Motion Technique. Aiondraes knew what to do. He shot a jet of boiling hot liquid from his mouth, to the spot where Xaphias had pointed. Then Aiondraes did a front flip in midair with such force that he catapulted Xaphias off his back, right at the hot spot. Xaphias accelerated like a comet, straightening his body to be as aerodynamic as possible. All the while, he stored earth energy into his sword, clutching the dark blue hilt with both hands.

Fifteen feet from the ground, Xaphias had built up as much earthly energy as his body could handle. Finally, with all his might, he stabbed right at the center of Aiondraes's soft spot.

"Ground Shredder!"

As the name foretold, the incredible force if the attack ripped through the earth like paper, breaking pieces of earth from its crust and pushing them aside. A red shockwave comprised of earth energy, triggered by Xaphias's mighty attack, tore through the gravel in a zigzag line one hundred meters long. The chasm was deep enough that people could see magma bubbling at the bottom. However, the job was not finished. Rohan appeared beside his comrade, and together they forced the chasm to open even wider, pushing with all their might. By the end of it, they were both exhausted.

"Nice. You can stop for now, Jadeleve. I'll take over." Lila relieved the soldier of her obligation. "Telekinesis!"

Lila forced Cataract's regenerating body into the chasm, deeper and deeper until he reached the bottom. After being submerged in magma, the regeneration process started again. Every time Cataract made progress, the constant flow of magma burned his body again.

They could keep him there forever. Finally, to conclude the plan, Xaphias and Rohan sealed the wound in the earth's crust again, granting Cataract one last look at the sky before sealing him away forever.

Silence. Following the crunching sound of the chasm's closing, there was only silence. They had won. They had endured years of training, traveling, and fighting. They had watched their friends and family die right in front of them, but somehow they picked themselves up and finished what they had started.

"Yeah!" Pupil cheered, pumping her fists in the air and breaking the silence at last. "We did it!"

Overcome with joy, the eleven remaining warriors and their two dragons met in the center of the battlefield and embraced each other with hugs and kisses. Tears fell freely. Laughs rang out. They had done it.

Yes … now you have done it, a raspy voice whispered. Cataract was using telepathy once again.

"What? No way!" Jadeleve howled, tearing herself from Xaphias's arms. Would this fight never end?

"Relax. You have beaten me. There is no way I can keep my regeneration up forever. I am here to answer any last questions before I go where I belong," Cataract rasped again, sounding defeated for the first time. A long silence followed again.

"Any last questions?" Zephyr looked like she wanted to strangle someone. She exploded in anger. *"You try to kill us all, and then you ask if we have any questions? Was this all just a game to you?"*

"Zephyr," Zenon said sharply, succeeding in calming her twin sister down. *"Interesting thing you asked us, Cataract, because there's always something I've wanted to ask you. Why did you do all this?"*

Absolute quiet enveloped the old battlefield for the umpteenth time while the weary warriors waited for their old enemy's response.

"As you wish, but let me tell you … my time is limited."

And so it began. Xaphias and his comrades sat down hard on the ground and began to listen to their foe's tale.

"*I am actually an Immortal Seer. I was born the eighth of July, 6543, the only child of my parents, and part of one of the final generations to fight in the First Last Eyebot War. When I was five, my father was killed in a horrific battle, and five years later, my mother followed his example, leaving me with an unwavering dream to end the war once and for all.*"

"*That's just like me,*" Lila mused, but then told Cataract to go on.

"*I was relocated from my home in the Land of Eyerobis to an orphanage in my same hometown. But I ran away after only a year. At the age of eleven, I set out on my own on a quest for power. I swore that day that I would train and grow strong enough to end the war that took so many lives. And that is where my path crossed with someone you may already know ... Master Dracon.*"

"*What? You knew Master Dracon?*" Xaphias gasped.

"*You sound surprised. He was my best friend and rival.*"

"*Wait! Who was Master Dracon?*" Teresa asked.

"*I am about to tell you. Before I tell you my story, it will make much more sense if I tell you the story of my rival's origin,*" Cataract replied without emotion. Xaphias sat in silence, listening carefully.

"*I traveled to the Land of Beings. The voyage took six months by submarine from the shore of my land, but it was well worth it. I reasoned that fighting with the mighty beasts would dramatically improve my fighting skills. I was sadly mistaken.*"

"*What happened next?*" Pupil prompted.

"*I was beaten. Many times. I got stronger naturally just from being tossed around, but I had progressed nowhere near the rate I wanted. Each day, I became less and less civilized. I almost lost track of time. But finally, one day, just before I turned thirteen, I encountered Dracon. Dragons are rare, you should know. Rarer than any other creature on this planet. Rarer than elves and fairies and leprechauns. And here was a young dragon that trained himself to use telepathy. Dracon told me how he was born in the waters on the west cost of the Land of See-Throughs in the Crescent Straight and how a man found him as an egg washed up on shore. The man treated him like his own son and even taught him the basics of fighting and energy control. Dracon, however,*" told the man as an adolescent dragon that he would fly to the Land of Beings to live on his own."

"Why would Dracon keep something so important from me?" Xaphias wondered.

"Dracon and I, having been around the same age, identified with each other and exchanged stories. We became training partners and battled through countless monster attacks together. But one day, everything changed."

"You both got eaten by sharks! Oh no!" Pupil squealed, but Jadeleve hushed her up.

"No. We discovered a prophecy written on the walls of a hidden cave in the middle of the jungle wilderness. It described how we could master a powerful technique that could crush all our enemies. It described achieving eyesight so remarkable that one could see to the edge of the universe and into the future."

"You guys were the first Immortal Seers?" Jadeleve gasped.

"Fools. Just because I am on my deathbed, you will believe anything I tell you. You think I will not lie? You weaklings could never survive in war. Everything I just said was a lie. I was reading your memories and came up with an elaborate story." Cataract chuckled.

A full thirty seconds of silence passed before anyone responded.

"What?" Zenon asked, incredulous.

"I knew we couldn't trust you!" Zephyr fumed.

"If everything you said was a lie, why are you killing people?" Lila inquired.

"Fools. My reasons make no difference. Killing is killing. You want a backstory so you can assess if my actions were justified or not. Say I had a troubled past and that led me to want to kill. Well, I will tell you now; you will never know my backstory."

"So you kill for no reason?" Jadeleve demanded, trying to suppress a deadly rage.

"I did not say that, but you will never know the truth. You will live in ignorance and die a fool."

"Cataract! Tell me!" Jadeleve roared. The zeal burst into action, extending higher and wider than Xaphias had ever seen it. Jadeleve clutched her head in agony, shaking violently, and began to weep. As the earth shook from the shockwaves, the group could feel Cataract's mind slowly slipping away. He was finally gone.

Jadeleve's tantrum had lasted only ten minutes, but she wasn't sure her if soul would ever heal.

"I knew that story was off. There's no way Master would hide something that important from me," Xaphias murmured as their group walked back toward Gato and Kuroski's bodies. Pupil and Iris went to retrieve their respective weapons so they could be buried with them. Then they gathered around to decide where they would bury them. There was an unspoken consensus that it would be nowhere near the island.

The group gazed down at their fallen comrades, searching their hearts for any last words.

"I felt like we never gave him a chance," Maelin sobbed, referring to Gato. She and Teresa began to weep together, starting a chain reaction in the group. Only Rohan and Xaphias did not cry.

"Kuroski ..." Xaphias started. "Sophfronia says hi."

Overcoming the Distance

"I've already missed almost two months of school. Can't I just stick with you guys?" Wayward complained.

"I wish, but we don't make the rules. Your mom does, and she'll be here any minute," Zenon explained.

In the past three weeks, their team had told Sophfronia about Kuroski's death, buried Gato and Kuroski with their weapons in the forest surrounding Origin Temple, where they had met, and recovered as best as they could at Yonderville's hospital.

"Don't take this the wrong way, Wayward, but you're pretty much dead weight. Not much an eight-year-old can do when it comes to saving the world. You would probably explode the second you touched the Zeal Orb."

Those were types of things that they said to him, teasingly, of course, but with an element of truth in there.

Also, there was much talk of the new course of action. Zenon had bought a new See-Through Zeal Corporation (SZC) transceiver for Lila so they could keep in touch. Rohan joined the Secondary Five on their quest to infiltrate the Land of Eyerobis. Lila would travel the world with Chalazia in search for the unused telepathy satellites to see if they could be used to serve their cause.

Yonderville was a port town on the northern edge of Fantasia County. From there, it would only take the Original Five about three months to reach No Man's Land in a submarine. It was a straight shot through the Odyssey Ocean. Ever since their group had defeated Cataract, the royal family stopped the Imperial Knights from restricting travel, now that there were no more formidable enemies to fear. Now, they could travel freely without having to fly under the radar.

However, ever since Jax and Retina claimed that *The Legend of the Zeal Orb* was just a fairy tale, Jadeleve was skeptical. They even reiterated their story when their team visited to bury Kuroski and Gato. Jadeleve did not want to be fooled again. She wanted to see No Man's Land with her own eyes before she made any judgments. If her parents had lied to her, then Jadeleve would consider the past two and a half years to be a waste.

On October 28, the Original Five and Secondary Five waited at Yonderville Train Station, almost ready for their respective adventures. Mrs. Kage was picking Wayward up, but she was also dropping off their means of transportation.

Chalazia and Aiondraes played together, racing through the clear blue skies. They had become good friends since the battle with Cataract, having been the same age and species. Jadeleve and the rest of the group passed the time in the train station by cracking jokes and playing board games. Never before had they felt so close, like a family. And even though they would have to part in just a couple of hours, and maybe never see one another again, it was one of Jadeleve's best memories of the trip so far.

Finally, at around eleven in the morning, after having waited at the station four about two hours (Mrs. Kage said her train would be there at nine, but trains were never on time), her train finally rolled around with only about thirty people on board. When Mrs. Kage finally stepped off the train in a khaki jacket, jeans, black boots, a black fedora, and a light green backpack, her blue eyes lit up like Ingrain Crystals when they gazed upon her youngest son.

"Wayward!" she screamed.

"Mom!" Wayward shouted. They rushed into each other's arms, and the moment they touched, it felt like everything was right with the world. Jadeleve had kept her promise to keep him safe.

"Oh, Wayward ... I'm so glad you're safe," she said, sobbing.

"Mom ..." Wayward muttered, equally emotional but wanting to look cool in front of his friends.

"Wow, you've grown a little, and so has your hair. It's even messier than before," Mrs. Kage whispered with a smile. These were tears of joy.

Slowly but surely, Mrs. Kage pulled away from her son, wiped away her tears, and embraced everyone else. She silently thanked the Original Five for keeping their vow to protect her son and stopping Cataract once and for all. But when she finally noticed Rohan, she froze. Jadeleve and the others had told her all about what he had been through and what he had done in the past few years, since he did not want to do it himself. She knew that he had killed and done all of Cataract's dirty work. However, she also knew how Rohan genuinely wanted to protect her; he just did not have the right role models. He was only nine when he was abducted. When she looked into her son's hesitant green eyes, which were just like his father's, she could see his guilt as plain as day. She wrapped her arms around him in a warm embrace.

"Rohan, you've grown so much. You're a young man now. I'm so sorry I couldn't protect you. I let Cataract get a hold of you. This was all my fault. But look at you ... you found your own way."

"Yeah, Mom, I guess I did." Rohan laughed. Now he was on the verge of tears. "Don't blame yourself. There's nothing you could've done. I needed a few years away anyway; you were always nagging me to stay inside." Rohan wept, bringing a small smile to his mother's face.

Once they were settled, or as settled a mother and son could be after not seeing each other for four years, they began to chat about what they would do next. Lila said that she would head back to Culloqui, her hometown, because Chalazia had said that the closest telepathy satellite was hidden somewhere in the forest near there (yes, Lila could read Chalazia's mind). Since there was no train station there, she would travel with her own power. She and Chalazia were the first to leave. Their group walked slowly to the edge of town where a large forest lay just ahead. Beyond that was the Battle Valley, and to the west, off the mainland, was Mind Fog Island.

"Guys, you're my best friends," Lila murmured. By the end of her spiel, tears glistened in her bright blue eyes. Her blonde hair fell over them like a curtain. "Keep in touch …"

After hugging each and every one of them, Lila reluctantly pulled Chalazia out of the pack by the reins of her new brown leather saddle.

"Arrriiii …" Chalazia rubbed her snout affectionately against Aiondraes's.

"Bye, Lila and Chalazia …" Iris sniffled. Jadeleve caught her irises turning a sorrowful shade of gray before she closed her eyes, buried her head in her hands, and cried. Jadeleve gathered her up and gave her a great big hug.

"Next time we see you will be on Saturn," Jadeleve promised. Lila gave a curt nod before finally turning around. She hopped onto Chalazia's back, and with one mighty flap of her wings against the dirt road, they lifted off into the sky.

Next, it was Wayward's turn. The group went back to the train station so he and his mother could head back home to Pearl Town. Mrs. Kage had gotten round-trip tickets.

"I'd almost forgotten. Here's your present, Rohan," Mrs. Kage said softly as she reached into the right pocket of her khaki jacket. She pulled out a zeal capsule labeled Boundless and gently placed it in her son's hand.

"You're giving me Dad's old submarine?" Rohan said.

Mrs. Kage nodded. "You can't get all the way to the Eyebots Land by flying. You take this to have a place to rest whenever you get tired. Make sure you keep it safe …"

Tears began to fall, and he rushed into his mother's arms.

"Thanks, Mom."

"I got one for you guys, too," Mrs. Kage told Jadeleve and handed her a capsule labeled Ocean Odyssey. "It's from Travel Atlas's underground section. I climbed over the Redundant Dungeon to get to Fiome like a normal person. Anyway, Jasmine said hi."

"Wow … thanks," Jadeleve said, somewhat uncomfortable.

"Good luck in the third grade, Wayward. Even though you're starting late, I think you'll do just fine. Take it from me, you're a genius." Zenon winked at him and messed up his hair.

"You think so?" Wayward giggled, and his face turned red. "You guys are the best!"

Wayward rushed into Pupil and Iris's arms, compelling everyone into a group hug. Aiondraes wrapped his tail around the perimeter.

"We love you, Way-Way." Pupil giggled and planted a kiss on his cheek.

When everyone pulled away, Rohan looked at his little brother. He looked like he had so much to say but could not put his thoughts into words. Luckily, he did not have to. Wayward and his mother spoke for him. As their three bodies pressed together, Rohan knew that his family would always be there for him. Half an hour later, Wayward and Mrs. Kage boarded their train back home, bound for a fresh start to life.

For the next few hours after they reached the shore, the remaining members of their group wandered around Yonderville's shore until they found the perfect place for Xaphias and his new team to depart: a secluded part of the Yonderville beach that was surrounded by trees. Teresa, who had never thrown a zeal capsule before, wanted to do the honors. Rohan handed the Boundless capsule to her, and she flung it into the rippling water. Once the capsule hit the rocky bottom of the shallow waters, it exploded into a huge white cloud of mist. When the smoke cleared, it revealed a brick-red submarine that was one hundred feet long, sixty feet wide, and sixty feet tall. Instructions for how to start and navigate the submarine also appeared, which Maelin snatched out of the sky.

"This is great and all but Aiondraes will outgrow this in two months tops," Maelin chuckled.

"Aiiiioooo!" Aiondraes protested. He flew around and perched on top of his new home, causing it to bang against the rocks of the shallow waters, and then quickly flew back.

"Yeah." Xaphias sighed, slightly embarrassed. "But it's all we've got."

After a few more farewells and another hour of figuring out how to work the submarine, Xaphias's group was finally ready to head out. Everyone in their group but Xaphias and Aiondraes had entered the submarine by four in the afternoon. He and Aiondraes decided that they wanted to fly for the first leg of their journey, but they would keep close to Rohan, who would steer his father's old vessel.

"So this time, I probably won't see you again until we make it to Saturn," Xaphias admitted.

"How are you getting there?" Zenon inquired.

"Either Mr. Dawn will teleport us when we're ready or we'll find a spaceship."

"Will you come back alive?" Iris pressed.

"Hopefully."

"We'll miss you!" Pupil bawled.

Now it was Jadeleve's turn to say something, but her heart was pounding. The thought of never seeing Xaphias again was too much to bear.

"Xaphias," she whispered, stunning everyone. She reluctantly let the tears fall. Surrounded by her family and friends, Jadeleve had never felt so alone. Recent events had left her empty inside.

"I know," he said. Before Jadeleve knew what had happened, Xaphias hugged her, kissed her forehead, and took off into the sky beside his partner. *Boundless* drifted off until the water was deep enough for it to submerge itself. Then, just like that, it disappeared from view, with Xaphias and Aiondraes following close behind.

Jadeleve waited uncomfortably for the expected teases from Zephyr, but they never came. When Jadeleve turned around, everyone seemed just as surprised as she was.

At last, it was the Original Five's turn to embark on their quest once again. Jadeleve threw the zeal capsule with their submarine into the water, and it appeared in a puff of smoke. It was a deep blue, identical in size to *Boundless*, but looked brand new. By five, they had boarded the submarine. The interior was spacious with four small rooms, a kitchen, bathroom, and gym. Zenon calculated that their fuel source would last eight months, which was plenty of time. Within minutes, she mastered the submarine, plotted out their course, and set *Ocean Odyssey* on autopilot. Now, there was nothing but ocean between them and their final goal.

TRUE POWER

J ADELEVE TRUDGED MINDLESSLY THROUGH THE frozen white powder, barely paying attention to her companions. Suddenly, Zenon's voice came through the communication device that was implanted in their orange heat suits, which were identical to space suits. Without the communication device, they wouldn't have been able to hear each other. Their heads were enclosed in soundproof glass globes.

"You okay, Jadeleve? You're acting like a zombie. Plus, you activated the zeal when there are no oncoming threats."

"What? Oh," Jadeleve murmured.

"Guess she's finally lost it. It took her long enough, but bad timing. We're so close," Zephyr chortled.

"Shut up," Jadeleve snapped. Zephyr's taunts had finally woken her up.

"I can see light now. Let's fly," Pupil suggested. A lime-green light began to illuminate the bleak gray sky and the snow-covered mountain faces. In order to avoid the even colder air at higher altitudes and a chilling breeze, the Original Five refrained from flight for most of their journey through No Man's Land. However, now they were finally close enough to their destination. At last, after three years, they had reached the Zeal Orb.

"I'll race you there, Iris!" Pupil said. Iris's eyes turned green with excitement, and she bolted after her twin in the direction of the light.

"Wait, guys! That's not the orb; those are just the northern lights. Stay with the group!" Zenon warned, but the two youngsters were already well out of earshot.

Now fully alert, Jadeleve took action.

"Slow down," she whispered. Using the Slow Motion Technique allowed her to focus her eyes on a single point so intently that any motion taking place in that area seemed to slow down. After activating the technique, Jadeleve teleported in front of her sisters and gathered them up in her arms before deactivating the attack.

"Whoa." Pupil gasped in astonishment after realizing what had happened.

"Don't go running off like that again," Jadeleve advised sternly.

"Yeah, yeah. Don't get all mushy on us." Pupil giggled.

"If you guys are done horsing around, let's get a move on. We've waited long enough for this," Zephyr said after she and Zenon had caught up.

The Original Five continued on, traversing the final miles of their nearly three-year trip. Even at this advanced stage in the process, however, there were still obstacles.

"Avalanche!" Iris cried.

"Where? Where?" Pupil exclaimed. Even with their exceptional visual prowess and the light of the Zeal Orb, the late-evening darkness masked the source of the avalanche. However, the sound was unmistakable. This was not the first time the crew had encountered an avalanche in their two-week trek through No Man's Land. They had come face-to-face with one on several occasions in the light of day and had learned to connect a distinct sound to the terrible natural disaster.

"One o'clock!" Zephyr roared over the howling winds, using her Pinpoint Technique to find the greatest concentration of energy in the massive snowslide.

"Thanks, sis! Blaze Cloak!" Zenon bellowed and activated a technique she had recently perfected. The Blaze Cloak harnessed internal heat energy and created a clock of fire that enveloped the body, heightening the strength of attacks that utilized heat energy. Zenon also drew power from her heat suit. Her heat suit, along with the clothes she was wearing on the inside of the thick orange jumpsuit, were all fireproof.

"Now, Fire Typhoon!" With the power of her attack increased, Zenon was able to vaporize the avalanche and the surrounding snow, leaving steamy mist in their absence. The Original Five avoided yet another catastrophe.

"Nice team work, guys. We can do anything!" Pupil cheered.

"Who's 'we'? All you said was 'Where, where?' Scaredy cat," Zephyr mocked, mimicking Pupil's earlier meltdown.

"Am *not!*" Pupil wailed. The whole group erupted with laughter. Except for Jadeleve.

The others tried to make light conversation with her to keep her occupied.

"What bad timing that we got here in January. It's cold enough as it is," Zenon joked.

"Shut up," Jadeleve said. Zenon tried to shrug it off.

"What's your problem, Jadel? You've been acting like a brat since we got here … since we left Fantasia!" Zephyr snapped.

"It's here," Jadeleve whispered. Now Zephyr's taunts could not even rouse her from her semicomatose state.

Nearly impossible to detect in the blizzard stood an ancient steel shrine that was covered in ice.

"This … this is the shrine they talk about in the legend. Where is it?" Jadeleve asked herself. "It's not here."

"Jadeleve, just calm down. We'll look for it," Zenon suggested.

"You and I both know that we could sense it if it's this close! It's not here!" Jadeleve raged, and her stress response activated again.

While Jadeleve exploded in anger, Iris, as quietly as she could, slipped Jadeleve's transceiver out of her backpack. As she was not quite strong enough to amplify her thoughts across such vast distances, she gave it to Zenon. Zenon, already knowing who to call, projected her thoughts into to the device.

Mr. Dawn? It's me, Zenon. Can you hear me? Zenon asked with her thoughts.

After a ten second long silence, someone responded.

Yes. It's me, Zenon.

Is this Mrs. Dawn? Why do you have this transceiver?

Silver is off fighting. I'm taking a break right now. So … you finally reached No Man's Land?

How did you know?

This is the first time you guys have called since you left.

You told us to wait until you called us.

It's only natural. Once they leave the nest, they never want to come back.

Hey, Zenon grimaced. *Anyway, we're here … but the Zeal Orb isn't. Where else could it be?*

No answer.

Mrs. Dawn? You still there?

Yes …

Is it true that the Zeal Orb, the actual, physical object, is just a legend?

No answer.

Please tell me. Jadeleve is going berserk.

Yes. It's true.

Okay, Zenon replied, not sure what else to say.

Let me talk to her, Mrs. Dawn requested, sounding like she was on the verge of tears.

Okay …

Zephyr and Pupil, who were unaware of what was happening, watched in confusion. They could eavesdrop on Zenon's mental conversation, but they chose not to get involved. Zenon walked over to Jadeleve and handed her the transceiver.

"It's your mom."

Jadeleve gasped and snatched the device from Zenon's hand. She used telepathy and projected her thoughts into the transceiver.

Mom?

Hey, Jadel …

Mom … what's going on here? We came all this way, and the Zeal Orb isn't here.

There's no Zeal Orb, Jadel. The Legend of the Zeal Orb … is a myth.

No way… There's just no way… Jax and Retina were right?"

What did they tell you?"

That zeal is the energy that started the Big Bang, that zeal is everywhere but it can't be drawn from in its purest form, that it can only be in one concentrated place at a time, and that I'm the first living Zeal Possessor.

That sounds about right.

So zeal capsules aren't actually zeal powered?

No.

And this power wasn't passed down to me by my ancestors?

No.

Is transflare even real?

Yes … and it is artificial … like Gold told you. What we didn't tell you is that transflare was derived from acedia. What your friends told you was half-right; both zeal and acedia created the universe. At the beginning of time, the entire universe was condensed into a single, infinitesimal orb of energy. This orb was made up solely of zeal and acedia. Zeal and acedia, being equal and opposite forces, pushed against each other, causing the orb to expand indefinitely in all directions. This is what humans call the Big Bang.

Acedia is as powerful as zeal. Like zeal, acedia is everywhere in the universe, but zeal is concentrated in stars and acedia is concentrated in black holes. As you know, zeal's aura is lime-green, but acedia's aura is magenta. Zeal has incredible destructive properties, and acedia has incredible absorption properties. Like zeal, drawing from acedia is almost impossible. In 10080, the Eyebots discovered a black hole that was close enough to Jupiter to extract acedia. But it's impossible to draw energy from a black hole alone. Black holes are resistant to energy extraction because they suck everything in. Also, they're so far away.

Practically the entire Eyebot race had to draw energy from the black hole to extract enough acedia. Of course, it wasn't enough acedia to power an entire army, so they combined the acedia with other elements and created transflare. They stored the transflare in an energy storage chamber, flew to Saturn, and set up their military base. After training for eight years, they declared war on us, and because of the royal family's rule to keep minimal contact with the other races, we weren't prepared.

The Eyebots have always believed that they were the superior race. They threatened to destroy Jupiter and all other races. They said they would colonize Saturn and start fresh. The royal family drafted all able-bodied adults between eighteen and fifty-five to fight in the See-Through army in 10088. Our troops arrived on Saturn in 10089. The royal family drafted again 10102, which is when your father left to fight. They'll draft again in 10116.

Acedia? There's an element as strong as zeal? Jadeleve thought.

Yes. They're equal and opposite forces.

Why did you hide so many things from me? All this time, I … Cataract was right … I'm so stupid. I thought I could finally … never mind.

Complete sentences, Jadeleve.

I'm so gullible I'd believe anything that people tell me.

I'm not "anyone." I am your mother, and I'm trying to protect you.

I don't need you to protect me! I need you tell me the truth! If you've been lying to us this time whole time, then … my friends died for nothing!

You wouldn't have made friends if you never left home.

How can you say that? I can't believe you just said that. She held the transceiver in her left hand and was clenching her right into a fist.

If you're not ready to see your loved ones die … you're not ready for war.

What kind of rule is that? Now that my friends are dead, I can come?

Over here, I'm helpless to stop hundreds of my comrades dying every day! If you can't handle the pain, you're not ready! You ... you haven't even unlocked your full potential.

What do you mean, Mom?

You haven't unlocked the zeal's true power ...

What are you talking about? I've used zeal my entire life!

Dad just brought Grandma back home, honey. She has served long enough. Go visit her. Go back home and clear your head, honey. You need to able to see these things for yourself, Jadeleve. Otherwise ... you'll never be ready, Mrs. Dawn concluded. Her stream of thoughts broke. Jadeleve could feel her mother's consciousness slip away.

What? Grandma's back? Mom? Mom! Don't go! Jadeleve pleaded, but it was too late. Jadeleve bent down and sobbed into her hands. Nothing made sense.

"Jadeleve," Iris whispered, wanting to console her sister, but Zephyr held her back.

"They died for *nothing*. All this was for *nothing*. *We haven't gotten anywhere!*" Jadeleve wailed.

A blinding white light lit up the sky. An incredibly powerful shockwave pushed the four girls back about two hundred feet, demolished the steel shrine, and triggered several avalanches. Extreme heat, which caused heat distortion, quickly melted the snow before it could fall. The harsh winds picked up even more, and thunder boomed.

Jadeleve howled. Her heat suit blew apart, and she was left with nothing but a purple T-shirt, black shorts, and bare feet. Since she was the force of the intense heat, the extreme cold of the land did not affect her. The ice she stood on quickly evaporated, forcing her to float. Her long golden hair blew wildly in the air. Her radiant golden eyes told of her furious rage. Finally, the once white light that enveloped her body turned a deep, dark indigo. Bright golden sparks danced around her aura like stars. The aura was at least ten times her size.

What? What is this? Jadeleve wondered, starstruck. She looked down at her teammates' faces, who had taken off their glass helmets in the intense heat. They were even more shocked. After five seconds, she put two and two together.

This ... this must be what Mom was talking about. It feels like I'm flying through space.

"Jadel ... What's that?" Pupil asked while she and the others trudged as closely as they could to Jadeleve.

"Zeal."

"That's zeal?" Zephyr gasped.

"If zeal is what created the universe like Jax and Retina said, it makes sense that its aura looks like space," Zenon explained. "Even your eyes ... they're gold and purple. They look like spiral galaxies with a black hole in the middle."

A long silence passed as Jadeleve looked off into the distance. The thunder died down, and the wind slowed, but the blizzard persisted.

"Are you okay, Jadel?" Iris finally asked the question on everyone's mind.

"No ... not really. Mom was right."

"You talked to *Mom*?" Pupil asked with bulging eyes.

"Yeah. She said I'm not ready for war."

"None of us are ready, Jadel. We're just kids. Nothing we've been through so far even compares to war," Zenon admitted.

Jadeleve hung her head in shame but lifted it a second later.

"What else did she say?" Iris inquired.

"She and Dad sent us on this quest to protect us."

"What about Saturn?" Zenon asked.

"Zenon ... I spent my whole life isolated in a forest, so when your dad told us about this mission, I was so excited. I just rushed in without thinking. Mom was right. We need more time."

"Hm. So what now, chief?" Zephyr sighed.

"We still have a lot to figure out, but for now, I think we should head back home and regroup. I want to see Grandma and Toto and Sila and Margarita. Now that I can use Dad's Solar Speed Technique, we could get home in two months. I haven't mastered the technique yet, so I can't fly us the whole way there, but if we use *Ocean Odyssey* to get us back to Fantasia, I could fly us the rest of the way," Jadeleve explained.

"That's a great idea. I second that." Zenon smiled warmly.

"Me too! Say, when are you gonna turn off the zeal, Jadel?" Pupil whined, panting because of the intense heat.

"I kind of destroyed my heat suit. If I don't keep this going, I'll freeze. Can we get going?"

"I thought you were the chief, Jadel!" Zephyr teased, walking back toward the submarine in slow motion.

"Shut up, Zephyr! Get moving!" Jadeleve screeched, but everyone laughed.

Once everyone had settled down in their rooms on *Ocean Odyssey*, Zenon put it on autopilot. They were heading south.

"Hey, Jadel," Pupil whispered. Both her little sisters had snuck into her room while she was taking a nap.

"What?" Jadeleve demanded and sat up in her bed.

"It's almost our tenth birthdays. Two more months …" Pupil started.

"And?"

"What're you gonna get us?"

"You're not gonna know until the day of. Sorry."

"You didn't get us anything, did you?" Pupil said.

"Of course I did. It's a secret." Jadeleve grinned.

"What could you have gotten? We've been in here for three months!" Pupil said.

"I got it months in advance, before we left," Jadeleve explained.

"Are you lying?" Iris asked, her eyes turning a suspicious, curious yellow.

"No. Of course not," Jadeleve promised, grinning. After five seconds of giving her the death stare, the twins relented.

"Okay! This better be good!" Pupil beamed. The twins scampered off, and Pupil slammed the door behind her.

Shoot. I've got to think of something fast, Jadeleve fretted.

We heard that, Pupil eavesdropped.

Shoot, Jadeleve thought. If she was careless, they could invade her privacy on a whole new level. The twins burst back into the room and wrestled her to the ground, and all three of them started laughing.

Printed in the United States
By Bookmasters